Praise for the novels of
#1 *New York Times* bestselling author
Debbie Macomber

"It's impossible not to cheer for Macomber's characters.... When it comes to creating a special place and memorable, honorable characters, nobody does it better than Macomber."
—*BookPage*

"Macomber's writing and storytelling deliver what she's famous for—a smooth, satisfying tale with characters her fans will cheer for and an arc that is cozy, heartwarming and ends with the expected happily-ever-after."
—*Kirkus Reviews* on *Starting Now*

"Debbie Macomber is...a bona fide superstar."
—*Publishers Weekly*

"Readers won't be able to get enough of Macomber's gentle storytelling."
—*RT Book Reviews*

"No one tugs at readers' heartstrings quite as effectively as Macomber."
—*Chicago Tribune*

"Romantic, warm, and a breeze to read."
—*Kirkus Reviews* on *Cottage by the Sea*

"The reigning queen of women's fiction."
—*The Sacramento Bee*

D0038115

DEBBIE MACOMBER

Always Dakota
and
Buffalo Valley

mira

mira™

ISBN-13: 978-0-7783-3397-5

Always Dakota

First published in 2019. This edition published in 2023.

Copyright © 2023 by Harlequin Enterprises ULC

Always Dakota
First published in 2001. This edition published in 2023.
Copyright © 2001 by Debbie Macomber

Buffalo Valley
First published in 2001. This edition published in 2023.
Copyright © 2001 by Debbie Macomber

For questions and comments about the quality of this book, please contact us at CustomerService@Harlequin.com.

Mira
22 Adelaide St. West, 41st Floor
Toronto, Ontario M5H 4E3, Canada
www.Harlequin.com

Printed in U.S.A.

Also available from Debbie Macomber and MIRA

CONTENTS

ALWAYS DAKOTA

To my
Aunt Betty Stierwalt
and
Aunt Gerty Urlacher,
for gracing my life with their incredible gift
for love and laughter.
I love you both.

Prologue

Bernard Clemens was dying and he knew it, despite what the doctors—all those fancy specialists—had said about his heart. He knew. He was old and tired, ready for death.

Sitting in the den of the home he'd built thirty years ago for his wife, he closed his eyes and remembered. Maggie had been his great love. His only love. Delicate and beautiful, nearly sixteen years younger, she could have had her choice of husbands, but she'd chosen *him*. An aging rancher with a craggy face and work-roughened hands. A man who had simple tastes and lacked social refinement. And yet she'd loved him.

God help him, he'd loved *her*, loved her still, although she'd been gone now for nearly twenty-seven years.

Her love had been gift enough, but she'd yearned to give him a son. Bernard, too, had hoped for an heir. He'd purchased the Triple C as a young man, buying the land adjacent to his parents' property, and eventually he'd built the combined ranches into one huge spread, an empire to pass on to his son. However, the child had been a girl and they'd named her Margaret, after her mother.

The pregnancy had drained Maggie and she was further weakened that winter by a particularly bad strain of the flu. Pneumonia had set in soon afterward, and before anyone realized how serious it was, his Maggie was gone.

In all his life, Bernard had never known such grief. With Maggie's death, he'd lost what he valued most—the woman who'd brought him joy. When they lowered her casket into the ground, they might as well have buried him, too. From that point forward, he threw himself into ranching, buying more land, increasing his herd and consequently turning the Triple C into one of the largest and most prosperous cattle ranches in all of North Dakota.

As for being a father to young Margaret, he'd tried, but as the eldest of seven boys, he had no experience in dealing with little girls. In the years that followed, his six younger brothers had all lived and worked with him for brief periods of time, eventually moving on and getting married and starting families of their own.

They'd helped him raise her, teaching her about ranching ways—riding and roping…and cussing, he was sorry to admit.

To this day, Margaret loved her uncles. Loved riding horses, too. She was a fine horsewoman, and more knowledgeable about cattle than any man he knew. She'd grown tall and smart—not to mention smart-mouthed—but Bernard feared he'd done his only child a grave disservice. Margaret resembled him more than she did her mother. Maggie had been a fragile, dainty woman who brought out everything that was good in Bernard.

Their daughter, unfortunately, revealed very little of her mother's gentleness or charm. How could she, seeing that she'd been raised by a grief-stricken father and six bachelors? Margaret looked like Bernard, talked like him and dressed like him. It was a crying shame she hadn't been a boy, since, until recently, she was often mistaken for one. His own doing, he thought, shaking his head. Had Maggie lived, she would have seen to the proper upbringing of their daughter. Would have taught their little girl social graces and femininity, as mothers do. Bernard had given it his best shot. He loved his daughter, but he felt that he'd failed her.

To her credit, Margaret possessed a generous, loving heart and she was a fine businesswoman. Bernard couldn't help being proud of her, despite a constant sense of guilt about her unconventional upbringing.

There was a light knock. At his hoarse, "Come in," the housekeeper opened the door. "Matt Eilers is here to see you," Sadie announced brusquely.

With effort, Bernard straightened, his fingers digging into the padded leather arms of his chair as he forced himself to meet his neighbor. "Send him in."

She nodded and left.

Less than a minute later, Matt Eilers appeared, Stetson in hand.

"You'll forgive me if I don't get up," Bernard said.

"Of course."

Bernard gestured toward the matching chair on the opposite side of the fireplace. "Sit down."

Matt obliged, giving Bernard his first good look at this man his daughter apparently loved. Frankly, he was disappointed. He'd seen Matt at social affairs, the occasional wedding, harvest dance or barbecue, but they'd never spoken. Somehow, he'd expected more substance, and he felt surprised that Margaret would be taken in by a pretty face and an empty heart. Over the past few years Bernard had heard plenty about his neighbor to the west, and not much of it had been flattering.

"I imagine you're wondering why I asked to meet with you."

"I am," Matt said, perching on the edge of the chair. He held his hat in both hands, his expression questioning.

"You enjoy ranching?"

"Yes, sir."

At least he was polite, and that boded well. "How long you been ranching the Stockert place?"

"Four years. I'd like to buy my own spread one day, but for now I'm leasing the land and building up my herd."

"So I understand." Bernard leaned back in his chair. His breath came slowly, painfully. "You have family in the area?"

Matt's gaze shifted to the Oriental rug. "No. My parents divorced when I was five. My father ranched in Montana and I worked summers with him, but he died when I was fifteen."

"Ranching's in your blood then, same as mine."

"It is," Matt agreed.

Bernard hesitated, waiting until he had breath enough to continue. "You know my daughter, Margaret."

Matt nodded.

"What do you think of her?"

The question seemed to take him by surprise. "Think of her? How do you mean?"

Bernard waved his hand. "Your general impression."

Slumping back in the chair, Matt shrugged. "I…I don't know what you want me to say."

"Just be honest," he snapped, impatient. He didn't have the strength—or the time—for word games.

"Well…" Matt paused. "Margaret's Margaret. She's… unique."

That was true enough. As far as Bernard knew, she'd only worn a dress twice in her entire life. He'd tried to get her into one when she was ten and the attempt had damn near killed him. "Did you know she's in love with you?"

"Margaret?" Matt sprang to his feet. "I swear I haven't touched her! I swear it." The color fled from his face and he shook his head as though to emphasize his words.

"I believe you… Sit down."

Matt did as asked, but his demeanor had changed dramatically. His posture was stiff, his face tight with apprehension and uncertainty.

"She's gotten it in her head that she's going to marry you."

Matt had the look of a caged animal. "I…I'm not sure what to say."

"You don't know my daughter, otherwise you'd realize that when she sets her mind to something, there isn't much that'll stand in her way."

"I…I…"

Bernard cut him off. He was growing weak and there was still a lot to be said. "In a few months, Margaret's going to be a very wealthy woman."

Matt stared at him.

"I'm dying. I don't have much time left." His gaze burned into Eilers. Then he closed his eyes, gathering strength. "God knows what she sees in you, but it's too late to worry about her judgment now. I raised her the best I could, and if she loves you, there must be more to you than meets the eye."

Matt stood and started pacing. "What makes you think I'd marry Margaret?" he asked.

Despite the difficulty he had in breathing, Bernard

laughed. "Because you'd be a fool not to, and we both know it. She's going to inherit this ranch. I own more land and cattle than you'll see in ten lifetimes. She'll give you everything you've ever wanted."

It was clear from Eilers's expression that he was shocked.

"I called you here today to tell you something you need to hear."

Matt clutched his Stetson so tightly, his knuckles whitened. "What's that?"

Bernard leaned forward. "You hurt my girl and I swear I'll find a way to make you pay, even if I have to come back from the grave to do it."

Eilers swallowed hard. "You don't have anything to worry about, Mr. Clemens. I have no intention of marrying Margaret."

Bernard chuckled, knowing otherwise. Eilers would marry Margaret, all right, but it wouldn't be for love. He'd marry her for the land and the cattle. No man with ranching in his blood would be able to refuse what she had to offer.

Yes, Matt would marry her, but it was up to Margaret to earn Matt Eilers's affection.

One

October

Margaret thought she was ready, as ready as any daughter could be to face her father's death. She'd been at his side, his rough, callused hand between her own, when it happened. For hours she'd sat with him, watching the intermittent rise and fall of his chest, waiting, wondering if this breath would be his last, praying it wasn't. Clinging to what little life was left in him.

Bernard Clemens had refused to die in a hospital and at his request, she'd brought him home. The hospice people had been wonderful, assisting Bernard in maintaining his dignity to the very end. Margaret had stayed with her father almost constantly the final week of his life.

She watched him draw his last shallow breath, watched him pass peacefully, silently, from one life to the next. Margaret wasn't sure what she'd expected to feel, but certainly not this torrent of agony and grief. She'd known he was dying, known it for months, and she'd thought that knowledge would blunt the sharp rawness of her pain. It hadn't. *Her father was gone.* She'd spent every day of her life with him, here on the Triple C, and now she was alone. In time, she realized, she'd be able to look back and see the blessing her father had been, but not yet. Not when her loss hurt as much as it did now.

She'd waited until she'd composed herself and then, dry-eyed, walked out of the large bedroom and awakened the sleeping family members, who'd gathered at the ranch. She'd announced that Bernard had died and his death had been peaceful. No tears were shed. That wasn't how grief was expressed in the Clemens family.

Almost immediately, everyone had found a purpose and the house was filled with activity. More and more people arrived, and then, two days later, it was time for the funeral. Bernard Clemens's three surviving brothers stood at the grave site with Margaret; they stayed long enough to greet folks and thank them for coming. Then they left, to return to their own families, their own lives.

The reception following the funeral was well attended. Nearly everyone in Buffalo Valley came to pay their respects. Hassie Knight, who owned Knight's Pharmacy, took charge of organizing the event. She'd been a family friend for many years. At least a hundred people had gathered at the large ranch house, and there was more food than Margaret could eat in six weeks. She never had understood why people brought casseroles and desserts for a wake; the last thing she wanted to think about was eating.

"Margaret, I'm so sorry," Sarah Urlacher told her, gently taking her hand and holding it. She was sincere, and her kindness touched Margaret's heart. Sarah's husband, Dennis, stood with her. His eyes revealed genuine compassion.

Margaret nodded, wishing she knew the couple better. It was her father who was well acquainted with the folks in Buffalo Valley. He'd been doing business there for years. Dennis delivered fuel to the ranch, so Margaret at least knew him, even if their relationship was just a casual one. Sarah owned and operated Buffalo Valley Quilts, a growing enterprise that seemed to be attracting interest all around the country. Margaret knew Sarah only by sight; they hadn't shared more than a few perfunctory greetings.

She wanted to thank everyone for coming—she really did appreciate their expressions of sympathy and respect—and at the same time find a way to steer them out the door. Making conversation with people she hardly knew was beyond her. She was polite, cordial, but a tightness had gripped her chest, and it demanded every ounce of restraint she could muster not to rush to the barn, saddle Midnight and ride until she was too exhausted to go farther.

Bob and Merrily Carr came next, with their little boy, Axel. They owned and operated 3 OF A KIND, Buffalo Valley's bar and grill. After that, the banker, Heath Quantrill, offered his condolences. Rachel Fischer was with him, and if Margaret remembered correctly, they were a couple now.

Ranchers and farmers crowded the house. So many people. There barely seemed room to breathe.

"Do you need anything?" Maddy McKenna asked with a gentleness that nearly broke Margaret's facade. Maddy was the best friend she'd ever had. If anyone understood, it would be Maddy.

"I want everyone to leave," Margaret whispered, fighting back emotion. The lump in her throat refused to go away and she had trouble talking around it.

Maddy took Margaret by the arm and led her down the long hallway to her bedroom. The two of them had spent many an afternoon in this very room; at Margaret's entreaty, Maddy had tried to instruct her in the arts of looking and acting feminine—feminine enough to attract Matt Eilers. Not that her efforts had been noticed. Not by him, anyway.

"Sit," Maddy ordered, pointing to Margaret's bed.

Without argument, Margaret complied.

"When was the last time you had any sleep?"

Margaret blinked, unable to recall. "A while ago." The night before the funeral she'd sat up and gone through her father's papers. He had everything in order, as she'd suspected he would. He'd realized months ago that he was dying.

"Lie down," Maddy said.

"I have a house full of company," Margaret objected weakly. It went against the grain to let someone dictate what she should or shouldn't do. With anyone else, she'd have made a fuss, insisted it was her place to be with her father's friends.

"You're dead on your feet," Maddy told her.

Margaret nestled her head in her pillow, surprised by how good it felt against her face. How cool and comforting. "I…I thought I was prepared," she said, her eyes closed. "I thought I could handle this."

"No one's ever ready to lose a father," Maddy said as she covered Margaret with the afghan from the foot of the bed. The weight of it settled warmly over her shoulders.

"Sleep now. By the time you wake, everyone will be gone."

"Nothing's ever going to be the same again," Margaret whispered.

"You're right, it won't."

Maddy's voice sounded soothing, even if her words

didn't. But then, Margaret could count on her friend to tell the truth. Already she could feel sleep approach, could feel the tension leave her body. "Matt didn't attend the funeral, did he?"

"No," Maddy said.

"I thought he would." She was keenly disappointed that he hadn't bothered to show up.

"I know."

Maddy was disappointed in him, too. Margaret could tell from the inflection in her voice. Few people understood why she loved Matt. If pressured to explain, Margaret wasn't sure she could justify her feelings. Matt Eilers was as handsome as sin, shallow and conceited. But she loved him and had from the moment she'd met him.

With Maddy's tutoring, Margaret had done everything possible to get Matt to recognize that she was a woman with a woman's heart. A few months back, she'd had her hair done and put on panty hose for the first time in her life. The panty hose had nearly wrestled her to the ground and the new hairdo had made her look like one of the Marx Brothers—in her opinion, anyway. The whole beautifying operation had been a unique form of torture, but she'd willingly do it all again for Matt.

"I'm sure he'll stop by later and pay his respects," Margaret whispered, confident that he would.

"He should have been here today." Maddy wasn't nearly as forgiving. "Don't worry about Matt."

"I'm not."

"Call me in the morning," Maddy said.

"I will," she promised, exhausted and grateful for Maddy's friendship. Her last thought before she drifted off to sleep was of the father she loved and how bleak her life would feel without him.

* * *

Jeb McKenna knew his wife well, and her silence worried him as he drove the short distance between the Clemens house and his ranch. Unlike the Clemenses and most other ranchers in the area, Jeb raised bison; Maddy owned the grocery store in town. Right now, though, she was staying home with their infant daughter.

"You're worried about Margaret, aren't you?" he asked as he turned down the mile-long dirt driveway leading to their home. Maddy had barely said a word after seeing Margaret to her room.

"She was ready to collapse," Maddy told him. "God only knows the last time she slept. Sadie said she'd been up for two nights straight."

"Poor thing." One didn't generally think of Margaret in those terms. She came across as tough, strong, capable. They'd been neighbors for about five years—ever since Jeb had bought the property—and he'd seen Margaret on a number of different occasions. It was some time before he'd realized Margaret was a *she* instead of a *he*. It'd startled him, but he wasn't the only person she'd inadvertently fooled. Maddy confessed that when they'd first met, she'd taken Margaret for a ranch hand.

"Bernard's death has shaken her."

Jeb understood. Joshua McKenna was in his late sixties now, and Jeb knew that sooner or later he, too, would lose his father. The inevitability of it made him feel a wave of sadness…and regret. He parked the car and turned off the engine.

"I'll talk to Margaret in the morning," Maddy said absently.

The October wind beat against him as Jeb climbed out of the vehicle and reached in the back to unfasten Julianne's car seat. At three months she was showing more personality than he would've thought possible. She gurgled and smiled, waving her arms as though orchestrating life from her infant seat. She'd proved to be a good-natured baby, happy and even-tempered.

Carrying the baby seat, he covered Julianne's face with the blanket and hurried toward the house, doing his best to protect his wife and daughter from the brunt of the wind.

Maddy switched on the kitchen lights and Jeb set the baby carrier on the recliner, unfastening Julianne and cradling her in his arms.

"I liked Pastor Dawson," Maddy said casually.

The Methodist minister had recently taken up residence in town. Although Larry Dawson had grown up in Buffalo Valley, Jeb didn't remember him. That wasn't surprising, seeing that the pastor was near retirement age. Dawson was slight in stature, his hair—what was left of it—completely white. He hadn't been in contact with Bernard Clemens for many years, but he'd given a respectable eulogy.

"The pastor invited us to church services on Sunday," she murmured.

Although it was an offhand remark, Jeb knew Maddy was interested in becoming involved with a church community. He hesitated; the drive into Buffalo Valley took at least fifty minutes, and that was on a good day. Going to church would consume nearly all of Sunday morning. He opened his mouth, about to offer his wife a list of excuses as to why it would be inconvenient to attend. Before he could utter a word, he changed his mind. The fact that she'd mentioned the invitation at all meant this was important to her and shouldn't be taken lightly.

When he married Maddy, Jeb knew there'd be a number of concessions on his part, but he loved her enough to make them. She'd certainly made concessions of her own—one of which was living so far out of town, away from her friends and the grocery she'd purchased a little more than a year ago. Church for Maddy would be a social outlet, and it would uplift her emotionally and spiritually. Women needed that.

Jeb and Maddy had met soon after she'd bought the one and only grocery store in Buffalo Valley. Her life-long friend, Lindsay Snyder, had begun teaching at the high school and married Gage Sinclair the following summer. Maddy had been Lindsay's maid of honor; the very day of the wedding she'd decided to settle in Buffalo Valley herself.

Jeb would be forever grateful that she had. His life changed the day he rescued Maddy during a blizzard. She'd been trapped in her car while delivering groceries and would have frozen to death if he hadn't found her when he did. He'd brought her home with him, never suspecting that their time together would have consequences affecting both their lives. Consequences that included an unexpected pregnancy… He'd fallen in love with her in those three snowbound days. After losing his leg in a farming accident several years earlier, Jeb had thought it would never be possible for him to live a normal life again—or to feel normal emotions, normal desires. Maddy had shown him otherwise. They'd been married four months now and he was so much in love with her he had to pinch himself every once in a while to convince himself this was real.

"What do you think about us attending church services?" she pressed, studying him closely.

"I think that's a fine idea," he said. It wouldn't hurt and might even do him some good.

Her smile told him how much she appreciated his response.

A few minutes later, Maddy efficiently changed Julianne's diaper, then settled into the rocking chair. She unbuttoned her blouse and bared her breast for their baby. Fascinated, Jeb watched as his infant daughter instinctively turned toward her mother and greedily latched on.

Maddy rocked gently and hummed a lullaby. It wasn't long before his daughter had taken her fill and Maddy carried her into the nursery to prepare her for the night.

Jeb had the television on, watching a news broadcast, when Maddy joined him. They'd decided to skip dinner, since they'd eaten the equivalent of a meal at Bernard's wake that afternoon. Now, sitting at her husband's side, Maddy picked up her knitting, a recently learned skill. Leta Betts, a devout knitter and Lindsay's mother-in-law, had taught both Maddy and Lindsay how to knit while they were pregnant. "I wonder what Margaret's going to do now."

Jeb glanced away from the television long enough to recognize that Maddy needed to talk about this. He reached for the remote control and muted the sound. "It wasn't as though Bernard's death came as a shock."

"I know. It's just that…"

"What?" he urged.

"I'm worried about what'll happen to Margaret without her father there to protect her."

"How do you mean?"

"She's alone for the first time in her life—and vulnerable."

Jeb frowned. He hadn't given the matter much thought, but Maddy was right. Margaret had lived a sheltered life, protected by her father and his name.

"She's easy prey for some man. Anyone with a good line can just step in and take advantage of her. Look at all the attention she got at Bob and Merrily's wedding."

Jeb had no recollection of anything about that night except Maddy. She'd been seven months pregnant with his child. It was the night he'd asked her to marry him and she'd agreed.

"Almost every single man in Buffalo Valley invited Margaret to dance."

It went without saying that the transformation in Margaret's appearance and manner was due to Maddy's efforts.

Maddy's knitting needles clicked more rapidly, signaling her anxiety. "Margaret is about to become a very wealthy woman."

"Credit her with some sense, Maddy," Jeb said. "She's intelligent and capable. Bernard made sure of that."

"I agree with you, except for one thing."

"What's that?"

"She'd marry Matt Eilers in a heartbeat. Don't ask me why, but she's in love with the man." The knitting needles were a blur by now. "He'd take advantage of her, too."

"You don't know that," Jeb said, although he suspected she was right. He wasn't any fonder of Matt Eilers than Maddy was. They'd never had any business dealings, he and Matt, so Jeb had no concrete reason to distrust the rancher. But he did.

"I hate myself for thinking ill of him," she muttered.

Jeb shrugged. He viewed Eilers as a weak man, although he wasn't sure exactly what had shaped that opinion.

Maddy's sigh was expressive. "Last I heard, he was dating Sheryl Decker in Devils Lake."

Jeb had never heard of her. "Who?"

"Sheryl Decker. She waits tables at a truck stop outside town."

"Maybe he'll marry her, then," Jeb suggested, hoping that would be the end of the discussion.

Maddy sighed and relaxed the knitting needles in her lap. "We can always hope."

"Matt," Sheryl Decker called from the bedroom. "Bring me my cigarettes, would you?"

Matt opened the refrigerator and grabbed a cold can of beer. Sheryl knew he didn't like her smoking, but his wishes didn't dissuade her.

He returned to the bedroom and tossed the pack onto the bed, the abruptness of his action telling her he didn't approve.

"You know how much I enjoy my smokes," she said, pulling open her nightstand drawer and reaching for a lighter. She placed the cigarette between her lips, lit up and blew a stream of smoke toward the ceiling.

Matt joined her on the bed and took a deep swallow of beer. He was upset with himself and with Sheryl. She knew he'd wanted to attend Bernard Clemens's funeral. He might not have liked the wealthy rancher, but Clemens was his neighbor and he felt honor-bound to pay his last respects. Sheryl, however, had other ideas, and like a fool he'd fallen under her spell—and not for the first time, either. Without much effort, she'd managed to lure him into bed; despite his best intentions, he'd let it happen.

"Are you still mad at me?" she asked, running her long fingernail down the length of his arm.

"No," he muttered. He couldn't blame anyone but himself.

"You know I have to work tonight, and this afternoon was the only time we could be together."

He did know. His mistake was in stopping by Sheryl's place at all. He'd come into Devils Lake for feed and had expected to get back before the funeral.

"You can still go to the reception, can't you?"

"No."

She wrapped her arm around his bare chest. "I'm really sorry," she purred like the sex kitten she was. Matt had never wanted this relationship to take the path it had. He'd started coming by once or twice a month for dinner and companionship. Occasionally he spent the night. They had an understanding, or so he'd assumed, one that provided mutual satisfaction. Lately, however, Sheryl had begun to bring up the uncomfortable subject of marriage. Matt didn't try to argue simply because it was easier to let her talk than to argue.

"I was thinking we should get married after the first of the year," she said, taking another deep drag of her cigarette.

Matt sighed. He didn't understand what it was with women and marriage. "Yeah, maybe. Whatever."

"Don't sound so enthusiastic," she said with heavy sarcasm.

"I can't figure out why women are always so eager to get married."

Sheryl stared at him incredulously. "Do you think I want to wait tables the rest of my life?"

To be perfectly honest, he'd never thought about it one way or the other.

"You planning to marry anyone else?" she demanded, then without asking helped herself to a long swallow of his beer.

"Margaret Clemens," he said, knowing that was sure to get a reaction.

"Margaret Clemens," Sheryl repeated with a harsh laugh. "That's a joke, right?"

"Not according to her father."

Sheryl twisted around so she could look him in the eye. "You talked to Bernard Clemens about marrying Margaret?"

"No," he said, disliking the cold tone of her voice. "He mentioned it to me."

"When did he do that?" She brushed the bleached blond curls away from her forehead.

"A few weeks back. He asked to talk to me and I went over to see him."

"And what exactly did he say?"

"He claimed Margaret's in love with me."

"Is she?"

Matt lifted both shoulders in a shrug. He hadn't told anyone about the conversation. He'd never considered Margaret in romantic terms, and it flustered him to think she held any such feelings for him. Not that he was interested. Margaret was, well…Margaret. He didn't even view her as a woman, like Sheryl, for instance, who was feminine from the top of her head to the tips of her crimson-painted toes. Although if memory served him right, Margaret had been dressed in something pretty the night of Buffalo Bob and Merrily's wedding.

"Her dad warned you off, did he?" Sheryl asked, apparently finding the question humorous.

Matt wasn't sure how to answer. "As a matter of fact, no. He seemed to think I'd marry her."

"For her money?"

Matt nodded. "According to him, Margaret's determined to have me."

"Really?" Sheryl made a low snickering sound.

"That's what he said." It wasn't something to brag about. Actually it was more of an embarrassment than anything. Ever since their conversation, Matt had gone out of his way to avoid Margaret Clemens.

"Are you going to marry her?"

"No!" His denial was swift and angry. How could Sheryl even suspect him of something like that?

She didn't say anything for several moments, then seemed to come to some conclusion that excited her. Tossing aside the blankets, she scrambled to her knees and a slow smile crept over her wide mouth. "Why *not* marry her?"

"Well, for one thing, I don't love her. For another…" He couldn't think of a second reason fast enough. "Hey, I thought you wanted me to marry *you*."

"You will, make no mistake about it. But you could marry Margaret first."

He couldn't believe his ears. "Why would I want to do that?"

"Why?" she asked as if that was the most hilarious question anyone had every posed. "Because she's *rich*."

"So?"

"You've been hoping to buy the Stockert ranch for years."

"Yes, but—"

"You can have it."

Matt frowned, beginning to sense what Sheryl was suggesting. "I hope you're not saying what I think you are."

"Sure I am. Marry her. She's already in love with you—isn't that what her daddy said? Give her what she wants, and then after a few months file for divorce."

Matt had never heard anything more heartless. "That's cruel."

"Matt, she has more money than she knows what to do with. Think of the months you're married to Margaret as a way to help her through her grieving. She needs someone and she *wants* you. All you'd be doing is giving her what she needs *and* what she wants. You'd just be…providing a service."

Matt's frown darkened.

"Why else do you think her daddy called you in for that little talk?" Sheryl continued persuasively. "He knew that Margaret was going to need you. In his own way, he was asking you to watch over his little girl. And once Margaret understands that, she'll be grateful. Grateful enough to buy you the Stockert place."

Matt didn't like the sound of this. "Bernard warned me not to hurt her."

"You wouldn't be hurting her, you'd be helping her through a difficult period in her life. Think about it, Matt. Bernard practically *ordered* you to step in and take care of his little girl. Besides, she's in love with you, so she'll do whatever you ask. It's only fair that you be compensated for what you're giving her. You'll just have to convince her that a year of marriage is worth the price of the Stockert place. And then…you'd have your ranch."

He wanted Sheryl to shut up; her plan was starting to seem plausible.

"I could quit my job and then the two of us could get married…"

Matt shook his head. "Forget it," he said. "Besides, once I married Margaret, what makes you think I'd want a divorce?"

Sheryl burst out laughing. "Two things," she said.

"First of all, we're talking about Margaret Clemens here. She's got about as much sex appeal as a bag of potatoes."

Matt couldn't really argue with that, especially when he looked at Sheryl, with her lush body, large full breasts and long legs. What he'd seen of Margaret, and that was damn little, was no comparison.

"You said two things," he reminded her.

Sheryl's sultry smile returned. "I'd make damn sure you wanted to come back to me," she whispered. As if to prove herself, she showed him exactly what she meant.

Two

*Minutes of the November 23rd meeting
of the Buffalo Valley Town Council*

As recorded by Hassie Knight, Secretary and Treasurer, duly elected.

The meeting was brought to order by council president Joshua McKenna with the Pledge of Allegiance to the American flag. Council members in attendance were Joshua McKenna, Dennis Urlacher, Heath Quantrill, Robert Carr, Gage Sinclair and Hassie Knight. Reverend Larry Dawson was an invited guest.

1. In the matter of old business, Joshua McKenna reported that a new siren has been installed by the Volunteer Fire Department. It will be used to alert the community in the event of a fire and to summon volunteers to the station. While the alarm was being tested, there were several complaints regarding the loud, piercing sound. Mrs. Summerhill, an elderly friend visiting Leta Betts, assumed the siren was an early warning of an air attack and was upset

to learn there were no bomb shelters in Buffalo Valley. Joshua McKenna suggested a sign be posted informing visitors about the meaning of the siren.

2. Also in the matter of old business, it was reported that the high school will not be putting on the annual Christmas play this December, due to the birth of Mrs. Sinclair's daughter. Gage Sinclair provided the council with the most current pictures of two-month-old Joy Leta Sinclair and reported that both mother and daughter are doing well.

3. In the matter of new business, the council officially welcomed Reverend Larry Dawson back to the community. Although his family has long since moved away, Larry has fond memories of growing up in Buffalo Valley. If all goes well, Larry and his wife, Joyce, plan to retire here. A buffet lunch was served following the meeting, catered by Bob Carr of 3 OF A KIND.

4. Joshua McKenna announced that the growth of Buffalo Valley has attracted the attention of our state government. He has been contacted by the governor's office, inquiring what actions town council has undertaken to bring about the changes. Further to this subject, Dennis Urlacher reported that Sarah now has five full-time employees and has expanded the business into the building connected to the one she now occupies. Because Buffalo Valley Quilts is attracting not only business, but tourists, Dennis suggested a beautification program, including stone flowerpots and flags on each

corner for the Fourth of July. The matter was discussed, but a vote delayed until after Christmas.

5. The meeting adjourned at twelve-thirty for the luncheon to welcome Reverend Larry Dawson.

Respectfully submitted,
Hassie Knight

"Bob! Bob!"

Merrily's cry jolted Buffalo Bob Carr out of a deep sleep. Hearing the panic in his wife's voice, he instantly threw aside the covers and bolted out of bed. She called him a second time but Bob was already staggering toward Axel's bedroom. The toddler had been fussy all night and they'd taken turns comforting him. Bob felt sure the two-year-old was coming down with another ear infection. Each bout seemed to be worse than the one before.

"What's wrong?" he asked, blinking the sleep from his eyes.

Merrily sat on the edge of the bed with Axel in her arms. "Look. He's got a rash or something. What is it?"

Bob rubbed his eyes, then stared at the child in the dim light. Axel gazed up at him, his brown eyes filled with fear. Merrily was gazing at him, too, her face anxious.

Bob let out a short, abrupt laugh. "That, my dear wife, is chicken pox. Axel has chicken pox."

Merrily framed the boy's face between her hands and studied him intently. "Where did he get them?"

Bob shrugged. "Who knows? It's contagious. Every kid gets chicken pox at some time or other."

"But he's miserable!"

Bob didn't know much about childhood diseases, but he knew chicken pox was a common enough ailment. "I'll go and see Hassie in the morning. I'm sure there's something she can suggest."

"Daddy, Daddy." Axel stretched his arms toward Bob.

"I'll stay with him," Bob volunteered, knowing Merrily had been up most of the night.

"Thanks," she whispered, and kissed Axel's head before she handed him to Bob.

With regret Bob watched her return to their bedroom, wishing he could join her. Instead, he slipped beneath the covers in the narrow single bed and cradled Axel against his chest. The boy rested his head there and whimpered softly. "Hurt, Daddy, hurt."

Bob pressed his hand against Axel's forehead and noted that he didn't have a fever. Merrily had probably already given him Tylenol. "Try to sleep," Bob urged.

Axel nodded. "Sing the song about nannytucket."

Grinning, he shook his head. Merrily didn't approve of his singing off-color ditties to the boy. Especially the one that started "There once was a man from Nantucket."

Instead he hummed a nursery rhyme the two had learned from a *Barney* video. Six months ago, if anyone had told him he'd willingly sit with a two-year-old to watch a purple dinosaur, Bob would have called that person a bold-faced liar.

Trusting and small, Axel nestled in his muscular arms. In the faint light, Bob ran his hand over the youngster's head, still humming softly. He loved the boy as dearly and completely as if they shared the same blood. However, his feelings for Axel hadn't started out that way.

Nearly four years ago Bob had been riding through

Buffalo Valley on his Harley when he met Dave Ertz. Dave owned the bar and grill, which was also the town's only hotel. He'd been trying to sell it, but when no buyers materialized, Dave—an inventive sort—had thrown a poker game with a thousand-dollar entry fee. The winner got the entire business, lock, stock and barrel. Bob won with three of a kind, hence the bar's new name.

Bob had been a loner and a drifter all his adult life. Because he rode a Hog, most people assumed he was part of the biker crowd. Bob enjoyed the reputation—he dressed the part, talked the talk—but he'd never been a gang member or participated in gang activities.

He'd been in business a few months, struggling to make ends meet the same way Dave had, when Merrily appeared. He'd recognized immediately that they were two of a kind. Now, with Axel, they were three of a kind. He grinned—three of a kind. Just like the bar.

Merrily had walked in one day looking for a job, and despite his lack of spare cash and customers, he'd hired her on the spot. Bob had sensed then that she was more than simply passing through his town—and his life.

They hit it off, and within weeks, Bob was entertaining thoughts of asking Merrily to move in with him, when suddenly she disappeared. That first time, the second time, too, had unsettled him. After that, he'd realized this was a pattern with her. Sometime around the third year, her visits came fast and furious and then one day, out of the blue, she showed up with Axel.

Bob knew the kid didn't belong to her. For one thing, the timing was all wrong. And whenever Bob asked her about Axel, she clammed up. Once, when he'd pressured her, she'd flippantly announced she'd won him in a poker game. Funny, real funny.

Not knowing the kid's background was worry

enough, but during those first few weeks, the boy was also a real pain in the butt. He constantly needed attention and no matter what Bob did, Axel refused to look him in the face. The toddler clung to Merrily, which proved to be downright frustrating to a man in need of his woman.

Little by little, the details came out, and Bob learned that the burn scars on Axel's thighs had come from his father. His parents had physically and mentally abused him; heaven only knew what would've happened had Merrily not been there to protect him. When it looked as though they were going to sell Axel to the highest bidder, Merrily had taken him herself. It went without saying that if the authorities were ever to find Axel, she'd be hip-deep in trouble. Him, too, seeing that he was part of all this now.

When he'd heard some of what the little boy had suffered at the hands of his parents, Bob's heart softened. He hadn't been keen on sharing Merrily, but she'd made it plain that she and Axel came as a package deal. Within a month he felt as protective toward the boy as Merrily did.

Soon Bob found himself looking forward to spending time with the child. At night, after Axel's bath, he often read to him. Merrily claimed that Bob's stories were the only thing Axel would sit still for. Bob had never felt completely responsible for another human being before; now he did. Now he had someone who needed him and loved him unconditionally. In the same way that Merrily was the only mother Axel had, Bob became his father.

After a trip to the doctor's office, when Axel developed his first ear infection, it became apparent that they were going to need a forged birth certificate. Bob had obtained one; that same day, he bought an engagement ring and asked Merrily to marry him.

She agreed, and their wedding was the best day of his life. The entire town of Buffalo Valley had celebrated with them. Bob had never known such happiness. Merrily was his wife and for all intents and purposes, Axel was his son. Life was good—and he should have known it wouldn't last. Should have realized that anything this perfect was bound to fall apart, probably sooner rather than later.

He and Merrily had been married only a few weeks when Bob learned that Axel's picture had appeared on a flyer sponsored by the Foundation for Missing Children. It had circulated throughout the country.

How many had turned up in Buffalo Valley, Bob didn't know. Most folks tossed them aside without looking carefully, and anyone who might have recognized Axel wasn't saying. But the fact remained: the authorities were searching for Axel. Not knowing what to do, Bob had discussed the situation with Maddy, who until recently had been employed as a social worker. Circumstances being what they were, Bob wasn't exactly able to disguise his predicament.

Maddy gave him the name of an attorney in Georgia she said he could trust. A man who specialized in difficult cases like this one.

Yes, Merrily had stolen Axel and transported him over state lines, but in doing so she'd saved his life. Bob's greatest fear was that if he approached the lawyer, he'd be in danger of losing both Merrily and Axel. His life wouldn't be worth living without them. But the crazy part, the incredible part, was that no one seemed to have connected Axel with the boy in the flyer. Within a few weeks, Bob began to believe they'd had a lucky escape, so he'd done nothing more. He hadn't called the lawyer. Why look for trouble? In the months since, the only people they'd allowed near Axel were townsfolk. No one had questioned either Merrily or him about the boy, and he trusted that the people in this town, whether they were aware of the truth or not, would protect the family as much as possible.

Axel stirred, and Bob could see that the boy had fallen asleep. Lovingly, he leaned down and kissed his forehead. No one was taking this child away. As God was his witness, he wouldn't let that happen.

"Sleep well, little man," he whispered, awake and alert.

Three weeks following the burial of Bernard Clemens, Matt Eilers decided to pay Margaret a condolence visit. Sheryl continually pestered him about it, wanting to know when he intended to see the dead rancher's daughter. She'd gone so far as to tell him what to say and how to act. The idea of marrying Margaret Clemens—or any woman—for money was repugnant to him. Sheryl tried to make it sound as though he'd be doing the poor girl a favor, but Matt wasn't naive enough to swallow that. He did, however, feel almost sorry for Margaret. She wasn't outright homely, but she wasn't pretty, either. Tall and skinny, she didn't have much of a shape. She was definitely lacking in charm and in social skills, and she seemed rather lonely.

Sheryl argued that Margaret was ripe for the picking and if Matt didn't marry her, then someone less scrupulous would. Of all the arguments she'd put forth, that one struck him as true.

Snow had fallen the week before, and his tires crunched on the gravel drive as he pulled to a stop in the Clemens yard. No one came out to greet him, so he moved onto the back porch and with his hat in his hand, waited for someone to answer his knock.

The housekeeper appeared. Her name was Sadie, he recalled from that first and only visit. It suited her—a plain, old-fashioned name. "You're here to see Margaret?" she asked, her gruff tone devoid of welcome.

"I'd like to pay my respects."

"Seems to me you're about three weeks late."

Matt let the comment slide. He knew one thing for sure: if he did marry Margaret, the first thing he'd do was hire a different housekeeper. The thought pulled him up short. Sheryl was getting to him. He *wasn't* going to marry Margaret, no matter how many arguments Sheryl advanced.

He remembered reading advice from Ann Landers years ago, in a newspaper he'd found in a doctor's waiting room. She'd said something to the effect that the people who worked hardest for their money were those who married for it. Matt wasn't in the habit of shying away from real work, and he didn't intend to live off anyone else. When he was able to buy the Stockert ranch, it would be with money he'd earned himself.

"Margaret's in the barn," the housekeeper told him. Her gaze narrowed as if she were Bernard Clemens himself warning Matt to tread lightly around his daughter.

"How is she?"

Sadie paused. "She has good days and she has bad days."

"She was close to her father, wasn't she?"

The housekeeper nodded. "Mr. Clemens was a good man. Margaret is a good person, too." With that, she slammed the door, leaving him to make his own way to the barn. Not that Matt needed anyone to draw him a map, but he would have appreciated at least the pretense of welcome.

He found Margaret inside the huge structure that put his own barn to shame. She was dressed in a heavy coat and thick boots; a knit cap covered her head. Her hair, which she'd grown over the past year, was pulled away from her face and tied at the base of her neck. He could see she'd had it curled. Working at a fast and furious pace, she pitched hay into an empty stall, her back toward him. Matt breathed in the satisfying scents of horses, straw and well-oiled leather.

"Margaret," Matt called softly, not wanting to frighten her.

She whirled around and when she saw him, she stood transfixed, as if she'd been waiting for exactly this moment for a very long time. "Matt!"

"I wanted to stop by and tell you how sorry I am about your father."

She stared at him with wide, adoring eyes, then raised her sleeve to her red nose, cheeks ruddy with exertion. So it was true, what Bernard had said—she was in love with him. But despite Sheryl's urging, he refused to do anything about it. He wouldn't lead Margaret to believe he reciprocated her feelings—or that they had any kind of future.

"I knew you'd come," she whispered.

He looked away, embarrassed that it'd taken him three weeks to make an appearance. "I meant to get here before this."

Her timid smile forgave him and he wanted to kick himself. Sheryl was right, even if her reasons were wrong; he should have come earlier.

"Your father was highly thought of around here."

Margaret nodded, and he could see by the way her

lip trembled that she was fighting back emotion. "I miss him something fierce."

"I know you do." Matt remembered when his own father died. He'd been fifteen, an age when it was difficult to express grief. He'd feared that if other kids saw him cry, they'd call him a sissy, so he'd lashed out at his mother. Why, he didn't know. Probably because his parents had divorced and he'd blamed her, always blamed her. She never knew—or perhaps she did—that he'd been the person who'd slashed her tires. He'd done it in a fit of rage, and that had been the beginning of trouble for him. Before he was out of his teen years, he'd had more than one scrape with the law.

Now his mother, too, was dead, and he carried a double load of grief—and guilt. He didn't think about his parents much, not anymore, but the memories never quite left him.

"Would you like to come inside?"

Her eyes were hopeful, and Matt didn't have the heart to disappoint her.

"I'd offer you a beer, but Maddy told me—" She closed her mouth abruptly and blushed. "Sadie keeps a pot of coffee on all day."

"Coffee would be fine. I can't stay long." Especially if Sadie was going to be giving him the evil eye. What had Maddy told her? he wondered next. That he drank too much? That he couldn't be trusted? Obviously, his reputation had preceded him.

Margaret led the way into the house, stopping just inside the heated porch to remove her jacket and boots; he did the same. She opened the kitchen door and they were greeted by an array of warm, inviting smells. Matt glanced around, relieved that Sadie was nowhere in sight.

Matt noted the coveralls Margaret wore. They were shapeless and about the most unflattering piece of clothing she could have chosen. Yet when she stood on tiptoe to reach for a cup in the top cupboard, he was stunned to see that she had a halfway decent body.

Scolding himself, Matt forced his gaze elsewhere.

"Sadie bakes the most delicious cookies," she told him as she opened the cookie jar and placed a dozen or so on a china plate. "I'd suggest we sit in the den, but neither of us is dressed for it."

Margaret slowly approached the table, carrying a serving tray with two small china cups, sugar, cream and the plate of chocolate chip cookies.

"I'll pour," she announced grandly, as if this feat required unusual skill. She left and returned with the coffeepot and filled each floral-patterned cup to the brim, then smiled hesitantly, apparently awaiting his approval.

"Thank you," he mumbled, uncertain what was expected of him. He felt nervous even touching the dainty porcelain cup, afraid he might snap off the delicate handle.

"This set belonged to my mother," Margaret explained as she sat across the table from him.

"It's very nice."

"It's all I have of her, except for the jewelry my father gave her, but I've never worn any of that."

Rather than risk breaking the cup, Matt gingerly lifted it with both hands. There was a long silence. "I hope you're adjusting," he finally blurted out. "To your father's death, I mean."

Margaret didn't reply right away, then said, "I'm trying."

"Is there anything I can do?" His gaze held hers. He was surprised to realize what pretty eyes she had.

Huge. A startling dark blue. Glossy black lashes. She stared at him, her expression completely rapt. Meeting her eyes for any length of time proved disconcerting and he promptly looked elsewhere. The girl had it bad, he thought with a sinking sensation. He wanted to warn her off, tell her she was making a mistake, but he couldn't find the words. The women he dated knew the score, but Margaret was as innocent as a newborn calf. Naive, too, and completely inexperienced; that was obvious. What he needed to do was leave, and the sooner the better.

"I appreciate the offer, but there's nothing anyone can do," Margaret told him.

It took Matt a moment to realize she was answering his question. He nodded. "Well…"

"The ranch is going to be all right," she went on.

Matt took a discreet sip of his coffee. "If you find you need anything, let me know."

Now it was her turn to nod. "I will. Thank you for offering."

"I'm sincere, Margaret," he surprised himself by saying. "You're a capable rancher and I don't mean to imply otherwise, but there are times when neighbors need to rely on one another. I'm here for you, understand?" He told himself he would have said the same thing to any local rancher who'd suffered a loss or some sort of crisis.

"And I'm here for you," she said in a low voice.

Matt downed the last of his coffee in one gulp, eager to be on his way. He'd stayed longer than he wanted, longer than required.

"You're leaving?" she blurted.

"It's time I headed out," he said. Matt could tell she was disappointed, but she didn't employ any clever means of detaining him. That was one of Sheryl's tricks.

He'd make noises about going home and she'd find some excuse to keep him with her. He had to give her credit; she was inventive—and often very sexy. Lately he'd been more conscious of her efforts and had become amused at the things she'd said and done to delay him. Sheryl could be one manipulative little devil.

"I'll walk you to your truck," Margaret told him, taking the coffee cups and tray to the kitchen counter.

He started to tell her that wasn't necessary, then changed his mind. Being stared at by a woman's adoring eyes was a flattering sensation, and Matt wasn't beyond enjoying it.

Margaret quickly put her mud-caked boots back on her feet. She buttoned her coat all the way to her chin and stuck a knit cap on her head without any concern about what it did to her hair.

"I appreciate your stopping by," she told him as they reached the truck.

"I'm sorry I didn't come sooner."

"I am, too." She blushed then, as if she regretted having said this.

"If you'd like, I could stop by again."

Her eyes flared with excitement. "I wish you would."

Matt wasn't sure what had prompted the offer. His ranch adjoined the Clemens property but this was only the second time he'd come to the house. Dropping by unannounced wasn't a habit he planned to cultivate.

"Come any time," she added, "any time at all." She sounded so pleased and excited.

What happened then was something Matt would always wonder about. One moment he was preparing to climb into his truck and the next he'd wrapped his arms around Margaret Clemens the way he would Sheryl. He kissed her. He wasn't sure why—curiosity, he supposed. He couldn't keep himself from finding out what it would be like to kiss her. Since she hadn't expected a kiss, it wasn't fair to judge. But he did, mainly because he was kind of shocked. As kisses went, it was pretty good. No, damn good. Uncomplicated and—he hated to use this word—sweet. With other women, those with experience, a kiss was never simple. It involved tongues and teeth and it was often explosive with passion and need. A kiss hadn't been innocent for him in a very long while.

He broke it off and released her. Margaret faltered and would have stumbled backward if he hadn't caught her by the shoulders.

An apology would be appropriate, but he wasn't sorry. If he was anything, it was confused.

"I'll check up on you later in the week," he managed to say.

She nodded and pressed the back of her hand to her lips. Her eyes were wide and jubilant, her lashes fluttering as if she didn't know how to react.

Matt drove out of the yard and was halfway down the driveway when he glanced in his rearview mirror. Margaret stood there unmoving, her hand still against her lips, staring after him.

"That's it," Matt said aloud, shaken and bewildered by his own actions. "I'm not coming back. Not for anything."

Calla Stern had expected her troubles to be over when she moved in with her father in Minneapolis. Her mother and Dennis Urlacher had publicly announced their engagement and hadn't even bothered to let her know beforehand. Although she supposed if they *had* approached her, it would have been a wasted effort.

She wanted nothing to do with Dennis, and no way did she want to be part of their perfect little family. Not in this lifetime!

Calla had always disliked Dennis. If it wasn't for Dennis, she told herself, her parents might have reconciled when she was younger. She detested them both—Dennis and her mother—for the things they'd done, sneaking around, pretending no one knew they were having an affair. When Calla learned that her mother wasn't even divorced at the time, she'd felt sickened by their disgusting behavior. Later, she'd been insulted and furious that they'd decided to get married and completely excluded her from their plans. Obviously they didn't want her in their lives. Well, that was fine with her; Buffalo Valley was such a hick town and she'd wanted to get out of there, anyway. So it seemed fitting that she'd run away the night Dennis and her mother announced their engagement.

Living with her father, however, had turned out to be less than ideal. She'd been five when her parents separated, and her memories of Willie Stern had been hazy. Over the past eleven years he'd sent her the occasional postcard and intermittently kept in touch. Without realizing it, Calla had placed him on a pedestal—from which he'd quickly tumbled. Her view of Willie Stern had completely changed by the end of her first week with him.

Despite that, she still felt she'd had no choice. After her mother decided to marry Dennis, Calla had packed her bags, borrowed her grandfather's truck and driven into Grand Forks, where she caught the bus to Minneapolis. It would be an understatement to say that Willie was surprised by her sudden appearance on her doorstep, but he'd let her move in with him.

For the first time in conscious memory, Calla had the opportunity to live in a real city with shopping malls, brand-name clothing stores and a school with more than twenty-five students. She didn't need to order an outfit on the Internet or from a catalogue but could walk into a store and try it on in a real dressing room. She had the opportunity to meet lots of other kids her own age, not just a handful. It didn't matter that her father had been such a bitter disappointment. Soon after her arrival she'd run away from Willie's place, but when her mother and Dennis came to collect her, she'd chosen to go back with her father rather than return to Buffalo Valley. She could put up with Willie more easily than she could accept the idea of Dennis Urlacher as her stepfather.

"You get those floors mopped?" Jason Jefferies asked.

Jason was only a year older than she was, but he was the manager of the BurgerHaven where Calla worked part-time. "Didn't you notice? I finished half an hour ago," she said, unable to contain her sarcasm.

"Don't give me attitude," Jason snapped. "I got three friends who'd jump at the chance to work here. You give me a reason to fire you, Calla, and you're outta here."

"Yes, sir," she said with a falsely sweet smile. Much as she hated to admit it, she needed this job. Her father's income was erratic, its source questionable. And he sure didn't share it with her. The reverse, in fact. Not waiting for a response, she turned and walked away.

Willie wasn't the only disappointment Calla had to face. The high school back in Buffalo Valley had twenty-five students. Twenty-five. The one she attended in Minneapolis had over three thousand—more people than lived in her hometown *and* the surrounding county. Finding her way from classroom to classroom before the bell rang was a major challenge. She'd already gotten nine tardy slips. One more and she'd be ordered to afternoon detention.

One teacher, Mr. Simon, had been totally unreasonable. She had swimming in fifth period, and her sixth-period algebra class was on the third floor in the east wing. A sprinter couldn't have covered that distance in five minutes! Mr. Simon docked her grade one full point every time she was late, and that was totally unfair. Her jaw tightened whenever she thought about it. The only classes in which she got decent grades were art and drama, because she'd volunteered to sew costumes for the senior production. They were doing *The Importance of Being Earnest*, and that meant lots of intricate Victorian dresses. Calla could lose herself in working with the patterns and fabric, in getting the details perfect.

Jason dimmed the lights and was ready to close the BurgerHaven.

Swallowing her pride, Calla approached him. "Any chance you could give me a ride home?"

He didn't like doing it, she knew, but waiting for the bus by herself unnerved her. A couple of men had harassed her one night, and she'd had nightmares about it ever since. She hated to ask Jason for a ride, but she didn't have any other means of getting home, besides the bus.

"You'll have to pay."

Calla nodded. What a jerk. He collected an hour's wages for driving her one block out of his way. If he charged her any more, she might as well take a taxi.

Jason wasn't the talkative sort and they rode in silence. Calla had hoped to make friends before now, but it hadn't happened. School had been in session nearly three months, and she didn't have one friend. Not even one. Trying to get to class on time was difficult enough.

Her father was sprawled in front of the television when she let herself into the apartment. She brought the mail and the free neighborhood newspaper in with her.

"You bring me anything?" he asked, not moving his gaze from the television screen.

"Not tonight."

That got his attention. "They throw away all the stuff that doesn't get sold, so why the hell not bring me a taco burger?"

Calla wondered if it ever occurred to him that they might not *have* leftovers. "There weren't any," she said, tired and out of sorts. *It's after ten*, she wanted to scream. *Leave me alone!*

"Damn! I was all set for a taco burger, too. I don't suppose you could get me dinner?" He looked beseechingly toward her.

Like she was a magician and could pull a decent meal out of a top hat. "Get you dinner?" she repeated. "With what?"

He leaned back and dug into his pants pocket and tossed her his car keys. "With these."

Calla left the keys on the floor where they'd fallen. She set down her books and sorted through the mail, although it was mostly dunning letters from bill collectors and a few advertising circulars. She paused when she saw the envelope with her mother's familiar writing. This wasn't the first letter she'd received, and her reaction was always the same—hope and excitement. Even though she didn't *want* to feel anything for her mother.

Sarah Stern had lied to her, and Calla refused to forgive her—for that and a truckload of other faults. The biggest of which was marrying Dennis Urlacher.

"You going or not?" her father demanded.

Calla barely heard him. A wave of homesickness threatened to drown her. She missed Buffalo Valley, missed her friends and her old job at The Pizza Parlor and even her old school. Her mother had ruined everything by marrying Dennis. Calla's entire life had been stolen from her and it was their fault.

"What's that?" Willie asked.

"A letter from Mom."

"She send me any money?"

Calla rolled her eyes. Willie insisted that if Sarah wasn't paying him the child support he thought he was entitled to, then Calla had to pay rent. Therefore, Calla paid rent.

"Well, aren't you going to open it?"

"Yes," she said, and headed toward her bedroom. When she did read the letter, she had no intention of doing it in front of him.

Sitting on the side of her bed, Calla stared at the envelope. It was thick, as if it included something extra. Her curiosity got the better of her and she tore it open. Inside were an airline ticket and a letter. She unfolded the letter.

Dear Calla,

I haven't been able to reach you by phone to ask about your plans for Thanksgiving. I'm hoping you can arrange to make it home for a few days. It would mean a great deal to me. I miss you, Calla. I realize I haven't been the world's best mother, and I've made plenty of mistakes, but I do love you.

On the chance you can get away, I've enclosed an airline ticket. The flight leaves Minneapolis Wednesday afternoon and returns on Sunday morning. Dennis and I would pick you up at the airport in

Grand Forks. If you're uncomfortable staying with
Dennis and me, then your grandfather wanted you
to know you could have your old room at his house.

Everything's going well here in Buffalo Valley.
Dennis and I bought the old Habberstad house.
The two of us rattle around in it, but we both
enjoy decorating it. With five bedrooms you could
have your pick if you decided you wanted to move
back home.

You haven't answered my letters or taken any
of my calls. I know you're angry with me, Calla,
and I'm sorry. It's time we settled all this. Don't
you think so, too?
Love,
Mom

"What did she have to say?" Willie asked, standing
in her bedroom doorway.

"Nothing," Calla muttered, stuffing the letter inside
her backpack.

"What's that?" he asked, pointing to the airline ticket
she'd set beside her on the bed.

"A ticket."

He laughed. "Home for Thanksgiving, right?"

Calla didn't answer.

"Home sweet home with Mommy and her new husband. You're not going, are you?"

"I haven't decided."

He glared at her. "I was hoping you and I could spend
the day together."

Calla recognized that for the bribe it was.

"It'll be the first Thanksgiving we've had in eleven
years. You aren't walking out on me now, are you, kid?"

"I said I hadn't made up my mind yet."

He leaned against the doorjamb, arms crossed. "Did she tell you she's pregnant?"

Calla's gaze flew to her father. He was baiting her and she refused to bite. It would be just like Willie to make this up, but at the same time Calla knew that Dennis wanted a family. She supposed her mother *could* be pregnant. Still, she wasn't sure she could trust Willie.

"She told me so herself," he muttered.

"I don't believe you."

"Ask her, then. She was saving it as a big secret, but she spilled the beans last time she called."

Calla frowned uncertainly. Her father had a habit of lying, of saying exactly what she wanted to hear. Or *didn't* want to hear, depending on the reaction he was after.

"I'll tell you what," Willie said, sounding bored with the subject. "You do what you want for Thanksgiving. Stay or go, it's up to you. But as for your mother having a baby, ask yourself what you think is true." With that, he left.

Calla stared down at the airline ticket. Then, with a deep sigh, jumped to her feet and threw it onto the rickety dresser beside the bed.

Her mother had made her choice, and she'd picked Dennis Urlacher over her.

Three

Rachel Fischer sat in a corner of her restaurant kitchen, where she kept her computer and desk. Writing out a check for the final payment of her loan from the Buffalo County Bank, she signed her name with a flair—and a deep sense of satisfaction. She ripped the check from the book, then stared at it, absorbing the significance of the moment. From this point forward, she was out of debt and free to pursue a relationship with Heath Quantrill, the bank president.

With the last of her bills paid for the month, she put on her hat and coat and headed for the bank. She walked briskly, facing the wind. Normally, the cold cut straight through her, but not today. She hadn't seen Heath in a few weeks and looked forward to personally handing him the check.

He served as the senior loan officer and manager and worked at the Buffalo Valley branch three days a week, spending the other two at the bank's headquarters in Grand Forks.

Rachel and Heath had an on-again/off-again relationship that she'd wasted copious hours analyzing. But over the summer their romance had grown serious and they saw one another exclusively. Since Rachel was a widow, much of her time went into supporting herself and her son. Heath wanted her to go out with him more often, but that was impossible and often a source of conflict. He'd suggested that if she invested as much time in their relationship as she did in her business, she need never worry about working again. The memory of that conversation infuriated her whenever she thought about it.

This past year had been difficult for them. She'd expanded both the hours and the menu of her weekend pizza delivery service—to reasonably consistent success. After paying off her original loan—for the pizza oven—she'd borrowed from the bank again to purchase tables and chairs and had turned her restaurant into a sit-down place serving dinner five days a week.

Her parents owned the building, so her rent was low. They'd operated the Morningside Café for many years, until the diner simply couldn't survive in such a difficult economic climate. It'd broken her mother's heart to leave Buffalo Valley and she'd pleaded with Rachel to join them in Arizona.

A recent widow at the time, Rachel had debated long and hard about uprooting her young son, and eventually decided against it. Mark had endured enough upheaval in his life after the loss of his father. Besides, every book she'd read on widowhood suggested she delay making a major decision for at least twelve months.

In order to support herself, Rachel drove the school bus and worked as a part-time bookkeeper for Knight's Pharmacy. She was barely scraping by when she came up with the idea of starting her own pizza parlor. Actually, it was her son who'd made the suggestion, claiming her homemade pizza was better than the pizza he'd eaten in a fast-food restaurant at a friend's birthday party in Grand Forks.

That was when she'd first met Heath Quantrill. Business plan in hand, she'd gone to the bank to apply for a loan. Heath had read over her application, and then, with barely a pause, refused her. True, she had nothing for collateral, although she'd offered her wedding band. She realized that on paper her business venture didn't look promising, but she was young, healthy, ambitious and determined. In addition, she'd been around the restaurant business her entire life. Heath had taken none of that into account.

The next few days had been bleak ones for Rachel. Then, to her amazement, Heath had phoned and announced he'd changed his mind. He'd never actually told her why, but she had her suspicions. Hassie Knight was good friends with Lily Quantrill, Heath's grandmother, and Rachel strongly suspected that Hassie had mentioned the loan to Lily, who had persuaded Heath to relent. Knowing Lily, she didn't think the persuasion had been of the gentle variety.

The bank was busy when Rachel walked in. Both tellers had lineups. Joanie Wyatt was there with her toddler son, and Steve Baylor, a local farmer, stood behind her. Even before she'd opened her restaurant, Rachel knew everyone in town. That wasn't saying much, though, since almost everyone knew everyone else. It was one of the advantages of living in a small town. And one of the disadvantages—when tongues wagged and other people got involved in her personal business. But for the most part she considered it a blessing.

Heath, who was in his private office, was chatting with Carl Hooper, the manager of the JCPenney catalogue store. His door was half-open, and he glanced up

when she came into the bank. He smiled, clearly pleased
to see her.

Content to wait, Rachel took a chair. The bank was
the only brick building in town, and one of the nicest, inside and out. Heath's grandparents had founded
Buffalo County Bank shortly after World War II and
over the years had expanded to ten branches across
the state. Their only son and his wife had died within
a short time of each other, leaving two sons, Max and
Heath. The elder, Max, was the one who'd revealed an
interest in the business and Lily, by now a widow, was
grooming him to take over as president. Then Max had
been killed in a car crash, and Heath, the playboy ad-
venturer, had returned from Europe to take his brother's
place. It hadn't been easy to step into Max's shoes, and
Heath had struggled with finding his own path these
past few years.

Carl Hooper left five minutes later and Rachel sprang
from her seat, then walked into Heath's office, approaching his desk.

"Hello," he said, standing to greet her. "It's good to
see you."

"Good to see you, too." Oddly, she felt almost shy
now that she actually faced him. They stared at each
other a moment before Rachel explained the purpose of
her visit. "I have two things for you," she announced,
pulling out the chair recently vacated by Carl Hooper.

"Two?" Heath raised his brows and sat down himself.

"First of all," she said, opening her purse, "this, as
far as I'm aware, is the final payment on my second
loan." She handed him the check, stretching her arm
across his desk.

"And as far as I'm aware, you're right," Heath said as
he took her check. He looked expectantly back at her.

"Also," she said, feeling flustered and excited, "I have an answer for you."

"Really." His voice became suspiciously unemotional. They'd talked about marriage a number of times, but Rachel had always managed to put him off. It didn't seem right to accept an engagement ring while she owed him money. Now the loan was paid off, she felt free to change that.

"I love you, Heath," she whispered, wishing she'd chosen the time and place more carefully. In her excitement, she'd rushed to the bank without careful thought. This *was* a public place, after all—not to mention that Heath's office door was still half-open.

"And?" he prodded.

"Aren't you going to tell me you love me, too?" she asked, thinking it was within his power to make this easier.

"No. If you don't know my feelings by now, then my telling you isn't going to make a damn bit of difference."

She could tell he was enjoying himself. He'd leaned back against his leather chair, playing the role of bank president to the hilt.

"If that's the case, I just might change my mind."

"Before you do, tell me what's *on* your mind," he cajoled.

Rachel figured he was entitled to that much. "Being your wife."

A smile exploded across his face, and he released a long, deep sigh. "At last."

Rachel agreed; it had been a long time coming, but now she was sure this was what she wanted, what was right for Heath, and for her and Mark.

"What took you so long?" he asked, coming around to her side of the desk.

He didn't know? Hadn't figured it out himself? "I made the last payment," she said, standing to meet him. "I couldn't agree to become your wife while I owed you money."

"Sure, you could have," he argued and then, right there in front of anyone who cared to look, he kissed her.

Rachel quickly became absorbed in the kiss, twining her arms around his neck, but not so absorbed that she didn't notice how quiet the bank had become. When Heath broke off the kiss, he gently disengaged her and hurried to his door. Flinging it wide-open, he called out, "We're engaged!"

His announcement was instantly followed by a chorus of congratulations and applause from staff and customers alike. Just as quickly the questions came.

"When's the wedding?"

"Does Lily know?"

"You aren't closing down The Pizza Parlor, are you?"

"You're going to live in Buffalo Valley, right?"

Rachel and Heath glanced at each other, but they didn't seem to have any ready answers. At least Rachel didn't.

"The wedding's soon. Very soon," Heath insisted, his arm around Rachel's slim waist. "Right?"

Rachel blushed and nodded.

"We'll tell Lily this evening," Heath continued, and once more looked to her for confirmation.

"I won't be closing the restaurant," she added. This had been the subject of repeated arguments between her and Heath. He didn't want her to work, but the restaurant was *hers* and she wasn't willing to give it up simply because she was marrying a wealthy man, although she did plan on hiring extra help.

"You won't?" Heath sounded surprised.

"No," she returned and elbowed him in the ribs.

"They aren't even married yet," Steve Baylor cried, "and they're already arguing."

"Every couple has issues they need to settle," Joanie Wyatt said calmly. Joanie should know; she'd recently reconciled with her husband after a yearlong separation. She and her husband, Brandon, were a good example of a couple who'd worked through the problems in their marriage.

"Rachel wants to stay right here in Buffalo Valley," Heath told everyone.

"I do," she concurred. She hadn't said anything to Heath yet, but she could see several needs arising in the community, prime business opportunities. With the success of her restaurant and Sarah's quilting company, Buffalo Valley was badly in need of a day-care center. Now that she had five full-time employees sewing for her, Sarah was expecting more women to come into town—some to buy quilts and some, eventually, to work for her. All of this meant the bank's, and therefore Heath's, increasing involvement with the town.

"You gonna kiss her again?" Steve asked.

Heath laughed. "I plan to do a lot more than kiss her. Come on," he said to Rachel, reaching for her hand. "If there was ever a time for a celebration lunch, this is it."

Rachel couldn't agree more.

Matt Eilers had kissed her. Even a week later, Margaret could hardly believe it had actually happened. In bed at night, she closed her eyes and relived the kiss. Nothing in the world could be more wonderful than Matt's wanting her.

Sure, she'd been kissed before. Well…onçe. By a ranch hand employed by her father. *Briefly* employed.

She'd been sixteen, physically underdeveloped, and as naive as they come. She was an adult now and eager to have Matt introduce her to adult experience. To show her what being a woman really meant.

For seven days she'd kept the kissing incident to herself, afraid that if she shared it with anyone else, something would be lost. But when she didn't hear from Matt again, Margaret knew she needed help in sorting out the significance of what had happened. Since Matt had kissed her once, surely that meant he'd be interested in doing it again—didn't it? But she hadn't seen her neighbor since. The only person she could ask about such things was Maddy Washburn McKenna.

Taking the truck, Margaret drove over to Maddy and Jeb's, hoping to catch Maddy when she wasn't busy with the baby. Margaret had been present when Julianne Marjorie McKenna was born, and she still considered it one of the most exciting days of her life. Over the years she'd helped a lot of calves into this world, but she'd never witnessed a human birth. Julianne's was exhilarating, a truly spectacular event in Margaret's existence.

She knew labor and delivery weren't easy on a woman; she'd been there to see Maddy's struggles. But after holding that precious baby in her arms, Margaret had understood why a woman would willingly undergo such pain.

As she rolled into the McKennas' yard and parked, Maddy waved to her from the kitchen window.

Margaret waved back. She hurried out of the cold and wind and onto the back porch, automatically slipping off her coat, hat and gloves.

"Margaret!" Maddy said, opening the back door for her. "I'm so glad to see you."

Maddy had a way of making everyone feel welcome

and...*special*, and Margaret wasn't immune to her enthusiasm.

"This is a wonderful surprise," Maddy went on.

"I'm not interrupting anything, am I?" Margaret was careful to avoid making a pest of herself. Jeb and Maddy hadn't been married long and there was the baby, too. Maddy was her closest friend, and she didn't want anything to disrupt their bond.

"This is perfect timing. Jeb's out with the herd and the baby's napping. How about a pot of tea? The water's already on."

"Sure." She didn't really want tea, but it was one of the rituals of their friendship.

A few minutes later, Maddy carried a steeping pot of tea into the living room and Margaret dutifully followed.

"How have you been?" Maddy asked. They'd spoken on the phone at least once a week, and Maddy always asked that question.

Margaret knew it wasn't her health Maddy was referring to, but her life now that her father was gone. She shrugged, saying what she usually did. "All right, I guess." After a moment's reflection, she continued, "A dozen times a day I find myself thinking I need to talk to Dad about this or that. When I realize I can't ever ask him anything again, this...this feeling of emptiness comes over me." She pressed her hand to her heart. "Some days don't seem as bad as others, but there *are* days I don't think I can go on."

"It takes time."

Margaret knew that. "I'm doing what you suggested the day of the funeral and that's to remember how fortunate I was to have him as long as I did. His life was a blessing to a lot of people."

"I said that?"

Margaret nodded. "Maybe not in those exact words."

Maddy poured the tea and smiled in amusement. "Sometimes I sound so wise, I astonish myself."

"You *are* wise—you understand about people. Actually that's the reason I came over," Margaret said, sitting back on the sofa and cradling her mug with both hands. She paused, hesitant to proceed.

Maddy said nothing, her expression quizzical.

"Matt Eilers stopped by last week to offer his condolences."

Maddy added a spoonful of sugar to her tea. "He's a little late, don't you think?"

"He apologized for that," Margaret said, quick to defend him. She took a deep breath. "When he was ready to leave, I walked him out to his truck…"

"And?" Maddy seemed to sense something important had happened because she gazed steadily at Margaret as she waited for her to go on.

"Well, before he left—" she paused a second time "—now, I don't want you to misjudge him… I realize Matt isn't one of your favorite people."

"I don't dislike him," Maddy assured her.

"But you don't trust him."

Maddy stirred her tea with no comment, then said, "I can be fair. You'd better tell me."

Margaret was dying to do so. "Oh, Maddy, he kissed me and it was just as wonderful as I dreamed it would be. At first, I didn't know what to think, since it was such a surprise and all. He started to open his truck door, then turned back, took me by the shoulders and out of the blue, he *kissed* me!"

"He kissed you," Maddy repeated in a low voice.

"Yes, and Maddy, oh Maddy, it was *wonderful*!"

"I'm sure it was…"

"I realize every other woman in the entire universe has more experience with men than I do." If it wasn't for Matt, she probably wouldn't care to this day. Being a woman, all that feminine stuff, was something she'd never had any interest in. She'd considered it trivial and, more than that, irrelevant. Most people blamed her father for not seeing to the proper upbringing of a little girl. But that was unfair. Few understood that she'd loved him so much she was determined to fulfill his every wish. Bernard Clemens had wanted a son, so Margaret had spent her entire life trying to be one.

The first time she'd felt a woman's emotions had been a shock. Matt Eilers was the reason for that revelation. One day she saw him and it felt as if she'd been hit over the head with a frying pan. He was the most gorgeous creature she'd ever laid eyes on and she wanted him in the worst way. Wanted him the way a woman wants a man.

"Now all I think about is Matt's kiss…except when I'm feeling depressed about my dad."

"Oh, Margaret…"

"No, listen, I'm happy he did it. Really happy—but I don't know what it means."

Maddy didn't appear to have an immediate answer herself. She kept stirring her tea until any sugar had long dissolved. "I don't know what to suggest," she said finally.

"The problem is, I haven't seen him since," Margaret murmured, unable to hide how discouraged this made her feel. "Do you think he didn't like the kiss—that I might have done it wrong?"

"No." At least Maddy sounded confident about that.

"What should I do?" she asked next. Her friend usually had answers.

"Do?" Maddy echoed, seemingly lost in thought. She set her cup aside and leaned forward, taking Margaret's hand between both of hers. "Listen carefully. I know how you feel about Matt."

"I love him," she stated simply.

"But I want you to promise me you'll be careful about starting any kind of relationship with him."

So Maddy was afraid Matt would take advantage of her. Margaret understood why her friend might react that way, but deep down, Margaret knew otherwise. She'd seen his surprised look after he'd kissed her. He hadn't come to seduce her; she would have bet the ranch on that. Nor was she as naive as others, including Matt, assumed. Inexperienced, yes. Naive, no.

They sat and visited for another thirty minutes before the baby cried and Margaret decided it was time to go. Maddy collected the still-sleepy infant and walked Margaret to the door, promising to call in a few days.

As she drove back to the Triple C, Margaret remembered something her father had often told her. *If you have a question or a doubt, go straight to the source.* She didn't know why she hadn't thought of that earlier. If she had any questions about Matt's kiss or his motives, all she needed to do was ask him.

With renewed purpose, she drove past her own ranch and headed toward his, pulling into the large yard. The Stockerts had been neighbors and friends of her father's for years, but had moved when beef prices plummeted dramatically. The house had sat vacant until Matt arrived, leasing the property from the retired couple. He'd started out small, which was smart, building his herd each year. The house needed plenty of repairs and a coat of paint. But why should he paint a house that wasn't his? Matt put everything he earned back into his herd.

Margaret parked the truck, then got out and glanced around. It appeared that Matt wasn't there. She was about to leave when she saw him walk out of the barn. Once again she was struck by his stunning good looks—stunning at least to her.

Suddenly Margaret felt insecure and self-conscious, and she experienced those emotions as a physical sensation. She didn't like the uncomfortable feeling that settled in the pit of her stomach.

"Margaret." He touched the brim of his hat in welcome.

"Matt." She touched her own.

They stood three feet apart with the cold drifting in around them. She supposed other people would gradually lead into the purpose of a visit, but she was beyond pretense.

"Why did you kiss me?" she asked, surprised by how cool and even her voice remained. The question had plagued her for days, had practically consumed her, yet she'd made it sound as if she was asking about the price of feed.

His eyes met and held hers. Then, looking discomfited, he shrugged. "I can't rightly say."

"You plan on doing it again?"

His gaze shifted away from hers. "What makes you ask?"

Wait a minute. *She* was the one asking the questions here. "Don't answer my question with one of your own. That's unfair."

"There are rules to this conversation?"

"You just did it again," she cried, exasperated.

At that, Matt burst out laughing.

Despite the seriousness of her concerns, Margaret laughed, too.

"You're fortunate you caught me. I was out on the range earlier, looking for stray cattle."

"We've had a lot of rain lately." They both knew what that meant. The wet weather could bring about symptoms of bloat in the calves; they required careful watching.

As it happened, Matt had brought a sick calf into the barn and before long, Margaret was down on her knees, checking him over.

"What do you think?" he asked.

If Margaret knew anything, it was cattle. "I'd get the vet out here if you hope to save him."

Matt nodded gravely. "I already put in a call to Doc Lenz in Devils Lake, but he said there's not much he could do that I haven't already done."

Talking softly to the sick calf, Margaret stroked his sleek neck. Hardened rancher or not, she hated to see anything suffer. She comforted the calf as it lay dying, tears springing to her eyes. She continued to stroke the calf's face long after it was gone. When she realized Matt was watching her, she got abruptly to her feet and glanced at her watch. "I'd better go home."

He stood, too. "I'll walk you out."

They strolled silently back to her truck, and she wondered if he was as reluctant to let her go as she was to leave. "You never did answer my question," she reminded him.

He grinned and shook his head. "You're right, I didn't."

"It isn't the proper thing for a woman to ask, is it?"

He buried his hands deep in his coat pockets. "I don't see why not. If you'd kissed me, I'd want to know why."

Really. Then perhaps she should do exactly that. Catching him by surprise, she reached for his collar, gripping it with both hands. Then, raising herself on her toes, she slanted her mouth over his, hungry to discover if a second kiss could possibly compare with the first.

Quick as anything, Matt's arms were around her waist, pulling her against him. He did it with such force that it drove the breath from her lungs. For one wild second, her eyes flew open. Matt quickly took charge of the kiss, seducing her with his lips, introducing her to his tongue and creating an ache in her that reached low into her belly. This was the kind of kiss that would make a woman want to lock the door.

When he released her, it was all Margaret could do to breathe again.

"I shocked you, didn't I?" he said, brushing the hair from her face.

Still breathless, she couldn't answer him.

"I figure you haven't had much experience at this."

His comment irritated her. He seemed to be saying her lack of sexual finesse was obvious.

"I…I should leave now," she murmured, doing her best to sound mature and unaffected, even though her knees were shaking.

"Feel free to stop by any time," he said, opening the truck door.

"By the same token," she said, climbing inside, "feel free to shock me any time."

He was still laughing when he closed the door and she started the engine and drove off. He was laughing and Margaret was smiling. *This could be the start of something good*, a voice inside her seemed to whisper.

The frantic hum of sewing machines filled the workshop at Sarah Urlacher's quilt company. Three machines were in use nearly eight hours every day. Two girls cut pattern pieces while Sarah was busy with the phones.

Orders continued to arrive and she was having trouble keeping up. Many nights she stayed late, dying the muslin, soaking the cloth in tea water and other natural concoctions made with lichen and berries and plants. She put in long hours, but she loved it with an intensity that was hard to explain. Quilting was her passion, and her love for it went into every quilt she sold.

No one was more amazed by the almost overnight success of her business than Sarah herself. It'd started out mainly as a hobby, something to occupy her time and employ her talents. Then she'd won first prize at the state fair and sold the quilt for an astonishing five hundred dollars. Soon other sales trickled in. Enough that she'd eventually realized she needed to expand, to move her business out of her father's house. That was when she created Buffalo Valley Quilts.

Although it was a risk, a leap of faith, she'd rented space in one of the abandoned stores on Buffalo Valley's main street. Having her own location with her business name painted on the window had brought her immense satisfaction—and pride. For the first time, she was doing something for herself. The success or failure of this venture rested squarely on her own shoulders. Everything else in her life had been controlled by circumstances, but this company was of her own making. And so was its success.

To be fair, she credited Lindsay Sinclair with those initial sales. Two years earlier, Lindsay had moved to Buffalo Valley and accepted a teaching job. With her, Lindsay had brought hope and vision to the community.

When Sarah started her company, Lindsay had contacted her uncle in Savannah about displaying the distinctive quilts in his upscale furniture store. The first had sold immediately, and everything since had been eagerly snapped up. Soon other retail outlets had approached her.

Already she had a handful of full-time employees and she could use more. But luring women into town to work for her was complicated. Farm wives were often needed at home, and with no day care available in town… A temporary solution was to hire them to do piecework out of their homes, but Sarah didn't feel that gave her the same quality control.

Her thoughts were interrupted by the jangling of the bell above the door. Hassie Knight walked in. The pharmacist visited often, usually without a specific reason; Sarah guessed she just liked seeing all the activity.

"It does my heart good," Hassie had told her once. "This town is coming back to life and it's starting right here in this shop." And then the older woman said something that brought a rush of pride to Sarah every time she thought about it. "I couldn't be prouder of you if you were my own daughter."

"Afternoon, Hassie," Sarah greeted her.

"I brought you a chocolate soda," the older woman said, handing her a tall metal container filled to the brim with ice cream and soda. "I'm betting you didn't eat lunch again today."

Sarah hadn't; she'd been too busy.

"We can't have you getting weak and fainting on us, now can we?"

There was little likelihood of that happening, but Sarah wasn't about to argue. Hassie made the best sodas she'd tasted anywhere. Until that moment, she hadn't realized how famished she was.

"Thank you," she said.

Hassie nodded, then left as abruptly as she'd come. Sarah stood by the window and watched her. Since her own mother's death, she'd considered Hassie both advisor and friend. In Sarah's opinion, Hassie Knight had held this town together. If not for her, the community would have shriveled up and died the way so many other prairie towns had in the last twenty years.

Sarah's gaze drifted toward her husband's service station. It was difficult even now, three months after speaking their vows, to believe they were actually married. Unfortunately, the joy she felt was almost immediately squelched by regret at her daughter's estrangement. For reasons no one fully understood, Calla disliked Dennis. When they'd announced their engagement, Calla had run away, choosing instead to live with her father in Minneapolis.

Sarah felt an oppressive sadness, a painful despair, whenever she thought about Calla. It was agonizing to see history repeat itself as she watched Calla make the same mistakes she had. Sarah felt so helpless. Nothing she'd said or done had brought Calla home. She shook off the memory; thinking about her daughter made it impossible to concentrate on work.

At five o'clock, her employees packed up and headed home. Sarah stayed behind, catching up on some long-overdue paperwork. An hour after she closed, Dennis joined her.

He walked into the back room, stood behind her, kissing her neck. "You ready to leave?"

He smelled of gasoline and grease, and spicy aftershave. Sarah closed her eyes and enjoyed the loving feel of his arms around her.

"I won't be long. Did you go to the post office?"

His hesitation told her he had.

"There's a letter from Calla," he told her.

Sarah's heart flew into her throat. She'd been so anxious to get a response about Thanksgiving.

"Open it later," Dennis advised.

Sarah whirled around, unable to believe he'd say such a thing. "Why?" He knew she'd been waiting for days to hear from her daughter.

"What if she tells you she won't come?" Dennis asked.

"Then she won't be here." Sarah's flippant reply suggested it didn't matter one way or the other. In reality, it meant everything. She'd only spoken to Calla a few times in the past five months. Despite her best efforts, every conversation had left her feeling guilty, upset and depressed. If only she could get Calla away from Willie's influence, talk to her, reason all this out.

Thanksgiving would be perfect. Her father and her brother, Jeb, along with Maddy and the baby, would be joining them. Even Dennis's parents were coming. A big family dinner, the kind they'd had when her mother was alive. Perhaps it was greedy of her, but Sarah wanted her daughter with them. Surrounded by family, Calla would surely feel the love everyone had for her, would surely realize how much they missed her. Realize how much Sarah needed her. Perhaps they'd even be able to break down the barriers and communicate as mother and daughter.

"Give me the letter," she told him, and held out her hand.

"Sarah…"

"Dennis, please."

His reluctance was obvious. She clutched the small manila envelope and was about to tear into it when she paused. "Perhaps you're right," she said, her voice shaking. All at once she was afraid of what she'd find inside.

"Open it," Dennis said now. "You might as well. Get it over with."

He was as ambivalent as she was. Sarah sighed deeply. Confronting her fear was more difficult than she'd expected. She opened the envelope, reached inside and pulled out half the airline ticket.

Sarah's chest tightened and for a moment she could hardly breathe. Calla had torn the airline ticket in two and returned both halves.

"No letter?" Dennis asked, sounding as discouraged as she felt.

Sarah looked again and shook her head. "Why would she do something so cruel?" she asked.

"Come on, sweetheart," Dennis said. "Let's go home."

"I don't know why she hates me so much," Sarah whispered. "If only she'd talk to me. If only…"

Four

Pastor Larry Dawson and his family had lived in fifteen different states in the past forty-three years, but he'd never thought of anywhere but Buffalo Valley as *home*. This was where he'd been born, where he'd gone to school, where he'd buried his mother and three years later, his father. From the day he left for the seminary, he'd planned to return to his childhood home—only, he hadn't expected that to take over forty years. He was near retirement age now, and it made sense that he pastor a church in the very town where he'd spent his youth. His life was about to come full circle.

For a time, his return had looked doubtful. It seemed that despite all of Joshua McKenna's and Hassie Knight's efforts, Buffalo Valley was about to be snuffed out, like so many other small towns that dotted the Dakotas. Then, unexpectedly, the community had sprung back to life. Larry was thrilled and had managed to convince the church hierarchy to send him to Buffalo Valley.

The only church available belonged to the Catholics. It'd been closed for a number of years, ever since Father McGrath, hampered by age and failing health, had retired. Despite circumstances, the elderly priest had continued to stop by every few weeks to celebrate Mass. Recently, however, Father McGrath had entered a retirement home in Minnesota and the Bishop was eager to sell the property. The Methodist Church had bought it.

Soon after Larry had accepted the assignment, he'd found a nearby house to rent. The spare bedroom served as his office. The house was smaller than he would've liked, but it was fine for the time being. Fortunately his three daughters were grown and settled in careers and raising their own families. Unfortunately, they lived in three different states—Connecticut, Nebraska and Oregon.

Larry's first official duty had been to officiate at the funeral of Bernard Clemens. He remembered the rancher, but it'd been years since they'd last spoken. The funeral, sad as it was, had been an opportunity to become acquainted with the people in town, those he'd once known and the younger people, whose families he often remembered. Larry had spent a good part of the day meeting and greeting his new neighbors.

In some ways, not much had changed in Buffalo Valley. When he'd left, there'd been a reserve toward strangers, a hesitancy. It remained in place to this day. The town...well, it *looked* better than he'd expected, but there was still much to be done. People were pleased with the most recent improvements and planning more. Then there was—

"Lunch is ready," Joyce called from the kitchen, breaking into his musings.

He'd met Joyce while he was in the seminary. His wife had been raised in Boston, but over the years she'd come to love small-town life.

"What are your plans for the afternoon?" she asked as she sat across the table from him. She'd prepared one of his favorites, a chicken salad made with cold noodles and tossed with a soy vinaigrette, but today he had virtually no appetite.

"I thought I'd go over and visit Joshua." A question about a couple he'd met at Bernard's funeral had been bothering Larry and he could think of no one better to ask than his old friend. After barely touching his lunch, he wandered over to Joshua McKenna's second-hand store. Joshua sold a little of everything. The sign in his window claimed there wasn't anything he couldn't fix, and Larry believed it.

"Good to see you," Joshua called out when the bell above the door announced Larry's arrival.

"I'm not disturbing you, am I?" Larry saw that Joshua was up to his elbows in grease, working on some kind of engine.

"Trust me, I welcome the interruption." Joshua reached for a wadded-up rag, tucked in his back hip pocket. "This," he said, gently patting the huge metal contraption, "is the engine to Gage Sinclair's tractor. Dennis had it two weeks and couldn't get it running. He threw up his hands and asked me to give it a try."

Larry knew that low prices were killing many of the small farmers in the heartland. Farmers kept their equipment running as long as possible, and then eked out another twenty thousand miles.

"Did you hear I was over at Buffalo Bob's?" Larry said as Joshua studied the engine. "Went there a couple of weeks ago, after I met them at Bernard's wake." Bob had talked him into trying his karaoke machine. Larry had no singing voice whatsoever, but bolstered by Merrily, he'd fallen victim. He was fairly confident they wouldn't invite him to sing again.

"They have a little boy, don't they?" Larry had noticed the child at the Clemens house but hadn't seen him since.

"His name's Axel."

"Unusual name."

Joshua nodded and continued to inspect the engine.

"Haven't seen him around much," Larry said.

"Seems to me Merrily said he's got the chicken pox," Joshua muttered.

"Poor little boy."

"I've never seen a couple crazier about a kid," Joshua said absentmindedly. He rubbed the side of his face, smearing a smudge of oil along his jaw.

"Bob seems to be a good father," Larry commented.

"He is," Joshua said. "Especially for being so new to it."

"Axel isn't his child?" Larry suspected as much, but then, he suspected a lot more.

"No. The boy belongs to Merrily," he said, and reached inside the engine with a long-handled wrench. "No one realized she had a kid until she showed up with him one day."

Larry's suspicions mounted. When he'd moved into the house, there'd been a pile of junk mail stacked in the post office box, waiting for him once he'd submitted his change-of-address information. Never one to toss a piece of paper without first looking at it, he'd come across some flyers, notifications of several missing and abducted children. The name Axel, being unusual, had stuck in his mind. Within a week he'd met Bob and Merrily and their boy...Axel.

"Come to think of it, I never saw Merrily pregnant, either," Joshua said. He twisted the wrench again and glanced up. "It used to be that Merrily would drift in and out of town. She'd stay with Buffalo Bob a few weeks, then disappear. He took her leaving real hard and never seemed to know when she'd be coming back."

"You never saw her pregnant?" Larry repeated.

Joshua paused. "Funny, I never thought about it before, but no."

"She didn't bring the boy with her on earlier visits?"

Joshua shook his head. "No, not once."

"You're sure the boy is hers?"

His friend looked uncertain. "It's clear he belongs to her," he finally said. He held Larry's eyes for an uncomfortably long moment. "If you've got something to say, then say it."

Larry wasn't sure this was the time or place to voice his suspicions. For many, he was a newcomer to the community; he had no intention of wading into an explosive situation without being sure of himself.

"Did Sarah hear from Calla?" he asked instead, purposely changing the subject.

"She did." Regret flashed across Joshua's face. "Apparently Calla's not coming."

Larry had been afraid of that. "Is Sarah upset?"

"Real upset. Frankly, I don't understand Calla. Makes me wonder what lies that no-good father of hers is feeding her."

"You might never know."

Joshua scratched his head, leaving more grease in his hair. "I told you how she ran away from his place, too, didn't I?"

Larry nodded.

"Sarah and Dennis tried to talk sense into her, but she wouldn't listen. Calla had a choice—either move back here to Buffalo Valley or return to her father. No one understood why she'd choose to live with Willie. I tell you, it's got us all worried sick. No one would object if you mentioned it the next time you're talking to God."

"I'll be glad to," Larry offered. And while he was praying for Calla and her mother, he intended to ask God about the situation with Axel and his parents, too.

In the past few days, Sheryl had phoned no fewer than seven times. She was hounding Matt about Margaret, quizzing him about the relationship and what he was doing to promote it. Heaven help him if she ever found out about those kisses! At first, he'd assumed Sheryl's talk about how he should marry Margaret for her ranch was nothing but that—talk. He'd been wrong. She was dead serious.

That anyone could so blatantly use another for such a mercenary purpose angered him. He should have realized from the beginning that Sheryl was trouble. The evidence was there. Sheryl had bragged about collecting on three frivolous lawsuits, as well as two minor car accidents and a workman's compensation claim. Every single time, she'd walked away with money in her pocket. It was a way of life with her. He'd been unimpressed and somewhat contemptuous, but until now, her proclivity for making easy money hadn't affected him. He refused to get involved.

Friday afternoon he drove to the truck stop, intending to tell her not to call him again. Her attitude toward Margaret Clemens irritated Matt. True, Sheryl was as pretty as a centerfold—and about as two-dimensional. Despite her lovely eyes, Margaret was plain, but unlike Sheryl she was both honest and kind. It surprised him that he felt so protective toward Margaret. One thing he knew for sure: he wasn't going to let Sheryl talk him into using her.

"Sheryl around?" he asked Lee Ann, one of the other waitresses.

"She worked the early shift today," Lee Ann told him. "But I know she'd like to see you."

Matt nodded, and ordered a beer. He wasn't in any hurry.

"Drop in at her house, why don't you?" Lee Ann said as she delivered his Bud Light.

Matt didn't reply. He would've preferred to see Sheryl here, where there were other people, rather than her place—where they'd be alone. She had her own special way of detaining him and he didn't want to fall into that trap. Instead, he went to a local watering hole and drank two more beers. Fortified by alcohol and a strong sense of what was right, he changed his mind and went over to Sheryl's rented house. He drove slowly and carefully, grateful for the lack of traffic—and always keeping an eye out for the sheriff. A drunk driving conviction was something he'd prefer to avoid.

"Where have you been?" Sheryl cried, her face lighting up when she opened her door. Without warning, she hurled herself into his arms, nearly knocking him off balance. "I've been missing you *so* much."

Although she'd been squawking about marriage, Matt was well aware that there were other men in her life. He let her think he was deaf and blind because it suited his own purposes. He was with Sheryl on *his* terms, no matter how much she liked to think she was the one controlling him.

"I haven't seen you in two weeks," she said.

"I've been busy."

"I'm sure you have," Sheryl said and led him into her cozy living room.

He sat down on the sofa and she poured them each a

stiff drink, Scotch over ice, bringing the tumblers to the coffee table. He didn't have time to reach for his glass before Sheryl crawled into his lap, straddling his legs.

"So you missed me, too," she murmured, wrapping her arms around his neck and settling her sweet little bottom directly over his crotch.

There was no denying that he had.

"Tell me how it's going with Margaret," she said.

Matt had come to Sheryl's to discuss Margaret, but not for the reason she assumed.

"You'd be a fool to let this opportunity slip through your fingers." She picked up her drink, sipping from it. Her eyes met and held his. "She needs you. Can't you see you'd be helping her?"

It was difficult to ignore his body's natural response to the things Sheryl was doing. His head was clouded with booze and desire, but he couldn't allow her to manipulate him. Bracing his hands against her shoulders, he spoke forcefully. "I'm here to tell you I have no intention of marrying Margaret or anyone else."

"Really?" Her eyebrows arched with the question. "What about me?" She squirmed in his lap, effectively reminding him of all she had to offer…and her willingness to do so. Setting aside her drink, she cupped his face between her hands and directed his mouth to hers.

This was a woman who knew how to bring a man to a full state of arousal—fast. Without the beer and the whiskey, he might have been able to break off the kiss and hold his ground, but his resolve was already weakening.

"I didn't say this was a hard-and-fast decision," he whispered huskily, his eyes closed.

"Good answer." She kissed him again, employing the full range of her talents.

By the time she'd finished kissing him, Matt was putty in her hands.

"I've missed you, cowboy," she said, leading him to the bedroom. "More than you know."

Matt doubted it, but he didn't care, not at that moment. There seemed little excuse to deny himself what he wanted most, and just then it was Sheryl.

The following morning, Matt woke with a hell of a headache. His entire head throbbed. The whiskey bottle, now empty, stood on the bedside table; one of the glasses lay on the floor. The other glass held several cigarette butts, floating in half an inch of melted ice. The sight disgusted him. So did Sheryl, naked beside him. Most of all, he disgusted himself.

Rolling onto his back, he stared up at the ceiling, and silently cursed himself for being so damn weak. He'd never meant for this to happen. He'd never meant to become this involved with Sheryl. But a man had needs—needs Sheryl was always happy to satisfy. What they shared was a mutually pleasurable sexual relationship; that was the extent of it. The more he got to know her, the less he liked her. He worked long, hard hours on his ranch, but every now and then he needed to let loose, indulge himself. Sheryl was always obliging.

"You awake?" Sheryl asked, rolling over and clinging to his side. Her fingers plucked annoyingly at his nipples.

Matt brushed her hand away.

"What are you thinking about?"

He didn't want to talk, and wished now that he'd showered and left before she woke.

"Nothing," he muttered and tried to get up, but she'd wrapped her leg around his and held him tightly in place.

"We need to talk about Margaret."

"She's off-limits," he said in no uncertain terms. His voice was cold, and loud enough to make his head pound even more. He tossed aside the sheet and despite her effort to hold him, Matt scurried out of bed and reached for his jeans.

"You like her, don't you?" Sheryl asked, sitting up and clutching the sheet to her breasts.

"It doesn't matter what I feel for Margaret."

Sheryl was suspiciously silent. "You don't have to marry her, if you don't want to," she said now. "It was just an idea."

"A stupid one."

Sheryl looked repentant. "All right, it was a stupid idea, but I was honestly thinking of her."

"Yeah, I'll bet you were."

"I was," she cried, sounding hurt that he didn't believe her. "This is a difficult time in Margaret's life. She's alone, and that's scary. She needs someone like you."

"I'm the last person she needs." He fastened his denim shirt, closing the snaps with more force than necessary. When he got to the bottom, he realized he had one snap too many.

"Oh, Matt, don't be in such a hurry to leave me," Sheryl said, smiling softly. Scrambling off the bed, she stood nude before him and unfastened his shirt, then refastened it correctly.

"I have to go."

"When will I see you again?" she pleaded. Pulling on her flimsy housecoat, she followed him to the front door.

"I don't know." That was what he told her, but he'd made his decision. He and Sheryl were finished. He didn't like the way she schemed to bring down another woman. It bothered him that she was so willing to hurt and humiliate Margaret on the patently false pretext of helping her. Sheryl was a user, and he'd been a fool to get involved with her.

The first thing Matt did when he arrived back at his ranch was take a long hot shower. He scrubbed hard to eradicate the scent of Sheryl's heavy perfume. By the time he stepped out of the shower, his skin was red and stung from the scouring.

The phone rang just as he was about to walk out the door. If it was Sheryl he'd tell her not to phone again. Their relationship was over. Finished. No more.

It wasn't Sheryl, though.

"Margaret." He couldn't hide his surprise. Ready to vent his anger at Sheryl, he was caught off guard by his neighbor's voice.

"I can call back if need be," she said.

"This is as good a time as any," he responded, wondering at the call. They'd been neighbors four years and she'd never phoned him before.

She waited a moment. "You doing anything Thanksgiving?"

The holiday was the following week. Matt wasn't someone who received a lot of invitations. "No."

"Do you want to come to my place for dinner?"

The truth of what Sheryl had said hit home. Without her father, Margaret was alone for the first time in her life. Sure, there were the housekeeper and the ranch hands, but they had their own families. Matt knew what it was to spend holidays alone. It wasn't a good feeling. "You cooking the turkey?" he asked.

"I'd be willing to give it a try, if you're willing to come."

Matt thought about the other ranchers he knew. They

all had families to share the holiday with or someplace to go and someone special to see. Matt didn't, and apparently Margaret didn't, either.

"I can bring the cranberries," he offered.

"Does this mean you'll come?" Her voice rose with unmistakable pleasure.

People generally didn't get excited about cooking him a meal. "I guess it does."

"I was serious about cooking the turkey, you know."

"I'm serious, too," he told her, grinning. He seemed to be doing a lot of that around Margaret. He'd come to know her a little, and every exposure left him feeling good, a sharp contrast to the way he'd been with Sheryl. "I'll bring a bottle of wine and we can talk."

"Talk?" This seemed to fluster her. "What do you want to talk about?"

"I don't know. Do we have to decide that now?"

She hesitated, as though measuring her words. "We could discuss those kisses…that is, if you want?"

"All right," he returned. It was easy to forget how direct Margaret could be.

"You know what I think?"

"What?"

"That you were just as surprised as me."

"At kissing you?" he asked.

"You liked it, didn't you? That's what threw you for a loop."

He didn't answer her, because he *had* enjoyed their kisses. And because she was absolutely correct: he'd been surprised.

"Am I right, Matt?"

He sighed and wondered if he dared admit it. Past experience had taught him it was better to hide a potentially dangerous fact.

"Why don't we save this discussion for later?" he hedged.

"Okay," she agreed, sounding eager.

The truth was, Matt was sure he'd disappoint Margaret Clemens. He understood why her father had talked to him. Hell, had their positions been reversed—had she been *his* daughter—he would have done the same thing.

Heath was finally going to tell his grandmother the news she'd been waiting to hear. Thanksgiving seemed the perfect time. During his youth, the two of them were often at odds. It had taken time and distance and more than one clash of wills for him to understand why. They were too much alike. She was a cantankerous old woman, but Heath loved her. He also respected her business acumen and valued her advice—even when it got a little too personal.

He left Rachel and Mark at his house in Grand Forks and drove to the retirement center where Lily Quantrill resided. As far as family went, Lily was all he had.

"I can't understand why you insist on taking me out to eat," she snapped the instant he arrived.

She was confined to a wheelchair now and he knew she hated it, but that was no reason to stay inside when the fresh air might do her some good.

"I thought you'd enjoy getting out for a few hours," Heath told her.

She wheeled toward him and reached for her hat. Posed in front of a mirror, which had been hung deliberately low, she set it on her head and pinned it in place. "Where did you say we were going?"

"I didn't," he reminded her.

Lily paused in her task and glared up at him. "You know I don't like surprises."

"Yes, Grandma."

"Then tell me where we're headed."

Heath sighed. "To eat Thanksgiving dinner."

Her pinched lips told him she wasn't pleased. He ignored her bad mood and laid the heavy winter coat across her lap. No need to put it on until he had her down on the first floor.

"It's a wonder Grandpa ever got to first base with you," he said as he wheeled her toward the elevator.

"Leave your grandfather out of this."

"Yes, Grandma."

"And don't patronize me, young man. I won't put up with it."

Hiding the smile in his voice was impossible. "I wouldn't dream of it."

The elevator arrived and the doors glided smoothly open. Heath maneuvered her chair inside and pushed the button for the lobby.

She twisted around and stared up at him. "Do you seriously think some restaurant is going to fix a turkey the way I remember it?" she barked.

"Thanksgiving is about more than turkey and pumpkin pie."

"Are you lecturing me, Heath Quantrill?"

"I wouldn't dream of it," he said again, his voice light with amusement.

"There was a day you wouldn't dare laugh at me."

"I'm not laughing," he assured her. The doors opened and he stationed her by the entrance while he went to the parking lot to bring the car around. When he returned, an attendant had helped her don her coat and wheeled her outside to meet him.

He didn't realize how thin and frail she was until he

lifted her into the passenger seat. Then the attendant folded her wheelchair and loaded it in the trunk.

"I can't imagine why you wanted to take me out to dinner," she muttered for at least the third time.

"Grandma," he told her, "there are women all over town who'd jump at the chance to have dinner with me."

"Well, I'm not one of them."

He glanced over and saw her lips quiver in a half smile.

"Have you been seeing Kate lately?" she demanded.

"No." Earlier in the year, Heath had gone out with a female bank executive a couple of times. The problem was, he'd already fallen in love with Rachel Fischer, but at that point her attitude had been completely and totally unreasonable.

"I've decided I don't like her," Lily informed him.

Heath chuckled. "Few women pass muster with you, do they?"

"Rachel did," she snapped, "but you tried to rush her into bed. It's no wonder the woman won't have anything to do with you." She glowered with disapproval. "What is it with you young people these days? You'd think God gave us Ten Suggestions instead of Ten Commandments."

"Yes, Grandma."

She grumbled something else he couldn't hear. Then, for the first time, she noticed that he wasn't driving in the direction of any restaurants. Instead, they were in a residential neighborhood.

"Where are you taking me?" she demanded again. "And don't give me that story about going to dinner. I want to know exactly where we're headed."

"You'll know soon enough," he promised.

Lily studied the landscape. "This is close to your parents' house, isn't it?"

"It is."

"You're living there, if I remember correctly."

"I am, and you do."

She appeared to relax with that. "How nice. We're having dinner at your home. I always did love that house." She paused. "Haven't been there since I got stuck in this blasted chair."

"I love the house, too." It was the reason he'd moved into it when he returned from Europe. His brother's death had hit him hard and he felt the need to surround himself with what was familiar. The house had been in their family for thirty years. Even now, when it involved a long commute into Buffalo Valley three days a week, he'd chosen to live in the family home.

He pulled into the driveway and paused, watching Lily. She stared at the house and her sharp features softened.

Transferring her from car to wheelchair went smoothly. Earlier he'd rigged a platform to get her up the stairs.

When they reached the porch, the front door opened, and Rachel's son, Mark, stood waiting. The scents of turkey and sage dressing and pumpkin pie were instantly recognizable. Rachel was one fine cook, and dinner promised to be everything he remembered from his childhood.

"Who are you?" Lily demanded of the boy.

Heath admired Mark for not flinching in the face of his grandmother's brusque manner.

"Mark Fischer," Mark returned politely.

"My son," Rachel said, coming to stand behind him, her hands on his shoulders.

Lily turned to look at Heath. "What's going on here?" she asked, but the question was hopeful, quite unlike her previous demands.

"Please, let me help you get comfortable first," Rachel said, "then Heath and I'll explain."

"All right." All the fire and irritation seemed to be gone.

Ten minutes later, they'd all gathered in the living room. Heath brought out a bottle of champagne and one of sparkling cider, along with four tall flutes. He sat next to Rachel and placed his arm around her shoulders.

Mark sat on Rachel's other side. "Can I tell her?" he asked Heath.

Heath nodded.

"My mom and Heath are going to be married!"

Lily didn't say anything for a moment. "This isn't a joke, is it?"

"No, Grandma," Heath explained, "last week Rachel agreed to become my wife."

Lily nodded, and tears shone in her eyes. "I suspect I don't have time left to hold a great-grandchild, but it'd do my heart good if God allowed me that." She looked away and sniffled, then dug inside her pocket for a fresh tissue.

"Why's she crying?" Mark asked his mother in a loud whisper.

"These aren't tears," Lily said imperiously. "I'm feeling sorry for your mother, that's all. She's going to have her hands full with this grandson of mine."

"I like Heath," Mark told her, leaning forward.

"Now that your mother's agreed to take him on, there's hope for him," Lily said and smiled at the boy through her tears. "This calls for champagne."

"I've already seen to that." Heath held up the bottle.

Lily held Rachel's look, then stretched her hand toward the woman Heath loved.

Rachel grasped Lily's fragile hand with her own.

"I'm so very pleased," she whispered.

"I'm happy, too."

"He loves you, you know."

"I do, and I love him."

"Hey, Grandma, I thought you said you didn't like surprises," Heath said.

"I'm flexible." Her smile was warm and full of love.

Five

Sarah and Dennis's house was brimming with activity Thanksgiving Day. This was exactly how Sarah had always dreamed the holidays would be. The turkey, browned to a golden hue, stuffed and fragrant, sat on the counter, ready to be placed in the center of the table. While she finished mashing the potatoes, her mother-in-law, Irene, arranged serving bowls on the large dining-room table, set with fine china, a pink linen tablecloth and matching napkins. Small ceramic pots filled with mauve and gold chrysanthemums were situated at intervals, to pleasing effect.

Maddy sat in a corner of the kitchen, nursing Julianne, an attentive Jeb at his wife's side. Sarah had never seen her brother happier or more content. Everything she'd ever hoped for him had come to pass.

The swinging door, which led from one room to the other, was tossed open every few seconds as Dennis's mother carried Thanksgiving dishes to the table, an embarrassing array of them. Sarah had been cooking for days, burying her disappointment at Calla's rejection in the meal preparation and in setting a table to rival Martha Stewart's. She'd hoped that if she didn't have time to think, it might be possible to forget. Unfortunately that tactic didn't work. Calla's absence left a giant hole in her heart, as impossible to ignore as it was to fill.

"Everything's on the table," Irene announced as Sarah brought the large bowl of creamy mashed potatoes into the dining room.

Dennis called the family to the table; no one needed further encouragement. Sarah watched as her brother tenderly placed his infant daughter in her carrier, then escorted Maddy into the room. So much had changed in all of their lives this past year.

Once everyone was seated, they joined hands and bowed their heads. Joshua waited a moment, then offered grace. His few simple words were followed by a soft chorus of "Amens."

No one mentioned Calla, although there was a place set for her, in case she changed her mind at the last minute. Sarah wanted everyone to know that her daughter continued to be a part of her life, even though she'd chosen to live with her father.

Soon dishes were being passed around and happy chatter took over. It astonished Sarah that a meal she'd spent days perparing could be consumed in less than an hour. Including dessert.

Once everyone had finished, Joshua looked around the table. His gaze settled on Jeb with Maddy and Julianne, then drifted to Dennis and her. He nodded once, then said, "It seems we have more and more to be grateful for each year."

"That's true," Dennis agreed and reached for Sarah's hand, gently squeezing it.

Jeb held Maddy's hand, as well.

"The only person missing is Calla," Joshua added, glancing toward the empty chair.

As soon as he mentioned her daughter's name, tears sprang to Sarah's eyes, mortifying her. She clutched her napkin and tried to hide the emotion that surged within her. Not only had Calla returned the airline ticket, she'd torn it in half, as if to say that being with her mother was the last thing on earth she wanted to do. She hadn't even bothered to include a letter. Not a single word. The brutal rejection ate at her, tarnishing this lovely time. She'd made mistakes, but she didn't deserve this.

Dennis's fingers tightened around hers. "It's all right, sweetheart," he whispered.

"No, it isn't!" Joshua declared, leaping to his feet. "I don't know what the hell's gotten into that girl, but I intend to find out."

"Dad?" Sarah had rarely heard her father so angry. She watched as he marched across the room toward the telephone. "Get me Willie's phone number," he demanded.

Without questioning him, Sarah did as he asked. Joshua grabbed for the phone and quickly punched in the number.

"What are you going to say?" Sarah asked, standing next to him.

"What someone should have said a long time ago. I'm going to tell her it's high time she came home where she belongs."

"But, Dad—"

He held up his hand and blinked, looking uncertain. "Is this the Willie Stern residence?" he asked. He cupped the receiver. "A woman answered. She sounds drunk."

"It isn't Calla, is it?" Horrified, Sarah placed her hand on his elbow.

Her father shook his head. "Willie Stern," he repeated, then glanced at Sarah. "She went to get him," he explained.

Even this far from the receiver, Sarah could hear the loud, discordant music. Apparently Willie was throwing a party. Sarah hated to think of Calla in that environment. A helpless, sick sensation came over her. Dennis seemed to sense it, because he moved to stand behind her. His hands rested on her shoulders.

Sarah closed her eyes, grateful for her husband's support, for his understanding and love.

"Willie?" Joshua asked, sounding unsure. He turned to Sarah and rolled his eyes. "It's Joshua, Joshua McKenna," he said loudly. "Listen, perhaps it'd be better if you talked to Sarah." With an apologetic expression, he handed her the phone.

Sarah took the receiver but she wasn't happy about it. "Hello, Willie," she said, trying to hide her disgust for her ex-husband.

"Sarah, how are you?" It was difficult to hear him above the music blaring in the background.

"Just great. Where's Calla?"

"Calla? Hold on, and I'll find out." He left and was gone several minutes. Sarah was about to hang up when he came back on the line. "No one knows for sure," he said in a thick, slurred voice.

He was stoned on something, probably a combination of drugs and alcohol. It was enough to make Sarah sick to her stomach.

"Don't you think it's important?" Sarah shouted, despite her best effort to hold on to her temper. With Willie stoned out of his mind, Calla could be missing for days before anyone realized it.

"She has to be around here somewhere."

"Find her," Sarah snapped. "I'm not getting off this line until I talk with my daughter."

"She's *my* daughter, too. You know what your problem is?" Willie asked. "You're uppity. I can't understand how I got involved with an uppity woman."

"I want to talk to Calla," Sarah demanded, barely able to remain civil.

"Fine, you can talk to her. Only I've got to find her first."

"Find her."

"Yes, your majesty," Willie taunted.

The phone made a clanking sound as if it'd been dropped. He was gone for several minutes and then returned. "She's at work," he said. "I forgot."

"Where does she work?"

"BurgerHaven. Not a bad job, either. I asked her if she could get her old man on, but they said I had to have a drug test first." This was followed by uproarious laughter, as if he found the suggestion amusing beyond words.

Sarah closed her eyes until the feeling of revulsion left. "Tell her I phoned."

His laughter died as suddenly as it had begun. "I might," he said.

"Never mind, I'll tell her myself," Sarah said, not wanting to feel beholden to Willie for anything, even the most basic of courtesies.

Everyone was watching her expectantly, especially Dennis's parents. Sarah replaced the receiver. She looked at Dennis, then her brother and her in-laws. "Apparently…Calla's working today." The words barely made it past her lips before she broke into sobs. Mortified, she retreated into the bedroom, hoping a few minutes alone would help her regain her composure. Normally she was better able to control her emotions.

"Sarah?" Dennis came into the room and closed the door.

"I'm so sorry," she whispered. "It's such a wonderful day and here I am crying... I'm so sorry."

Her husband sat down on the edge of the bed beside her. "You don't have anything to apologize for. Not one damn thing."

"But I embarrassed you in front of your parents—"

"Don't even think that." He placed his arms around her, and Sarah turned into his embrace, breathing in the warm scent of him, loving him until she felt as if her heart would burst. "I don't deserve you," she whispered.

He wove his fingers into her hair and tilted her face toward him. "No, it's the other way around..."

She shook her head. "I don't know what I did for Calla to hate me so."

"You married me. I'm the one she hates."

Sarah wrapped her arms around him, and they clung to one another. Then, sobbing, she pulled away and wiped the tears from her cheeks. "I didn't mean to tell you like this...but, Dennis, I think... I'm fairly sure I'm pregnant."

He stared at her, his face uncomprehending. "You're pregnant?"

She nodded, smiling through her tears.

"When did you find out?"

"Just yesterday... I talked to Hassie and she recommended one of those home pregnancy tests and...and the stick turned blue."

Dennis let out a shout of joy so loud it echoed in the room. Racing to the bedroom door, he hurled it open and stuck out his head. "Mom, Dad, we're pregnant!"

Racing back to her side, he took hold of both her hands. "Oh, Sarah, you don't know how happy this makes me."

She knew Dennis wanted children when she married him. Her doubts were multiple, especially since she didn't seem to be a very successful mother; Calla's attitude proved as much.

"You're pregnant?" Irene asked when Dennis and Sarah reappeared. She held her hands to her mouth, tears trickling down her face.

Sarah nodded.

Irene hugged them both. "This is just *wonderful* news! Just wonderful."

"It is," Maddy agreed, embracing Sarah. "I'm so pleased Julianne will have a cousin close to her own age."

"Congratulations, sis," Jeb said, hugging her, then slapping Dennis on the back. The two men clasped hands.

"Another grandchild," Joshua said, tucking his thumbs inside his suspenders. "Now, this is welcome news. Very welcome." He took a turn and hugged Sarah, too. "I don't suppose anyone would object if I helped myself to a second piece of pumpkin pie."

"I'll join you," Jeb announced.

"Don't mind if I do myself," Norm Urlacher said, trailing Jeb and Joshua into the kitchen.

"I should probably supervise," Dennis said, following the others. "I want whipped cream on mine," he called, halfway through the door.

"We just ate," Sarah complained to Maddy and her mother-in-law. How anyone could get up from a table laden with a meal fit for royalty and be hungry less than half an hour later was beyond her.

"While they're in there," Irene said, "let's suggest they do the dishes."

"Good idea!"

Soon the three of them were laughing, their excitement about the pregnancy dulling the pain of Calla's rejection.

Margaret Clemens's housekeeper wasn't at all pleased that Margaret had taken it upon herself to invite Matt Eilers to Thanksgiving dinner.

Sadie muttered disparaging comments under her breath all morning as she worked in the kitchen, cooking the turkey, peeling potatoes, slicing green beans and making pumpkin pies.

"You can go now, Sadie," Margaret told her when she'd finished preparing the last of the vegetable dishes and had set a pie on the counter to cool.

"And leave you alone with that scoundrel?" she bellowed, fists digging into her wide hips. "I think *not*."

"Sadie." Margaret could be just as stubborn. "Matt is a gentleman. Now, go home. Your family's waiting."

Still the housekeeper hesitated.

"Go," Margaret insisted, shooing the older woman out of the kitchen. Sadie had been with the family for as long as Margaret could remember and was as close to a mother as Margaret had. She'd been a blessing, for sure, but distrusted strangers and single men. It didn't help that Matt fell into both categories. He might have lived and ranched in the area for nearly five years, but as far as Sadie was concerned, he wasn't one of them and shouldn't be trusted.

With obvious reluctance the housekeeper removed her apron. "If you need help, you phone."

"I will," Margaret assured her, and edged her toward the door. As soon as Sadie was gone, Margaret sighed with relief, thankful she'd finally managed to get Sadie out of the house. This dinner was important, and the last thing Margaret wanted was a chaperone, especially since she was hoping Matt would see fit to kiss her again.

Her guest arrived promptly at four, the time they'd agreed upon. He brought a bouquet of flowers, along with a can of cranberries and a bottle of wine.

"Thank you, Matt," she murmured, smelling the yellow and bronze mums. Feeling self-conscious, she led him into the kitchen, where she placed the bouquet in a vase. Might as well tell him now and be done with it. "I have a confession to make."

"Already?" he asked, frowning. "I just got here."

"I fell short on my part of the bargain." It probably would have been better if she'd waited until later to own up. "I'm not a very good cook. I'd hoped—actually, I'd planned—to whip up the entire meal on my own, but Sadie convinced me to start with something less demanding before tackling a five-course holiday dinner. So..."

"So in other words Sadie made the turkey?"

Margaret nodded. Well, the turkey and everything else. It hardly seemed surprising that she was pretty much of a lost cause when it came to finding her way around a kitchen. After all, she'd never spent any time learning those skills—she was a rancher, not a cook. The important thing was that, dinner aside, he'd chosen to spend the day with *her*.

Matt glanced at the table already set. "I'm glad not to be alone today. That's what really matters—not the turkey."

His words seemed to echo her thoughts, which flustered her so much, she said the next thing that popped into her mind. "Would you like a beer before we eat?"

"Sure."

Hands and heart trembling, she removed two cans from the refrigerator, emptied them into tall tumblers, then took him to the library. It was her father's favorite room, and hers, too. They sat in the high-back leather chairs, on opposite sides of the brick fireplace. She'd laid a small fire earlier and lit it just before he arrived. It provided a comforting warmth…and a sensation of intimacy.

At first the silence between them was awkward. Then Matt asked her a question about a new worming product for cattle, and before she knew it, they'd talked nearly an hour. Matt seemed as delighted as she by how easily their conversation had gone.

"I don't generally talk cattle with women," he told her, drinking the last of his beer.

Margaret wasn't sure what he was telling her. He seemed to be implying that he didn't think of her as a woman, which she found downright depressing. Especially since she'd taken pains to put on a dress. A dress, panty hose, the whole nine yards. It was the same outfit she'd worn for her father's funeral, although he wouldn't know that, seeing he hadn't attended the services.

"I'd better check on dinner," she said, bolting out of her chair.

"Margaret." He stopped her as soon as she stood. "Did I say something wrong?"

She shook her head, then decided he probably wanted the truth. "If you don't talk cattle with other women, then what *do* you talk about?" She sat on the ottoman facing him, staring at him intently.

Her question appeared to pull him up short, and he

avoided eye contact before responding. "We talk about this and that. Nothing important."

"Oh."

"I enjoyed our conversation if that's what concerns you."

The tension eased out of her shoulders. This was as good as a compliment. She blushed and looked away. "I enjoyed it, too." At ease once more, she said, "I'll check on dinner and get us another beer." She reached for the empty tumblers.

"Good idea," Matt called after her.

She wasn't gone long and when she returned they chatted again, this time on a variety of subjects—Buffalo Valley's past and present, the feasibility of raising bison, like Jeb McKenna did, politics, religion and Western movies. The beer loosened her inhibitions, and soon they were sharing a few jokes. It felt good to laugh, and to know he considered her a friend. The only other person she felt as comfortable around was Maddy McKenna. But this was different. Better.

"Are you planning to kiss me again?" The beer had given her courage to ask what had been on her mind for weeks.

"Do you want me to?"

"Oh, yes." She nodded eagerly. "In the worst way."

He cast his gaze down at his beer. "I don't know if that's such a good idea."

As far as she was concerned, it was a helluva great idea. "Okay, okay, maybe we should eat first, then check out how we feel afterward."

It didn't help her ego any to see the blatant relief on his face. His attitude was playing havoc with her theory that he'd enjoyed their kisses.

Dinner was superb. Sadie might not have approved

of Margaret's inviting Matt for Thanksgiving dinner, but that hadn't stopped her from preparing one of the finest meals in recent memory.

"More wine?" Margaret asked.

"I'll pour," Matt said, reaching for the bottle of chilled chardonnay before she could.

After two beers and two glasses of wine, Margaret's reserve slipped even further. Propping her elbows on the table, she leaned toward Matt. "I want to talk about us kissing again, all right?"

"Margaret…"

"Please. You have to understand that something like this doesn't happen to me every day. I have questions."

He shifted, clearly uncomfortable.

"What did you think?" she blurted.

"Think?"

"You know. How was it?"

He held his wineglass by the stem and seemed to carefully consider his response. "It was…nice."

She couldn't hold back a smile. "It was fabulous for me, too," she said, trying to sound mature, striving for sophistication. At the moment she was too pleased to care whether she succeeded or not. Hot damn, but he was a looker.

A silence followed, and she guessed he didn't know what to say next. From her father, Margaret had learned to respect silence. It didn't always need to be filled, particularly not with chitchat or superficial comments. She let several minutes pass, watching him, enjoying his nearness.

"Do you know the first time I saw you?" she finally asked.

Matt shook his head.

"It wasn't too long after you moved here. I was round-ing up strays and I came upon you and one of our men. You were knee-deep in mud, freeing a calf and you were arguing with this hand Dad had recently hired."

His face went tight. "I remember."

"Neither of you realized I was watching. As I recall, he accused you of attempting to steal that calf."

"We threw a couple of punches," Matt said, frowning. "You were watching?"

"I was." She picked up her wineglass. "You two really got into it."

"We had a history."

She'd suspected as much, and would have wagered money that the history they shared was a woman.

"You beat him in a fair fight."

He nodded, but didn't look especially pleased with himself. He should've been, she thought, seeing that he'd come out on the winning side. The other man had hit the dirt after two solid punches. As if the confrontation was irrelevant, Matt had returned to the calf and finished freeing him. His actions told her more about Matt Eilers than all the gossip she'd heard before and since.

"That hand wasn't much of a cattleman," Margaret muttered. "Dad fired him soon after."

"Last I heard, he was working for a fuel distributor in Texas. I think he always liked trucks better than cattle. Not everyone's cut out for ranch life."

That was true enough, and perhaps Margaret should have left it there. She probably would have if not for the drinks she'd had. "I fell in love with you that day," she confessed, "and more so every time I saw you. You might think it's 'cause you're handsome as sin, and that's got something to do with it, but there's more. You're a good person, Matt Eilers. You don't like people to know that—I haven't figured out why. Deep down you're honorable. You don't cheat and I've never heard you say a bad word about anyone—not even when they deserve it."

If Matt had seemed uncomfortable earlier, it didn't compare to the way he responded now. He half rose from his chair, his eyes filled with dread.

"Women aren't supposed to tell a man that, are they?" Margaret said quickly.

"Ah..."

"It's all right," she assured him, regretting that she'd embarrassed him, but not that he knew the truth about how she felt.

"You don't know me," he said. "You don't know what I'm really like, what I've done..."

"I know enough." Matt was no saint, especially when it came to women; she'd seen clear evidence of that. But, as she'd said, he had a good heart. She'd never told anyone what she'd seen that day. Not only had he freed the calf and returned it to its mother, but he'd given the man he'd beaten a hand up, too.

Matt stood and took his wineglass with him.

"I was thinking," she began, then fortified her courage with another sip of wine, "that I'd like to marry you, Matt Eilers."

Matt downed the rest of his wine in one giant gulp. He looked stricken, confused and utterly baffled. Margaret had never intended to propose marriage, but it'd happened and now that it had, she wasn't sorry. If anything, she felt released from a burden.

"I think it's time I left," Matt announced.

"All right," she whispered, and followed him to the kitchen door. Already he had his hat in his hand.

"Dinner was very nice."

Certain she'd embarrassed them both enough, she didn't say or do anything to delay his departure. It'd been a risk; she'd taken her best shot. In all likelihood, she wouldn't see or talk to him again for a long time. That part saddened her.

"Goodbye, Matt."

Without saying anything, he opened the door. The wind moaned and whistled and in its high-pitched rush, she heard it call her a fool. Matt bowed his head against the force of it and hurried toward his truck, parked on the far side of the yard.

Margaret stood at the window and watched as his headlights dimly illuminated the driveway.

Discouraged, she walked back into the dining room and cleared the table. Like her daddy, she was a risk taker, but usually a cautious one. Bernard had always been philosophical about the chances he took. She'd come by his believe-in-miracles-but-don't-bet-on-them attitude naturally. Only this was one miracle she'd really wanted.

An hour later, after she'd cleaned the kitchen and soaked out her disappointment in a hot bath, she heard someone pounding on the kitchen door.

When she went to investigate, she saw it was Matt Eilers. Dressed in her thick flannel robe, she unbolted the lock and hurriedly let him in. His face was red with cold, his jaw tight.

"All right," he said abruptly.

Not understanding, she stared at him.

He grasped her by the shoulders and brought her close. His kiss was as wild as his eyes and revealed none of the finesse she'd experienced in their earlier kisses.

"You want me for your husband?" he demanded

roughly. "Fine, I'll marry you, but you don't have a clue what you're getting yourself into. Not a clue."

"Don't be so sure," she told him, her pulse going crazy. His dark eyes burned into hers. Reaching for his collar with both hands, she jerked his mouth back to hers and kissed him with the same urgency.

She'd waited her entire life for this man and wasn't about to be shortchanged now. If anyone was in for a surprise, Margaret reasoned, it was going to be Matt Eilers.

Merrily had never thought of herself as an especially perceptive woman, but when it involved Axel she was almost psychic. The Monday following Thanksgiving, she found Pastor Dawson and Bob deep in conversation. They sat at a table on the far side of the restaurant, hunched together, talking quietly.

He knew.

This churchman had figured out that she'd stolen Axel. He knew she and Bob were hiding the boy from his birth parents and from the authorities. What he didn't know was all the whys and wherefores. She doubted the circumstances made any difference to nosy do-gooders like Pastor Dawson. If he'd guessed the truth, he was sure to consider it his God-given duty to call the state police and have her arrested.

That meant she and Bob had no choice. None. They had to protect their son and Merrily was prepared to do so at any price.

Thankfully, Axel was down for his nap when Pastor Dawson finally left. Merrily could barely wait for the other man to walk out the door before she confronted Bob. Her husband still sat at the table, his hands in his hair, staring blankly at the wall.

"He knows?" She whispered the question.

Bob nodded.

"How?"

"Does it matter?"

Weak and shaky, Merrily pulled out a chair and literally fell into it. Having Axel taken away was her greatest fear. He was her son. He might not have been born from her body, but he was as much a part of her as if he had.

Bob rubbed his hands down his face, glanced at her and then looked away. Something was wrong, she could see it in his eyes.

"What?" she pleaded.

Her husband shook his head.

"Tell me!" she demanded.

Bob continued to stare at the wall. "Pastor Dawson didn't know for sure... He asked a few questions..."

"Yes?" she prodded.

"I told him about Axel."

It took a moment for the implication of what he'd said to sink in. "You told him!" The anger inside her was explosive. "Why would you do such a thing?" Bob knew how dangerous that was. He'd purposely put their son at risk. She wanted to lash out at him, slug him, cause him the same kind of pain he'd caused her.

"He'd already guessed."

"You couldn't keep your mouth shut?"

Bob's eyes were empty, his complexion ashen, as if he were about to be violently ill. "He knew, Merrily, he already knew. He just didn't have proof. He asked if there was anything he could do to help. He saw the flyer, recognized Axel's name. He didn't threaten to turn us in..."

She started to tremble, and struggled to control the

panic that threatened to overwhelm her. "What kind of questions did he ask?"

"Questions that told me he's figured out what we've done. He knew you weren't Axel's biological mother... that I wasn't his father."

"But how?"

"Because of the flyer. And probably because we've made such an effort to keep Axel out of sight lately."

"That's crazy!" None of this added up to Merrily. Besides Axel had suffered with chicken pox. It was only natural that they not expose anyone else to the illness.

"He asked about Axel's family and when I didn't answer—"

"You could have explained that we didn't know each other—that you weren't in my life at the time."

"But you were, and he knew that, too."

This minister had become a threat to everything Merrily held dear. "You should have lied!" she shouted.

"Aren't we living a big enough lie already?" Bob shouted back. "I told him the truth because it's the only way we're ever going to be able to live a normal life. Look at us! Axel isn't even three and we're already afraid of what'll happen if anyone recognizes him. Afraid he might be taken away from us. Afraid someone might turn us in. Constantly looking over our shoulders. That's no kind of life, Merrily. Not for Axel and not for you and me."

"You don't mean that."

"I do mean it." All at once he was on his feet and pacing. His boots made hard, heavy sounds against the floor.

"We're his parents!" she cried.

"Yes, but burying our heads in the sand is wrong. Wrong for us and wrong for Axel. I love him as much as you do," Bob said. "I'd never purposely do anything to hurt him, but our fear is going to smother him. I can see it happening."

Merrily wasn't sure what to believe anymore. "How can you say you love Axel after what you did?" came her high-pitched cry. She looked at Bob, seeing him with fresh eyes. She'd trusted him with everything, her heart, her son, her very life. He'd betrayed that trust. The immensity of it burned like hot coals inside her.

"I did it because I love Axel and I love you."

Using both hands, she brushed the hair out of her face. Then, taking in a deep breath, she forced the panic from her heart. "Okay, Pastor Dawson knows. Exactly what's he going to do about it?"

Bob continued pacing, but his steps grew slower.

"Bob?" she asked, when it was clear he hadn't heard her. "He's not going to keep our secret, is he?" That would be too much to hope for.

"He didn't say he was going to do anything. He offered to help."

"By turning us in to the authorities, no doubt." It was what she expected, what she knew to expect.

"He said if we wanted, he'd be willing to contact the authorities on our behalf."

"Dear God." It felt as though the world had been jerked upside down.

"He wants us to take a week and think it over."

"A week?" That meant they had a full seven days to run. In that length of time, they could disappear somewhere in Canada. Bob was good at saving money, better than she was. They could take the cash from their bank account and run.

"Pastor Dawson assured me he wouldn't say anything to anyone," Bob explained.

"Thank God," Merrily whispered. "That gives us

time." Already her mind was racing with where they could go and the story they could make up. They'd need a lie that was convincing; they'd have to create a believable background. It would mean a name change, too, for all three of them.

Bob's eyes met hers. She saw his pain, right along with the unasked questions. "What do you mean?"

"We have seven days, don't you see? That's long enough to find a place to hide out, to—"

"Merrily, we can't do that. What kind of life would that be? For any of us? Our lives are here in Buffalo Valley."

"The hell we can't run. Are you nuts? That's exactly what we're going to do! It's our only option." Thanks to him. Thanks to what he'd done.

"Merrily—"

"Do you seriously believe I'm going to wait around for the cops? The social workers? You know me better than that. There's no way in hell I'm going to hand over our son to some stranger. Axel *needs* me. He needs us both."

Bob paled even more. "We're going to fight for him, Merrily, with everything we have. He's our son, and we're going to make a stand right here, surrounded by our friends."

For the first time, the pain gripping her heart lessened, but she still resisted. "It's our only chance. We can make a new life in Canada—or anywhere you want. Running's our only chance."

"Don't you understand that it's only a matter of time before we're found? It's inevitable."

"We can hide—"

"Until the next time. Until someone else figures out that Axel isn't ours."

She slapped at his hand as he reached out to console her. "You broke a trust! You betrayed Axel and me."

"Are you saying I don't love you?" Pain flashed from his eyes. "After everything I've done, after the months we've lived together as husband and wife? Nothing means more to me than you and Axel."

Merrily was sobbing openly now. "My baby, my baby," she whimpered.

Bob embraced her and she buried her face in his shirt.

"I don't want to lose my baby," she wailed.

"I don't, either."

"They'll take him."

"Over my dead body. I'm not going to let it happen," Bob returned adamantly.

Heaving in a shaky breath, she raised her eyes to meet her husband's. In him she saw resolve and determination. He wasn't just going to fight to keep Axel; he was determined to win.

Six

When Margaret went after something, she did so in what could only be called a headlong manner, Matt reflected as he arrived at the Triple C the day of their wedding. She sure didn't let any moss grow under her feet. No sooner had he accepted her proposal than she had them driving into Grand Forks to apply for the marriage license. Shifting schedules, the earliest possible day for the wedding was December seventh. He tried to forget that this was the same day the worst military defeat in U.S. history had occurred.

It didn't help that on the morning of their wedding day, the weather dipped to record cold temperatures. The Grand Forks newscaster stated that it could be the coldest day of the year. One of her uncles, who lived in South Dakota, had planned to attend the ceremony, but he'd phoned that morning to cancel because of the weather. Her other two uncles sent their love and best wishes; since they'd recently made the long trip for Bernard's funeral, they weren't able to come for another visit so soon.

Margaret, never shy, met him at the door, and quickly

ushered him out of the piercing wind and into the warm house.

"You haven't changed your mind, have you?" she asked, looking worried. The wind wasn't nearly as penetrating as her eyes. She seemed to gaze straight through him.

"I'm here, aren't I?" The truth was, he *had* changed his mind. Four or five times in the past few hours, in fact, but each time he'd managed to set aside his guilt and his doubts. He was marrying her for all the wrong reasons—and all the right ones. No woman had believed in him the way Margaret did. None had looked past the polished exterior and seen his heart. And dammit, there were all those beautiful cattle. And the land. It wasn't like he could ignore what she had to offer.

Now that he was at the Triple C, he had every intention of going through with the ceremony. If he was making a mistake, then he was doing it with open eyes.

Sadie's disapproval was all too evident and implied that Margaret was the one making the mistake. She didn't even try to hide her distaste for him. He felt her censure the instant he walked into the room. But no matter what the housekeeper thought, it wasn't anything Matt hadn't been saying to himself since the moment he'd agreed to this.

Margaret ignored Sadie, but Matt suspected the two women had done verbal battle over the impending marriage. Clearly Margaret had won the war, but he figured there'd been more than one battle from which she'd walked away wounded. She wanted him and she'd been willing to fight for him; that said a great deal.

"Pastor Dawson is already here," Margaret announced, leading Matt by the hand into the library. "Jeb and Maddy are on their way. Gage and Lindsay are coming, too."

"Hassie?" he asked, and swallowed tightly.

Margaret nodded. "And Leta Betts. Joyce Dawson's here with her husband, as well."

Matt wore his best clothes, a ten-year-old suit, and made small talk with Pastor Dawson while he waited for their guests. He was tense and tried to hide his nervousness, talking far more than usual. Everyone arrived within the next fifteen minutes. Soon they all gathered in the very room where Bernard Clemens had warned Matt against hurting his daughter. Now he was marrying Margaret and God help him, he sincerely liked her, but he didn't love her. Not the way she deserved to be loved.

Glancing around uneasily, Matt was certain everyone knew why he was doing this. He felt sure that Margaret's friends believed the worst of him, that the words *money, cattle, land* echoed in their brains. It was almost as if they all knew about Sheryl and her scheming ideas, although he swore he wanted no part of that.

Margaret loved him. Bernard Clemens had said as much and Margaret had told him so herself. In time, he hoped to love her with the same intensity. In fact, he was counting on that. He didn't yet, but he would. Dear God, he prayed that would happen.

"Is everyone ready?" Larry Dawson asked. He stood before them, his open Bible in his hands.

Margaret looked at Matt with such adoration, it was all he could do not to turn and bolt from the room. It amazed him that she couldn't see the truth. He half expected someone to step forward and stop the wedding, claiming he wasn't a fit husband. But he *hoped* to be, wanted to be.

Margaret's friends and neighbors were as somber as if they were attending a funeral. No one seemed happy except Margaret, who, oblivious to the tension in the room, beamed with joy.

His bride wore a long white dress and held a small bouquet of pale rosebuds. White…she wore white. He closed his eyes, barely able to concentrate on Pastor Dawson's words.

Margaret was a virgin. In all his life, Matt had never slept with a virgin. His women were as experienced as he was. He understood there was pain involved when a woman made love for the first time, and the one thing he didn't want to do was hurt Margaret. Marrying her might appear heartless, but he did care for her. She was giving him so much—her life, her trust—and little as he had, he would willingly offer that up to her.

"We are gathered here this afternoon to share in the…"

Matt blocked out the minister's words, his thoughts whirling. This was wrong. He knew it even as he repeated his vows, his voice flat and barely audible. Not wrong for him, but for her. Margaret's loving him was the best luck of his life, but marrying her, pledging himself to her, proved that everything she'd said about him was a lie. A man who was honorable and decent wouldn't do this.

Matt tried to concentrate on the words, but his mind soon drifted. He remembered how love had changed Jeb McKenna and Gage Sinclair. Jeb had been a surly, bitter man until Maddy came into his life. He recalled how Gage and Lindsay Snyder had been continually at odds. Every time Matt talked to him, Gage had predicted that Lindsay would abandon the town after the first snowfall. Yet, months later, when she really was about to go, he'd driven his tractor across a freshly planted field in an effort to stop her. Yes, love had changed both men. The only thing Matt expected Margaret to change in *his* life was the state of his bank account.

Margaret's eyes shone as she held Matt's hand and repeated her vows, her voice loud, clear, distinct.

After they'd exchanged plain gold bands, Pastor Dawson proclaimed them married. His emotions in turmoil, Matt brought his bride into his arms and kissed her lightly, almost as if they were brother and sister. He saw the disappointment in her eyes and feared this was only the first of many.

It didn't surprise him that none of their guests seemed eager to stay. The ceremony was followed by cake and champagne, and a couple of halfhearted toasts. The weather was a perfect excuse to rush home. They were all polite, cordial, but Matt realized he hadn't fooled anyone, with the exception of Margaret.

A half hour following the ceremony, they were alone.

"Hello, husband," Margaret said, happiness radiating from her. She threw her arms around his neck and gazed lovingly up at him.

"Wife," Matt said. Deception was never his strong suit. He kissed her and felt the muscles of his stomach tighten with dread.

"I don't know about you, but I'm starving. All I've had today is wedding cake."

It was all he'd eaten, too. He couldn't force anything into his stomach earlier, and had skipped both breakfast and lunch.

As they headed into the kitchen, Matt saw that his wife had thought of everything. She had dinner ready to serve, along with wine and music. Nor did Matt need to worry about carrying a conversation. Margaret talked animatedly throughout the meal, bouncing from one subject to the next, asking one question after another; he had merely to reply. They chatted about the ranch, about how he'd give the Stockerts notice and move his things into the house, about combining their herds.

The wine helped relax him, but the tension returned as soon as Margaret mentioned bed. Matt had never experienced problems performing sexually, but with Margaret, his doubts were rampant. His biggest fear was that she'd guess his true feelings and hate him. He had other fears, too. The fact that she was a virgin intimidated him. Any pain he caused her would undoubtedly be followed by plenty of angst—and regret. The mere thought of what might happen was enough to drive away any hint of desire.

"Matt," Margaret whispered, studying him.

He finished the last of his wine and looked up at her.

"I might not be beautiful—"

"It's not that," he said, wanting her to know she wasn't the problem. "You're an attractive woman. Your eyes are lovely. Your hair..." He let his words drift into silence. His hesitation was due to his own failings, which, at the moment, seemed too many to count.

He toyed with the idea of suggesting they put off the wedding night, but couldn't come up with a plausible reason. If she didn't love him so much, Matt thought he could have found a viable excuse, could have invented one. It was out of the question, though, and he firmed his resolve. He would make love to his wife. He was destined to be a disappointment to her in the future, but he was going to give her a wedding night she wouldn't soon forget.

She steered him into the bedroom, then reached over and turned out the light. Matt drew her into his arms and kissed her fully, expecting—he wasn't sure what, but certainly not this strong surge of passion. Her mouth was soft and moist and pliant, her eager response innocent and sweet. What had intimidated him earlier excited him now.

"Margaret," he groaned, shocked at the quick passion she'd created within him. His fingers worked at unfastening the many buttons of her dress. That was a difficult enough task with only the light from a bedside lamp, but nervous as he was, Matt faltered, all thumbs.

"Here," she breathed and whirled around, flipping her hair out of the way. "I told Maddy this dress would be impossible."

Matt chuckled and patiently unbuttoned the dress. Driven by desire, he slipped his hands inside the bodice and cupped her breasts. He was pleasantly surprised to find her lush and full. A sigh escaped him, echoed by a soft groan from her.

"Margaret... Margaret."

"Oh, Matt, this feels so good," she whispered. "I didn't know it would be like this."

He closed his eyes, astonished by the intensity of what he was experiencing.

"You make me feel so beautiful." She turned to face him, the dim light revealing the shape of her features, the perfection of her skin, the brilliance of her eyes.

"You are," he whispered, and she was. It stunned him that he'd ever viewed her as plain, because it simply wasn't so. Her eyes glowing with love, she brought her palms to his cheeks. Rather than trying to understand the curious mix of emotions that swirled inside him, Matt kissed her. Soon they were devoid of clothes. He pressed her down onto the bed, his engorged penis throbbing.

"I don't want to hurt you," he whispered, his voice husky with need.

"That would be impossible."

"But, Margaret…"

"Love me, Matt, just love me."

He brought her satisfaction with his hands and his mouth, reveling in her shudders and cries. Then he poised himself above her, his arms and legs trembling at the knowledge of what he was about to do. Apparently unwilling to wait any longer, Margaret slid her arms around his neck. He murmured, "Not yet," and reached for a condom in his wallet, which he'd tossed onto the bedside table.

As he slipped on the condom, she lifted her head just high enough for their mouths to meet. Urging him with soft sighs, she opened her body to him, giving herself completely. Afraid of causing her pain, Matt kept his movements slow and shallow. Feeling her body suddenly tense, he froze, uncertain how to proceed. It was Margaret who urged him forward, and afterward, it was his sweet, generous wife who comforted him.

Her innocence had been something Matt dreaded, but now he felt honored and more than that, deeply moved.

Usually when he slept with a woman, she clung to him, reluctant to let him go, but with Margaret, he was the one who needed to hold her close. He was determined to be a good husband. He might not have married her for love, but he planned to do his utmost to make their marriage beneficial to them both.

Matt woke at dawn, from years of habit, with Margaret's warm body tucked against his. His arm was around her waist and he grinned, delighted that beneath the ill-fitting jeans and bulky shirts lay the delectable body of a woman. He'd had a hint of it once, during that first visit to her house, but the reality was so much more impressive.

"Morning," she said with a yawn and rolled onto her back. "Morning, husband."

"Good morning, wife," he said and kissed her cheek. "How about I rustle us up some coffee?"

"That sounds wonderful," she said, raising herself to a sitting position. "But before you do, I thought we should talk."

"Talk? Before coffee?" He frowned. Experience had taught him that when a woman sought conversation, she was generally unhappy about *something*. They hadn't been married twenty-four hours. Had he failed her already? "This can't wait?"

She took a minute to mull over his question, then shook her head.

He sat upright and tensed. "Okay, shoot."

"I love you, Matt. I've loved you for nearly five years, and I'm fully aware that you don't love me."

He'd reached for his pants, but let them drop as he sat on the edge of the bed. She knew, and had married him, anyway. "Then why'd you go through with it?" he demanded, not sure if he should be relieved or depressed.

"Isn't that the question I should be asking *you*?"

He shook his head. The answer was obvious.

"I already know you married me for the ranch," she told him. "I'm not so beautiful, but those cattle of mine certainly are. I'm not naive enough to think you've fallen head over heels for me in such a short time."

He said nothing, silenced by her honesty.

"It's always been important to me to make everything as clear and above-board as possible," she stated simply, as though reading his mind.

He nodded.

"I had to say these things because I don't want you feeling guilty. I knew how you felt when I asked you to be my husband. It was a risk I was willing to take. Naturally, I hope you'll have a change of heart and that eventually you'll love me as much as I love you."

Matt stared at his wife, hardly able to believe that he'd been fortunate enough to marry a woman as forthright and plainspoken as Margaret.

"Do you think you *can* learn to love me?" she asked quietly.

Margaret was almost completely unfamiliar with feminine wiles and manipulative behavior. She was innocent and trusting. Over the years he'd had more than his share of beautiful women and he'd learned that beauty usually faded. Prolonged exposure to a woman he'd once found gorgeous inevitably resulted in disappointment. Look at Sheryl, for instance—as vain and selfish as she was beautiful. Margaret was the first woman he'd ever known who possessed such genuineness.

"I believe I'm halfway in love with you already," he said. Then, because it seemed the most natural and perfect thing to do, he made love to his wife.

Sarah sensed almost immediately that there would be problems with the pregnancy. At three weeks she started spotting and, terrified she was about to miscarry, she called Dennis at work.

Her husband, ashen with fear, raced her into the doctor's office in Grand Forks, cursing the lack of a medical facility in Buffalo Valley. After a careful examination, Dr. Leggatt, who'd been the attending physician for both Lindsay Sinclair and Maddy, had ordered complete and total bed rest until at least February, and maybe longer. If Sarah hoped to deliver a healthy infant, there was no alternative.

Never in all her life had Sarah spent this much time in bed.

"Do you need anything before I head out to work?" Dennis asked this particular morning. It was Wednesday in the third week of December.

She managed a smile and casually waved him on his way. So far, she'd been able to occupy herself with designing new quilt patterns. Buffalo Valley Quilts had developed to the point that she felt safe venturing beyond the natural-dyed muslin designs she'd started with. These days, she experimented with bright, bold colors and complex patterns.

With Christmas approaching, the company was busier than ever. Jennifer Logan, who'd worked the longest for Sarah, made trips to and from the house twice a day. It helped Sarah stay involved with what was happening. Jennifer, whom Sarah had recently promoted to manager, had a good head for business. Together they talked over every aspect of the daily schedule. If Jennifer was going to be late or needed an immediate answer, she phoned.

The telephone was set up next to the bed for just that reason. When it rang, Sarah knew it was either Jennifer or Dennis.

"Hello," she said, hoping to sound cheerful and in good spirits, although she'd grown weary of forced bed rest. She followed her physician's orders because she very badly wanted this child. Nothing in her life had ever come easy and she'd learned that what she treasured most often brought her the greatest pain.

"Mom."

Sarah's heart froze at the sound of her daughter's voice. "Calla?"

"What are you doing home? I called the store and Jennifer told me you weren't at work. Are you sick?"

Now, their first conversation in months, wasn't the time to tell her about the pregnancy. Instead, she avoided the question. "Oh, Calla, it's so good to hear from you! How are you?"

"All right." Her voice was flat, dull, and Sarah could only imagine what had been left unsaid.

"Me, too." She'd say anything just to keep the conversation going. "Where are you?"

"Home."

Sarah had to bite her tongue to keep from insisting that Calla's home was and always would be with her. She didn't bother to ask why her daughter wasn't at school this time of day.

"I bought a phone card. Dad doesn't have long-distance service."

Probably because he couldn't be trusted to pay the bill, but Sarah didn't say what was already obvious.

"Juliet said you called on Thanksgiving."

Juliet must have been the woman who'd answered the phone at Willie's place. "Your grandfather did—we were hoping to talk to you."

"I was working." Calla sounded none too pleased about that. "Juliet's moved in with Dad, but I doubt it'll last," she added, almost in afterthought. "It never does."

"What about Christmas?" Sarah asked, plunging ahead, hoping Calla would consider joining them, if only for a few days. "Will you be working then, too?"

"I...I was sort of thinking about coming back to Buffalo Valley around then."

Sarah's relief was so great, it was all she could do

not to break into sobs. She didn't dare reveal too much emotion. Not to Calla. She cleared her throat. "That would be fabulous. We'd love it if you could."

"Just for a visit, Mom, so don't go hyper on me."

"I won't," Sarah promised, although she wasn't entirely sure what she was agreeing to.

"How's Jessica?" Calla asked about her best friend next.

"Jessica? Good, great," Sarah reported. She closed her eyes, trying to remember the last time she'd talked with the girl. It must be months now. She'd been so busy with the business; she rarely had any opportunity to see the people who'd once been close to her daughter. Jessica and the others hadn't asked about Calla, either. After so many months of not hearing from her, they'd given up.

"What about Joe?"

"Joe Lammermann?" It was a mistake to ask, but Sarah didn't realize that until it was too late.

"Of course Joe Lammermann. I went to the Sweetheart Dance with him last February, remember? You're supposed to be my mother. I thought real mothers remembered details like that."

Sarah stiffened. "Mothers, even real mothers, aren't perfect."

"So I've noticed."

"Neither are their children."

To Sarah's surprise, Calla laughed. "Touché."

While Calla was still in high spirits, Sarah decided to finalize the details of her visit. "It wouldn't be difficult to exchange the airline ticket I sent you for Thanksgiving." She wasn't actually sure that was true, but she'd gladly purchase another ticket, if necessary.

"I wouldn't have to stay with you and…and your

husband, would I?" she asked. "You told me before that Grandpa said I could have my old room back."

"I'm sure he'd be willing to make the same arrangement," Sarah assured her, hoping her excitement didn't show.

"In that case, I'll come home, but only for Christmas."

"Just one day?" Sarah shouldn't be greedy, but she wanted Calla to stay much longer. A week, possibly two. Her heart's desire was that her daughter would recognize that she'd been wrong to leave.

"I might be able to stay a bit longer than one day," Calla offered, her tone suggesting she'd bestowed a tremendous favor.

"How long?" she asked warily, fearing Calla would use the opportunity to hurt her.

"A week," Calla announced tautly, as though she expected an argument.

"That would be perfect." Sarah couldn't quite disguise her delight. "I'll call the travel agent in Grand Forks today and have the tickets sent to your father's."

"Ah…Mom, listen, would it be possible for you to get the ticket mailed to my job? You know what a slob Dad can be. Things have a way of turning up lost or missing at his place…so it'd probably be best if I could pick up the ticket at the BurgerHaven."

"All right." She reached for a pen and paper and wrote down the address. Then, because she was curious as to why Calla had rebuffed her previous gift of an airline ticket, she asked, "Why didn't you want to come for Thanksgiving?"

Calla hesitated. "Dad told me you were pregnant. I thought it was a ploy to keep me with him, but I wasn't sure."

Sarah closed her eyes and swallowed tightly. It *had*

been a lie, but it wasn't now. Clearly this wasn't the time to mention her pregnancy.

"He was lying, wasn't he?"

Willie had lied. He couldn't possibly have known; she hadn't known herself. Sarah suspected it wasn't the first time he'd misled their daughter. "That's why you didn't come here?" she asked, not answering Calla's question.

"No…the ticket went missing, and well, that's the reason I wanted you to have it mailed to the Burger-Haven."

"The ticket went missing?" Sarah repeated.

"Dad said it must have gotten lost…"

That rat! He'd returned the ticket himself and let Sarah believe Calla had heartlessly rejected her offer.

"I'll make sure the new ticket's mailed to the Burger-Haven," Sarah promised. "Or you could pick it up at the airport," she suggested, but Calla seemed to find that an intimidating prospect.

"I want it right here, in my hot little hands," she joked. They spoke a few minutes longer and although Sarah didn't want to end the conversation, Calla's telephone card had nearly expired and Willie was due home any minute.

"I'll see you next week then," Calla said quickly.

"Next week." Sarah replaced the telephone in its cradle and if she hadn't been ordered to rest, she would have danced around the room. She had to let her daughter know about the baby, but she'd bide her time and choose exactly the right moment.

Buffalo Bob pressed the telephone hard against his ear, listening intently. He'd never met Doug Alder, the Savannah attorney Maddy McKenna had recommended, but had talked to him several times over the phone. The case involving Axel was complicated, to say the least, and Doug had decided to work with a California law firm, which meant additional fees and a larger retainer.

During a conference call earlier in the month, both Bob and Merrily had talked to the attorneys regarding their situation.

Merrily had done most of the talking. Her reluctance to work with the authorities was obvious. She didn't trust the lawyers any more than she did Axel's birth parents.

"Well?" she muttered now, looking to Bob for an answer.

Still listening, Bob held up his hand and shook his head. It was difficult enough to understand the complexity of what Doug was saying without Merrily's constant interruptions.

"As we decided, I contacted Child Protective Services for the state of California on your behalf," Doug Alder continued.

"You didn't mention where Axel was, did you?" Bob demanded.

Merrily's eyes flared wide.

"No…no. I did exactly as we agreed. You tell Merrily I kept my promise to her."

"I will," Bob said, relieved. He'd wanted this to be another conference call, had wanted to include his wife in the meeting, but she'd refused. The first call had ended abruptly, with her nearly in hysterics. Bob had felt trapped—between Doug's recommendation and Merrily's need for comfort and reassurance. He didn't know how she'd cope if they lost Axel.

"I explained the situation," Doug went on, "but it's messy. Merrily not only took Axel, she drove him across state lines. That's a federal kidnapping charge, a serious offense."

Bob realized that if they weren't careful, his wife could end up serving jail time. He wouldn't be exempt from charges himself. His hand tightened around the receiver. "I know there are...problems."

"It doesn't help matters that she didn't get in touch with the authorities when she learned Axel's father intended to sell him."

"She doesn't trust the so-called authorities!" Bob shouted, losing his patience. "Besides, Merrily *did* report what was happening. She called Child Protective Services, but by the time they arrived the bruises were gone. Merrily tried to tell them, and the woman took a report, but nothing ever came of it." If anything, her reporting the abuse had made matters worse. Shortly afterward, Axel's parents had decided to sell him to the highest bidder.

"It's understandable, considering her history." Doug sighed. "Merrily's drug conviction could hurt our case."

Bob's eyes flew to his wife. "I know." He could barely choke out the words. She had a drug conviction—and she'd kept it hidden from him! Throughout the entire ordeal, Bob had been nothing but forthright and honest with Merrily. He'd risked everything for her and the boy, and she hadn't trusted him enough to reveal the truth about her background.

"That's not all."

A hard knot formed in Bob's chest. "There's more?"

His question was followed by another heavy sigh. "In the time you've had Axel, his father's landed in prison on a drug charge."

This was good news as far as Bob could see. After

the way the bastard had abused his own child, prison was exactly where he belonged.

"He has a twenty-year sentence, but he's already been in trouble—fighting with other inmates. It doesn't look like he's going to be paroled any year soon."

"Good."

Merrily watched him the way an animal does its prey, pacing back and forth, from the far edge of hope to the brink of despair, frantic to know what was being said, yet afraid to listen herself.

"About Axel's mother—"

"Don't know her, but Merrily does."

"Did," the attorney corrected. "She died of an overdose."

Bob suffered no regret on her account, either. The woman wasn't fit to be called a mother. From what Merrily had told him, she'd willingly agreed to sell Axel and she'd made no effort to end the abuse.

"This has to be good news, right?" Bob asked. "For us, I mean. Axel has bonded with Merrily and me. We're the only family he knows."

"It *would* be good news if Merrily hadn't stolen the boy."

"She was protecting him," Bob cried. Anyone with half a brain would see that she'd taken the only possible course of action. The child was being physically and psychologically abused. Merrily had contacted the authorities and—because of circumstances, perhaps because of her own lack of credibility—that hadn't resulted in a damn thing. But if she hadn't taken Axel when she did, there was no telling what would've happened to the boy.

"Now listen," Doug said, "I know this is going to be difficult, but I want you to trust me."

Bob could feel it coming. He sensed it the same way he did an approaching storm.

Doug Alder waited as if giving Bob time to adjust to what he was about to say. "The state has asked me to hand Axel over to them."

"No!" Bob's response was loud and instantaneous. "No."

"Bob, listen, if you and Merrily are going to have a chance at adopting Axel yourselves, you have to do this."

"No."

Merrily's eyes had gone wild. She couldn't hear what was being said, but his reaction told her they were in danger of losing their son.

"The state will send a social worker to collect Axel. The courts have appointed what's called a guardian ad litem. That's generally another attorney whose job is to look after the child's best interests. Basically, you have a strong case. Axel loves you and Merrily, and if he's bonded to you, the courts should be willing to consider you as adoptive parents."

Buffalo Bob sat down, his knees too weak to hold him upright. "How…long?"

"How long would Axel be away from you?"

"Yes." His voice shook with the depth of his emotion. This shouldn't be happening. He'd hoped it could all be resolved without Axel's being taken from them. More than hoped, he'd counted on it.

"I can't answer that," Doug told him quietly. "It could be a matter of weeks, but it might take several months."

"Tell me!" Merrily demanded, grabbing Bob's arm. "They want to take him away, don't they?"

He nodded, then gestured for silence.

"It's up to you," Doug told him. "I haven't given the authorities any information that would lead them to you, but I don't think continued secrecy is what you want. You wouldn't have called me if you didn't want to clean up this mess with Axel, and make everything legal and above-board. You said it yourself. You're tired of constantly worrying about being found out."

"Either we face it now or we face it later." Bob repeated his own words, although the conviction had gone flat.

"Exactly."

Doug made it sound easy. Made disclosure sound like the only choice they had. If that was the case, then why did his heart feel as though it was being ripped from his chest? If that was the case, why was his wife sobbing at his side?

"The decision is yours."

Bob put down the phone. He looked to Merrily and held open his arms and she came to him. As he held her tight, she stared up at him expectantly, silently begging him not to let them take her baby.

"We have to hand him over until the adoption can be completed," he told her.

Merrily bit down on her lip so hard, blood oozed from between her teeth. "He doesn't know any mother but me."

"He isn't going to forget us."

"But…"

"We have to do this."

Merrily closed her eyes and slowly nodded, sobs shaking her shoulders almost uncontrollably.

"Tell them where we are," Bob whispered into the phone. His resolve was stronger now than ever. It wouldn't be long before they had their son back, before he and Merrily were Axel's legal parents. The interim, the weeks or months without him, would be hard on them both, but that couldn't be avoided.

The state of California scheduled a social worker to pick up Axel two days before Christmas. Doug had tried to talk the authorities into waiting until after the holidays, but his request was denied. Buffalo Bob and Merrily had no choice but to relinquish their son.

Merrily had barely spoken to Bob in days. On the morning of December twenty-third, she silently, dutifully, packed Axel's clothes and toys.

Bob got up early that day, unable to sleep. He found it impossible to stay in one place for long. The flight was supposed to land in Grand Forks at noon, which meant that Beth Graham would arrive between one and two. Maddy McKenna, Hassie and Pastor Dawson arrived at 12:30, hoping to provide comfort and support, but no one seemed to have much to say.

Bob saw the rental car the minute it pulled into town. "She's here," he told Merrily. A few moments later, an older woman walked into the restaurant. She stood at the entrance in her inadequate trench coat, her shoes wet with snow. Despite her obvious discomfort, she had a kind face and her expression was sympathetic.

At the sight of her, Merrily's eyes welled with fresh tears. Bob reached for Axel. "How's my man?" he asked in a choked voice. He held out his palm and Axel slapped his small hand against Bob's. He laughed and hugged Bob tight around the neck.

Bob kissed him, then handed him back to Merrily.

She clung to the boy, sobbing uncontrollably. Axel squirmed in her embrace, not understanding.

The social worker advanced into the room. "I'm Beth

Graham from California C.P.S.," she said softly. "I'm here for Axel."

Bob merely nodded.

"No…no! God, please don't take my baby from me! Please!" Merrily screamed as the woman approached.

"I'm sorry, Mrs. Carr."

"Somebody, please… Bob, don't let them do this." Merrily was crying so hard it was difficult to make out her words.

"We have to give him up for now," Bob said as gently as he could. "It'll only be for a little while."

"You promised me it'd never come to this. You promised…"

"I'm sorry." Surely she could see this was just as hard for him.

In the end, Bob was forced to pry Axel away from Merrily's grasp. Thankfully, the social worker left almost immediately. Merrily ran out of the room, and Bob collapsed in a chair, burying his face in his hands. He felt Pastor Dawson at his side, Maddy and Hassie, too. Through blurry eyes, he squinted at the Christmas decorations in the bar, so at odds with the way he felt.

Somehow they made it through the evening, and that first night. Bob didn't sleep and he knew Merrily was awake, too, but they didn't speak. Their emotions remained raw, confused.

Come morning, Christmas Eve, the sun woke Bob. He was surprised to discover he'd drifted off, but he didn't feel he'd gotten any real rest. His heart ached for Axel and for Merrily, who'd placed her trust in him. Difficult as it was, he'd done what he believed to be right.

Rolling onto his side, he reached for his wife and discovered her side of the bed empty. Thinking she'd decided to sleep in Axel's bedroom, he went to look for her. Merrily wasn't there, either.

Nor was she downstairs.

A sick sensation came over him. Hurrying up the stairs, he ran back to their bedroom. The closet door was half open and he could see at a glance that Merrily's clothes were gone.

His wife had done what she always did. She'd run away.

Rage filled him, and with a wild shout Bob plowed his hand into the wall. His fist slammed into the plaster and as luck would have it, he hit a stud. The last thing he heard before he crumpled to the floor in pain was the sound of cracking bones.

Seven

When Calla arrived in Buffalo Valley on Christmas Eve, she was shocked by how different the town looked after six months away. Christmas lights were strung across Main Street and although it was still daylight, they glowed a festive red and green. The pharmacy windows were painted with a cheery winter scene, and at Maddy's Grocery the entire parking lot was decorated with strings of glittering rope and blinking lights. Even the new beauty shop and the catalogue store had an inviting display of Christmas joy.

Never in her life had Calla seen the town look prettier. She was excited to be back but wasn't admitting it, at least not out loud. In fact, she'd decided to stay cool and impassive and not let anyone know how she felt about being home.

"What do you think?" Jessica asked as they pulled onto Main Street. She'd ridden along with Calla's grandfather to collect her from the Grand Forks airport. Although Calla was curious as to why her mother or Dennis hadn't come, she wasn't about to complain. Actually she was so glad to see her friend that nothing could ruin her good mood.

"The town looks all right," Calla said noncommittally. In reality she thought it was delightful—like driving through a Christmas card. A fresh snowfall had dusted the road and frosted the buildings, and the nostalgic beauty of the scene brought her close to tears.

"You aren't going to get this kind of cozy feel in Minneapolis," Jessica murmured, wrapping her arm around Calla's.

Calla nodded, blinking rapidly.

Jessica couldn't possibly have any idea how glad Calla was to be away from the big city. Phoning her mother had been the hardest thing she'd ever done, but she couldn't tolerate living with her father any longer. She hadn't asked about moving back home yet, but that was what she hoped would happen. If anything, these months away from Buffalo Valley had taught her the importance of checking out a situation before plunging into it. Had she known what her father was really like, she would never have gone to him, would never have made the mistakes she had.

The week before she called her mother, Calla had narrowly escaped being arrested. Her father had held another of his infamous parties. Luckily, she'd been on her way to work when the place was raided. Ten minutes earlier and Calla would have been there when the narcotics officers arrived. The worst of it was that her father had taken the money she'd saved from her job to help bail himself out. Every cent was gone. That money had been her freedom fund, her chance to escape.

Following his arrest, her father had turned ugly. It'd gotten so bad, Calla was ready to swallow her pride and move back to Buffalo Valley. Naturally, she wasn't telling her mother or Dennis the real truth about Willie; if she did decide to stay, she wanted her mother to be grateful.

"Everyone's dying to talk to you."

That bolstered Calla's ego. In six months she hadn't managed to make one good friend in Minneapolis. Between school and her job at BurgerHaven, there hadn't been much opportunity to cultivate friendships. All this time, she'd assumed that attending a big city high school would mean lots of advantages—interesting programs and people she'd never see in a hick town like Buffalo Valley.

True, she had access to programs far beyond the reach of anything offered at school here. Unfortunately, participation in many of those programs required money and time, neither of which was available to her. She could go to Europe with the German class, for instance, but she had to pay her own way. Like her father was ever going to fork over any money! That was a joke. Half the time *she* was the one who supported him.

Calla didn't know why it'd taken her so long to figure it out. Her father was an irresponsible freeloader—and worse.

"Do you want to see your mom a little later?" her grandfather asked when he stopped at his house—the only home Calla had ever known.

"You mean she's not here?" Calla had assumed her mother and probably Dennis would be at her grandfather's waiting, with dinner all ready and a decorated Christmas tree with wrapped gifts beneath it. She felt more than a little hurt that they weren't. She'd been hoping for a resumption of the family's traditional Christmas festivities as part of her "welcome home." She hadn't realized until now how badly she'd wanted that.

"Your…mother hasn't been feeling well lately."

Both her grandfather and Jessica looked at Calla, waiting for a response.

"Is she all right?" Apparently, whatever was wrong seemed to be lingering, because her mother had been at home the day she'd phoned.

"She's fine."

"Actually, everyone's heading over for Christmas Eve service at the church later. You'll come, won't you?" Jessica pleaded.

"Father McGrath is here for Christmas Eve?" Calla asked. The old priest only came into town occasionally, and never for Christmas Eve, not since the church had closed.

"We have a new minister," Jessica told her eagerly. "He used to live here."

"Larry Dawson," her grandfather cut in. "He was a good friend of mine."

Calla had never heard of him.

"He's great, too," Jessica continued. "There's plans to start a teen group after the first of the year. Everyone's excited about that."

"The whole family's going tonight," Calla's grandfather said. "You comin'?"

"I'll go, I guess."

"Sit by me, okay?" Jessica urged.

Another time, an earlier time, Calla would have found the request childish, but after the trouble she'd had making friends, it felt good to be wanted. "Sure."

"Joe Lammermann will be there."

Calla shrugged as though that was of little concern. Actually she was dying to see him. A year ago they'd gone to the Sweetheart Dance together, but soon afterward Joe had dumped her for some cheerleader over in Devils Lake.

"He's asked about you a few times," Jessica told her, as they walked into her grandfather's house.

"He has?" Joe's interest was the best news yet. She had to hear this, and she didn't want her grandfather listening in. "I'll put everything in my room," she told him, then grabbed Jessica's hand and led her back to her old bedroom.

Everything in her room was just as she'd left it. She wasn't sure how she felt about that—other than grateful.

"What did Joe say?" she asked, hopping onto the bed and sitting there cross-legged.

"He said…" Jessica bit into her lower lip. "You don't want to know."

"Yes, I do."

"All right. He said you were a fool to leave."

Her old boyfriend's remark wasn't far from the truth, and Calla had no problem accepting it.

"But the only reason he said that was because he misses you," Jessica added quickly.

"He's not dating anyone…special, is he?"

"No." Jessica glanced at her watch. "Listen, I've got to run or my mom will kill me. Meet me at the church at seven, okay?"

"Sure." Calla walked her friend to the door and watched as Jessica raced toward the pharmacy where she'd parked. Calla realized she hadn't asked her about Kevin, the one true love of her friend's life. Jess hadn't mentioned him, which suggested that things weren't what they had been. Kevin Betts attended art school in Chicago, and it was difficult to maintain a long-distance relationship. Not long ago, Calla had envied him the opportunity to escape Buffalo Valley.

"Gramps," Calla called, seeking him out. "Do you know if Kevin is still dating Jessica?"

"Don't have a clue," Joshua McKenna muttered.

For the first time Calla looked carefully around the house. Now that her mother was married and living with Dennis, the house wasn't as homey as it used to be. Her grandfather had put up a Christmas tree, but it was a small aluminum one that sat on an end table. That was the extent of any holiday decorations. Her mother had always gone overboard with Christmas and Calla was surprised to realize how much she missed it. She missed silly things, like the two cotton-ball snowmen she'd made in sixth grade. She missed the crocheted and starched snowflakes that added a festive air to the house. Sarah had been ridiculous about the holidays—even placing lights in the windows, including an old gas lamp that had once belonged to Calla's grandmother—and Calla knew now that she loved all the Christmas traditions as much as her mother did.

"I'll bet Mrs. Sinclair could tell you about Jessica and Kevin," her grandfather said. "You'll probably see her at church tonight."

But it would be awkward to ask her old teacher, especially there. Rather than wait, Calla reached for the portable phone and retreated to her bedroom.

Mrs. Sinclair sounded pleased to hear from her. "I didn't mean to bother you," Calla said, getting to her point immediately, "but I need to find out about Jessica and Kevin before I say something I shouldn't."

"Oh, Calla," Lindsay Sinclair breathed, "we've all missed you so much."

"I've missed you, too."

"Are you going to stay?"

"I—I…" Calla could see no reason to delay talking about her problems with school. "I've…my grades haven't been the best. I don't know if I can graduate this year and it'd be too embarrassing to come back and not graduate."

"Yes, you can," Mrs. Sinclair insisted. "I've been on maternity leave and Mrs. Folsom from Devils Lake filled in for me. But I'll be returning after the first of the year. We'll work together and you can get caught up, but it'll take effort on both our parts."

"You'd do that for me?" Calla felt like weeping. She hadn't wanted to say anything, but not being able to graduate with her class was her biggest concern. Because she'd been tardy so often, she'd flunked two classes and her grades other than drama weren't that good. Not the way they'd been here in Buffalo Valley.

"We'll do whatever is necessary to get you back on course. Don't you worry."

"That'd be great."

"Now, listen, about Jessica and Kevin, they broke up in September. Jessica's been dating Bert Loomis."

"Bert?" One of the Loomis twins. That didn't seem possible.

"They're quite an item."

Calla was astonished and tried to hide it.

"You're coming to the Christmas Eve service, aren't you?"

"I thought I would," she murmured, still adjusting to the thought of her friend dating Bert Loomis. Funny Jessica hadn't said anything herself.

"I'll see you later, then, and if you want, we can talk some more about school right after the holidays."

"Sure," Calla returned eagerly. They exchanged Christmas greetings, and Calla hung up, feeling a great sense of relief. Her homecoming was going so well, she could see no reason to delay visiting her mother. She wouldn't have admitted it to anyone, but she *had* missed her. A thousand times she'd wanted to call and beg to come home, but had resisted because of Dennis.

"You ready to head on over to visit your mother?" her grandfather asked when she came out of her bedroom.

"I guess." She shrugged, as if to say she'd eventually need to confront her mother and might as well get it over with now.

Calla donned her coat and stuffed a hat over her hair, pulling it down past her ears. They walked the few blocks over to the old Habberstad house. The place had been vacant for a couple of years and was one of the nicest in town. Calla had always liked the two-story Victorian structure, especially the wide veranda. It was the kind of house she'd always thought about living in one day, perhaps when she was married.

Dennis opened the door and shared an enigmatic look with Joshua before greeting Calla. "Merry Christmas."

"You, too," she said, stepping past him. She wasn't actually rude, but she was well aware that her behavior bordered on it.

"Calla!" Her mother was sitting up with her feet on the sofa, her legs covered with an afghan. She held her arms open for her daughter.

Frowning, Calla hugged her, and briefly closed her eyes, wrapped in the warm embrace. Sarah seemed so pale and thin. "What's wrong?" she asked as she straightened. "Did you break your leg?" Surely that was something her grandfather should have mentioned.

"You'd better tell her," Joshua said, nodding at Sarah and Dennis.

"Tell me what?" She stared at her mother, who looked like she wanted to weep. Dennis came to stand by her and, placing his hand on Sarah's shoulder, he gazed directly at Calla. "Your mother's pregnant. There's been some trouble with the pregnancy and the doctor's ordered bed rest."

Her mother had lied.

"I know what you're thinking," Sarah said hastily, "but I didn't know I was pregnant until the day before Thanksgiving—your father *couldn't* have known. He lied to you."

"Yeah, but you knew when I phoned," she challenged.

"Yes, I did, but it didn't seem the right time to tell you."

Calla glared at her mother. She should have realized. Sarah wasn't any better than Willie. "In other words, you *both* lied to me!"

"Do you have anything you want to say?" Gramps interrupted, coming to stand between Calla and her mother.

"Say?" Calla repeated with a short laugh.

"Like *congratulations, I'm pleased for you*," Gramps suggested.

"You want me to be happy about this? In your dreams." With that, she raced out of the house. Calla could hear her mother's frantic shouts, begging her to come back, but she ignored her, desperate to get away.

Whatever hope there'd been of rebuilding their relationship was gone now. Completely destroyed. As soon as the new baby arrived, Calla would be old news. They wouldn't want her around. She'd stay in Buffalo Valley, not because she wanted to but because she didn't really have a choice anymore. Her grandfather had said she could live with him and she would until she graduated, but not a minute longer. Once she had enough money for a car and a life of her own, she was leaving Buffalo Valley.

Next time, she wouldn't be back.

* * *

Margaret smiled to herself as she sat at her desk doing paperwork, thinking about her life since her marriage. It was the first full week of the new year. Matt was busy working on his truck engine. He enjoyed tinkering with cars. Margaret was fully capable of changing oil and doing other basic maintenance, but it wasn't her favorite task. Matt, on the other hand, seemed to like it.

In the very beginning, she hadn't been sure what to expect from married life. Still wasn't. However, Christmas had turned out to be a wonderful day. Since this was the first Christmas without her father, Margaret had thought the holidays would depress her. But Matt had been sensitive in unexpected ways. Instead of ignoring her father's absence, he'd asked her questions. Before long, she was telling him about holidays from years past. Early on, some or all of her uncles had come, but eventually they'd all married and scattered throughout the country. Then it'd just been Margaret and her father. Matt had talked about his early years with his family, and she'd formed a picture of a small boy torn apart by his parents' divorce. A couple of times she'd been tempted to shed a few tears—for both of them. Even then, her husband seemed to understand and encouraged her to vent her grief.

They'd spent Christmas Day together, just the two of them. They'd eaten a turkey dinner Sadie had left for them—reminiscent of their Thanksgiving repast. And they'd exchanged small, simple gifts. In retrospect, she was pleased they'd been alone.

Marriage to Matt was even better than Margaret could have anticipated. Clearing away any misconceptions regarding his feelings for her, or lack of them, had been a calculated risk. Confronting him the morning after their wedding could easily have backfired. Matt could have lied, could have tried to convince her of his undying devotion. But they both knew he didn't love her. The lie would have oppressed them both.

Margaret realized she should never have proposed when she did. It'd been much too soon, but she loved Matt and needed him. Mostly, she was unwilling to wait. Without her father, she was terribly lonely. Perhaps if Matt hadn't kissed her, she would have been more patient, but he had—and the kiss had been…incredible. So she'd taken a risk and it had paid off.

In the weeks since their wedding, their lives had fallen into a pattern of working side by side. They'd each sold off the better part of their herds rather than feed them through the winter. But that didn't mean they could idle away their time. Most mornings they were either in the saddle or the truck, riding out to check on their breeding stock.

Matt was an experienced cattleman, and they often became involved in lengthy conversations about ranching and cattle. Margaret could hold her own in any such discussion. Matt loved listening to stories about her father and laughed with her, bringing Bernard's memory to life in a way that made her happy rather than sad.

In the evenings, they talked over the events of the day during dinner, then played cribbage. It was a game she enjoyed, one her father had taught her. Almost every night she and Bernard had sat across from each other and counted out the cards, moving the pegs on a huge board he'd made one winter more than thirty years ago. Margaret had been gifted with good card sense; Matt, too, was an accomplished player and they were evenly matched.

Cribbage didn't occupy the entire evening. They sometimes watched television, but not often. Matt had a program or two that he liked and so did she, but for the most part the television was off.

It seemed to her that most of their time together was spent in bed. Margaret had taken to wearing silky concoctions to entice her husband. During the day it was coveralls and flannel, but the nights were made for lace and perfume.

The physical delights of the marriage bed had turned out to be an extraordinary bonus. Margaret supposed it was natural they'd make love often, since they were newlyweds. They were both young and healthy. Although she could have asked Maddy or even Lindsay, sex was a subject she found herself oddly shy about discussing. If what they were doing was too much or not enough—if the intensity and frequency of their love life wasn't "normal" or "average"—she didn't want to know, because it suited her and Matt, and they were the only ones who mattered.

All the books and manuals she'd read about sex had page upon page of description. Although none of the so-called experts had come right out and said it, the implication was there, plain as day. The authors seemed to imply that sex was overrated. Not in Margaret's opinion.

Perhaps because she hadn't had many expectations, she'd been pleasantly surprised by how much she liked it. Apparently Matt did, too, because he was as eager for her as she was for him. He often told her she was a fast learner. Margaret was convinced she'd taught him a thing or two herself, although he probably wouldn't admit that.

Her husband might not have married her for love, but she was determined to win his heart. Every day she grew more and more encouraged. Eventually he *would* love her; she was sure of it.

The phone pealed and Margaret automatically reached for the receiver on her desk.

"Hello," she said in her usual no-nonsense tone.

Sadie picked up at the same time. "Hello."

"I'm calling for Matt Eilers." The voice on the other end of the line was decidedly female. Decidedly sexy.

"I've got it," Sadie said gruffly.

Margaret was about to replace the receiver, but hesitated, listening for a moment longer while Sadie informed the woman that Matt was out for the day. Lately, she noted, the housekeeper made a mad dash for the phone any time it rang. Now Margaret wondered if there was a reason she knew nothing about.

"Have you given Matt my messages?" the other woman asked, her voice defiant and angry.

"I have." This came from Sadie.

"But I have to talk to him!"

"I told Mr. Eilers about your calls and he said he didn't want to speak to you. He asked that you not phone here again."

"Then you tell him that either he gets in touch with me soon or he'll live to regret it."

Margaret had already listened to more than she should have. Quietly putting down the receiver, she kept her hand poised over the phone. She should be pleased Matt didn't want to talk to another woman but she wasn't. She wanted to know more.

Before doing anything rash, she tried to reason out her feelings, sorting through the days for any evidence that her husband had been unfaithful. She knew for a fact that he hadn't been with anyone else since their wedding. There hadn't been a day in which they weren't together almost every hour.

Jealousy burned in her. Margaret had never thought of herself as the suspicious type, but she couldn't just ignore this. Her father had taught her to go to the source and that was exactly what she intended to do.

Margaret got up and retrieved her hat and coat from the hallway, then marched outside.

Matt had pulled his truck into one of the outbuildings and was bent over the side, working on the engine. He didn't hear her approach or if he did, he was too involved in what he was doing to acknowledge her.

"Who's the woman who keeps phoning the house asking for you?" Margaret demanded.

Matt straightened and reached for a rag to wipe the grease from his hands. "I thought you were clearing your desk."

"I did, but the phone rang."

"Oh." The red in his ears wasn't from the cold; Margaret would have wagered money on that.

"You'd better tell me." Her eyes hardened and she refused to release his. Anger settled in the pit of her stomach. She knew what people said about her marriage. She didn't want to look any more of a fool than she already did.

"Maybe we should wait and discuss this later," Matt suggested.

Margaret shook her head. "We'll talk about it now."

He stared at her a moment, then a slow, sexy grin widened his mouth. He was obviously about to say something.

She didn't give him a chance. "Nor am I willing to be sidetracked."

Matt sighed. "Dammit, Margaret, there's nothing for you to get upset about."

"I'm not upset." She crossed her arms, disliking this unpleasant feeling that came over her.

"She isn't important—"

"Does *she* have a name?"

Matt met her gaze straight on. "It's Sheryl, but I swear to you I haven't seen her in weeks."

The uncomfortable tightness in her chest lessened slightly. "Have you seen her since we've been married?"

"No." He was adamant about that. His face softened and he offered her a second, tentative smile. "You're all the woman I can handle."

Slowly Margaret grinned. It could be a ploy to bolster her ego, and if so, it had worked. She felt better already. "I—I never knew I'd be a jealous wife."

"You don't need to be, I promise you that."

She relaxed.

"Any more questions?" he asked.

"No." She started toward the house, but a few feet away she turned back. "You don't plan on seeing Sheryl again, do you?"

"No," he said. "Not on purpose, anyway."

"One more question." She looked down, embarrassed to be asking it, but needing to be sure. "Am I really all the woman you can handle?"

He took his time answering. Meeting her eyes, he didn't say anything for a long moment. "In all my life I've never had anyone believe in me the way you do. Without conditions. Without expectations. I figured I was lucky to marry you, but I had no idea how damn lucky."

He didn't kiss her, didn't so much as touch her. Without another word, he returned to the truck and resumed his task.

Reassured, Margaret headed back to the house. Sadie was waiting in the kitchen. "Did he tell you about her?" the housekeeper demanded as soon as she hung up her coat and hat.

"This is between me and Matt," Margaret told her, tired of the same old argument, resenting the housekeeper's disapproval of her marriage.

"He's playing you for a fool." Sadie made a soft belligerent sound. "Mark my words, you're going to rue the day you ever laid eyes on that man."

Rachel and Heath were married in a private ceremony the third week of January. The reception that followed was in a posh Grand Forks hotel. Against the advice of her physician, Lily Quantrill attended both the wedding and the reception, looking frailer than Heath could remember.

The reception was well attended, with friends from Buffalo Valley as well as Grand Forks. The Sinclairs were there and Hassie Knight and the McKennas and more. Best of all, Rachel's parents had flown in from Arizona. Heath divided his attention among his bride, his guests and his grandmother.

"I think it's time you went back to the retirement center," he told Lily, ready to call for the attendant. Heath didn't want to make a fuss, but he was worried. Her health had declined rapidly in the past few weeks.

"Would you kindly allow me to make my own decisions?"

"Grandma…"

"What are you doing spending time with me, anyway? You have a bride."

Heath glanced toward Rachel who stood in the center of a group of men, his business associates, completely winning them over. "She'll have me the rest of my life," he countered. But he didn't know how much longer he'd have Lily.

"Before I go, there's something I want to tell you," Lily said.

Heath had to strain in order to hear her and crouched by her wheelchair so they could look eye to eye. "Then you'll go back to the center and to bed?"

"You make me sound like a disobedient child," she muttered, scowling at him.

It was a scowl he knew well. She'd been critical of him nearly his entire life. In his youth, Heath had watched his parents and brother kowtow to Lily Quantrill. He never had. He viewed her as cantankerous, opinionated and wonderful, but he'd always been his own person, even as a boy.

"What's so important that you have to say it right now?" he asked.

Lily reached out and touched his cheek with an arthritic finger. "You always were my favorite."

"Me!" The shock of it nearly bowled him over.

"You were the only one with enough grit to stand up to me."

"That being the case, you might've occasionally let me win an argument."

Lily's face beamed. "You won your fair share."

Heath had never thought of it that way.

"Rachel will make you a good wife."

Heath smiled at his bride, loving her with an intensity he'd never known. "I think so, too."

"I'm proud of you for not settling for second best."

He'd been tempted a number of times to search out another woman, especially when it seemed Rachel wasn't interested in him.

"You've made me proud in more ways than one, Heath," she continued. "I'm confident that Buffalo County Bank will prosper with you as president." Her eyes were steadfast on his.

"President?"

"You're ready. You have been for a long time."

Heath looked at Rachel. They'd decided, because of her restaurant and Mark's school, to make their home in Buffalo Valley. His grandmother was moving him into the leadership of the bank, and the head office wasn't in Buffalo Valley. Such a promotion would mean many long hours on the road, commuting to and from Grand Forks, not to mention the other eight branches across the state.

His frown must have said it all.

"Your grandfather and I started the business in Buffalo Valley," she reminded him.

He nodded. "Yes, Grandma," he murmured, "I know that. But things are different now..."

Her smile was fleeting. "You'll figure it out. Michael and I did, all those years ago." Her eyes were tired and slowly drifted closed. "Now I think it's time I went home."

Long past time, but Heath had already said so earlier. As it was, she seemed to have fallen asleep in her wheelchair.

"Heath?" Rachel joined him. He stood and slid his arm around his bride's waist, taken aback once again by her beauty.

"Lily's tired," he whispered. "She needs to go home."

Rachel pressed her head to his shoulder. "Perhaps you'd better see her out."

"You don't mind?" He hated to leave his wife of only a few hours. She'd been more than patient already.

"Lily needs you."

Grateful for Rachel's understanding, Heath kissed her cheek and accompanied his grandmother to the car the home had sent for her. Not allowing the attendant to place her in the vehicle, Heath gently lifted her from the chair himself and set her inside.

As the car pulled away from the curb, it occurred to him that he was now officially the president of Buffalo County Bank. For nearly three years, he'd served on the board of directors, sat in on meetings, offered his recommendations. Apparently his grandmother was confident that he was ready to take over.

This was no small matter. In his hands she'd placed fifty years of banking history and the future of one of the largest financial institutions in the state. Along with faith, love and trust, she'd presented him with a huge personal dilemma.

"You're a crafty little devil," he whispered aloud. "Your favorite relative, am I?" Then the laughter came, bubbling up inside him. He was her *only* relative. And he doubted very much that he'd *always* been her favorite, as she'd claimed. Still, that made no difference. He adored Lily Quantrill as much as he ever had—more— and was thankful for the influence she'd had on his life.

Rachel was waiting for him when Heath returned to the reception. "Is everything all right?" she asked.

Heath nodded. "Just fine," he said, and unable to resist, he kissed her.

"How much longer do you think we're going to have Lily?" Rachel asked.

Heath shrugged; he'd been wondering the same thing all evening.

The question was answered a week later when Lily Quantrill died quietly in her sleep.

Eight

It soon became apparent to Matt that Sheryl had no intention of staying out of his life. Sadie took considerable delight in letting him know his "girlfriend" continued to phone the house. Her pinched lips suggested it was all she could do to keep her opinions to herself.

"If she calls again, hang up on her," Matt instructed.

"Very well," Sadie returned flippantly. Everything the housekeeper said and did spoke of her disapproval. If it was up to him, he'd fire the woman, but she'd been with the family for years, and Margaret felt a strong loyalty toward her.

"I think you should know she isn't going to give up easily," Sadie told him. This was the day after his confrontation with Margaret, and Matt was particularly sensitive to the subject of Sheryl—and sick of it. "She wanted me to tell you that if you didn't see her soon, you'd regret it," the housekeeper intoned with far too much pleasure.

Great. It'd come down to threats, had it? Matt didn't know what the hell he was supposed to do. Margaret wasn't a woman who'd casually accept a dalliance on his part. Not that he had any desire to cheat on his wife.

In fact, this entire marriage had turned out to be a shock. He'd respected and liked Margaret when he'd married her, but he hadn't really *known* her. He'd discovered since that every day with her was an adventure. The best kind of adventure. Not only did she know cattle and ranching, but she was one hell of a worker. She put in twelve-hour days without complaint, working as hard and long as he did. There was something about having a partner, an equal partner, that lightened the load and allowed him to find enjoyment in ordinary things. At night Margaret proved she was one hell of a woman, too. She'd been a virgin when they got married, but her appetite for the physical side of marriage was strong and inventive.

When he married Margaret Clemens, Matt hadn't known what he was getting. He hadn't expected to acquire a knowledgeable and intelligent partner any more than he'd anticipated finding a best friend. That was what Margaret had become. His wife, his partner and his best friend.

The first week of February, Sadie fended off two more calls from Sheryl. Matt knew the housekeeper had reached the end of her limited tolerance when she pulled him aside to suggest he "take care" of the situation. For once Matt found himself agreeing with the woman. Enough was enough. He decided to talk to Sheryl himself and put a stop to her harassment.

Late the following afternoon, when Margaret went over to visit Maddy McKenna, Matt hopped in the pickup and headed into Devils Lake. This was better done in person; he'd settle matters with Sheryl and when he was finished, there'd be no room for doubt. Whatever had once been between them was long over. He was married now and he wasn't interested in a relationship with anyone else.

He would never have believed Sheryl was capable of this. The closer he got to Devils Lake, the angrier he became.

Pulling into the parking lot at the truck stop, he saw that the place was crowded. Five o'clock on a Friday—he should have known it would be. Although the bar and grill catered to truckers, it was a favorite watering hole. The locals often came by for a reasonably priced dinner and a couple of beers to wash it down.

The bar was filled with cigarette smoke so thick it stung his eyes. He thought he saw Sheryl by the bar and he edged past a burly cowhand to get there.

"Matt!"

He whirled around to see Sheryl's friend, although for the life of him, he couldn't remember her name.

He shouldered his way over to the waitress, who wore a cowgirl outfit with a too-short skirt and a fringed vest. "Sheryl's going to be so happy to see you," she said as Matt reached her. "Stay here and I'll find her for you."

He was close to the bar, and would have stepped up to it and ordered a beer if there'd been room. On second thought, maybe that wasn't such a good idea, since he didn't intend to stay any longer than necessary.

"Matt." Before he had time to respond, Sheryl hurled herself into his arms. "I knew you'd come. I told Lee Ann you'd come by and I was right." Her heavily made-up face was bright with happiness.

"We need to talk," Matt said, tugging her arms free from his neck. He surveyed the room and realized it would be impossible to hold a private conversation.

Sheryl seemed to realize the same thing. "Follow

me," she said, and when he hesitated, she reached for his hand, linking their fingers. She led him behind the bar, pausing long enough to lean forward and whisper something to the bartender. The other man glanced at Matt, frowned, then reluctantly nodded.

"Sam said we could talk in his office," Sheryl said, dragging Matt through the kitchen.

He walked past two chefs and the stove, obediently following Sheryl. Still, he argued with himself every step of the way. What he had to tell her would only take a minute. He'd rehearsed his statement on the drive in: They'd shared a short-term relationship that was mutually enjoyable while it lasted, but it was over. It'd been over well before he married Margaret, he'd tell Sheryl, and he'd explain that he planned to honor his marriage vows.

Sheryl turned to smile at him. She opened the office door and laughing, yanked him inside, closing the door after him. The room was pitch-dark. His back was against the wall, and before Matt had a chance to find his bearings, Sheryl's arms were around him.

"Oh, Matt," she cried. "I've missed you so damn much." She moved against him, seducing him with her body, kissing him while her breasts massaged his chest.

"Sheryl…"

He wasn't allowed to finish. Her mouth was all over his, open, moist, insistent. He jerked his head back and forth, but all that did was encourage her. Backed against the wall, he couldn't easily pull away.

"Tell me you've missed me. I need to hear it," she begged.

"Sheryl, stop!"

"No," she whimpered, "I need you so much." Sheryl's

hands were busy in the dark, tugging his shirt free of his waist. Then she was rubbing her palms up his bare chest.

"Stop!" he shouted, gripping her hard by the shoulders, finally disengaging her with a shove.

Breathing hard, Sheryl went still.

"I don't want to do this," he told her, struggling to hold back his irritation.

"I know this isn't the ideal place to make love, but I'm so hungry for you, I—"

"I'm not making love to you, Sheryl. I'm married now."

He heard her sigh. "Don't I know it. But that doesn't have to change anything. Not with you and me. We have an understanding."

"No, we don't."

"You don't mean that," she insisted, sounding close to tears.

By this time, Matt's eyes had adjusted to the dark, but he still had trouble making out details. He felt behind him for a light switch. Nothing.

"You want me," Sheryl whispered. "Your body tells me you do." As if to prove her point, she started to unbuckle his belt. He stopped her.

"Like I said, it's over. Don't call me again."

"Oh, am I causing problems between you and Margaret?" she asked in a falsely sweet voice.

"The only person you're causing problems with is the housekeeper."

Sheryl obviously thought that was a joke and laughed softly. "Okay, okay, but I had to see you."

"No, you didn't. And like I said, I don't want you phoning the Triple C again."

"It got you here, didn't it?"

Matt groaned, understanding her game. She intended to use those phone calls to blackmail him. Either he went along with her little scheme or she'd continue making trouble for him.

"Come on, Matt, give me what I want." Her arms began to slither around his neck.

He closed his hands on her wrists and wrenched himself free before she could kiss him again. As it was, he feared the heavy scent of her perfume would cling to him. He didn't want to think how Margaret would react if she happened to catch a whiff of that. His sole purpose in being here was to get Sheryl out of their lives, not to create more problems.

"I mean it," he growled. "Don't call me again."

"You can't be serious." Her voice held a sharp edge.

Good! Maybe she'd finally believe him. "I'm not the right man for you."

"The hell you aren't," she snapped. "Don't tell me you've forgotten our plan."

"Plan? We didn't have any plan."

"You were going to marry Margaret, and then divorce her in a year and marry me."

Matt shook his head firmly. That he'd even listened to anything so outrageous nauseated him.

"You married her, and there's no way in hell you'll ever convince me you did it for love."

"I'm not divorcing Margaret," he insisted. "Certainly not for you."

Matt winced as Sheryl swore, using language he'd rarely heard, even from the toughened cowhands. "You can't cut me out of this now," she yelled.

He was astounded—she honestly believed he'd followed through with her callous scheme. "It's over, Sheryl," he said quietly. "Way over."

"That's what *you* think," she said in vicious tones. "We haven't even started yet. No one double-crosses me. No one. You're going to be sorry you did this, Matthew Eilers."

"Yeah, whatever, but I'm telling you for the last time that I'm not going to let you blackmail me. If you're thinking of telling Margaret about our so-called plan, then feel free. She knew I didn't love her when we got married. And you know what? It doesn't matter to her. Nothing you say now will make one bit of difference." Not caring if he stumbled over furniture, he blindly moved forward, arms outstretched. With a minimum of fuss he located the door, and jerked it open.

Squinting against the bright hallway light, he hurried through the kitchen and bar, eager to make his escape. He regretted ever coming to Devils Lake. The first thing he wanted to do when he got home was have a long, hot shower—to wash every trace of Sheryl from his skin.

If only he could as easily remove her from his life.

The biggest news in Buffalo Valley after the first of the year, Calla learned, was that Joanie and Brandon Wyatt were opening a video rental store. He'd continue to farm, and Joanie would manage the store. Apparently they'd been able to buy the inventory of another store in a nearby town, one that was going out of business. In addition to renting videos, Joanie would be carrying a number of craft items, such as knitting yarn and cross-stitch supplies.

The new store created quite a buzz. Calla enjoyed crafts and actually showed a talent for that kind of activity, which she supposed wasn't surprising, since her mother was artistic. The one bright spot about attending school in Minneapolis had been the drama class and her work designing and sewing costumes. Her projects had received high grades and lots of praise.

The very best thing about the video store was that Joanie hired Calla part-time. Calla loved it. She could have spent her entire paycheck on craft supplies. In fact, the first week she collected her pay, she discovered she actually owed the store money.

Between her job and school, with the extra assignments Mrs. Sinclair had given her in order to make up the credits she'd lost while living in Minneapolis, Calla didn't have time to worry about her mother. They'd talked maybe twice since she'd moved back, but their conversations had been stilted and uncomfortable. Calla had the impression her mother was glad to be rid of her.

Not that it mattered. She lived with her grandfather, and that was working out all right. Without her mother to see to his meals and the other household duties, Joshua McKenna was in pretty sad shape. He needed her, and frankly Calla needed him. Not only that, life with Gramps was a thousand times better than it'd been at her father's. Calla wouldn't even consider living with her mother and Dennis. No, the situation at her grandfather's house was fine; it suited them both.

Friday afternoon, Calla was leaving the video store when she ran into Joe Lammermann. She played it cool with Joe these days. He kept his distance from her, too, although he was friendly whenever they happened to meet.

"How's it going?" he asked, stopping in front of her. He wore a too-big jacket and a knit cap that fit over his ears. He'd grown taller since she'd left and now stood a full head higher than Calla.

"All right," she responded without a lot of enthusiasm.

"You thinking about going to the Sweetheart Dance this year?"

"I guess so," she said with a casual shrug. If he was inviting her to attend the dance with him, he'd left it till the last minute. Either it'd taken him that long to find the courage, or she wasn't his first choice. She found neither option acceptable.

"I thought I'd go," Joe muttered.

"Great. I'll probably see you there." She stepped around him and moved on without giving him the opportunity to invite her, if that had indeed been his intention.

With her spirits high—Joe was still interested in her!—Calla walked over to Knight's Pharmacy. She was out of mascara.

"Hi, Hassie," she called as she came through the door. The pharmacist stood at the back, behind the counter where she filled prescriptions.

"Hey, Calla," Hassie greeted her. "Good to see you. Listen, could I impose on you to do me a favor?"

"What?" Calla had learned the hard way to ask what kind of favor first. Her stay in Minneapolis had made her wary of even the most innocent-sounding requests. She strolled purposely toward the far side of the store, where Hassie displayed several lines of cosmetics.

"I've got a new prescription for your mother," Hassie told her. "Would you drop it off for me?"

Calla placed the mascara on the counter and pulled a wad of dollars from the hip pocket of her jeans. "Can't Dennis get it for her later? Let him do it." Calla wasn't stupid. Hassie was trying to manipulate her into visiting her mother—something Calla would prefer not to do.

Her response seemed to stun Hassie. Not saying a word, she stared at Calla with a directness that made her squirm.

"Oh, all right," Calla said irritably. "I'll take over the

prescription." But she was annoyed Hassie had asked her to do this, and made her feelings very clear.

Muttering under her breath, she grabbed the small white sack and her change and slammed out of the store. Still annoyed, she walked the few blocks to the old Habberstad house.

She stomped onto the porch, where she paused to ring the doorbell. Then, without waiting for an answer, she let herself inside. "It's me," she shouted, stepping into the house.

Her mother lay on the sofa where she'd been the other two times Calla had talked to her.

"Calla!" Her mother's eyes lit up when she saw her.

Calla hated that and she loved it. She wanted her mother to be happy to see her, but at the same time, she didn't want to feel anything for Sarah. Nevertheless, Calla had to admit that she did, and she resented it. "Hassie asked me to drop off this prescription," she said, wanting to be sure her mother realized this wasn't a social call.

"Thank you." Sarah was pale and drawn, much paler than she'd been on Calla's last visit.

"How are you?" Calla hesitated, then set the small package on the coffee table.

Her mother glanced up toward the ceiling. "I'm going stir crazy. Another month and everything should be better, but this inactivity is so boring. I've read every book and magazine in the house, until my eyes feel like they're about to fall out of my head."

"Can't you work on the quilts?"

"Some," her mother said, "but my concentration is so poor these days."

"You could always watch TV or videos."

"I could," she agreed. "But there's very little I want to see on television."

"Daytime television is the pits," Calla murmured, remembering her own attempts to watch it in Minneapolis. She also remembered that her father had found it enthralling, especially the sports channels. He could sit in front of the TV for eight hours straight.

"I'll manage," Sarah insisted.

Calla frowned. "One would think Dennis would be happy to get you some videos, then," she said waspishly, eager to put her stepfather in a bad light.

"He would if I asked," Sarah returned.

"Why don't you?"

Sarah looked down, shaking her head. "He has enough to do with keeping up the house, cooking, cleaning, plus working all day. I don't want to ask anything more of him."

Calla walked about the room and picked up discarded sections of the newspaper. It didn't look like Dennis was all that great a housekeeper, but she didn't say so.

"Dennis should spend more time with you," Calla muttered instead, her tone challenging. He was the one responsible for this—her mother being pregnant and all. The least he could do was be there for her.

"He tries."

Calla snorted softly, hating the way her mother was so quick to defend him. "In my opinion, he doesn't try hard enough." She picked up the empty juice glass on the table and carried it, along with the newspaper, into the kitchen. The sink was filled with dirty dishes. There was no excuse for that. It wouldn't take three minutes to load the dishwasher. If her mother saw the state of the kitchen, she'd have a conniption.

Calla ran the sink full of hot, soapy water, rinsed the

dishes and loaded them, then wiped down the counter. She should probably leave this mess for Dennis but knew how upset her mother would be if she were to see all these dirty dishes.

"What are you doing in there?" Sarah called.

Not wanting to admit she was washing dishes, Calla made up an excuse. "I thought you'd enjoy a cup of herbal tea."

"Oh, Calla, how thoughtful. I'd love one."

She hadn't wanted her mother to think of her as thoughtful, but there was no help for that now. Feeling as though their roles had been reversed and *she* was the adult in the situation, Calla brewed a pot of mint tea and carried it out on a tray—with a cup and saucer and a plate of cheese and crackers. Her mother should be gaining weight, not losing it. She looked wretched, almost gaunt.

"Calla," her mother whispered, "this is lovely. Thank you."

She shrugged, dismissing the gratitude.

"Could you stay a few minutes and talk?" Sarah implored.

"What's wrong with the baby?" No one had bothered to explain it to Calla—but then she'd made a point of not asking until now.

Her mother seemed happy to supply the answer and outlined what the physician had told her. Apparently, what she had was called an irritated uterus, which was a broad term describing the symptoms. It'd started with spotting early in the pregnancy. During even the slightest activity, the uterus underwent contractions. When Sarah lay down and kept still, the baby was safe, but the minute she was up and about, her uterus reacted. Sarah spoke about this at greater length than Calla considered necessary; it made her realize how lonely her mother was, how hungry for company.

Calla had intended to leave almost immediately, but now she was glad she'd stayed. Her mother was going crazy with all this unproductive time on her hands, and Calla discovered that she enjoyed being useful—and appreciated. Before long, she had a cup of tea herself.

She reached for a cracker with cheese. "Joe asked me about the Sweetheart Dance," she commented, unsure why she mentioned the fact. It was something to talk about, she decided, something noteworthy.

"Was he inviting you?" Sarah's look held hers.

Calla set the teacup aside and tucked her hands beneath her thighs. "If he was, I didn't give him the opportunity to ask."

"He's a little late, isn't he, seeing that the dance is next week?"

Calla nodded. "That's what I thought. I didn't want to give him the impression that he could ask me at the last minute and I'd leap at the chance to go out with him again." Calla lowered her gaze. "But I would."

"You're still interested in him?"

Calla shrugged. Joe had hurt her, dumping her the way he had. He'd made her feel foolish...and undesirable. It wasn't because of the things they'd done physically that she felt bad, although she had regrets in that area, too, but because she'd shared her thoughts. He'd gotten her to talk about her feelings and her problems. He'd seemed to understand and sympathize. She'd felt close to him, closer than she had to anyone, when out of the blue he'd announced that it might be best if they started seeing other people. Translated, that meant he'd met a cheerleader type with a lot more sexual experience. A girl who was willing to put out.

"I'm over Joe," she said, although that wasn't entirely true. "What I want is for him to be sorry that he broke up with me."

To her surprise, when she glanced up she found her mother smiling. Calla bristled. "Is that funny?"

"No, no," Sarah said, obviously hurrying to correct the impression. "It's just very human. Everyone feels like that when someone's done them wrong."

They talked more about Joe, and drank another cup of tea. This was the longest conversation Calla had had with her mother in years. When she checked her watch, she was shocked to see how late it was.

"Would you like me to get dinner started?" She'd found a roast defrosting on the kitchen counter. If she stuck it in the oven now, it'd be done by about 7:30.

Sarah looked amazed at the offer. "That would be very nice. Meals have been pretty haphazard recently."

Calla could well imagine. She knew what her grandfather was like when he came home from work; the last thing he wanted to do was cook dinner. Apparently Dennis felt the same way. Calla was absolutly certain that until she'd returned, her grandfather had eaten every meal out of a can or the freezer, unless he went over to Buffalo Bob's or The Pizza Parlor.

Thirty minutes later, just as Calla was about to leave, the back door suddenly opened and Dennis walked in. He paused when he saw her, almost as though bracing himself for a confrontation.

"My mother's too pale," Calla said, accusing him.

"I know," he muttered, frowning. "The blood test showed she's anemic. That's what her new prescription was for." He looked around the kitchen. "You clean up here?"

She nodded. "Someone had to do it. My mother

doesn't like a mess. You're her husband, you should know that."

"I do—I just wish there were more hours in a day."

Calla wasn't interested in listening to his excuses. "You take care of her, understand?"

"You'd better believe it," Dennis said grimly. Then he paused. "Listen, Calla. You and I might have our problems, but we do have one thing in common."

Calla doubted it.

"We both love your mother."

Five weeks after Axel had been pulled from her arms, Merrily woke up in Oklahoma City, sleeping in a cheap hotel and working at a job she hated. More and more, her thoughts were of Bob and Buffalo Valley, and the life she'd abandoned. She'd left with no intention of returning, but now, going back was all she thought about.

It was a revelation to her: she'd lost the taste for running. Despite what she'd been telling herself every day of these five miserable weeks, the only place she wanted to be was with Bob, her Buffalo Man in North Dakota. Somehow, without her noticing it, Buffalo Valley had become home.

Merrily believed Bob had betrayed her. So she'd done what she'd always done—and that was to escape. To run as far and as fast as she could. If Bob had kept his mouth shut, they'd still have Axel. If he hadn't insisted they work this out through the legal system, no one in California would ever know what had become of the boy. Not a single person there cared that Axel was being abused by his father. Not until it was too late and the evidence was gone. The state had refused to listen when she'd reported that his mother was a drug addict.

Because of her own previous conviction? Why should that matter? No one gave a damn about Axel—not the police and not Child Protective Services—until she'd risked everything and taken him. Overnight she was a criminal.

The people of California should be thanking her for saving his life; instead they called her a kidnapper and threatened her with a jail term that would make her an old woman by the time she was released.

What hurt most was that her husband, the man she loved, was responsible for this, the biggest loss of her life. He'd insisted they couldn't be constantly looking over their shoulders, worrying, wondering.

Bob didn't want anything hanging over his head; he hated living like a fugitive. He was also braver than she was, more trusting. Apparently he hadn't gotten kicked in the teeth as many times as she had. He actually seemed to believe that once the courts heard the evidence, the two of them would get Axel back.

Merrily tried not to think about Axel, because every time she did her eyes filled with tears. In the past five weeks, she'd shed more tears than she would've guessed possible. They'd taken away her baby and despite all the promises, despite all the reassurances, she knew deep in her heart that she'd never see Axel again.

That was why she'd run. When the pain got too bad, that was what she always did. Her entire life had been spent racing from one "geographical cure" to another, seeking a new beginning, a fresh start, a way out. Not until she'd met Bob had she ever returned to one place. One man.

Sitting on the edge of the thin mattress, Merrily rubbed her face. She missed Bob and their home. She missed Axel, too, but there was nothing she could do about that, and the ache in her heart was even worse without Bob.

It didn't take long to stuff her belongings in a bag. She paid the bill with cash, then worked an eight-hour shift at the all-night diner. Before she left, she filled her car with gas and headed north to Buffalo Valley. Headed home.

Not until she reached Sioux Falls, South Dakota, did she allow herself to wonder what Bob would say or do when he saw her. After five weeks of no contact, she couldn't be one-hundred-percent sure of her reception.

Bob had made it plain when he married her that from this point forward they were partners in life. Her disappearing acts were over. She'd agreed to those terms, welcomed the opportunity to be a wife and…a mother to Axel. She would have done anything, signed any contract, to ensure a stable life for her son.

In the weeks she'd been away, a whole lot could have changed. Merrily didn't know what Bob had told their attorney about her being gone, or if he had. All that money spent and for what? It wouldn't get Axel back. Nor did she know what awaited her in regard to possible jail time. There was every likelihood that there'd been an arrest warrant issued in her name. That was all part of the risk she was taking. Nevertheless she headed back because the life she had now was no life. With Bob there was a chance—there was love.

It was late when she hit Buffalo Valley. Almost midnight. The only light came from the streetlamps, which she saw even before she turned off the highway. Bob would have closed the restaurant for the night, but the bar might still be open.

Sure enough, the neon sign for 3 OF A KIND glowed in the window. Merrily studied each store, each business, on Main Street. So Joanie Wyatt had gone ahead and opened a video rental place. Although the sign was turned off, Merrily saw the storefront. In the years she'd known Bob, she'd watched this town grow. She'd taken comfort in that, seeing the changes in Buffalo Valley, believing they paralleled the changes in her own life. Changes for which she thanked Buffalo Bob Carr.

Winter in North Dakota was dark and cold. Barren. Snowbanks lined the sides of the streets. Merrily parked with difficulty and climbed out of her car, then walked the short distance toward 3 OF A KIND. A look through the window revealed a couple of men sitting at the bar, drinking beer.

Bob was nowhere in sight.

Taking a calming breath, Merrily stepped inside. She saw him immediately and just as importantly, he saw her.

His eyes narrowed as he paused, a beer mug in one hand. That was when she noticed the cast on his right arm. Apparently he'd broken it. A chill went through her that couldn't be attributed to the cold or the wind; she knew it was brought on by the realization that the man she loved had endured terrible pain.

"What happened?" she asked, walking toward him, her gaze on his arm.

His eyes held hers. "You left."

The two men sitting at the bar stared at her and then each other. Merrily had seen them before, but she didn't remember their names. She ignored them and they turned away and pretended to ignore her.

"I'm back now," she told Bob, hoping he understood that this time it was forever.

"Should I throw a party?" he asked.

She deserved his sarcasm. "I realized something im-

portant," she said in a low voice. "I don't belong anywhere but with you."

He looked as though he didn't believe her and she
couldn't blame him. "I love you, Buffalo Bob Carr."

He set the frosty mug down and turned away. "I'm
sorry, fellows, but I'm closing up early tonight. I got a
problem here that's going to demand my full attention."

"Sure thing, Bob."

"Yeah. I should be leaving, anyway. See ya, Bob."

Both men left cash on the counter, although he hadn't
presented either one with a bill. Casting a wary eye in
her direction, they ambled out the door.

After the men had gone, Merrily stood in the center
of the room, waiting. Unable to read Bob's response,
she wasn't sure what to do.

He frowned, standing behind the bar as if it offered
him some defense. "I risked everything for you, and
then you walked out."

"I know—I thought you'd betrayed me."

"I was protecting you, protecting Axel. Protecting us."

She didn't want to hear it, hadn't traveled all this way
to argue. "I'm not leaving again."

"I've heard that before," Bob muttered.

"This time I know there's nothing out there that isn't
a thousand times better right here." She stepped toward the end of the bar, hoping for a sign that would
tell her he wanted her back. That he'd been as miserable as she had.

Merrily's arms had felt empty from the moment Bob
pried Axel from her embrace. They'd ached for five very
long weeks. "I'm so sorry," she whispered and broke
into sobs.

It was the sound of her tears that seemed to break the
spell. Bob stepped around the bar and strode toward her,

and she fell into his arms, the tears burning her eyes, streaming down her face.

The instant Bob's arms closed around her, Merrily felt the throbbing pain in her heart diminish. For the first time since Axel had been taken from her, she felt as though she didn't stand alone. Her husband was with her, and to her amazement he loved her. Still loved her. He was willing to forgive her, and take her back.

They clung without words, like the lone survivors of an accident, trembling and in shock. The cast on his right arm dug into her back, reminding her that she should find out what had happened. Had he fallen? Been in a fight?

"I lost Axel," Bob whispered, "and then you."

"Oh, Bob." He didn't understand that he hadn't lost her. Couldn't. Not anymore. She was a part of him and he a part of her.

"Don't leave me again… I can't bear it."

"Never," she promised, and this time she knew it was true.

Nine

"You ready?" Jeb asked, coming inside, out of the cold, to collect his wife and daughter. In addition to a number of business-related errands she needed to do, Maddy planned to visit Sarah—and she was anxious to talk to Buffalo Bob and Merrily. They'd phoned the night before and asked if she could stop by for a few minutes to answer their questions. They were looking for advice to help them win back Axel.

"Ready," Maddy told her husband, carrying a bundled-up Julianne in her combination car seat/baby carrier. Jeb had thoughtfully gone out to start the car for her.

He took Julianne's carrier from Maddy and tucked their daughter safely into the Bronco's back seat. Maddy waited by the driver's side and glanced at her watch. It was now 12:30. "I'll be back by four," she told him.

He nodded, his eyes serious. "Drive carefully."

"I will," she promised, and they briefly kissed before she climbed into the driver's seat. The vehicle was warm inside; she was grateful to Jeb for that. She didn't know if she'd ever become accustomed to the frigid winters in North Dakota. The blizzard a year earlier, in which she'd almost died, had been an accurate indication of what the weather could be like.

Jeb remained standing in the driveway, watching her leave. Although he'd encouraged her to talk to Bob and Merrily, she knew he'd rather she stayed off the icy roads. But he, too, was concerned about the couple.

Maddy had been the one who'd recommended Doug Alder. From her work with Child Protective Services in Savannah, Maddy knew and trusted the attorney. He was the best—compassionate, yet tough and realistic. The situation with Axel was complicated, but she'd seen Doug succeed in similar cases. Still, the main thing Bob and Merrily—*all* of them—needed to remember was that Axel's welfare came first.

Bob had sounded worried when he'd phoned. Maddy wasn't sure if she should stop by to see him right away or wait until she'd talked to her sister-in-law, Sarah Urlacher. Sarah's pregnancy continued to have problems, and between boredom and physical weakness, she found the required bed rest increasingly difficult.

Rather than delay talking to Bob and Merrily, Maddy decided to drive over to 3 OF A KIND immediately. Merrily hugged her, and it seemed she clung an extra moment before she left to get Bob.

The three sat at a table in the restaurant, nursing cups of coffee. Nine-month-old Julianne sat in the high chair, gnawing contentedly on an arrowroot cracker. Several times Maddy caught Merrily glancing toward the infant with a look of longing.

"We heard from Doug Alder," Bob explained. He met his wife's eyes and she reached for his hand. He clasped her fingers tightly.

"I think I told you Axel's father is in prison," Bob went on.

Maddy nodded. "And his mother is dead."

"From what we understand, Axel has been made a ward of the state and is now available for adoption."

Maddy's heart leaped with gratitude. The possibility of adoption was what she'd hoped for. She'd also learned from Bob that the lawyer in California had talked to the prosecutor before they'd surrendered Axel. He'd worked a minor miracle in having the federal kidnapping charges against Merrily reduced to a suspended sentence; she wouldn't have to serve any jail time.

"Axel's in a foster home now," Merrily blurted out. Her knuckles were white from the pressure with which she held on to her husband's hand.

"Apparently he isn't doing well," Bob added.

"We asked Doug to get us a report…" Merrily paused, and tears filled her eyes, threatening to spill over. "He was able to talk to Axel's caseworker and she said he isn't eating or sleeping well."

"You've applied for adoption?" she asked, certain they had.

"We've spent two days filling out all the forms," Bob told her.

"Doug thinks that given our history with Axel, we'd be seriously considered," Merrily said.

"But he also explained that it was no guarantee we'd be chosen," Bob pointed out. "Apparently there are very few children available for adoption these days, but no lack of applicants."

"Axel loves us as much as we love him," Merrily rushed to add. "I'm sure the judge will take that into consideration, don't you think?"

"Naturally the caseworker will be interviewing us," Bob said, not giving Maddy an opportunity to respond to Merrily's question. "We were hoping you could tell us what they'd want to hear."

"I'll be happy to help in any way I can."

"Pastor Dawson has been...helpful," Merrily said with a guarded smile. "He said we'd done a brave thing and that he respects and admires us for the way we've handled the situation. He...thought it might help if he got a letter-writing campaign going. You know, having people from the community write letters of recommendation on our behalf."

"That's an excellent idea." Maddy would gladly send one herself.

"We have to travel to California for the interview, of course."

Maddy knew this entire process was expensive. Attorney's fees were high, and it had to be costing them plenty, along with all the fees involved in the adoption process.

"The church took up a donation to help with the traveling expenses," Merrily told her. "We weren't expecting anything like that. We were really touched by what they did."

Julianne had been running a fever the previous weekend, so Maddy had missed Sunday services and hadn't heard about the collection.

"Everyone's been great," Bob said, his voice gruff with emotion. "I don't know what we would've done without all our friends."

"The town wants you to bring Axel home, too."

Merrily nodded tearfully. "I can't tell you how much everyone's support has meant to us."

Bob stood and disappeared for a moment, then returned with a file. "This is the paperwork we've completed for the state of California." He handed it to

Maddy. She read through the questionnaire and was impressed with the straightforward, honest way in which he'd revealed his past, including his run-ins with the law. At the end of the application, he'd listed improvements he'd made in his life during the past few years, since taking ownership of 3 OF A KIND. He described how he was now a successful businessman, a member of the town council, a member of the school board, a married man. The letters of recommendation Pastor Dawson was collecting would underline those constructive changes.

Merrily's portion of the form supplied all the necessary details, plus a heartfelt plea that the judge make her and Bob legally what they already were in every other way, and that was Axel's family.

"You've done an excellent job with this," Maddy said when she finished.

"Would you let us adopt Axel if you were the one making the decision?" Merrily asked.

It was a difficult question, especially since she knew how badly they needed to hear a positive response. The fact that they both had police records didn't help their case. But anyone who bothered to read their application would be able to tell how much they loved Axel. The child had clearly bonded with them, which was also in their favor.

Bob and Merrily studied her, anticipating her response. She nodded and smiled. "I think I would. I believe you have an excellent chance."

For the first time since her arrival, they both smiled.

"That's what Doug told me," Bob said, sounding vastly relieved.

"Now, let's go over the kinds of questions that are

likely to be asked in the personal interview," she suggested.

When she'd spent an hour or so rehearsing questions and answers with Bob and Merrily, Maddy left, their effusive thanks echoing in her ears. She'd take care of her errands next, then drop in on Sarah. She walked across the street to her grocery, planning to discuss some business issues with Pete Mitchell, her manager. She wanted to switch one of her suppliers, plus try out some new inventory-control software. As well, she and the Loomis boys were going to talk over their ideas for a Valentine's display. She missed the everyday interaction with people in town, but loved her role as wife and mother. In time, she'd return to the store, but for now she was content. She had an excellent manager and the Loomis twins were an unexpected asset.

"Afternoon, Maddy," Pastor Dawson called out when she entered the grocery.

"Hello," she called back. Julianne rested against her side and cheerfully waved her arms in greeting.

"My goodness, Julianne is growing," he said as he approached them.

"She's going to be walking any day now." Maddy wasn't sure if she should be thrilled or not that her daughter was an early walker.

"You talked to Bob and Merrily?" Pastor Dawson asked.

"I did. What you're doing with the letters is extremely generous."

The minister brushed off her praise. "You'll write one on their behalf, won't you?"

"Of course. I'll have it to you before the end of the week."

"Terrific." He hesitated, his expression sober. "What do you think of their chances?"

That seemed to be the question of the hour. "I don't know... I'd like to believe the judge would take into account more than meets the eye. More than their police records, in other words."

"Merrily stole Axel," the pastor said bluntly.

"There were extenuating circumstances." She sighed. "But..."

"Do you have doubts?" he asked.

Maddy shifted Julianne from one side to the other while she considered his question. What *were* the chances of Bob and Merrily being selected as Axel's parents? Worrying her lower lip, she slowly shook her head. "I just don't know."

"We'll leave it in God's hands," the pastor told her.

That sounded like the best solution to Maddy.

As February drew to a close, Sarah grew more and more restless. She'd hoped to get back to her normal life after the first of the year, but the doctor advised against it. He felt that continued bed rest would give her baby the optimum chance of a safe delivery. On this particular Monday, she picked up the remote control and turned off the television. Another four months of this forced inactivity and she'd go stark raving mad. If not for her designing board, she'd have reached that point long before now. Thankfully, she'd had plenty of company in the past two months. Maddy visited her once a week, and even her brother had deigned to stop by and chat. Now, that was a rare treat.

Jeb was happy—happier than he'd been in years. Maddy was perfect for him, and Sarah felt vindicated; she'd recognized it long before her hardheaded brother did. Marriage and fatherhood required a serious adjustment, but he genuinely loved Maddy and was crazy about their baby.

Within a few months she'd be a new mother herself, but it didn't seem quite real to her. Although Dennis was thrilled with the pregnancy, he worried constantly. He'd waited for this child a long time and, God willing, she'd give him the family he wanted.

Unfortunately, he was short-staffed and worked long hours. Her being trapped in the house made his life more difficult. Not only was he responsible for supplying fuel to the outlying areas, but he owned and operated the only gas station in town. After a full day he came home and had to see to her needs, both physically and emotionally. Sarah knew he worried about her when he was on the road, and tried to check in at least twice a day. Some days it just wasn't possible.

Leta Betts and Hassie Knight made frequent visits, and for that Sarah was grateful. Leta had decided it was time Sarah learned how to knit, and had undertaken to teach her, the way she had so many others. Joanie sold more yarn than anything else, and she had Leta to thank for that. Despite Sarah's aptitude with a needle, though, knitting didn't come naturally. Leta had encouraged her, and soon had her working on a blanket for the baby. However, looking at her humble effort now, Sarah realized she must have done something wrong because it resembled a triangle more than it did a square. Until she saw Leta again, she'd have to set the project aside.

Releasing a deep sigh, Sarah closed her eyes, attempting to nap. She was on the verge of falling asleep when the doorbell chimed. She raised her head as Calla walked into the house.

"Hi," Calla said, sounding only slightly belligerent.

"Hi," Sarah returned, hardly knowing how to respond to her anymore. She was afraid her daughter would know how pleased she was to see her and decide not to visit again. Either that, or she'd be outraged that Sarah hadn't revealed the proper delight. Sarah just couldn't predict her reactions.

"I brought you some videos," Calla announced in an offhand manner, as if it embarrassed her to admit she'd actually thought of Sarah. She stepped forward and set the plastic sack on the coffee table, then quickly stepped back, hands in her pockets.

Stunned into speechlessness, Sarah stared at her daughter.

"I thought…you know, watching movies might help kill time."

"That's so nice of you."

Calla shrugged off her gratitude. "I work at the video store, Mother. It's no big deal."

Sarah reached for the bag and sorted through the titles. These were the very ones she would've chosen if she'd picked out the movies herself. The original *Sabrina* starring William Holden, Audrey Hepburn and Humphrey Bogart. *The Rainmaker* with Katharine Hepburn and Burt Lancaster. Plus *Father Goose* with Leslie Caron and Cary Grant.

"Oh, Calla, these are perfect!"

"They're old movies—no one ever rents them."

"Get my purse and I'll pay you. I wouldn't want you to take this out of your own wages."

"No need to do that." Calla sat on the edge of the chair, as if she anticipated needing to make a quick escape. "Joanie told me to tell you there's no charge. She's been meaning to come by and visit but hasn't had a chance."

"That's so sweet of her."

Calla looked about the room and frowned. Sarah could only imagine what displeased her now.

"Is Dennis treating you any better?"

She opened her mouth to argue but decided that wouldn't help. "He's been his usual self." Which was wonderful, gentle and patient, but her daughter didn't want to hear that.

Calla snorted. "That's what I thought." She jumped up from the chair and went into the kitchen. "Look at this!" she cried, sounding disgusted.

"What?" Sarah called out to her.

"Did you know he stacks dirty dishes in the sink?"

Sarah was a meticulous housekeeper and no one knew that better than Calla. Before she could respond, she heard running water. Apparently her daughter had taken it upon herself to wash those unsightly dishes. Calla was more like her than she cared to admit.

The child moved within her and Sarah pressed her hands against her abdomen. "That's your sister making all the racket out there," she whispered. Almost five months into the pregnancy, and the baby moved quite a bit now. Sarah found it reassuring. Feeling her baby eased her worries somewhat.

"Do you want me to put in one of those movies for you?" Calla asked a few minutes later.

"Please." Sarah was definitely in the mood to be entertained.

Calla reappeared and grabbed the top video. Using the remote control like an expert, she slipped the video into the VCR and set it on Play.

"Have you ever seen *Father Goose*?" Sarah asked as the credits rolled and the music began.

Calla shook her head, implying that any one of these movies would be completely boring to a girl her age.

"It's quite humorous."

The opening scenes came on, and Calla watched the first couple of minutes. "This takes place during World War II?"

Sarah nodded.

"We're reading about that in our history class. Did you know Hassie's husband fought in the war?"

"Yes. So did other men from this area."

"Hassie had a son who died in Vietnam, too. His name was Vaughn. She came to talk to us last Friday and brought pictures of him. I knew she was the one who put up flags at the cemetery every Veterans' Day, but I never really understood why."

Sarah was sure she'd mentioned Hassie's son at one time or another. Perhaps not.

"She had photographs of him when he was in high school. He was a really good football player. He wasn't bad-looking, either."

"She doesn't talk much about Vaughn anymore," Sarah said. "I think she still finds it too painful."

"Hassie told us how his girlfriend stayed in touch with her for years after Vaughn died, even after she married someone else and had children. She named one of her children after him—Thomas Vaughn. That has a nice sound, doesn't it?"

Sarah nodded.

"When she left, Mrs. Sinclair talked about the effect war has on people," Calla said quietly.

The Friday afternoon sessions at the high school had been a real hit with the community, for a number of reasons. Lindsay regularly invited people to come in and talk to her students—about their jobs or their family histories or their interests. Sarah had spoken herself and her father had, too, more than once. Almost everyone in the community had. Farmers, cattlemen, business owners. Everyday people. Lindsay was a master at convincing folks they had something beneficial to contribute. And in doing so, she'd helped foster the town's new and growing sense of pride.

"Would you like some popcorn?" Calla asked.

Taken aback by the question, Sarah blinked. "Sure."

"Me, too." She put the VCR on Pause and walked out to the kitchen.

Calla was staying? Sarah could hardly believe it. Soon the popping of kernels could be heard from the microwave in the background, and the scent drifted through the house.

Calla returned a few minutes later with a small bowl for each. "Do you have a name picked out for the baby?"

"Not yet." Both she and Dennis had gone around and around about names. "Do you have any suggestions?"

"Me?"

"Sure, you might as well put in your two-cents' worth," Sarah said. "Everyone else has."

Calla munched on her popcorn, seemingly deep in thought. "I'd suggest that if it's a girl you name her after Grandma, but Jeb and Maddy beat you to the punch."

"I thought of that already."

"What about Denise? Isn't that the female form of Dennis?" Calla asked with a sneer. "Doesn't he want to name the baby after himself?"

Sarah ignored the sarcasm. "Denise…" she murmured, trying to come up with a middle name.

"Denise Sarah," Calla threw out. "Might as well get your name in there, too."

"What about a boy's name?"

Calla mulled that over for a moment, then said, "I've always liked the name Joseph."

Sarah wasn't fooled. Calla was thinking about Joe Lammermann, who'd been her first love. She hadn't mentioned him much lately, but Sarah knew her daughter still cared for Joe. Through the grapevine, Sarah had learned that Calla and Joe had both showed up at the Sweetheart Dance without dates and then spent most of the night dancing with each other. She'd also heard from her father that they'd gone out to the movies one evening last week.

"I've been dating Joe again—well, sort of dating him." This information was offered casually.

"You always did have a soft spot in your heart for him."

"A soft spot in my head, you mean," Calla muttered. "I promised myself that if Joe ever asked me out again, I'd take real pleasure in rejecting him. Then he called to invite me to a movie and I couldn't say *yes* fast enough. Sometimes I don't know what's wrong with me," she said in disgust.

"The same thing that's wrong with most of us when it comes to men," Sarah said wryly. Calla nodded without comment and pressed Play, as though to end a conversation that was becoming too personal.

They were silent for a few minutes as the movie began again. Soon they were both laughing.

"This isn't such a bad movie," Calla commented, sounding surprised.

"It's actually pretty wonderful," Sarah added, glancing from the television screen to her daughter.

Calla's visit felt like a gift to Sarah, an unexpected and welcome surprise. The baby moved, this time for several moments as if exploring his or her cramped space. As Sarah cradled her stomach, she noticed Calla staring at her, but she said nothing.

The movie was almost over when Dennis returned from work. He saw Calla in the living room with Sarah and stopped short. "Hello," he said cautiously.

"Hi." Calla's greeting was equally stiff. "I brought my mother a few videos."

He looked at Sarah and she saw the merest hint of a smile. "I heard you were working for Joanie," he said.

"Yeah," she said and stood. "I'd better be going."

"Don't let me rush you off," Dennis told her. "I've got to shower and then make something for dinner. Stay as long as you like."

Calla wavered, visibly unsure about what she should do. "I'll just watch the end of the movie."

Before Dennis turned away, his eyes caught Sarah's and he winked. Humming, he walked down the hallway to the bathroom, wearing a huge grin.

There were already hints of spring, and it wouldn't be long before the first calves of the season arrived. When Margaret woke Monday morning, she suggested they work on cleaning out and preparing the calving barn. Matt agreed. After breakfast, they started, working side by side, laughing and teasing one another.

"How many calves have you delivered?" Margaret asked.

Matt doubted it was as many as his wife. He was about to answer when Sadie appeared, looking more than a little displeased.

"Phone call," she said in that spiritless monotone of hers. "For you," she added, pointing at Matt.

Matt could easily guess who the call was from. Sheryl.

"Take a message," he said curtly.

"Who is it?" Margaret wanted to know, staring from her housekeeper back to Matt.

"The call is for Mr. Eilers," Sadie responded diplomatically.

"Matt?" Margaret looked at him. "Problems?"

"No," he muttered, and without another word, followed Sadie toward the house. His steps were heavy with dread. When he hadn't heard from Sheryl for several weeks, he'd hoped that meant she'd accepted his decision. Apparently not.

The phone was just inside the kitchen, and by the time he reached it, he was furious.

"Hello!" he half yelled as he picked up the receiver.

"Matt…"

It was Sheryl, all right, and hearing her voice was enough to set him off.

"What does it take, Sheryl? I can't be any more blunt than I was before. There's nothing between us and there won't be in the future. Don't call here again, understand?"

"But, Matt—"

He didn't wait to hear her response; instead he slammed down the phone. Sadie stood with her back to him, slicing vegetables, but Matt knew she'd heard every word. Good. He wanted the housekeeper to realize he wasn't cheating on his wife.

"Sadie."

She turned and for the first time since he'd married Margaret, he thought he saw her smile. "I told you before, if Sheryl phones again, hang up on her."

"Hang up?" The housekeeper gave him a sour look. "I didn't know if you meant it or if that was just for show."

"I meant it, all right. Would you please do as I ask?"

Sadie muttered an unintelligible response, and Matt wondered, not for the first time, if the woman was trying to make trouble.

Margaret was waiting for him when he returned to the calving barn. "Who was that on the phone, Matt?" she demanded the moment he walked into the stall he'd been hosing down with antiseptic.

"Just now?" he hedged.

"Of course just now!" She scowled. "It was a woman, wasn't it?"

He was tempted to lie. That would have been an easy out, but then he remembered what Margaret had said—she considered him an honorable and decent man. He felt obliged to live up to that, even if it cost him. He lowered his gaze and nodded.

Margaret didn't say anything else, simply turned her back and continued to work.

"It's not like it sounds…" Matt tried, hating the look of hurt and disappointment in her eyes, hating the way her shoulders slumped forward. "I was hoping you'd hear me out."

"Answer me another question first," she insisted, slamming the pitchfork into the ground.

"All right," he said, determined to be as forthright with her as he'd been with Sheryl.

"Is this the same woman you went to see a little while back?"

The question caught him off guard. So much so, that he literally took a step in retreat. Margaret knew he'd driven to Devils Lake to see Sheryl? It was the first she'd mentioned it.

"You think I didn't smell her on you?"

"Ah…" He'd worried about that.

"Wasn't I supposed to figure out why you suddenly

felt the overwhelming urge to take a shower the instant you walked in the house?"

She had him there.

"What's her full name?" Margaret asked. "Sheryl what?"

"Margaret, listen…"

"Don't give me excuses." She was stiff with anger. Rarely had Matt seen her in such a rage. If he didn't watch out, she was liable to stab him with the pitchfork.

"Her name's Sheryl Decker."

"Sheryl Decker," she repeated as if the sound of it was repugnant. "Did you sleep with her, too?"

"No." His response was immediate. From the moment he'd taken his wedding vows, he'd been faithful to Margaret.

"Do you love her?"

"I swear to you that I don't."

"Then why's she calling you?"

"I don't know," he cried, and it was the truth. "I don't *want* to know. I didn't talk to her just now and I won't. I told her not to call here again and I slammed the phone in her ear. You can ask Sadie if you don't believe me." He didn't entirely trust the housekeeper, but surely she wouldn't tell an outright lie. "I swear to you I didn't sleep with her."

Margaret blinked a couple of times, her face vulnerable, uncertain.

He held out his palms, silently imploring her to believe in him.

Margaret cast down her eyes. "I don't like this feeling," she said, her voice low.

"What feeling?" If he could get her to talk about it, perhaps they could come to an understanding. He desperately wanted her to believe him, needed her to. She was the only woman who'd ever really loved him. The one thing she'd asked of him was that he marry her. Even then, she seemed to think *he* was doing *her* the favor. That was incredible enough, but then he stopped to consider what she'd brought into the marriage—the cattle, the land, the house and everything else. It was more than Matt had expected to accumulate in a lifetime.

"The feeling here," she said, pressing her hand to her heart. "I hate it when I think of you with another woman. It makes me want to be sick."

"No, Margaret, no..." He didn't care what she did with that stupid pitchfork, but he wasn't keeping his distance any longer. He walked right up to her and backed her against the wall. Before she could argue, he kissed her. By this time they were lovingly familiar with each other's bodies. Matt savored the taste of her lips, inhaling the smell of hay and fresh soap—as seductive as anything he'd ever encountered.

"You wearing your lace underwear?" he whispered.

She nodded, then said, "Don't try to sidetrack me."

"I'd never do that," he murmured. As he spoke, he opened her coat and made short work of the buckles holding up her coveralls. Before long, her breasts were in his hands.

"This is unfair," Margaret protested, but he noticed she didn't say it with real conviction.

"Is it now?" he asked, kissing away any further objection.

An hour or so later, Sadie came to the barn to call them in for lunch. The housekeeper's eyes narrowed when she saw them.

"We'll be there right away," Margaret promised.

"Take your time," Sadie muttered, pulling a piece of

hay from the back of Margaret's hair. Then she glanced at Matt and shook her head, as though to suggest he ought to know better.

That afternoon Maddy McKenna came for an unexpected visit. The two women disappeared into the house and Matt busied himself with routine chores. At the sound of a car engine, he peered outside the barn—and froze. It was Sheryl.

His heart went into a tailspin. So, it had come to this, had it?

She'd parked the car and started for the house when he stopped her. The last thing he wanted was a confrontation in front of Margaret and her friend. "What do you want?" he demanded, letting her know he wouldn't tolerate her interference.

"Want?" she asked with a short, humorless laugh. "I don't want anything from you, Matthew Eilers."

"Good." Then she could be on her way and out of his life.

"I'm here to give you something," she told him, opening her purse. She withdrew a thick envelope and slapped it into his palm.

"What's this?"

"I'm serving you with papers."

"Papers?" She was *suing* him? For what?

"It's a paternity suit. I'm pregnant, Matt, and you're the father."

Ten

*Minutes of the March 20th meeting
of the Buffalo Valley Town Council*

As recorded by Hassie Knight, Secretary and Treasurer, duly elected.

The meeting was brought to order by council president Joshua McKenna with the Pledge of Allegiance to the American flag. Council members in attendance as listed: Joshua McKenna, Dennis Urlacher, Heath Quantrill, Robert Carr, Gage Sinclair and Hassie Knight. Reverend Larry Dawson and Rachel Quantrill sat in as observers.

1. In the matter of old business, Joshua McKenna reported that he'd heard back from the Doctors' Clinic in Grand Forks, and it has now been confirmed that Buffalo Valley has been chosen as a branch site for the health organization. This means that a general practitioner will be scheduling regular office hours in Buffalo Valley three days a week, starting the first week of April.

2. This is a major step for Buffalo Valley, and a much-needed service. Council members congratulated Joshua on his persuasive efforts and the many hours of meetings that went into convincing the Doctors' Clinic to choose Buffalo Valley.

3. Also in the matter of old business, Heath Quantrill stated that he will be working four days a week at the Buffalo County Bank and traveling into Grand Forks only one day. He was asked about his announcement from last month's meeting. Heath explained that a consulting firm has been hired by the ten-branch bank to explore the possibility of moving head office from Grand Forks to Buffalo Valley. Heath did explain that this is only in the beginning stages and that, if it does happen, it would be two to three years before the move is completed.

4. In the area of new business, Hassie Knight suggested that the community should plan a celebration. Buffalo Valley has experienced tremendous growth in the last three years. Her idea is to have a Summer Fest.

5. Heath Quantrill has other news. His grandmother's will has recently been read, and she donated two square blocks of land to Buffalo Valley, with the stipulation that the town utilize the property as a park. Robert Carr (Buffalo Bob) added that with the number of marriages and births taking place, a park would benefit families and draw more people into town.

6. Much discussion followed, and the idea for the Summer Fest and the park were shelved until next month. The meeting adjourned at one o'clock.

Respectfully submitted,
Hassie Knight

Bundled in her coat, gloves, scarf and boots, Hassie stood on the sidewalk outside the pharmacy that had been in the Knight family for more years than she wanted to think about. Her daughter had been after her to retire, move to Hawaii and spend the rest of her days soaking up the tropical sun. As if Hassie could do such a thing! In all her life, she'd never been one to sit back, relax, take it easy. She'd be bored to death. Valerie loved Hawaii and often mailed postcards of the turquoise-colored water, white beaches and sloping palm trees, hoping to lure her to the islands. Hassie wouldn't be opposed to another visit, but all that sunshine would be more than her system could handle. No, Buffalo Valley was her home, and recent events here were downright exciting.

The Doctors' Clinic was open for business now. Joshua McKenna could be proud of that. The council president had negotiated long and hard to convince the clinic to set up a branch office in town. Hassie knew that Sarah's troubled pregnancy had been his incentive; both he and Dennis were worried about her and the baby. The town needed a doctor, and even one on a part-time basis was better than none. At the rate Buffalo Valley was growing, it made sense to plan for a clinic that would eventually have office hours five days a week.

The Doctors' Clinic wasn't the only new sign on the block. Harvey Hendrickson had sold his farm, and instead of moving his family out of the area, he'd opened a hardware store. The town needed that almost as badly as it did the clinic. The entire Hendrickson family had moved into Buffalo Valley, and with six children, they had plenty of homegrown employees.

"What's so interesting out here?" Leta asked, coming outside to stand on the sidewalk with Hassie. She wore several layers of clothes and only her nose was visible beneath the thick woolen scarf tied around her head and draped across her neck.

"I was just taking a gander at Main Street," Hassie explained. It was a joy to look up and down the street and see new businesses popping up every few weeks.

"I heard talk that Rachel's thinking about building a drive-in hamburger place."

Hassie grinned. She'd heard the same rumor herself. Rachel had a good head for business; the success of The Pizza Parlor proved as much. "My guess is she'll set it up across the street from the proposed park."

"Ready to go in?" Leta led the way back into the warm store. "This town could use a fast-food restaurant. The teenagers would love it. Families, too. And tourists in the summer."

"What do you think of Rachel as the new council president?" Hassie asked. The annual election was coming up, and Hassie had been giving some thought to potential candidates. Who was the best person to take this town into the future? The person who kept rising to the top of her list was Rachel Quantrill. Hassie walked to the back of the store, where she removed her coat and reached for her white pharmaceutical jacket.

"Wouldn't Joshua take exception to that?" Leta asked, after shedding her own coat.

Hassie shook her head. "I doubt it. He's commented a

number of times that he's ready to retire from the council. Can't say I blame him. He's been president nearly five years now."

"I think she'd do a good job," Leta said.

Hassie agreed; Rachel loved Buffalo Valley with the same passion and loyalty as Hassie. Like so many other towns across the Dakotas, Buffalo Valley had seen its share of troubles. But overall, living here had been a blessing. Even during the very worst times, a sense of community, of neighborly cooperation, had never entirely disappeared. And now…now things were looking up.

"How's Sarah doing?" Hassie asked, knowing Leta had recently been to visit.

"Better, I think. Her mood was good."

"Calla's stopping by more often, is she?"

Leta nodded. "Thankfully, yes. She tries to avoid Dennis, though. Sarah said she always has a convenient excuse for coming over. Usually it's something to do with the video store. Either she's dropping off a movie or picking one up. Although, as I understand it, she usually doesn't stay long."

"Still, they're communicating."

Leta flashed her an easy smile. "So it seems. You know who I haven't seen much of lately? Margaret Clemens."

"It's Eilers now," Hassie reminded her.

"Right." Her tone conveyed her lack of enthusiasm for Margaret's choice of husband.

To be fair, Hassie had entertained her own doubts about Margaret's marriage to the rogue rancher. The girl deserved better. Bernard had certainly been unimpressed by him. Hassie recalled a time, nearly a year ago now, when he'd sat at her soda fountain and asked Hassie her opinion of Matt Eilers. Hassie hadn't been sure what to say. She knew who Matt was, knew his reputation, but not much more.

Most people tended to think of him as an outsider, the same way they'd looked at Lindsay Snyder and Maddy Washburn when they'd first arrived. It hadn't taken Lindsay long to win the respect and affection of the townspeople. Maddy, either. Matt was a different story. He'd been part of the community far longer but was less well known, and certainly not as well liked.

Anyone with a lick of sense knew he hadn't married Margaret for love. Apparently Margaret knew it, too. And this was the kicker—it didn't seem to matter to her. She'd been blinded by hormones, Hassie suspected. Poor thing. However, Hassie had to admit she'd seen a softening in Margaret since her marriage.

"Lots of changes..." Leta was saying.

Distracted from her thoughts, Hassie paused, wondering what she'd missed.

"Changes in Margaret and for that matter Matt, too," Leta went on.

"Change isn't always bad, you know."

Leta's smile said she agreed. "In their case, I think it's for the better. Those two actually seem happy. I would never have believed it, but I'm delighted."

Hassie was pleased for them, too, and hoped that whatever they'd found would last.

If ever there was a time Matt Eilers needed a drink, it was now. He stepped into the Doctors' Clinic for the scheduled blood test that would dictate his future and claimed a seat in the waiting room. The collar of his shirt felt like a noose around his neck and his hands sweated with the agony of the unknown. He hadn't come by choice, that was for damn sure. He'd been ordered here by the court.

A number of people sat in the waiting room, most of whom he didn't recognize. Thank God. The last thing he wanted was for Margaret to get wind of this. He'd taken a chair as far removed from the others as possible. He felt so worried that he was sick to his stomach. He removed his hat and, for something to do, rotated the brim while he waited for his name to be called.

Under normal circumstances, Matt wasn't a praying man, but today he was. He'd willingly fall to his knees before the Almighty if this blood test proved he wasn't the father of Sheryl's baby.

Needless to say, he hadn't mentioned the paternity suit to Margaret. Hell and damnation, he couldn't tell his wife of only a few months that he might have gotten another woman pregnant. Seeing how Margaret had reacted to Sheryl's phone calls, Matt didn't want to even *think* what she'd say or do if he told her about the pregnancy. He gripped his hat tightly and prayed like never before.

Okay, so he'd slept with Sheryl, but he wasn't fool enough to believe he was the only one. And, yes, there'd been a time or two when they'd been careless about birth control. That made him feel both weak and stupid. Sheryl had a reputation—and not just for being an easy lay. He knew about her opportunistic and frivolous lawsuits, her willingness to lie and manipulate others. More fool he for ever getting involved with her.

"Matt Eilers."

At the sound of his name, Matt nearly stumbled out of his chair in his eagerness to get this over with.

"Hello, Mr. Eilers." The nurse greeted him cordially, leading him to a small cubicle at the end of the hallway. She motioned for him to take a chair. "I understand you're here for a court-ordered blood test."

"Yes." Matt nodded for good measure. "Isn't this a bit unusual? I thought the normal procedure was to wait until after the baby's born to determine paternity?"

"Generally, yes," the nurse informed him. "It *can* be decided early, but for the baby's sake, that's not recommended. It causes a risk to the pregnancy." Frowning, she glanced down and read over the court document. "Apparently, in this case, the mother insisted paternity be determined right away and went against the advice of her physician."

It was already clear that Sheryl was bent on getting revenge—and money—as quickly and efficiently as possible. It was equally clear that the well-being of her baby was not her priority here. Matt swallowed hard and tensed.

"If you'll roll up your sleeve?"

He did as instructed.

The procedure took only a minute. The nurse then taped a piece of gauze to the inside of his elbow, and Matt rolled down his sleeve, refastening it at the wrist.

"How long will it take before I get the results?" he asked. He had no doubt that Sheryl would be on his doorstep the minute the report came in. She was willing to put the baby at risk to prove that he was the father, just so she could drain every possible penny from him. He'd already received the bill for her test, which had been done at the Grand Forks hospital. Thank God he'd intercepted the mail that day!

"It shouldn't be more than a week."

So all he had to do was live with this threat hanging over his life—and his marriage. A few more days of repressed anger and pretended normalcy. Margaret *couldn't* know.

When he was finished, Matt walked over to 3 OF A KIND, needing a stiff drink. To his surprise, the building was locked up tighter than a bank.

"What's going on?" he asked Steve Baylor, who happened to be walking by.

"You didn't hear?" Steve asked.

Obviously he hadn't, or he wouldn't be asking. "Hear what?"

"Buffalo Bob and Merrily are in California. They're looking to adopt that kid."

"They closed down completely?" Matt needed something to calm his nerves. That and some quiet to think about this situation.

"I understand they won't be back for several days."

He muttered a curse under his breath. "Anyplace else a man can get a drink?" He wasn't aware of one, but Steve had lived in Buffalo Valley his entire life and would know better than he did.

Steve lifted the brim of his hat, frowning heavily. It shouldn't be this difficult, Matt thought irritably.

"Hassie's," Steve said, after a moment.

"She serves beer?"

"Root beer," Steve answered and laughed. "But she makes a mean chocolate soda. If you're desperate you might check it out."

Matt didn't have much choice. Really, the drink wasn't that important. What he needed most was a few minutes to compose himself before he returned to the ranch and Margaret.

Matt had lived in the vicinity of Buffalo Valley five years, and not once had he been inside Hassie's place. No reason to before now. His ranch was equidistant from

Buffalo Valley and Devils Lake. Most of the time he steered toward the larger of the two towns. Not so with the Clemenses. They seemed to have some link with Buffalo Valley.

"Hello there, Matt," Hassie said in a friendly voice when he walked through the pharmacy's glass door, past a couple on their way out. "What can I do for you?"

He ambled over to the soda fountain and sat down. "I heard you make an exceptional soda. I've been meaning to try it," he said, hoping not to give himself away. He didn't need Hassie reporting to Margaret that he'd come in looking drawn and worried.

"That I do," she agreed, striding around the counter. "Business has been good the last few days with Bob gone."

"Do you have anything stronger than root beer?" Might as well ask.

"Afraid not." She reached for a tall glass. "So, you interested in one of my famous sodas?"

"Sure," he agreed. Why not?

"You're not such a bad guy," she said casually, bending forward to scoop up the ice cream.

Matt could have asked her what she meant, but he wasn't in a talkative mood. Not today. Once he had his soda, he'd make sure Hassie knew he was looking for privacy.

"A lot of us had our doubts when you married Margaret."

Matt could well imagine. "She's one helluva woman," he said, wanting Hassie to know he appreciated his wife. Okay, so Margaret had her faults. He laid claim to a fair share of his own.

"Where is she?" Hassie asked.

Matt lowered his eyes, wishing he could come up

with some plausible reason for being in town while Margaret was busy at the ranch, fighting the cold and wind as she and a couple of the hands rode across the north and east pastures, checking for early calves.

He stared up at Hassie and realized she was waiting for him to answer. "She's home… I had to come into town for a doctor's appointment." That much was true. He'd told Margaret the same thing.

"Like I was saying," Hassie continued as she assembled the soda. "I'm really pleased about the way things have turned out between you two."

"I'm pleased myself," Matt said, just to be conversational.

"I've always been fond of Margaret. Her daddy used to bring her into town, back when she was a little girl."

Matt listened, wondering what his wife had been like as a child.

"She used to try to imitate Bernard's walk. It was the cutest thing I've ever seen. She dressed just like him."

Still did for that matter, Matt mused, grinning to himself. He'd never known a woman more comfortable in coveralls, but it was what she wore underneath that enthralled him.

"I'm not sure how well you knew Bernard Clemens."

Matt wished now that he'd had the opportunity to know Margaret's father. He felt sure he would have enjoyed a friendship with the man.

"His wife, Maggie, was nearly twenty years his junior and as pretty as a picture. I remember when he brought her into town the first time. He was the envy of every man in the county. Maggie was a gentle creature, very elegant and refined. It damn near killed him when she died." She shook her head. "I don't think he ever recovered from her death."

Matt's heart ached for the father-in-law he'd only briefly met. "He had Margaret."

"That he did. And to give him credit, he did the best he could with her, but I've often wondered what her life would have been like had her mother lived."

One thing was certain: she wouldn't be married to Matt.

"It's worked out for her, though."

Caught up in his own thoughts, Matt had lost track of the conversation. "Beg your pardon?"

"For Margaret," Hassie said as she set the bubbling soda in front of him.

"What's worked out for her?" he asked.

"Well…you fell in love with her, didn't you?"

Her words hit him like a fist in the face and he blinked back his surprise. Circumstances being what they were, he didn't feel he'd done Margaret any favors. "I'm not sure what you're getting at," he murmured.

Hassie gently patted his hand. "You love her."

Matt nearly swallowed the straw. *Love Margaret?* He narrowed his eyes, wondering what the old woman knew that he didn't.

"You seem a little shocked," she said, apparently finding his reaction amusing. "But you couldn't hide your feelings if you tried. She's got you, Matt Eilers, hook, line and sinker."

Until Hassie said it aloud, Matt hadn't thought about it, but she was right. "I do love her," he said, and found it only slightly amazing that the first person he told was a busybody old-lady pharmacist.

The person who deserved to hear this was Margaret. The woman he loved. His wife.

* * *

"We can't put it off much longer," Rachel said, finishing her breakfast coffee.

Heath nodded, wandering into the living room. He knew his wife was right, but he didn't think he was emotionally capable of sorting through his grandmother's things. She'd been gone two months, and he was only now becoming accustomed to her loss.

For three years, he'd talked with her on a daily basis. Until the very end, she'd been involved in the business. Countless times Heath had gone to his grandmother for advice and guidance. She'd shown him that he possessed every bit as much financial sense as Max, although she'd rarely mentioned his brother's name. There'd been a valid reason for that.

Neither Lily nor Heath would ever forget Max—that would have been impossible—but his older brother's death remained a painful subject for them.

Max had been the one with the brains. The brother who'd been groomed from his school days to take over the bank. Then, in an instant, Max was gone.

Heath had hurried home to North Dakota.

Lily hadn't been easy on him during those early years. The first thing she'd done was appoint him loan manager at Buffalo Valley. In the beginning he'd been insulted. Outraged. He was the only surviving heir, and his grandmother had sent him to work at a minor branch in a town that was all but dead. Every farmer in the area needed money. It was a terrible position to find himself in, and after a few months he'd hardened his heart. Being appointed to this less-than-desirable job had been a punishment, he guessed, for having left, for not allowing her to control his life the way she had Max's. They'd started off on hard ground, the two of them, but Heath soon recognized that Lily was teaching him some of the most important lessons he'd ever learn about the banking business.

"I can help if you want," Rachel said, coming into the living room and sitting across from him. "But you really need to do this soon."

"You're right, I shouldn't put it off any longer," Heath replied without enthusiasm. The retirement center had already packed up everything in Lily's small apartment and Heath had stored it all in the large basement of his parents' home. He'd eventually be selling the place but wasn't ready to let it go quite yet.

"So do you want me there?" Rachel stood behind him and wrapped her arms around his waist. Heath breathed in her familiar scent and realized that having her with him was important. He not only wanted her company, he needed it.

His stepson had spent the night with a friend and wasn't coming home until late in the afternoon, which gave him and Rachel at least half a day. They drove into Grand Forks, chatting as they went.

Midmorning they arrived at the family home. Until their wedding, he'd been living in this very house and he still maintained it, but most of the time he stayed in Buffalo Valley with Rachel and Mark.

Cartons were stacked all about the recreation room in the house's daylight basement. "Where would you like to start?" Rachel asked, hands on her hips. She'd pinned her hair up and wore faded blue jeans, ready to tackle the work with the same energy she brought to everything else.

Heath glanced at the first stack of boxes. There was no need to keep Lily's clothes, which he intended to pass on to a charitable organization. But he wanted to be sure he wasn't unintentionally giving away something personal.

They worked silently for an hour before Rachel commented, "Look, this box has your name on it."

"Mine?" Heath didn't think he'd left behind anything of importance when he'd gone to Europe.

"Aren't you curious?"

He had to admit he was. He lifted it down and slit open the sealed top with a knife, then peeled back the cardboard. To his amazement, he discovered an assortment of expensive leather-bound scrapbooks. His name was embossed in gold on the cover of each one.

"These are yours?" Rachel asked.

"No." Heath had never seen them before. He opened the top book and his breath caught at the newspaper photograph on the first page. He was in his high-school basketball uniform; he and three other players were grinning wildly, clutching a trophy.

"Heath," Rachel breathed in awe. "Is that you?"

They sat down together and flipped through the pages. Each one showed Heath. If not a picture or an item from the local newspaper, then the school paper. Every program of every game he'd ever played was there. High school and college.

"I had no idea you were a sports star," Rachel said, smiling at him.

Heath didn't remember being especially talented; certainly he wasn't the star. He'd been a member of the team and a hardworking athlete, but he hadn't sought the glory.

"Your mother kept these scrapbooks?"

Heath suspected she hadn't. Most likely it'd been Lily.

When he didn't respond, Rachel tucked her arm through his. "Lily?"

He nodded. The second book revealed every letter and postcard he'd mailed home. Lily had kept them all. Treasured each one. All this time, all these years, she'd loved him. It shouldn't have come as such a shock, but it did. For much of his adult life, Heath had considered himself the black sheep of the family. The one who didn't fit in and probably never would. Max, his intelligent, perfect-in-every-way brother, had been the Quantrills' golden boy.

Then Heath recalled his wedding day and those few minutes when he'd stolen away to be with Lily. She'd been weak, growing more and more feeble. He remembered her taking his hand and whispering, telling him he'd always been her favorite.

Heath had listened with skepticism, considered her words the rambling of an old woman at the end of her life, holding on, clinging to her family. But she *had* loved him, loved him from the first, long before he was ready to accept that love.

If it hadn't been for Max's passing, he might never have known.

Eleven

Margaret knew something was terribly wrong with Matt. She sensed it. Felt it in every pore, every nerve, especially when she lay in his arms. As always, he was loving and attentive, but a part of him was missing—that was the only way she could describe it. Lacking confidence, she assumed the problem, whatever it might be, originated with her. If not, perhaps that other woman was somehow involved; she was afraid to find out, afraid of what it would do to her and Matt. To their marriage. For the first time in her life, she felt like a coward.

The only person Margaret could talk to was Maddy. She couldn't stand this silent tension between her and Matt. It terrified her.

Not bothering to drive over, Margaret saddled Midnight, a favorite gelding, gaining purpose as she rode, her face to the wind, her shoulders hunched. The cold stung her eyes, and her lips were badly chapped, but she hardly noticed. She'd entered this marriage convinced that her love for Matt was the only thing that mattered. As long as he was her husband, she'd believed she could accept whatever happened. Naturally she'd hoped that one day he'd love her, too.

When they were first married, everything had gone so well, but lately—in the past couple of weeks—she felt she'd failed both Matt and herself. The worst of it was not knowing what she'd done or why Matt had closed her out. Outwardly he behaved as if their lives were the same as always, which made it difficult for Margaret to broach the subject.

"Hi, Margaret!" Maddy called out from just inside the kitchen. She'd scooped Julianne into her arms, and the child gurgled happily in greeting.

"I shouldn't have come unannounced." Margaret felt a bit awkward now that she was here. "I…I could come back later."

"Don't be silly. I'm dying for company and Jeb's out with the bison." She steered Margaret toward the kitchen table and buckled Julianne into her high chair.

Margaret should be with her own herd. Matt was probably wondering where she'd vanished, and why. Not wanting him to worry, she'd told Sadie where she was, asking her to pass the message on. Margaret didn't think she could face Matt herself. Not right now.

"How about tea?" Maddy asked, already filling the kettle and setting it on the burner.

"Sure," Margaret answered.

"I baked cookies this morning. We'll indulge in those, too," Maddy said as she brought down two cups and saucers from the high cupboard.

"That'd be nice," Margaret said politely. Some emotion must have echoed in her voice because Maddy abruptly turned around.

"I take it this isn't a social call?"

Margaret shrugged.

"What's wrong?" Being the good friend she was, Maddy abandoned her task and moved to Margaret's side, taking the chair across from her. She clasped Margaret's hands in her own.

"If I knew what was wrong, I wouldn't be here," she snapped, and instantly regretted her outburst. "Maddy... something's not right between Matt and me, and I don't know what it is."

Maddy stared at her in silence for a moment, eyes narrowing at the pain and confusion Margaret didn't bother to hide.

The kettle started to whistle, and Maddy quickly rose and tended to it. She let the tea steep, then poured it and brought the cups to the table. Margaret said nothing all this time, sunk in her own misery. Maddy slowly stirred in a heaping teaspoon of sugar, still frowning.

"I'm positive Matt's keeping something from me. At first I thought it had to do with a woman, but now I'm not sure," Margaret finally said. "I've asked him what's wrong, and he just tells me I'm imagining things."

"You aren't."

"I know I'm not," she muttered.

"Trust your instincts," Maddy said. "But what could he be holding back? Do you have any idea?"

"The only thing I can think of..." She hesitated, afraid to even say the words aloud. "There might be another woman."

Maddy's eyes widened. "You mentioned something about a woman."

Margaret nodded. "She was phoning the house for a while."

"No longer?"

Margaret shook her head, then quickly lowered her eyes. "Matt came home one afternoon, smelling of perfume."

"Did you ask him about it?"

"Not right away, but he swore all he'd done was tell her to leave him the hell alone."

"You believe him?"

Call her a fool, but she did. Once more Margaret nodded.

"Whatever's wrong will eventually come out," Maddy said. "If you trust him, and you say you do—"

"Yes, but…" Margaret stopped and bit her lower lip.

"But what? Are you afraid this is all tied to some lacking on your part?" Maddy asked gently.

"Yes!" Margaret was astonished that Maddy knew her so well. "I'm afraid I'm not woman enough to keep him happy."

"Nonsense!"

"But—"

"Don't allow your own insecurities to blind you to what's really happening. I'm pretty sure this has nothing to do with you. Men aren't very good at sharing their troubles—unlike women. Most of them prefer to handle things alone, at least in my experience. In his own male way, Matt is asking for space and time. Men seem to need that. Step back and give it to him."

"But—" Stepping back was the last thing Margaret intended to do. She wanted to hog-tie her husband and not release him until he told her what was wrong. She wanted Maddy to advise her to confront him—until she suddenly realized the wisdom of what her friend was telling her.

"You love him, you trust him," Maddy said simply. "Now prove it."

Margaret exhaled a deep sigh. Already she felt better.

"I was talking to Hassie about Matt the other day," Maddy continued. "Hassie mentioned the positive changes she's seen in him since the two of you got married."

"What kind of changes?"

"First, Matt used to spend a lot of time away from his ranch. If he wasn't at Buffalo Bob's, then he was drinking in Devils Lake. That's not to say he wasn't a hardworking rancher, but he didn't let his responsibilities stand in the way of a good time."

Margaret couldn't say anything in his defense because it was true.

"He used to be a real loner, although he certainly had acquaintances—mostly in bars. He's a lot friendlier now, much more part of the community."

Margaret had noted that herself.

"Those are only a few. But it's the changes I've seen in *you* that I mentioned to Hassie," Maddy surprised her by adding.

Margaret pressed her hand over her heart and attempted a smile. "Me?"

"There's a softness in you I've never seen before," Maddy said. "A...sweetness."

"Sweet? Me?" Margaret was ready to laugh out loud and would have, if not for the challenging look from her friend.

"It's true! Oh, Margaret, you mean to say you don't see it? I do. So does Hassie. Marriage is what's made the difference. When you announced that you were marrying Matt, I have to tell you I had my doubts. I prayed you were making the right decision. Without even thinking, I could come up with a dozen men who would, in my opinion, have made you a better husband."

"But I love Matt!"

"I realized that. Which is why I knew it wouldn't do any good to try to change your mind."

Margaret couldn't argue. She wanted Matt and no other husband.

"Actually I'd planned to phone you later in the week," Maddy said. "Jeb and I wanted to invite you and Matt over for dinner next weekend."

Margaret felt her heart lighten. "Yes... I mean I'll ask Matt to make sure he doesn't have a conflict, but it should be fine." This was exactly what Margaret had hoped would happen. She yearned to be like other couples, to make close friends in the community, to belong.

Not long after she finished her tea, Margaret returned to the house, looking forward to telling Matt about the McKennas' invitation. When he saw her, Matt immediately came out from the barn to meet her.

"Where'd you go?" he asked, although Margaret suspected he already knew.

"I went to Maddy's for tea," she said, as if it was a very womanly thing to do and she regularly took part in such activities.

"You might have mentioned it."

"I might have," she agreed as she led Midnight into the barn and unsaddled him. "In fact, I asked Sadie to let you know."

Hands in his hip pockets, Matt followed her as she went about her tasks of rubbing down the gelding and feeding him oats.

"I didn't talk to Sadie," he muttered.

"Well, it's no big mystery. I just needed to get away," Margaret confessed as she gave Midnight a final pat and let herself out of the stall.

"Any particular reason?"

"Actually, I was worried about us."

Her husband tensed. "Us?"

"It's all right, Matt," she said, and slipped her arm around his waist to hug him. "Really. I don't know what's bothering you, but I can tell that something is.

I'm giving you space to deal with it in your own way. When you're ready to discuss it with me, I'll be here."

He stared at her as though he wasn't sure he should believe her.

"If you choose not to tell me, that's fine by me, too."

He frowned. "You're okay with that?"

"I'm fine with it."

He looked down at her, shaking his head. "I don't know what I ever did to deserve you," he said, his voice low and barely controlled. "But whatever it was, I'm grateful."

Sarah and Dennis sat in Dr. Leggatt's Grand Forks office and anxiously awaited his decision. "I'm feeling much better," she told him. The cramping and contractions had lessened over the weeks of continued bed rest.

"The pregnancy seems to be progressing normally," Dr. Leggatt said, sitting across the desk from Sarah. She looked at her husband and flashed him a huge grin.

"Then I can go back to being a regular person again?" That might be pushing her luck, but she couldn't help asking.

"Back to work?" he repeated with a short laugh. "Not quite."

"I can leave the house?"

He hesitated. "Some."

Her shoulders sagged with disappointment, and Dennis's hand tightened around hers.

"You're the best judge in this situation," the doctor said. "No one knows better than you exactly how much activity you can undertake. As soon as you feel any contractions, you know what to do. The most dangerous time has passed, but we still have to be careful if you're going to carry this child to term."

Sarah wanted that more than anything, even if it

meant risking her sanity. This afternoon was the first time in weeks that she'd stepped outside. The first time she'd stood in the afternoon sunshine and breathed in fresh spring air. It made her feel nearly giddy with happiness. Giddy with love. It turned her thoughts to her husband and how long it'd been since they'd last made love.

They rode the elevator to the lobby and as luck would have it, they were alone. "Dennis, I want you to kiss me."

"Here? Now?"

This joy was almost more than she could contain. "Yes, right here. Right now. Hurry." It didn't matter that she was five months pregnant or that the elevator could stop any second.

"Sarah, I..." Dennis paused, glancing over his shoulder as though he half expected someone to suddenly appear, then wrapped his arms around her. The kiss started gently but quickly grew as wild as their passion. Sarah slid her hands around his neck and gave herself fully to this man she loved beyond reason. One kiss, however, wasn't enough. Their dilemma was ironic; before their marriage they'd made love often and with abandon. Now that they were legally husband and wife, their relationship was strictly platonic, for fear lovemaking might disturb the troubled pregnancy.

By the time the kiss ended and the elevator doors opened, Sarah was weak with longing. Somehow they managed to step out and allow others to enter. Smiling to herself, she wondered if anyone had noticed. Dennis didn't look any more in control than she felt.

The ride back to Buffalo Valley was jubilant. The tests showed the baby was healthy and developing at the proper pace. The release of tension and worry was enough to make Sarah feel light-headed. With caution, she could carry the baby to term and they'd have the child they both wanted so much.

"I'd like to go to the shop," Sarah told her husband as they drove into town.

He frowned in her direction and seemed about to object, then changed his mind. "Dr. Leggatt said you'd know your own endurance."

"And I do," she assured him.

Dennis pulled into a parking space in front of Buffalo Valley Quilts. Although Sarah talked to her manager every day, she hadn't actually been inside the shop since December.

No sooner had she walked in than she was surrounded by her staff. Everyone was talking at once. Most of her life, Sarah had maintained a distance from people, but none of that reserve was in evidence this afternoon. She felt free and alive and very much in love with her husband.

Jennifer proudly showed her the quilts in progress. Sarah examined each one, amazed at their beauty and the talent of her staff. She couldn't have done a better job herself and said so.

Dennis stood at her side, his arm about her waist. He, too, appeared impressed with the work that had been done in Sarah's absence.

The doorbell above the shop chimed and Sarah glanced over her shoulder to see Calla. Her daughter looked upset and near panic.

"Jennifer," Calla cried, "does anyone know where my mother—" She stopped talking when she saw Sarah.

"I'm here," Sarah said and stretched out her arm to her daughter.

Calla hesitantly advanced toward her. "I stopped at

the house after school and you weren't there. I...I didn't know what to think."

"I'm fine," Sarah told her, struggling to hold back tears. This was the first sign she'd seen of Calla's love in a very long while. "I should've let you know I had a doctor's appointment this afternoon."

"I'd better get back to work," Dennis said, and squeezed her hand, aware of Calla's feelings toward him. Whenever possible, he tried to give her plenty of breathing space.

"You'll get a ride home?" he asked. "Lie down for a couple of hours?"

Sarah assured him she would, although at the moment she felt like celebrating, not resting.

"I...I didn't mean to interrupt anything," Calla said, sounding self-conscious. She backed away from her mother as though she'd suddenly remembered their estrangement.

"You didn't. How about one of Hassie's sodas?" Sarah asked, and then for incentive, she added, "Just you and me. I'll tell you what the doctor had to say."

Calla shrugged as if to imply that she didn't have anything better to do.

"Great." Sarah smiled at Jennifer, then walked over to Hassie's with her daughter.

Unfortunately Hassie was gone for the afternoon, but Leta Betts put together a darn good soda herself. She served them, then hurried to help a customer who seemed bewildered by the different kinds of film on display.

More like longtime friends than mother and daughter, Sarah and Calla sat on the padded stools and sipped their sodas and chatted. "The baby's going to be all right?" Calla asked.

"So far, so good."

Calla's lips formed a smile. "What's it like being pregnant?" she asked.

"Actually, it's pretty incredible."

"Do you really feel the baby kick?"

"All the time."

Calla's questions revealed thought and sensitivity. Apparently she'd done quite a bit of thinking about this baby. That pleased Sarah. In the last months, Calla had revealed no indication of jealousy or sibling resentment.

Then, in a carefully casual voice, Calla said, "Dad phoned the other day."

Involuntarily, Sarah tensed. If Willie had gotten hold of Calla it could be for only one reason. He wanted something. It didn't take a brain surgeon to figure out what it was, either. He was after Calla's hard-earned paycheck.

"Do I dare ask why he called?"

"He said he needs money. A loan."

"You didn't give it to him, did you?" It wasn't any of Sarah's business, but she'd blurted out the question before she could think better of it.

"Mother, please," Calla returned, rolling her eyes. She held on to the straw with one hand and the glass with the other. "Do I look like I was born yesterday?"

So Willie didn't get a dime. "Good for you."

Calla didn't say anything for a couple of moments, then glanced in Sarah's direction, her eyes sober. "It wasn't easy, you know?"

Sarah did know. Calla was Willie's daughter and any daughter sought her father's approval, even if that father was as inadequate as Willie. Refusing him money must have been difficult.

"He asked me to get it from you," she added. "He seems to think you'd give it to me if I asked."

Willie was right; if Calla had asked for money, Sarah might well have forked over her own cash without asking a lot of questions. She would have seen it as a way to build a bridge in their relationship, a way she could prove her love.

Calla was staring at her, waiting. Then Sarah understood. Her daughter was asking. Despite everything Willie had done to her, Calla wanted to help him.

"I won't give you money for your father," she said flatly.

Calla looked away.

Feeling she had to explain, Sarah said, "It's as hard for me to turn you down as it was for you to say no to your father. I understand what you must have felt when he pressured you, because that's how I feel right now."

Calla looked back and surprise flickered in her eyes.

"I love you, Calla. You're my daughter and the fact that you've decided to live apart from me hurts. It hurts really badly. I'd do just about anything to regain your affection."

That seemed to require some digesting on Calla's part. "You won't give my father money?"

"No."

Calla's eyes narrowed. "Because you're married to Dennis."

"I did marry Dennis, but my decision has nothing to do with him." She paused, trying to make sense of Calla's reactions. "I wasn't choosing Dennis over you, if that's what you're thinking."

By now Calla's eyes had turned cold. "Think what you like, Mother, but that's exactly what you did." She slipped off the stool and stalked outside, as though she couldn't get away fast enough.

Buffalo Bob felt good. Better than good. He felt terrific. He'd taken the biggest gamble of his life by contacting the California authorities about Axel. Even bigger than buying into that poker game when he won 3 OF A KIND from Dave Ertz. He'd made an honest go of the business in a town that was practically dead. Now, as March progressed, he had real hopes that the courts would choose him and Merrily as Axel's adoptive parents.

Merrily rushed into the kitchen. "Pastor Dawson is here."

Bob nodded and carried a tray laden with an assortment of baked delicacies into the restaurant. His cast had been removed several weeks before but his arm was still weak, and several people rushed to take it from him. Everyone he'd contacted upon his return had shown up. Bob figured this meeting was the best way to thank the community for all the help and support he and Merrily had received.

The low buzz of chatter died down when he walked out of the kitchen. He set the tray on the counter, alongside the large urn of coffee.

"Help yourselves, and once everyone's served, Merrily and I will tell you about our trip."

"I'm not shy," Hassie announced as she reached for a plate.

"Me, neither," Joshua McKenna said and followed suit.

Soon Lindsay and Gage Sinclair, along with Maddy, had helped themselves to the pastries and cookies. Bob noticed that it was difficult for Merrily to keep her eyes off the two infants. His wife hungered for their son, but Bob didn't think it would take much longer for Axel to come home.

"First of all," Bob said after everyone was seated again, "Merrily and I want to thank you from the bottom of our hearts for the way you've stood by us and supported us."

Merrily's arm was around his waist. "It meant more to us than you'll ever know to have your letters of recommendation there before the judge. We know he was impressed."

"He said he was," Bob told them and noticed the quick exchange of smiles. He grinned at Pastor Dawson, who'd originally come up with the idea. "The money the church collected was a huge help, too."

"California is expensive," Merrily said. "Compared to North Dakota, anyway."

"What else happened?" Pastor Dawson asked.

Merrily cleared her throat and when she spoke, the muscles in her face tightened. "I—I had to stand before the judge because of what I did."

Even with the plea bargain in place, Merrily had been terrified. The federal kidnapping charge was a serious crime. It was only the testimony she'd provided in the plea agreement regarding Axel's natural father that had saved her from jail.

"Did you see Axel?" Leta Betts asked.

"No," Merrily replied, and that one word revealed a world of pain and regret.

Bob put his arm protectively around his wife's shoulders. This had been the hardest part of the entire ordeal. Merrily had assumed she'd have some time with Axel. Bob had, too, but it didn't come to pass.

"We talked to the social worker and it was felt that a

visit from us now would do him more harm than good," he explained.

"He's...doing better, we understood." Merrily forced a brave smile.

Bob loved her all the more for trying to conceal her bitter disappointment. He saw several heads nod in agreement and noted the pained looks their friends shared with him and Merrily.

"We were able to get a couple of pictures of him, though," his wife added excitedly. She went from table to table, showing off the latest snapshots of Axel. "I couldn't believe how much he's grown."

"You're being considered for adoption?" The question came from Gage Sinclair.

"Yes, oh, yes." Again it was Merrily who responded.

"We were interviewed individually," Bob said

"And then together," Merrily told him.

"Are they doing a home study?" Maddy asked.

"Apparently so." Bob explained that the last thing he'd heard from Linda Beck, the social worker assigned to Axel's case, was that she'd be getting in touch with them soon about a home study.

Grinning, Maddy flashed them a thumbs-up.

"If she wants to interview character witnesses, give her my name," Pastor Dawson said.

Bob felt his wife's arm tighten about him. "You'd do that for us?"

"Of course."

Each person in the room made the same offer. Bob was deeply moved by these actions of genuine friendship. Never would he have guessed that he'd meet such good people in this down-on-its-luck town. Everyone here was as much family as he'd ever hoped to find.

"Bob and I are grateful, but the battle hasn't been won yet," Merrily went on to say.

"We'll do everything we can to help," Hassie called out.

Their friends lingered for another hour, asking questions and making suggestions. Before they left, each one in turn hugged him and Merrily.

Before she went home, Maddy said that with the state willing to do a home study, it was advisable to make their living quarters as attractive as possible. An apartment above a bar probably wouldn't be considered the best environment for a toddler. Maddy hadn't come right out and said that, but Bob had gotten the message.

Axel's old bedroom could use a fresh coat of paint. Merrily had thought of a dozen ways to add homey touches about the place, too. Funny, he'd never given the matter much thought, but Maddy was right. Their living quarters could definitely use a bit of sprucing up. Nothing extravagant. They couldn't afford that.

The attorneys' fees, plus the trip out west, had set Bob back plenty. The fact that they'd been forced to close down the business while they were away didn't help, either.

"Notice any changes?" Merrily asked when he walked into their bedroom later that night.

Bob looked around, not sure what was different. "You'd better tell me," he suggested tiredly.

"I removed the painting."

Bob's gaze flew to the wall. He loved the painting that depicted a saloon in the old west, with men crowded around the bar, their shot glasses raised in a silent toast. The bartender reminded Bob of himself, only his belly wasn't as big and his hair was longer. Above the bar was a painting of a naked woman posed to reveal the most seductive parts of the female anatomy.

"You moved my picture?" he cried, unable to disguise his outrage.

"We can't have the social worker walking into the bedroom and seeing a picture of a naked woman."

"It's more than a painting of a naked woman," he argued. Certain things were worth fighting for, and that picture was one. "What's that?" he asked with disgust, pointing to the still life of some fruit bowl she'd replaced it with.

"Fruit."

"I know that. It's insipid. Stupid."

"You like that naked woman?"

"Damn straight I do."

Merrily arched her brows, then slowly released the sash holding her silk robe together. "I was hoping you'd find a *real* naked woman more enticing than a painting."

"Oh, no, you don't," Bob said. He wouldn't be that easily dissuaded. He wanted his picture back. Okay, okay, he'd move it for the home study, but not until absolutely necessary.

"I'll rehang it after the interview if you insist." Merrily shrugged her shoulders and the robe pooled at her bare feet. He'd been with Merrily for years now, and there were damn few secrets when it came to his wife's naked body. Nevertheless, Bob found himself as eager to make love to her as he had the very first time.

"You'd put it back later?" he asked, surprised at how weak his voice sounded.

"I would."

"Then I can't see any harm." As he spoke he threw off his own clothes with an urgency that left him trembling. "Come to your Buffalo Man," he coaxed.

His wife didn't need any further encouragement.

Twelve

Sarah didn't take one minute of her newfound freedom for granted, limited though it was. Wanting to protect her pregnancy and at the same time have some semblance of a life, she paced herself carfully. Mornings were spent at Buffalo Valley Quilts.

Orders for her quilts continued to pour in and the thrill never waned. People loved her simple designs and the fact that each quilt was individually constructed, each unique in its own way. At noon she returned to the house for what she called quiet time. Dennis assumed she napped, and sometimes she did, but mostly she worried about her relationship with Calla and wondered what she could do to repair the damage.

In the afternoons she prepared dinner and if she was feeling up to it, she took a short walk or went to visit friends. The last week of March, Sarah stopped by Joanie's video store. It had only been open a few months and was an unqualified success. Sarah had gone there two or three times in the past weeks, but catching Joanie during a quiet moment was rare.

Sure enough, Joanie was busy ringing up a sale when Sarah stepped in. She liked the way the videos were displayed; Brandon had built the cases himself. In the back of the store was an area set up for crafts. Needle-point kits hung from a peg board on the wall and there was a bulletin board filled with demonstration greeting cards created with rubber stamps. Joanie had bins of yarn and pattern books, with a completed sweater hanging up on display. Even while making the most of her space, she'd managed to create a homey and comfortable atmosphere. A couple of big, overstuffed chairs marked the entrance to the crafts section, issuing a silent invitation to sit down and relax.

"Hi, Sarah," Joanie called out when she'd finished with her customer. "It's great to see you."

"You, too," she called back. "I'm admiring your store."

Joanie walked toward her. "The crafts are where my heart is. Brandon and I both felt the videos were where we'd make the most profit, but I've always loved crafts. Can I help you find anything?"

"No, thanks. Actually I was hoping we could chat for a few minutes."

"Sure." Joanie glanced at the front of the store, where two people were choosing videos.

"Whenever it's most convenient for you," Sarah suggested, knowing that if she were to attempt the conversation now, they'd be constantly interrupted.

"Would you like me to drop by your house on my way home?" Joanie asked. "Calla comes in about four. I could be there shortly after that."

"Perfect."

By the time Joanie arrived, Sarah had made tea and baked currant-filled scones. "Oh, this is lovely," Joanie said, joining her in the living room.

Knowing she was taking Joanie away from her family, Sarah came directly to the point. "To begin with, I wanted to thank you for sending me videos while I was laid up. I can't tell you what a difference they made."

Joanie brushed aside her gratitude. "It was no problem, and truthfully, the idea was Calla's."

Sarah had suspected as much, and her spirits soared at Joanie's confirmation. Despite her overtures, her relationship with Calla remained fragile and tentative. Anytime she saw progress, something would happen to upset Calla. Almost every conversation seemed to end with her angry. Regretfully, Sarah realized that nothing she could say now would undo the past. All she could do was swallow her irritation and hope that Calla would look beyond her failings as a mother. Sarah wanted her daughter to know that no one would ever love her as much as she did. Calla could trust her, talk to her, come to her. Anytime. Anyplace. Unfortunately, with a girl as moody as Calla, that kind of trust didn't come easily.

"Calla's a good kid," Joanie said.

Sarah nodded. "What I really wanted to talk to you about is a day-care center," she said, diverting the conversation from the uncomfortable subject of her daughter.

"Really? Rachel Quantrill mentioned starting one, too."

"Did she?" This was welcome news to Sarah.

"There's definitely a need. I'm driving over to Bellmont every day to drop Jason off with a friend who has a toddler herself. Brandon picks him up in the afternoons, but it's inconvenient all the way around."

Sarah had her own concerns. She had to find more employees, and she couldn't do that unless there was someplace women felt comfortable leaving their children. With orders coming in at such a steady pace, her quilt company was having trouble meeting the demand. But it wasn't only her business she was thinking of.

Within a matter of months, she'd need someplace she could leave her own baby and feel confident that he or she would receive the best possible care.

"I've been meaning to talk to Rachel," Joanie said. "Perhaps we both can."

"That'd be great."

Joanie reached for her scone and broke it in half. "I realize you invited me over to discuss day care, but you're worried about Calla, too, aren't you?"

Sarah's distress must be more obvious than she'd realized. A lump thickened her throat and she nodded; it was the only reply she could manage.

"I meant what I said about her," Joanie murmured.

"She *is* a good kid, but we just don't seem to get along," Sarah whispered, then averted her gaze, embarrassed and dismayed that everything had gone so wrong between her and Calla. "I can't tell you how many times I've tried." She weighed the advisability of baring her soul to someone she viewed more as acquaintance than friend. But keeping everything to herself, the way she had in the past, hadn't worked, either.

"Calla feels I chose Dennis over her. You see…" Sarah hesitated. "I wasn't legally divorced when I first got involved with him and…" She stopped rather than allow her emotion to take control. After a moment to compose herself, she continued. "I know you and Brandon were separated for a while and I'm so pleased you worked out your problems, but—"

"But," Joanie finished for her, "a reconciliation isn't always possible. I know that better than anyone. I loved Brandon and he loved me. We had a lot of years and three children invested in this relationship. Neither one of us wanted a divorce, but we simply couldn't continue the way we were."

"You see," Sarah whispered, fearing her voice was about to crack, "I loved Willie, too—or the man I thought he was. I was young and stupid, and in the beginning I put up with a lot more than I should have. I guess I was hoping he'd…change… It seems ridiculous now, but deep down I prayed he'd realize how much he loved Calla and me. Needless to say, that didn't happen. When it became obvious that I didn't have any choice but to leave, I moved home. I should have gone ahead with the divorce then, but I put it off. There were complications with money that made it easy to delay."

"Dennis didn't know?"

Admitting she'd lied to him was a painful thing. "I didn't tell anyone, not even my father. I let everyone assume I was divorced. A few years later—once I started seeing Dennis—I desperately wanted out of the marriage, but by then I was trapped in the lie." She reached for her tea, humiliated to be confessing her sins.

"Is this why Calla's so upset with you?" Joanie asked softly.

Sarah shrugged. "Partly. Willie never bothered to keep in touch with her, and because she wanted a father who loved her and cared about her, she built him up in her mind. He became the perfect father—a complete fantasy. Later, when she discovered we *weren't* divorced, she felt I'd purposely withheld her father from her."

"That was why she moved in with him?"

Sarah nodded, putting down her cup. "There was more to her decision to run away. She was furious with me for…being involved with Dennis while still legally married to her father."

"You can't beat yourself up over that. We all make mistakes. It's part of life, part of the maturing process.

Trust me, I've made plenty of mistakes with my own children."

"I'm sure you can understand why Calla believes I chose Dennis over her." It didn't help that they'd announced their engagement without talking to Calla first. Neither of them had intended to slight her, but they'd suffered the consequences ever since.

"None of us are perfect parents," Joanie reassured her. "We try, but we're only human."

"I wish I could get her to look at things differently..."

"Calla's still young. And she's got some issues to resolve. Teenagers don't have much perspective, anyway, but toss in divorce and what she assumes is betrayal, and you end up with the kind of confusion Calla's feeling."

Sarah didn't know how to react to Calla's contradictory emotions. Her daughter's coming to her, asking for money to give Willie, had hit her hard. Even knowing the kind of man he was, Calla had wanted to rescue him and planned to use Sarah to do it. She was afraid that Calla had given Willie her own meager paycheck. If she had, Sarah would prefer not to know about it. She just couldn't handle that right now.

"Is...is she dating Joe Lammermann?" Sarah hated to ask, but Calla hadn't been exactly forthcoming about the on-again off-again relationship.

"She hasn't seen much of him since the Sweetheart Dance. In fact, I'm fairly confident she's interested in Kevin Betts."

"Kevin?"

"I can't say for sure, but last month she told me they were writing."

"When did that start?"

"Not long ago. I do know the letters have been coming fast and furious lately."

So Calla was corresponding with Kevin. Sarah experienced a sadness that was difficult to define. Having always liked Kevin, she was pleased, but at the same time, she wished Calla had mentioned this to her. She couldn't help wondering when she would. If she ever did.

The Doctors' Clinic had told Matt he should have the results of the blood test within a week. He'd figured they'd either phone him or mail him, but it was almost two weeks now and he hadn't heard. From anyone.

No news was good news, or so he'd always been told, but as the days progressed, his thinking took a decided turn toward reality. No news was no news.

When he couldn't stand the suspense any longer, he invented an excuse about needing something from the hardware store and drove into town. The receptionist at the clinic glanced up as he approached the desk. His heart pounded with dread.

He gave his name, then said, "I'd like to talk to Dr. Kaplan."

The middle-aged woman ran her finger down the appointment schedule. "I'm sorry, but I don't see your name. What time was your appointment?"

"I don't have an appointment," he said with controlled impatience. "All I need is a few minutes of his time."

"But…"

"I don't mean to cause a ruckus, but I *will* talk to Dr. Kaplan."

The woman heaved a deep sigh, and Matt knew she'd gotten his message. "If you'll wait here, I'll see what I can do."

"Thank you." He remained standing at the desk.

A minute later, the receptionist returned. "Please take a seat. He'll be with you as soon as possible."

Kaplan's ASAP turned out to be ninety minutes. Twice Matt was ready to walk straight through the door and corner the physician, but he managed to curb his irritation. He'd waited this long; a few more minutes wasn't going to matter. What surprised him was the number of people coming in and out of the clinic— including several he recognized. Apparently the place was doing a good business.

"Dr. Kaplan will see you now," the receptionist announced.

Matt stared at her and his legs refused to budge. After waiting more than two weeks and ninety minutes, he'd expected to race inside when the opportunity presented itself.

"Mr. Eilers?"

"Yes…thank you." He stood and followed her inside as she led him past the cubicles to the physician's private office.

He was pacing when the harried doctor walked in. "I understand you have a problem," he snapped.

"I was told," Matt said, his own voice raised, "that I'd get the results of my blood test a week ago. I've heard nothing. As you might well understand, I'm anxious to know the verdict."

"You haven't received notification?" He flipped open the chart.

"Not a word."

"Ah." Dr. Kaplan glanced up. "The results were sent to the court. They'll send you notification soon. It's our policy—"

"Tell me." Matt wasn't willing to wait until he was contacted by an attorney. He needed to know if he'd fathered Sheryl's baby. He'd come this far and wouldn't retreat now.

"Mr. Eilers—"

"Either you tell me or—"

"All right, all right."

The physician must have recognized that Matt was frustrated, stressed out and damn near sick with worry.

Sitting down at his desk, Dr. Kaplan pushed up his glasses and read through the report.

"Well?" Matt demanded in a growl.

"The test is positive. You're the child's father."

It was as though Matt had suddenly been tackled from behind. His legs simply went out from under him and he slumped into a chair. If there hadn't been a cushioned seat to catch him, he would have fallen to the floor. "There isn't any chance of a mistake?"

"None."

The shock was almost immediately replaced with a numbness that quickly spread to his extremities. He'd always thought that if and when he ever learned he was going to be a father it would be a joyous moment. Instead, he felt a sense of impending doom. His life as he knew it was about to change drastically—and not for the better.

He should have realized the happiness he'd found with Margaret wouldn't last. Nothing this good ever did. Dear God, how was he going to tell his wife?

"Mr. Eilers?"

He looked up and noticed that Dr. Kaplan was standing beside him.

"Thank you for letting me know." He managed a hoarse whisper and staggered out of the chair. When he walked outside, the cold air hit his face but he was only distantly aware of it. Sheryl was having his baby.

After leaving the Doctors' Clinic, Matt sat in his truck, hands clenching the steering wheel while he mulled over what to do next. Obviously he had to tell Margaret. His wife wasn't going to take this news well and he couldn't blame her. Briefly he considered hiding the truth from her until he was better able to deal with it. Until *they* were better able, he amended.

The numbness started to dissolve, replaced with an anger that began to build in the pit of his stomach. Sheryl had purposely gotten pregnant. Nothing would convince him otherwise. She was the one who'd suggested he marry Margaret, then obtain a divorce and marry *her*. He cringed every time he thought about that ridiculous scheme. He remembered that when he'd teasingly asked Sheryl why he should leave a wealthy wife to marry her, she'd claimed she had ways of bringing him back.

She had ways, all right. Getting pregnant was the trick she'd held up her sleeve. She planned to use this child as a weapon against him. He clenched his jaw so hard his teeth ached. *A child.*

It became clear to him that he had no choice but to tell Margaret and the sooner the better. If he didn't, Sheryl would take great delight in doing it for him. The woman wanted to make as much trouble for him as she could. What was the old expression about a woman scorned? He had to protect his marriage from Sheryl's fury, and that meant, first and foremost, telling Margaret the truth.

Decision made, he closed his eyes, wondering how he'd ever find the strength to face her with this news. Two minutes later, he was out of the truck and inside 3 OF A KIND. This task required the kind of courage only hard liquor provided.

"What can I do for you?" Buffalo Bob asked as Matt approached the bar.

"Give me a shot of whiskey."

"Ice?"

"No." He needed fortification—the courage weak men found in the bottom of a bottle.

Bob eyed him suspiciously as he set the shot glass down on the counter. "You don't look so good," he commented. "You sure you want this? I've never known you to drink anything but beer."

Matt's response was to reach for the whiskey and toss it down his throat. It burned, and he shook his head in an effort to cut the effect. "Another."

Bob hesitated.

"What's the matter?" Matt demanded. "Isn't my money good enough?"

"It isn't your money I'm worried about."

"Just give me the damn drink." He downed that glass, then shook his head again, coughing violently. He heard his name shouted from outside the restaurant.

"Matthew Eilers, come out here!"

Margaret? He whirled around and found his wife looking straight at him through the large window. One glimpse of the anger and outrage that flashed from her eyes told him he could stop worrying about breaking the truth to her. She already knew.

No sooner had he stepped out the door than she sprang directly in front of him.

"Is it true?" Her anger was fierce, unrelenting. "Is it true?" she screamed again.

"Margaret, perhaps we should talk about this someplace less public." He glanced around, and it seemed everyone in town was watching. A couple of store owners stood in doorways. People crowded nearby, wanting to know what all the noise was about.

"Answer the question, dammit!"

"Is what true?" he repeated, buying time while he could.

The words had barely left his mouth when she grabbed hold of his shirt collar and jerked him toward her. Her face was scant inches from his own.

"You know what I'm talking about, so don't play dumb with me."

Matt closed his eyes and nodded.

"You son of a bitch." She dragged out each word—and then slammed her fist into his belly with enough force to double him over.

Too stunned to react, Matt staggered backward only to have her immediately plow her fist into him a second time. Clutching his middle, Matt fell to his knees and groaned.

He looked up, silently pleading with her to let him explain, but he could see it would do no good. Nothing he had to say now would make a damn bit of difference. He closed his eyes, expecting her to kick him next.

Instead she whirled around and stalked off.

"You okay?" Buffalo Bob asked as Matt rose painfully to his feet.

Not only had Margaret slugged him as hard as a man, she'd humiliated him in front of the entire town.

"You need a place for the night?" Bob asked.

Matt shook his head. He was going after his wife, and they'd talk this out. Sheryl might try to screw up his life, but by God, he wasn't going to let it happen. He loved Margaret and would do everything in his power to save his marriage.

He couldn't have been more than ten minutes behind her, but by the time he pulled into the yard, she'd managed to drag the contents of his closet outside and dump it all on the ground.

Matt parked and advanced cautiously toward her. "Margaret…"

In return she glared at him with such ferocity he swallowed his plea.

"I want you out of here, understand?"

He raised both hands in a pleading gesture. "Can we talk about this?"

"No!"

"All right. I can see you're upset… Perhaps this isn't the best time for us to—"

"I want you off my land! Now get the hell out."

Matt rubbed his face. He felt as if he'd walked directly into a full-blown nightmare. "Margaret, I know you're angry. I don't blame you, but the least you can do is hear me out."

"The *least* I can do? That's rich." Her laugh was high and hysterical. Next she proceeded to stomp all over his clothes, grinding them into the mud and dirt. "Get out…of my sight…before…I do something I regret."

The tears in her voice damn near broke his heart. Not caring what she did to him, Matt moved toward her, taking her in his arms. As he knew she would, Margaret started to pound at his chest with her fists. He took each hit, not caring about the pain, more concerned with the agony he'd caused her.

Margaret was sobbing now. Matt felt like weeping himself. He tried to hold her, but she wouldn't allow it. She pushed away from him with such vigor that she stumbled backward. He reached out to balance her, but she slapped at his hands.

"I hate you!" she cried vehemently. "I can't believe I could ever have loved you."

"Margaret, please…"

Shaking her head wildly, she burst into sobs and raced toward the house.

Matt hurried after her, not knowing what he'd say or do if he happened to catch her. He didn't have a chance to find out. Margaret got to the porch first and slammed the door in his face.

Resting his head against the screen, he bent over, balancing his hands on his knees as he exhaled. His head swam, and he was beginning to feel sick to his stomach. Sick enough to step off the porch and heave into the bushes. It wasn't long before he lost what remained of his lunch, plus the whiskey.

Wiping his mouth, he walked over to where Margaret had dumped his clothes. He crouched down to pick up a shirt. The door opened and he glanced up, hoping it was Margaret.

Sadie stood on the porch, hands on her broad hips. "Quite the mess you've gotten yourself into."

He straightened. "Is Margaret okay?"

"No, but there's nothing you can do now."

Even with all the evidence to the contrary, he had to say it. "Despite what she thinks or what anyone says, I love her."

"You have a fine way of showing it."

"I never touched another woman after we were married." Sheryl had tried to tempt him, had kissed him, but he'd wanted nothing to do with her. He'd always known what a conniving bitch she was. Why had he ever gotten involved? What an idiot! He kicked at his clothes, disgusted with himself.

Sadie snickered.

"Go ahead and say it," he yelled. "You never approved of me. The old man didn't either."

"You don't deserve her."

Matt hauled what clothes he could to the bed of his pickup, throwing them inside.

"You running?" Sadie taunted.

"No. Like I said, I love my wife and by God, I'm going to fight to save this marriage."

"So you're leaving?"

"She kicked me out."

"There's always the bunkhouse."

Matt hadn't thought of that and appreciated the suggestion. He nodded. "Thanks."

"You've accomplished quite a feat, Matt Eilers," the housekeeper commented as he grabbed another bundle of mud-caked clothes.

Frowning, he looked in her direction. "What makes you say that?"

"You've managed to get two women pregnant at the same time."

Because his head was reeling and his heart was aching, it took him a moment to understand. Shock raced through him. "Margaret's pregnant?"

"Two women at once. You must be real proud of yourself." With that, she returned to the house.

Matt heard her turn the bolt, locking him out.

Curled up tightly in the middle of the bed, Margaret wrapped her arms around her middle and stared at the wall. Sleep was out of the question. Every time she thought about the letter that had arrived in the mail— a letter addressed to them both—the pain started all over again. Sheryl hadn't missed a trick. She was after Matt—and Margaret's money.

After spending several minutes sorting through the legal jargon, she'd realized it was a paternity suit against Matt. Not only was Sheryl Decker looking for child support, she sought income to cover her expenses during the pregnancy, plus all medical costs. Seeing that Matt had married a wealthy woman, the amount Sheryl's attorney requested was a substantial sum.

Margaret wasn't stupid. She tallied up the numbers and figured out that she and Matt weren't married yet when he'd slept with Sheryl. But that didn't make the pain any less. He'd fooled around before the wedding, and she couldn't trust that the affair hadn't continued afterward. He'd lied to her! Hadn't he claimed that he'd never slept with Sheryl?

Margaret felt like an idiot. How she'd loved him, wanted him. All the years she'd wasted pining for him. She'd been willing to do *anything* to get Matt to notice her. All the work and effort she'd put into changing her appearance had been for him. Why? So he could devastate her? Betray her trust? He'd humiliated her, publicly humiliated her! Margaret didn't know how she'd show her face in town again.

Dear heaven, she had no idea what to do.

The tears came in earnest then. Margaret hated that she couldn't make herself stop crying. Hated the way her nose ran and her eyes hurt and her shoulders shook. All her emotions were out of kilter. Because of the pregnancy, no doubt. She blamed Matt for that, too, taking risks with birth control. He'd gotten her pregnant—her *and* his lover.

Closing her eyes, she forced herself to try to sleep, but only managed to doze fitfully.

"Margaret." Sadie's voice gently woke her.

Her eyes flew open. Sunlight poured into the room. Her mouth felt dry and her eyes ached. Propping herself on one elbow, Margaret looked around. "What time is it?" she demanded.

"Long past the time you normally rise."

Throwing off the covers, she reached for her jeans, but stopped when the room started to sway. She fell back onto the bed.

"Don't hurry. Everything's under control."

"What about the men?" This was calving season; she had responsibilities.

"Matt's with them."

At the sound of his name, Margaret clenched her fists and vaulted upright. "What's he doing here? I told him to get the hell off my land!"

"He's your husband," Sadie stated calmly.

"Thanks for reminding me."

The housekeeper smiled sardonically. "You're welcome."

With her head swimming and her stomach heaving, Margaret grabbed the bedpost and hung on, certain she was about to be ill. It took a determined effort to breathe normally.

"I'd like you to make an appointment for me with the best divorce attorney you know," she said.

Sadie calmly shook her head. "I'm your housekeeper, not your secretary."

"Fine, I'll do it myself." She'd assumed Sadie would be only too happy to comply.

"You're the one who married him."

"Go ahead, rub it in. I was stupid, but believe me, this isn't a mistake I plan to repeat." She'd already made one colossal error in judgment and she'd pay for it the rest of her life. She'd learned her lesson. Love wasn't what it was cracked up to be. It was like a wild animal that you thought you'd tamed—you could never completely trust it.

"What about the child?" Sadie asked, focusing her gaze on Margaret's abdomen. "That's his child, too."

"Are you sticking up for him?" Margaret cried. Not only had her husband lied to her, now her staff had taken his side.

Sadie grimaced. "Matt Eilers is a bastard and he deserves to be shot."

"Let me be the first one to volunteer," Margaret said, and she'd let Sadie guess exactly where she intended to aim the gun.

"You married him."

If Sadie reminded her of that one more time, Margaret thought she'd scream. "It was a mistake!"

"Yes," the housekeeper agreed, "but not nearly as big a mistake as divorcing him would be."

"How can you say that?" Margaret asked. The one person she'd counted on was Sadie. They weren't close, but the housekeeper had known her longer than anyone. This betrayal cut her to the bone; surely Sadie could see that. She needed comfort and sympathy, not judgmental comments and bad advice.

"Right or wrong, you married him, and you loved him. The child you carry is his. The baby deserves a father."

"Tell Sheryl that."

"That's something I'll leave up to you and Matt," Sadie said gravely. "That's for you to work out."

Thirteen

Matt thought he'd lose his mind if he spent another night sitting in the bunkhouse staring at the wall. It was April now, and Margaret hadn't said a word to him in two weeks. Correction. She'd said several words he didn't care to repeat. Every effort he'd made toward reconciliation had been rebuffed.

He'd realized early on that his wife wouldn't react well to the news of Sheryl's pregnancy, but he'd had no idea that the line between love and hate could be so thin. Margaret passionately hated him. He felt it in her contemptuous stare every time he met her eyes. She wanted him off her ranch, and after two weeks of constant rejection, he was at his wits' end. Perhaps it would be best if he did leave. Margaret had made her intentions clear: His life would be hell as long as he stayed there. She'd personally see to it.

His friends were few, and not knowing where else to turn, Matt headed into Buffalo Valley. He didn't have any place to go, so he went to 3 OF A KIND. The music was blaring and Buffalo Bob had cranked up the karaoke machine.

Some cowhand belted out an off-key version of a

Jim Reeves hit. Matt didn't know him, and didn't plan to seek out any company. He took a table in the back of the room, letting it be known that he was there for the booze and not for local chitchat. It wasn't long before Merrily approached.

"How you doing?" she asked, friendly as ever.

His reply was a forced smile. "I could use a beer."

"Coming right up."

Sitting in the shadows, Matt nursed three drinks, one right after the other, but they didn't make him feel any better. If anything, he was more miserable now than he'd been when he arrived. Margaret wasn't his only worry; already Sheryl and her attorney were determined to bleed him dry. She was after child support, money for her medical bills and living expenses. It wouldn't stop there, either. He knew damn well this was only the beginning. She was going to exploit this situation for every dime she could get, just like she had in those lawsuits she'd filed in the past. And if she didn't get any money out of Margaret, she'd try for whatever she could get out of him. It was all about money for Sheryl. She didn't give a damn about the kid.

It must be near closing time. The bar was mostly deserted and Bob was counting out the till. Matt should be clearing his own tab and moving on, but the thought of returning to the ranch held little appeal.

Trapped in his own murky thoughts, Matt didn't notice Bob walking over to his table.

"I'll settle up with you now," Matt said, reaching for his wallet.

"Anytime is fine. I'm in no hurry," Bob said, and surprised him by pulling out a chair and taking a seat. "Seems you got something on your mind."

Matt didn't respond. He hadn't meant to be this

obvious—but what did he expect after half the town had seen Margaret beat the hell out of him in the middle of Main Street?

"Trouble at home?"

Matt stiffened. "That's my business."

"I don't mean to pry," Bob continued, sounding apologetic. "Nor am I about to offer you advice—"

"Good," Matt said, cutting him off.

"But," Bob went on, unfazed, "I don't think it's a good idea for you to be driving."

"I only had three beers."

"It's not the alcohol I'm worried about, it's your state of mind. You look about as low as a man can get. Merrily thinks it'd be best if you spent the night, and I agree. We have a room for you—on the house. In the morning, if you feel like talking—"

"I already said—"

"You don't have to discuss your troubles with me," Bob said, holding up both hands. "But if you *want* to talk, I'm here, and there are others, too."

Matt frowned. "Who?"

"Hassie for one. She won't judge you. And the new pastor. He's been a real help to Merrily and me." Bob looked down at the floor. "You might've heard our boy was taken away from us."

Matt had heard about it, but not the details.

"We were both pretty upset, as you can imagine."

"That was when you broke your hand?"

Bob smiled briefly. "Put it through the wall. I was feeling worse than I've ever felt. I'm embarrassed to admit it now, but for a while there, I wondered if life was worth living."

"I can't see myself talking this out with a pharmacist." He didn't want to hear what a preacher would have to say, either. Especially when it wasn't four months ago that Larry Dawson had officiated at his wedding. Just married, two women pregnant—there had to be an entire section of hell ready and waiting for the likes of him.

"Just think about it," Bob advised. "It might help."

"Thanks for the suggestion."

"I don't know what I would've done without my friends during that time. They got me through some rough days when I didn't care what the hell happened to me anymore."

With Bob's words echoing in his mind, Matt took the room key and wandered up the stairs. Normally he wasn't one to accept charity, but even in his pain he recognized that Bob offered friendship and understanding, not pity.

The phone on the nightstand seemed to taunt him. He would have given anything to call Margaret. Anything simply to talk to her and share bits and pieces of their day, the way they had for those few months. She represented everything that had ever been good in his life. He was weak, but her love made him strong. Without her, he was nothing and never would be.

Sitting on the edge of the bed, Matt buried his face in his hands. Margaret was having his baby and this should be the happiest moment of his life, but whatever glimmers of joy he experienced were tainted by Sheryl. Dear God, could he have screwed up any worse?

Things didn't look much better in the morning. Matt thanked Bob and Merrily, left the room key on the counter and headed toward his truck. Part of him wanted to escape. Change his name, move to a different town, start all over again. The thought was tempting, but he knew running was a coward's trick. Besides, it wouldn't solve a damn thing.

On his way out of town, he drove past the old church, same as he always did, went a block farther, then abruptly stepped on the brake. He skidded to a stop.

That he'd even consider talking to the minister was evidence of how deep his troubles went. Just as fast as he'd braked, he put the truck in Reverse and turned around. He parked outside the church, suddenly besieged by second thoughts. He sat in his vehicle while he weighed the idea of spilling his guts to a man he figured would likely condemn him—despite Buffalo Bob's claim to the contrary.

He might have changed his mind and driven on if Pastor Dawson hadn't walked out of the church that very moment. Figuring he had nothing to lose, Matt climbed from his truck.

"Pastor Dawson?" he called.

Larry Dawson turned around. "Good to see you, Matt," he said warmly. "What can I do for you?"

"Do you have a few minutes?" he asked.

"Of course. Come inside. I'll ask Joyce to bring us some coffee."

Like a schoolboy headed into the principal's office, Matt followed the minister. A few minutes later, he was sitting in a comfortable chair, a mug of hot coffee in his hand.

To his relief, the pastor didn't drill him with questions. Matt needed a few minutes of silence and false starts to dredge up the courage to tell him about Sheryl. He was sick at heart by the time he finished.

"Go on, say it," Matt murmured.

"That you're a fool?" Larry Dawson asked, then surprised him by laughing. "Why would I call you a fool when you've already done that half a dozen times yourself?"

"I don't know what to do," Matt confessed, leaning forward and bracing his elbows on his knees. "Margaret isn't speaking to me… Hell, I don't blame her. I try to think how I'd react if I learned she was pregnant with another man's child." He closed his eyes, unable to bear the thought. Yet that was the very thing he'd done to her. The relationship with Sheryl had taken place before he married Margaret, but somehow that didn't make it hurt any less—especially since his dishonesty had left her feeling so betrayed.

"First thing you need to do is get yourself an attorney," Pastor Dawson said with the authority of a man who'd advised countless others. "You have legal rights, too. I suspect you're correct in guessing that Sheryl did intentionally plan the pregnancy. From everything you've said, it looks like she'll try to use the child as a means of controlling you. As much as possible, don't let it happen."

Matt nodded. That had been his own thought, but he'd felt too helpless and confused to think clearly. An attorney was necessary and he wondered why he hadn't considered hiring one sooner.

"Another thing. Don't let Sheryl drive a wedge between you and Margaret. If you're thinking about moving out, don't."

"I am," Matt confessed. "Every time Margaret deigns to speak to me, she lets it be known that she wants me out of her life." For the first time in days he managed a small if genuine smile. "My wife has her own way of expressing her wishes."

Larry Dawson's look grew intense. "If you love her the way you claim, then it's time you proved it."

"I'd do anything to make this right with Margaret,"

Matt told him, feeling the first signs of optimism since he'd learned about Sheryl's baby.

"Be patient," the minister continued. "Do what you can to make amends. But remember, it isn't going to be easy. Show her how committed you are. If you love her, though, stick it out."

"I do love her… I'm not giving up on our marriage," Matt said. He stood and offered the pastor his hand. "Thank you." Larry Dawson had been refreshingly non-judgmental, kind and helpful. He'd told Matt what he needed to hear, given him a plan of action and promised to pray for him.

Leaving the minister's, Matt drove into Grand Forks, met with an attorney he chose from the Yellow Pages and began to feel some hope. He arrived back at the ranch just as Margaret was leaving the barn. He paused when he saw her, wondering if he should say anything.

Scowling at him, she removed her gloves. "I thought I was finished with you once and for all."

"I spent the night in town. Had some thinking to do."

She snickered as though she didn't believe him.

Matt followed her to the house and stopped on the front step. "I thought you should know I saw an attorney this afternoon."

"Good. When's the divorce final?" She looked straight through him, her face emotionless.

"It wasn't a divorce attorney."

"More's the pity." She started inside.

"Margaret, for the love of God, would you listen to me?"

She hesitated, her back to him. "I have the distinct impression I'm not going to like what you have to say."

"What will it take to make this right with you?" he shouted.

"Take?" she shouted back, finally confronting him. "You think you can buy your way out of this? Do you think I can pretend this never happened? Do you seriously believe I can put it out of my mind? Haven't you figured it out yet? *Nothing* you say or do could possibly make this right with me."

"Look, I realize it isn't an easy situation. I'd give anything to have spared you this, but it happened and I can't deny it. Keep in mind that I wasn't married to you at the time, and once we got married I didn't see Sheryl again. Still, we're both going to have to deal with this pregnancy. I'm sorry. Sorrier than you know."

Slowly, thoughtfully, she shook her head, dismissing everything he'd said. "What about *my* pregnancy, Matt? What about *my* baby? This should be a happy time for us... But all I can think about is that another woman's having your baby, another woman is giving you a child first." Tears shone in her eyes and she seemed about to say something else. Instead, she stormed into the house and slammed the door.

More than ever, Matt had the feeling he was going to need the prayers Pastor Dawson had promised.

Dennis Urlacher and Jeb McKenna had been friends most of their lives. When he wanted to talk about Sarah's pregnancy, Dennis figured the one person who'd understand his fears would be her brother.

Driving out to the bison ranch for a fuel delivery, Dennis couldn't stop worrying about his wife and child. Sarah's pregnancy had been difficult from the start. They'd feared with the first spotting that she'd miscarry. The trauma of those few weeks had taken an emotional toll on them both. When Sarah became bedridden, it'd been a hardship in more ways than one.

In the last months, the pregnancy had taken a turn for the better and Sarah was allowed to get around to a limited degree. After a huge number of expensive tests, it was determined that the baby was developing normally. For Dennis, relief alternated with panic about what *could* still happen. He desperately wanted this child; he'd waited a long time for a family and he deeply loved Sarah.

Knowing he was due to deliver fuel that afternoon, Jeb was waiting for him when he arrived. Dennis wasn't usually one to chat. Jeb knew and understood that. Perhaps it was one reason they'd remained such good friends—they didn't need a lot of conversation to be content.

Marriage had changed Jeb. After the farming accident that cost him his leg, he'd become something of a recluse. But in the months since he'd married Maddy, Dennis had seen the old Jeb, with his subtle sense of humor and gruff charm, reemerge. There was a brightness in his eyes again, a sense of life that had virtually disappeared. A laugh that came more easily now and a pride that shone every time Jeb mentioned Maddy or their daughter.

Dennis parked his gasoline truck close to the tank he was scheduled to refill. Jeb didn't run much farm equipment anymore; as much as anything, filling the tank was an excuse for them to visit. Dennis noticed that men needed excuses to get together. Not so with women. They seemed to throw a party for every reason imaginable.

"About time you got here," Jeb said by way of greeting.

Dennis grinned as he pulled out the nozzle and went about his business. "You talk to Sarah lately?" he asked casually a couple of minutes later.

"Last week."

"How'd she sound to you?"

Jeb shrugged and his brows came together in a frown. "Same as always. Is everything all right?"

Dennis wished he knew. "I think she's doing too much. She won't slow down. The doctor said she should use her judgment, but... I'm worried. I've tried to convince her to let me do more around the house—she won't hear of it."

"How's the pregnancy going?"

"Supposedly everything's as it should be. But..." Dennis sighed. His fears were rampant. He didn't go to sleep without worrying about Sarah and the baby. He feared the unknown, feared some unexpected complication that would cost him either the life of his child or that of his wife. Perhaps both. There were nights he'd lie awake for hours, consumed by dread.

Dennis wasn't the kind of man who could bear the grief of losing a wife or child. He wasn't the kind of man who could ever get over it, whose personality would remain intact.

"You want me to talk to her?" Jeb asked.

"I want you to tell me everything's going to be all right with her and the baby," Dennis snapped. He ran his hand over his face and glanced apologetically at his friend. "Sorry."

Jeb slapped him on the shoulder and waited until Dennis had finished with the pump. He sat on the fuel truck's bumper, where Dennis joined him.

"I worried about Maddy, too," Jeb said quietly.

"She had complications?"

"No," Jeb admitted, "but that didn't keep me from worrying. When I learned she'd gone into labor and refused to leave for the hospital without me, I nearly lost it. Luckily everything turned out all right. I told her never again, but she's already after me to have another baby."

"So soon?"

"She was an only child and she wants to be sure Julianne has siblings." Jeb stood, paced two or three steps, then turned around. "The problem is, Maddy knows there's damn little I can refuse her, so give or take a few months I figure she'll be pregnant with our second baby."

Dennis chuckled.

"What's so damn funny?"

"You. I never would've believed a woman would get to you like this."

"Maddy isn't just a woman. She's…Maddy."

Dennis nodded, understanding far better than he let on. He felt the same about Sarah. He was crazy in love with her. Nothing could change that.

An advancing car sounded in the background, and Jeb peered around the fuel truck. "That's Calla."

A heaviness settled over Dennis's heart. "Did you know she was coming?"

"She called earlier and mentioned stopping by this afternoon sometime."

Dennis stood. "You might have said something."

Jeb frowned. "Why? She's your stepdaughter."

"True enough, but we don't get along, never have. I don't know what I did that was so horrible—other than love her mother." He shrugged helplessly. "She seems to think we're in competition."

Calla parked her grandfather's truck and climbed down. Dennis noticed her hesitation when she saw him, as though she wasn't pleased to be running into him, either.

"What's he doing here?" she demanded of Jeb.

"I have a name, Calla," Dennis said mildly.

She glared at him. "Whatever."

"No, it's Dennis, and like it or not, I'm your step-father."

She sighed, signaling that she was bored with the subject. "Whatever," she said again, infuriating him with her rudeness.

"Dennis is here delivering fuel," Jeb said, coming to stand between them, obviously accepting the role of peacemaker or at least buffer. "He's also my friend, and I expect you to treat him with courtesy."

Calla ignored him. "Is Maddy around?"

Jeb walked toward her. "She's visiting Margaret Eilers. She shouldn't be long. You can wait if you want."

Looking disappointed, Calla headed for the house, then apparently changed her mind. With her hand on the railing she scowled at Dennis. "I hope you're happy."

"Thrilled," he snapped back, although he had no idea what she was talking about. Not that *she* needed any excuse to start an argument.

"You finished up here?" Jeb asked, clearly wanting to usher Dennis on his way and thereby avoid a confrontation.

"Yeah," he muttered.

"Oh, Dennis is *more* than finished," Calla sneered.

Dennis shook his head. "What the hell is your problem?" he asked angrily. "Where do you get off talking to me like that?"

"I don't think right now is the time for this," Jeb muttered, glancing anxiously from one to the other.

Dennis knew Jeb was uncomfortable, but he'd had it with Calla. Had it with her gibes and her attitude. Had it with her altogether. If she wanted to be miserable, then fine, but leave him and Sarah out of her sick little world.

"If anything happens to my mother, you'll pay."

"You think I'd hurt *Sarah*?" he yelled. "Are you insane?"

"You got her pregnant, didn't you? She told me how much you wanted a family. Well, I hope you're happy when you have your precious son. If the pregnancy kills my mother, why should *you* care?"

Dennis saw red and would have started for her if Jeb hadn't spoken. "Don't be ridiculous, Calla," he said sharply.

"Why don't you go back and live with your father?" Dennis suggested. The months Calla had lived in Minneapolis had given him the only peace he'd had in years.

"Dennis!" Jeb looked at him as if stunned.

Calla went pale.

Knowing what had happened at Willie's, Dennis regretted the outburst. If not for his uncontrolled fear and his lack of sleep, he would never have said something so immature, something so worthy of Calla herself.

"I think it's time you both cooled your tempers," Jeb said, not hiding his distress at the exchange between them.

Dennis agreed. He needed to remember who was the adult here. "That last comment was uncalled for," he muttered. "I apologize."

"You're an ugly, cruel man, Dennis Urlacher," Calla shouted after him as he walked toward his truck.

"You might take a look in the mirror yourself," he shouted back, then leaped inside his cab and gunned the engine.

Margaret could no longer avoid a trip into town. She had an appointment in Grand Forks with the gynecologist, where she discovered her weight was down five pounds. Dr. Leggatt wasn't pleased with her, but seemed to sense that her weight loss had little to do with the pregnancy and everything to do with her state of mind. She left after the brief examination.

In no rush to return to the ranch, she went to Hassie's for a soda first. No one, other than Maddy, knew she was pregnant. However, she couldn't help wondering how many people in Buffalo Valley knew about Matt and Sheryl.

She hadn't told anyone. Couldn't. It was too mortifying, too humiliating. Married less than five months, and already she was sure she'd made a terrible mistake. Matt claimed his affair with Sheryl had taken place before the wedding. That was supposed to make her feel better? Well, it didn't. He should have told her!

Maybe she was being unfair, but she couldn't help how she felt. He was right about one thing: they'd eventually have to deal with this, but just now Margaret was too caught up in her own disappointment, her doubts and fears. She hated the things she'd said to him yet she couldn't seem to stop herself from saying them, from thinking them.

Hassie greeted Margaret as warmly as always. "You look like you could use one of my sodas," the older woman said.

"That's why I'm here." Margaret slipped onto the stool and glanced out the window. People had begun to gather outside 3 OF A KIND. "What's going on at Buffalo Bob's?" she asked. She hadn't seen that big a crowd since the night of Bob and Merrily's wedding.

"You didn't hear?" Hassie asked, adding soda to chocolate ice cream.

"They're getting Axel back?" It seemed a shame that the boy had been taken away from them, and she sincerely hoped the court had seen fit to return him.

"Bob and Merrily are going through the adoption process, the same as anyone else. The state of California sent someone out to interview them and see the home." Hassie set the soda on the counter. "The social worker's there now. Been with them an hour or so."

"Why's the crowd milling around outside?" That seemed odd to Margaret.

"Moral support. People in Buffalo Valley have taken a real liking to Bob and Merrily. I remember the first time I met him. He called Buffalo Valley a dead-end kind of town. It made me mad, but you know, at the time he was right."

"It wasn't dead-end enough to stop him from taking over the bar and grill, though, was it?"

"That's what's so humorous. He was thrilled, claimed he'd do whatever he could to help save the town, and by golly, he stuck to his word."

"Are they going to be able to adopt Axel?"

Hassie thought that over for a moment. "If there's such a thing as fairness in this world, then Axel will come back here, where he belongs."

For the sake of the couple, Margaret hoped Hassie was right. Unfortunately her current mood was anything but optimistic. Tears blurred her vision, and she brushed them aside. She didn't know if her mixed-up emotions were due to her pregnancy or to her good-for-nothing husband. These days, she didn't need an excuse to cry; her tears were so near the surface. A sentimental television commercial could reduce her to a puddle of emotion in seconds.

"I wish them well," Margaret whispered as she sipped.

Hassie stared at her, eyes narrowing. "Margaret Clemens Eilers, are you crying?"

Margaret's bottom lip started to tremble. She opened her mouth, ready to deny it, but decided that was useless. "I'm pregnant."

Hassie's face lit up with delight. "Margaret, that's wonderful!"

"That's a matter of opinion," she muttered.

Hassie frowned in surprise. "You don't want this baby?"

Somehow the question had never entered her mind. When she'd first suspected she was pregnant, she'd hidden the news from Matt, wanting the pregnancy confirmed before she told him. Every time she thought about the baby, she felt a happiness she'd never experienced before. And yet there was something missing, something crucial. She couldn't share this pregnancy with her husband. Matt and his girlfriend had robbed her of that joy.

"I want my baby," Margaret whispered, her voice faltering. Embarrassed by the tears, she used the back of her hand to dash them from her face. Eager to leave, she reached inside her pocket for cash.

"It's on the house," Hassie told her.

Any other time, Margaret would have insisted on paying. She regretted the stop in town now and knew she was only postponing the inevitable. Matt would be waiting for her when she returned to the ranch. Despite Margaret's instructions, Sadie was giving him information; she was convinced of it. He seemed to know she was going to the doctor's when she left and had asked her to give him an update on the pregnancy when she got home.

Sure enough, he met her when she climbed out of the truck.

"What did the doctor have to say?" he wanted to know.

She noticed the shadows beneath his eyes. So he wasn't sleeping well. Good. She wasn't, either.

"I'm fine. The baby's fine. Kindly leave me alone." She pushed past him and made her way toward the house.

"I'm wondering if you remember what you said the day we were married?" he called out after her.

"What I said?"

"Our wedding vows," he reminded her in clipped tones. "You promised to love me for better or for worse. Okay, so the worse part is here. Are you going to stand with me, Margaret?" His eyes pleaded for understanding and forgiveness.

The irony of his quoting their wedding vows was almost more than she could take. "I can't believe you'd have the audacity to mention our vows."

"I never broke them," he said, "not once."

Unable to stop herself, she snorted. "You never *meant* them! You want to quote vows at me, then include *love* and *honor.* Are you trying to convince me that you feel *anything* for me? You're only interested in my cattle and my land. I'm just a means to an end— that's all I ever was and that's all I am now. Admit it, Matt, if not to me, then to yourself."

"You're wrong, Margaret!"

Sadly she shook her head. "Are you now claiming you *did* love me? You expect me to believe you would've married me if I didn't have a dime to my name?"

He lowered his gaze. She had him there and he knew it.

"It didn't hurt that you inherited the ranch. I won't lie about that, but it wasn't the only reason." He hesitated and swallowed convulsively. "You were the first person who ever believed in me. I told you that before, and it's the truth. You had faith in me. I've never had anyone stick up for me the way you did. Never had anyone look past my faults and love me despite them. Not like you—not with such sweetness...such innocence."

"In other words, I was a naive idiot."

"I never meant to hurt you. If I could go back and change any of this I would."

Margaret couldn't look at him and not feel the urge to forgive—but she refused to do that. He'd hurt her too deeply. "You can't change the past."

He gripped his hat with both hands and boldly held her eyes. "You got what you wanted."

She frowned in confusion. "I wanted this kind of pain? I wanted this agony? Never in my life have I hurt more! It wasn't this bad when my father died, and now you're telling me it's what I *want*? You're crazy!"

"You wanted me, remember?"

Unfortunately she did remember, all too well.

"I'm no prize. You knew that when you married me."

"All I want..." she sobbed "...is for all this pain to go away."

"If I could make that happen, I would. But I can't." He moved toward her, then stopped when she tensed. "I've talked to Sheryl and her attorney. The baby's due the end of June and she'll be my responsibility."

"It's a girl?"

He nodded.

"You've spoken to Sheryl?" She couldn't keep the dejection out of her voice.

"It was while I was in the attorney's office, and it wasn't a friendly conversation. Mostly I let him do the talking..."

She swallowed the huge lump that filled her throat.

"You're right, I didn't love you when we married. I'm

guilty of that crime, but I didn't marry you just for the ranch. I needed someone to believe in me, and even if it was only for these five months, all I can do is thank you. I've learned to love you, Margaret. Heart and soul, I love you."

She could feel herself being drawn toward him, being lured back into his arms. Despite her own intentions, she was affected by his sincerity. "You love me," she repeated doubtfully. "That's mighty convenient, isn't it?"

"Assume what you want, but it's the truth."

Margaret needed to think, needed to sort through the pain and all the confused emotions. It was too easy to allow herself to be swayed.

Pressing her hands to the sides of her head, she closed her eyes. "I can't think now."

"Take all the time you need. I'm not going anywhere. When you're ready to talk, I'll be here."

That was fair, and necessary. She nodded, turned her back on him and walked inside.

Fourteen

Sarah couldn't sit still. She paced the living room and glanced at the clock every other minute, waiting for Dennis to come home. She would have driven down to the service station and confronted him, but it was his day to make fuel deliveries. Briefly she considered waiting for him there. However, when she was this angry, she preferred to discuss the matter in private.

An hour later, the door off the kitchen swung open and Dennis came in, still wearing his grease-smeared coveralls. From the way he dragged his feet, she knew he'd had a long, hard day, but that didn't stop her. She had to know.

"Did you and Calla have an argument last week?" she demanded.

Dennis snapped his head back, as though her sharp words had caught him by surprise.

"Did you have it out with my daughter?" she asked again, with the same outraged intensity. The anger had been festering inside her since morning and wouldn't easily be quelled. Not until she'd heard from her own husband exactly what had happened.

Not responding, Dennis walked into the bathroom and proceeded to climb out of his coveralls.

"Don't pretend you don't know what I'm talking about," she cried, refusing to be ignored.

"I'm not." He turned on the shower and started to undress.

"Answer me, will you?" After waiting all afternoon to talk to him, she wasn't willing to be put off.

"We'll talk about this when I've had a chance to unwind." With that, he eased her out of the bathroom and shut the door.

Standing in the hallway, her arms crossed defiantly, Sarah blinked. He'd actually removed her from the room, then calmly closed the door in her face.

Not knowing what else to do, she returned to the kitchen and chopped green peppers and tomatoes for the dinner salad. By the time she'd finished, the vegetables looked pureed.

Ten minutes later, Dennis entered the kitchen, his hair damp from the shower. He wore a clean pair of jeans and a short-sleeved shirt, suitable for the unseasonably warm May weather.

"Are you ready to talk now?" she asked, doing her best to hold back her irritation.

"In a minute." He got himself a beer from the fridge, poured it into a glass. Then he sat down at the table. "All right," he finally said with a beleaguered sigh, "what do you want to know?"

"Did you or did you not have words with Calla?" She was incredulous that it'd taken nearly a week for news of the confrontation to get back to her.

Dennis nodded.

"You didn't say anything about it to me," she accused him, furious that he'd hidden this from her.

"I couldn't see the point. I knew it would upset you, and—"

"You're damn right I'm upset! I can't *believe* you'd do something like this." In all the years of their relationship, Sarah had never known Dennis to lose his temper. She couldn't imagine what had happened, what Calla had said or done that would evoke such a reaction from her husband. And she worried that this might further damage her own fractured relationship with her daughter.

"Did Calla tell you?" Dennis asked, his eyes narrowing.

"No!" Calla rarely shared anything with her, and dammit, that hurt. Now Dennis was excluding her, too, and that hurt even more.

"Jeb?"

"No, Maddy happened to mention it. But she didn't do it maliciously." Her sister-in-law didn't have an unkind bone in her body. The conversation had occurred earlier in the day, when Maddy had driven into town on some business concerning the grocery. She'd stopped at the quilt shop to say hello and innocently asked about Calla. Reading between the lines, Sarah soon understood that her daughter had visited the ranch the week before and been upset and shaken by a confrontation with Dennis. Apparently Calla had talked to Maddy about it at length.

"I suppose you want to hear my version?" Dennis asked in a tired voice.

"Of course I do!" Since Calla's return from Minneapolis, Sarah had slowly but surely been rebuilding their relationship, taking one small step at a time. In the space of a few minutes, her husband had ruined months of effort.

"She insulted me, and—"

"What did she say?" Sarah broke in, not allowing him to finish.

Dennis cupped the glass with both hands. "For starters, she asked Jeb what I was doing at the ranch."

Still pacing, arms folded, Sarah frowned, sure she'd misunderstood. "That was an insult?"

"I was standing right there. The least she could have done was address the question to me."

Sarah felt sick.

"Sit down, Sarah," he urged, pulling out a chair. "All this anger can't be good for the baby."

"Let me worry about the baby."

"It's my baby, too!" He took a deep breath. "Look, Sarah, I've stayed out of the situation with Calla because that's what you wanted. You insist on handling everything yourself, carrying the full load. I'm your husband—"

"Then start acting like one," she cried. She saw the hurt in his eyes, but ignored it. "Don't you realize how hard I've tried with Calla? Everything is so tentative with her... Your little outburst might have destroyed everything I've worked so hard to build."

"Then so be it," Dennis shouted, shocking her by banging his fist on the table.

She leaped at the unexpected noise. "What's gotten into you?"

"Calla. You. Everything. I've stood silently by, put up with her bad moods and insults for years. I'm not having a teenager talk to me like I'm scum, nor will I allow her to insult my wife."

"She's my daughter—"

"I'm your husband."

"Don't you see—"

"All I see," Dennis said, rising to his feet, "is the two

of us walking on eggshells in an effort to appease her. I'm fed up with it, fed up with watching what she does to you—the way you feel whenever she rejects you."

"I was the one who lied to her... I should have told her..."

"You were protecting her just like you are now. She doesn't need your protection anymore. Furthermore, she doesn't want it. She was seventeen last month and it's time she grew up. Time she accepted responsibility for her own life instead of blaming everyone else."

"But—"

"You're allowing the guilt you feel about your first marriage to affect our lives. I won't stand for it any longer."

Trembling, Sarah sank into the chair. "I can't believe you're saying these things. Don't you realize... Don't you understand?"

"I understand that you've placed me in an impossible position. If Calla can't treat me with the respect due another human being, then she's no longer welcome in my home."

"This is my home, too."

Dennis sadly shook his head. "I've told you the way I feel. How you respond is up to you, but if Calla's ever here when I come home, I guess that'll be my answer, won't it?"

"She's my *daughter*..." Sarah didn't know why it was so important to keep reminding him of that, especially when the girl had chosen to live elsewhere. Calla had repeatedly turned her back on Sarah. The situation just never seemed to get better, despite all her efforts, and now it was creating tension in her marriage.

Dennis reached for his beer, raised it to his lips, then

put it down. "I need to think," he said. "I'm going out for a while."

"You're leaving?"

He was already halfway out the door. "Yeah," he said, "I'm leaving."

Sarah watched him go, then buried her face in her hands. The entire conversation had gone badly. She'd been angry and frustrated and she'd taken everything out on Dennis.

Sarah felt sick again, both emotionally and physically. She was trapped between the two people she loved most in this world. Calla had been rude and spiteful to Dennis all along, going out of her way to cause problems.

If that was her goal, then she'd succeeded.

Sarah acknowledged that her daughter had inflicted numerous cruelties on Dennis and that Dennis had never let her goad him into overt anger. Maybe it *was* time for some decisive action. Maybe Sarah had to stand up for her husband and say no to Calla.

Dennis didn't return for dinner. Because of the baby, Sarah forced herself to eat, but she could only stomach a few small bites. At ten, she turned out the lights and went to bed. After years of sleeping alone, she was surprised to discover that a bed could feel so empty.

Sleep was impossible. Shortly after midnight, when she heard the front door open and the floor creak, she tossed aside the covers and hurried into the dark living room.

"Dennis?"

"I'm here." He switched on a table lamp, casting the room in a muted glow.

She flew into his arms, hugging him. "I'm so sorry," she wept, "so sorry."

He nuzzled her neck, his hands in her hair. "I'm sorry, too. I'll try to be more patient with Calla." He breathed the words, as though it'd taken great effort to speak them.

"No you're right. We can't let Calla behave this way. I won't let her come between us."

Dennis held her face tenderly between his hands and kissed her. "I love you, Sarah Urlacher."

"I love you, too," she said, and slid her arm around his waist. She led him toward the bedroom, knowing she'd be able to sleep now that she'd made peace with her husband.

"I'm supposed to do *what*?" Jeb demanded of Maddy as they drove into Buffalo Valley.

"We're having a meeting about the town park," Maddy reminded him patiently, although he was well aware of the purpose of this venture into town. "I told you about it last week, remember?" And the week before, as well. She'd quickly learned that her husband conveniently forgot things when it suited his purpose.

Jeb glanced at her and sighed expressively. "You know how I feel about meetings."

"Yes, I do," she said, and slipped her arm through his. Leaning her head against his shoulder, she reflected that his being part of this committee was no small thing. He'd agreed when she'd first mentioned it. Only later did he start muttering, and Maddy had the feeling it was mostly for show. Gage and Lindsay were also on the committee, along with Rachel and Heath Quantrill, and Joanie and Brandon Wyatt.

The weather was lovely and Maddy was convinced that, with a minimum of effort, they'd be able to get a group of volunteers together right away. She and Rachel Quantrill were spearheading the project. Everyone seemed to be waiting for someone else to do it. Maddy understood; people were busy with their own lives. Well, she, for one, was determined to see this park become a reality.

"I wouldn't do this for anyone in the world but you," Jeb muttered, his voice gruff.

"I know, honey, and I appreciate it."

"Is Dennis going to be there?"

Maddy shook her head. "Not that I know of."

"How come he gets out of this and I don't?"

"Would you kindly stop your complaining? If all goes well, by the end of the summer, we should have a real park."

He muttered something else, but she noticed he didn't complain again as they continued the hour-long drive into town.

Lindsay and Gage were the only people already at the vacant lot when they arrived. Gage was carrying his daughter, Joy, and Julianne automatically went into Jeb's arms when he removed her from the car seat. Not long from now, the girls would both be walking. It seemed impossible to Maddy that just a year ago she'd been pregnant. So many wonderful changes had come into her life since the move to Buffalo Valley.

Lindsay and Maddy immediately started chatting. Now that they were both married, they didn't have nearly as much time as they would have liked to maintain their friendship. They found themselves depending on phone calls and even email; at least they could stay caught up on news.

Gage and Jeb had their heads together, too.

"Hmm. There's a sight you don't see every day," Hassie commented as she approached the small group.

"What?" Lindsay asked.

"Two men, holding their baby daughters on their hips. I gotta tell you, it does my old heart good to see those two married and settled down."

Maddy and Lindsay glanced at each other and shared a smile.

"Is everyone prepared to work hard to make this park happen?" Hassie asked loudly. "It isn't going to come together by itself, you know."

"Maddy," Jeb called.

She walked over to him and he handed her Julianne. "Gage says he can get the tractor out here to churn up the land and get the grass planted."

"You'd be willing to do that?"

Lindsay stepped next to her and elbowed Maddy's side. "Don't look a gift tractor in the mouth. He volunteered, didn't he?"

"I can set aside some time next week," Gage told her.

"Wonderful." Maddy beamed at him.

"Harvey Hendrickson from the hardware store volunteered wood for a couple of picnic tables," Hassie added.

"I could build those," Jeb chimed in.

Joanie and Brandon Wyatt arrived, followed by the Quantrills, and Maddy updated them on what had been discussed.

"We need playground equipment," Hassie said next. "If families are going to come here for a picnic, they'll want something to keep the youngsters entertained."

"It wouldn't take much to put up a few swings." Maddy looked around. "Swings would be nice."

Heath and Rachel nodded.

"One of those big timber play sets would be good, don't you think?" Rachel asked.

Maddy liked the idea, but knew they were expensive. She mentioned the price listed in a brochure she'd read and watched the enthusiasm of her committee wane.

"And that doesn't include assembly," Lindsay said.

Brandon Wyatt cleared his throat. "I never thought of myself as much of a woodworker, but I did a fairly decent job constructing the display shelves for the video store."

"You did a fabulous job," Rachel insisted.

Maddy had admired his workmanship, too, and said so.

Brandon flushed at their praise. "Well, if the town could come up with money for the materials, I could build a jungle gym for the park."

"Consider it done," Heath said. "You order whatever you need and send me the bill."

It was all Maddy could do to keep from clapping her hands. Then she noticed Hassie, who seemed to have something else to say.

"Hassie?"

"Listen," she began, "I know I'm older and I won't have grandchildren living here to enjoy the park once it's completed."

"That doesn't matter," Maddy assured her. "If you have a suggestion, we'd like to hear it."

A number of people nodded in agreement.

"Everyone here knows I lost my son in Vietnam. I'm not the only mother to lose a son in war. I want this town to remember that there were a number of fine young men from right here in Buffalo Valley who died for their country and the freedom we enjoy." She paused, and Maddy could tell by the way her throat worked that she was swallowing the tears brought on by painful memories of her only son's death.

"Would you like a memorial built to honor those who died in war?" Maddy asked, taking Hassie's hand and squeezing her fingers, letting her know she understood. "The First and Second World Wars, Korea, Vietnam?"

Hassie returned the squeeze, then reached inside her sweater pocket for a handkerchief and blew her nose. "That would please me very much. Now, I know a memorial's going to cost a lot of money, but I'm prepared to pay for it myself. I've got a few dollars set aside and I can't think of any better use for it."

"If you'd like a sculpture, what about having Kevin work up a few designs?" Gage asked. "He'd be honored if you asked him to submit a drawing for this memorial."

Hassie nodded. "Kevin would be my first choice."

Maddy and Lindsay smiled at each other again. It'd been Lindsay who'd encouraged Kevin Betts to pursue his love of art, and now his artistic skills would serve the town. There was something very satisfying in that.

Matt sat at the kitchen table and watched Sadie as she fussed about the kitchen. Strangely enough, the housekeeper had turned into the best ally he had. Although she didn't actually give him information about Margaret, she was kind enough to drop hints now and then. If it wasn't for Sadie, he wouldn't have any idea what his wife was thinking.

This latest tidbit, however, worried him.

"You want a refill on that coffee?" the housekeeper asked, nodding toward the ever-ready pot.

"Sure." Although he'd already drunk two cups, he didn't want to leave, and the coffee provided him with a convenient excuse to linger. Although God knew if

Margaret caught him inside the house, there'd be hell to pay.

"She's not suffering from morning sickness, is she?" he asked for at least the third time. Sadie had already told him that Margaret didn't appear to be experiencing any discomfort as a result of the pregnancy.

"She's in good health—physically," Sadie told him and then scowled in his direction, letting him know that her *emotional* health was a different matter. As if he wasn't already aware of how much his wife was hurting. Dammit, he was hurting, too.

"You don't know why she drove into Grand Forks, then?" This was as bold as his questions had gotten. Right after breakfast, Margaret had left without a word. Sadie had told him it wasn't a doctor's appointment; those were marked on the office calendar. When Margaret hadn't returned by lunchtime, Matt figured something was up.

Sadie finished pouring his coffee. "I have my suspicions about where she went."

Matt did, too, and it bothered him plenty. Banished to the empty bunkhouse with nothing more than a radio to keep him occupied, Matt was left to his own devices once work was through for the day. Most nights he lay on his bed, staring up at the ceiling. He worried about Sheryl and Margaret and their babies, about his marriage and whether he had any chance of saving it.

Pastor Dawson had told him to fight for Margaret, and Matt had taken the advice to heart. If his wife assumed he was going to roll over and play dead, then she didn't know him nearly as well as she thought.

"You're *sure* she didn't have a doctor's appointment?" he asked again.

"Positive."

Matt's stomach churned. His biggest fear loomed before him. "She's seeing an attorney, isn't she?"

Sadie returned to the sink, where she peeled potatoes with the skill of many years. The brown skins curled away from the sharp blade in a perfect spiral, falling toward the sink. "I can't rightly say if she's with an attorney or not."

"But you said you have your suspicions."

"I do."

The sick feeling was back in the pit of his stomach.

The sound of a car door closing echoed through the kitchen. Margaret must be home.

Sadie and Matt exchanged looks. For an instant he toyed with the idea of sneaking out the laundry-room door, but just as quickly, he rejected the thought.

"Let me talk to her for a few minutes," Matt suggested.

"You telling me to leave this kitchen?" Sadie asked, fire flashing from her dark eyes.

"No," he said quickly. "I'm asking you to give me a few minutes alone with my wife."

Sadie hesitated, then dropped the potato in a pan of cold water. She dried her hands on her apron and walked out of the room. No sooner had she disappeared than Margaret entered the house.

Seeing Matt, she went rigid, eyes narrowed. "What are *you* doing here?" she spat.

"I want to talk to you."

She ignored him and rushed into the long hallway. Not easily dissuaded, Matt followed. Margaret headed for the bedroom and would have slammed the door if he hadn't stopped her by planting his foot in the way. They met face-to-face, their eyes blazing.

"I have nothing to say to you."

"Hear me out. Then if you want me to leave, I will."

She folded her arms and pretended to be bored. "Did Sadie let you in?"

"No."

"Liar."

"I let myself in, so don't blame Sadie."

Frowning, she pinched her lips together. "Say what you have to say."

"All right." He'd known this wouldn't be easy. Running his hand across the back of his neck, he decided to make his first volley an aggressive one. "I need to know where you were this afternoon. Because if you were seeing an attorney, there's something you have to understand."

"Where I was and who I saw are *my* business."

"Not anymore."

"Like hell, Matt Eilers! I don't owe you any explanations. I don't owe you anything."

"This isn't a matter of owing anyone. Fine, don't tell me and I'll just go ahead and speak my piece." After a deliberate pause, he said, "If you saw an attorney with the intention of filing for divorce, then you should know I plan to fight you every step of the way."

She glared at him, as if to say she welcomed the challenge.

"I admit the situation is unfortunate. You regret our marriage. I can appreciate that. But you were the one who chose to marry me and by God, we're going to stay married."

She blinked and looked away.

"I've got regrets, too," he continued. "A whole truckload of those. Unfortunately, there's not one damn thing I can do to change the circumstances now."

His words fell into the silent room. Matt wasn't sure

what he'd expected, but not this…this utter lack of emotion. It was as though she'd completely closed him out.

"Are you finished?" she asked curtly.

"No," he surprised himself by saying. "You're my wife, dammit, and it's high time you started acting like it." He could tell his words had hit their mark when the fire leaped back into her eyes.

If looks could kill, there'd be a funeral in Buffalo Valley that night. "I beat the hell out of you once, Matt Eilers, and I have no compunction about doing it twice."

He nearly laughed out loud, which would have been a big mistake. "If it'll make you feel better, then you're welcome to try." She'd caught him off guard before, but she wouldn't again.

Instantly she pulled back her clenched fist, and swung at him, but Matt caught her fist with his open hand. Despite her outrage and anger, her struggle was futile.

"Did you have an appointment with an attorney?" he demanded.

"Yes," she hissed back.

The admission so deflated and discouraged him, he released her hand and slumped against the bedroom door.

She could have slugged him then and he wouldn't have cared. He sincerely doubted he would've felt anything beyond the numbness that had taken hold of his heart. She wanted a divorce.

Breathing hard, Margaret stood in front of him. "I didn't originally contact him about filing for divorce," she said after a long pause.

Puzzled, he chanced looking up. Her hands were braced against her hips, but the defensive stance was gone, replaced with a more guarded one.

She surprised him by suddenly moving into the room,

sitting on the end of the bed, her back toward him. "I did talk to an attorney. Divorce was one of the options he presented."

Matt swallowed hard. "That isn't what I want, Margaret."

She snickered softly. "At this point, I'm not overly concerned with your wishes."

He suspected that was true.

"I needed to know what my legal rights are in regard to Sheryl and her...baby."

"I talked to an attorney, too."

"I knew that," she said, sounding matter-of-fact. "But I wasn't interested in talking to the same attorney you had."

Rather than question her reasoning, he asked, "What did your attorney say?"

"Nothing that I didn't already know. We're financially and emotionally responsible for your...daughter. It'll mean you and Sheryl will have to develop a parenting plan. The child will be spending time here, vacations, holidays—for at least the next eighteen years. She'll be part of our lives."

"She's my responsibility, I'll—"

"Get real," Margaret snapped. "If we're married, she'll be in this house, eating, sleeping, calling you daddy right along with our child. She's going to need your love—and mine."

As Margaret had just reminded him, he wasn't the only one involved in this. The child would be a constant reminder of his faults, of the pain he'd caused his wife. More than that, he was asking her to love his daughter. No wonder Margaret was feeling overwhelmed. So far, all he'd sought was her forgiveness, her acceptance. That had been paramount in his mind. Everything else—the ramifications of fatherhood and of Margaret being his child's stepmother—had escaped him.

"You're right."

She didn't respond. Her back was to him so he couldn't see her face, couldn't read her thoughts or gauge her feelings.

"Do you want out of the marriage?" he asked bluntly.

"I don't know yet."

"I said I'd fight for you, fight for our marriage, and I meant it." He exhaled sharply. "But if you really want out, then I'll abide by your wishes."

He stood and started to walk away.

"Why the change of heart?" She seemed genuinely curious.

"It's asking too much of you... I wanted, needed, your forgiveness, but this goes beyond that. Way beyond..."

"Yes," she whispered brokenly, "it does."

With nothing more to say, Matt left the bedroom. Sadie was back at the sink peeling potatoes when he walked through the kitchen.

She glanced at him and then did a double take. "What happened?"

He shook his head, unable to answer.

"That bad?"

"That bad," he echoed.

Fifteen

Buffalo Bob replaced the telephone receiver, but continued to grip the phone. He needed to hold on to something. Anything.

Pain, followed by escalating anger, charged through him. He felt breathless, as though he'd been kicked in the gut. Not knowing what to do, he sank into the chair and waited for the shock to pass. He had to be in control of his own emotions before he could deal with Merrily's.

"Bob, I—" Merrily came into the office and stopped short when she saw the look on his face. In that instant she must have known. "What is it?" she asked, her voice small and fragile.

For the life of him, he couldn't answer her. Not yet.

"Bob?" she cried.

"That...that was Doug Alder," he whispered hoarsely.

"He heard about the adoption?"

Bob nodded and slowly got to his feet. "Sit down, sweetheart."

"Sit down? Does that mean you have something to tell me I don't want to hear? Is that what you're trying to say?" She clutched her stomach and lowered herself into the wooden chair. Her arms still clutched her middle as she stared up at him. Her eyes, her big beautiful eyes, were wide with fear.

"We knew when we applied to adopt Axel—"

"Just tell me!" she shouted, tears already brimming, ready to spill down her pale cheeks.

Bob felt like sobbing himself. "The judge decided on another couple as the adoptive parents for Axel. Two doctors who've been waiting five years to adopt a child. They're…good people."

"And we're not?" she sobbed. Leaning forward she started to rock gently.

"Neither one of them has been arrested on drug charges," he muttered, repeating what their attorney had told him. Bob had hoped and believed and trusted that he'd done the honorable thing when he contacted the authorities about Axel. He'd known the risks, but he'd been willing to take them because he'd truly thought that in time Axel would be returned to him and Merrily. They were his parents. The only family he knew. They loved the boy.

His wife was sobbing now. She covered her face with both hands and continued to rock with grief. Had he been able to, Bob would have reached out and comforted her, but his own pain was too great. He had nothing to give her, nothing to help her through this.

"It's all my fault," he whispered.

"Why did this happen?" Merrily wailed. "Why?" she demanded again when he didn't answer.

"We each have a police record."

"That was years ago—it shouldn't matter anymore. Is the court honestly going to hold a five-year-old drug arrest against me for the rest of my life?"

"There's more… Doug said we displayed a less than ideal home environment." He shook his head hopelessly.

"Less than ideal what?" Her voice echoed the outrage he'd felt when he'd first heard the words. "Did they say I wasn't a good enough mother? Is that it? That I didn't love Axel enough? Because I couldn't have loved him any more than I already do right now. Bob, Bob, what am I going to do without my baby?"

Bob had no answers or reassurances, as desperate as Merrily was to hear them. Apparently, the judge didn't feel that living above a bar was the proper environment for a child. Or that Bob had potential as a father. Or Merrily as a mother, despite her love, despite the fact that she'd saved Axel's life.

He shook his head again, unable and unwilling to repeat what was sure to bring her more pain. "We both loved him enough…"

"Then why?" Her sobs made the words almost indistinguishable.

Bob wished it was possible for him to cry, to vent his own bitterness and sense of loss. Instead he shoved all the emotion deep inside.

"Blame me," he told her.

Merrily stared at him, her face streaked with tears, her eyes imploring him to untangle the court's message. "You?"

"Remember how the caseworker examined the new plaster on the wall?" he asked. He didn't wait for Merrily to respond. "She asked me about it, and I made up some excuse."

"You lied?"

"Yes, dammit, I lied. I couldn't very well admit that I rammed my fist through the wall, could I? Only it didn't do any good. If anything, it hurt us. These people are trained observers, and she put two and two together fast enough, especially since I'd recently been in a cast and she saw that, too."

"Oh, Bob."

"In her report, she concluded that I'm susceptible to fits of anger."

Merrily gasped. "The only reason you punched the wall was because I'd run away."

"It doesn't matter why I did it." He couldn't, wouldn't tell Merrily what else the report said. No need to rub salt into her wounds. In making his decision, the judge had also cited Merrily's tendency to run away when confronted with problems.

"What are we going to do?" She sobbed. But he had nothing to suggest. He'd never felt so inadequate.

"The attorney said the judge told him the decision was a difficult one." As though that was supposed to make them feel better. It didn't. Nothing would.

Without another word, Merrily stood, and he watched as she wandered blindly out of his office, then drifted upstairs. He watched her mount the stairs, one by one, her steps slow and uncertain. She headed toward their living quarters and didn't look back.

Unable to deal with customers, Bob closed the bar and restaurant for the day and sealed himself inside his office. He sat dazed with shock and pain, unable to do more than stare at the wall. He didn't know how long he remained there before the sound of someone knocking invaded his grief.

Reluctantly he went to check, and discovered Hassie standing outside the locked door, peering through the window.

"Let me in," she demanded.

"I'm closed."

"Well, open up. Folks are worried about you."

Bob frowned. How could people already know—
then again, maybe they didn't. With no enthusiasm, he
turned the lock and stepped away from the door.

Hassie didn't wait for an invitation. She hurried inside and closed up after herself. "This is about Axel,
isn't it?"

Bob nodded, unable to meet her gaze. Eventually the
town would discover the truth. He and Merrily couldn't
hide the fact that their son, the boy they loved, had been
given to a different family.

"The judge awarded him to another couple," Bob
said, figuring that was explanation enough.

A look of sadness came over her, and she gave a
deep sigh. "No wonder you've closed up shop. Where's
Merrily?"

"Upstairs."

"Come on," Hassie said, and led him into the kitchen
as if she were steering a child. "I remember what it was
like when those two young men from the Army came
to tell me my son was dead. I couldn't think, couldn't
eat, could barely function for days. Now listen, you sit
down here and I'm going to make us all a pot of tea."

"Tea?"

"I know it sounds ridiculous. You lost your son and
I'm boiling water, but it will help. Trust me on this,
there are few things more soothing to the spirit than
a cup of tea."

As soon as the kettle whistled, she had the tea leaves
steeping. "Stay here, I'm going to check on Merrily."

Grateful, he nodded. He hadn't meant to abandon his
wife, but he couldn't help her, not when he was hurting
so badly himself. His heart actually ached. The lump in
his throat was so large, he found it difficult to swallow
or breathe normally. The telephone conversation had

hit him hard. Until that moment, he'd been living with expectation, with the hope and promise of joy. It felt as though a bomb had gone off, devastating their lives.

Reality was slowly sinking in. Axel would now look to another man and call him daddy. The boy Bob loved, who'd found his way into Bob's heart, would belong to some other man, a stranger who had more to offer him than Bob did. A physician, a wealthy man who could give Axel material goods. Perhaps so, but no one—*no one*—would love Axel more than Bob and Merrily did. It wasn't possible. They'd risked everything for the boy; surely that must prove something. Surely the courts had taken into account the courage it'd required to step forward, to risk losing their son.

The gamble, the giant gamble, hadn't paid off.

It was a long time before Hassie came downstairs. Her eyes were red, and Bob knew she'd sat and wept with Merrily. Their friend had held and comforted Merrily when Bob couldn't.

Silently, she poured him a cup of tea. "There isn't any pain in this world worse than losing a child. I know this situation is different from mine. You aren't going to stand there and watch Axel being lowered into the ground, the way I did my boy. But the pain is the same."

"He might as well be dead. He's dead to Merrily and me."

"True enough. You had him for a short while and changed his life. You have a great deal to be proud of. You and Merrily gave that boy the love he desperately needed."

"Merrily—is she all right?"

"No," Hassie said as she set the steaming tea in front of him. "She needs you, but she won't ask."

He suspected his wife was waiting for a convenient

moment to disappear. Come morning, he fully expected to wake and find her gone.

Bob sipped the sweetened tea. It was too hot and burned his throat, but he didn't care. He tried not to think, tried to put Axel out of his mind. And couldn't.

It wasn't supposed to happen like this. By all that was right, they should be Axel's adoptive parents. Instead he was financially crippled by attorneys' fees, his heart was damn near ripped from his chest and his wife was upstairs sobbing. But how could he give her peace when he hadn't found any himself?

"What am I going to do now?" he asked Hassie. She'd lived through this; she would know. "What happens next?"

"Pain, lots of pain, but eventually you and Merrily are going to release your son," she said.

"Release him?" This was a sick joke. They'd lost Axel five months ago, only they hadn't realized it until this morning. The boy would never be theirs again.

"Not from your heart," Hassie was quick to amend. "That would be impossible. Never from your heart."

Early Friday afternoon Maddy was at the grocery. She generally came in once a week to check on her store, although most of the everyday management was handled by Pete Mitchell.

This arrangement worked well with Jeb and Julianne, too, and gave her husband one afternoon a week to spend with their daughter. Jeb had proved to be a wonderful father. Maddy delighted in watching her husband with Julianne and the tenderness that suffused his face as he rocked her to sleep.

Maddy was just finishing up some paperwork in the small cramped office when she heard Margaret. Her loud voice carried all the way to the back of the store. "I'm here to see Maddy," Margaret insisted gruffly.

On their most recent visit, Margaret had broken into tears and told Maddy about her husband fathering a child with Sheryl Decker. It'd nearly broken Maddy's heart to hear such pain. When she'd finished telling her story, Margaret had asked for advice. Sadly, Maddy didn't know what to tell her. She was disappointed in Matt, but the fact that he'd fathered a child didn't distress her nearly as much as the heartache he'd caused her friend.

"Margaret?" Maddy came out of the room, not knowing what to expect. She discovered her friend barreling down the produce aisle with all the grace of a lumberjack on his way to the mess hall.

"Maddy," Margaret cried, "I've been looking all over for you!"

"Didn't Jeb tell you where I was?"

"He did, but I thought you'd be home and—" She paused, dragged in a deep breath. "I need to talk… Can you spare me a few minutes?"

"Of course." Maddy stepped aside to allow Margaret into the compact quarters.

She fell into the chair, looking pale and about as forlorn as Maddy could remember. Maddy sat down, too, and waited, certain Margaret would tear into her reason for coming. When she didn't, Maddy decided to prompt her.

"Did something happen?" she asked, deciding to take the direct approach.

Margaret put on a brave smile. "I… Matt moved out this morning."

Maddy was sure she'd misunderstood. "Moved out?"

Margaret nodded. She blinked a few times and Maddy

knew she was struggling not to break into tears. "I didn't know who else to turn to for help," she blurted out.

"I, uh, take it this came as a shock?" Maddy didn't know what else to say.

Margaret shook her head, then nodded just as emphatically. "I didn't ask him to leave, if that's what you're thinking." She hesitated, and as though embarrassed to admit it, she said, "But it was what I wanted, and I made sure he knew it." She bit her lower lip. "He said he was going to fight for me, for our marriage, but apparently he didn't mean that any more than the other things he claimed."

"You wanted him out of your life, right?"

Margaret swayed, and Maddy felt a moment's alarm, especially considering the pregnancy. But Margaret rallied and took a deep breath. "Some days I wanted us to patch up our differences," she said, "and then I'd start thinking about him with that woman and I'd get so damn mad I wanted to scratch his eyes out." She shook her head wildly, as though to dislodge the mental image of her husband with Sheryl Decker.

"Did something trigger this?" Maddy asked, hoping to shed light on the current situation. "The fact that he left, I mean?"

Margaret looked down and nodded. "I saw an attorney."

"You did?"

"I wanted to know my rights. Not Matt's. Mine."

"Okay, I understand."

"Matt and I talked afterward and…and it didn't go well, but then nothing has since that paternity suit. You notice Sheryl Decker included me in that lawsuit? She wants everything she can get from me… Maddy, if you'd read her demands, why, it'd make you sick to your stomach. That woman plans to use her baby like a...like a weapon against Matt and me."

The picture was beginning to take shape in Maddy's mind.

"You know who's caught in the middle of this, don't you?" Margaret continued. "Matt's daughter. The situation's horrible."

"Oh, Margaret."

"And now he's gone. He did it for me," she whispered. "He left to spare me any more grief."

Maddy sensed that in talking it out, Margaret had been able to gain control of her feelings, and perhaps a measure of understanding.

"A divorce isn't what you want, is it?" she asked quietly.

"No." Margaret stood, her back straight, her shoulders square.

Maddy got to her feet, as well. "You love Matt, don't you?"

Margaret didn't so much as hesitate. "With all my heart." Then as if it was all more than she could handle, she slumped back in the chair.

"I remember when you first told me about loving Matt Eilers," Maddy reminded her, hoping the memory would somehow help her friend—bring her comfort and resolve. "Frankly, I took your declaration with a grain of salt. I assumed your feelings were basically a schoolgirl crush." Maddy sat down again so they could meet eye to eye. "Then you said something I won't forget. You told me you knew Matt was no saint, but you loved him, faults and all."

The merest hint of a smile touched Margaret's mouth as Maddy repeated those fateful words.

"I don't like what's happened—with Sheryl and her

baby. I'm not sure I can accept there being another child in our lives."

Maddy's heart went out to her. The situation was painful and difficult.

"But I want to save this marriage," Margaret said forcefully. "My baby's going to need his father and... I need Matt, too."

Maddy knew it wasn't easy for Margaret to admit needing anyone or anything. Emotionally, Margaret Eilers was one of the strongest, most self-sufficient women Maddy had ever known. "So what are you going to do about it?" she asked.

Margaret's shoulders sagged. "I don't know where he moved—where he is. Oh, Maddy, all I want is for this pain to go away." She stopped and swallowed hard. "When I realized he'd left...I felt this burst of relief... and then almost immediately this horrible emptiness. Nothing means anything to me without my husband."

Confused and anxious—and pregnant. Margaret had every right to feel unsettled.

Joshua McKenna didn't have much confidence in his skills as a father. Both his children had grown up to be decent, hardworking adults, but he accepted none of the credit for that. Marjorie had seen to the rearing of Sarah and Jeb, and he'd done little more than pay the bills.

Sarah had been a rebellious teenager, just like Calla was these days. History seemed to repeat itself. Marjorie had sat up many a night worrying about her failings as a mother, the same way Sarah fretted over how she'd failed Calla.

Jeb had always been an intelligent child—and much easier on his parents than his sister had been. Even before the accident that cost him his leg, he'd been an intense, quiet man. Joshua had watched with amusement the changes in his son since he'd married Maddy. She was everything Joshua had hoped Jeb would have in a wife. If only Marjorie had lived long enough to see their son this happy.

After nearly twelve years, Joshua still missed his wife. He realized he hadn't appreciated her nearly as much as he should have. A sad but all-too-typical commentary on marriage, he supposed.

He poured himself a cup of coffee and then sat in the recliner in front of the television, hardly thinking about dinner or what he'd eat. Probably something from the freezer. Sarah had lived with him for so many years that he'd grown accustomed to having someone else cook. He'd hoped Calla would see to his meals the way her mother had, but the girl was rarely home. If she ate, it was generally with friends.

Last Christmas when Calla asked if she could live with him, Joshua had welcomed the prospect. The house felt downright empty after Sarah had married Dennis and they moved into a place of their own. So he'd invited his granddaughter to move in. Calla needed a home and he needed the company.

These days Joshua wasn't so sure it was a good idea. According to Jeb, Dennis and Calla had exchanged words not long ago. Sarah had been upset about it. Joshua couldn't exactly miss the fact that something was seriously awry. Calla hadn't been herself for days but, like him, she kept her troubles to herself.

Joshua wasn't one to intrude; for that matter he seldom even offered advice. He wouldn't say anything now, except that he felt it was necessary. Someone had to step in, and since Calla lived with him, he was the only real choice.

The back door banged and Calla walked into the house. "Evening, Grandpa."

"Calla." He set his coffee aside. "Do you have a minute?"

"Ah…sure." She came into the living room, and Joshua reached for the remote control and turned off the television.

"Sit down," he ordered.

Calla complied and sat on the edge of the sofa, obviously eager for this to be over so she could make her escape.

"How long have you been living with me now?" he asked.

She shrugged. "Practically ever since I can remember."

"That's right. I've seen you grow into a beautiful young woman."

"Grandpa!"

His praise flustered her and she seemed ill-at-ease with it, but he ignored that.

"I've stood by and watched what's happened between you and your mother for a lot of years. For the most part, I've stayed out of it, but I'm beginning to believe that was a mistake."

Her face was now devoid of emotion. "If you don't mind, I'd rather not discuss my mother."

"I do mind," he countered flatly. "In fact, I mind quite a bit."

She folded her arms, signaling her resistance. Joshua didn't care; he fully intended to speak his piece whether she wanted to hear it or not. How she responded was entirely up to her.

"Even though you rarely heard from your father, you placed him on a pedestal. Your mother didn't say or do anything to enlighten you. Wisely, she understood that you loved Willie and needed your father—or an image of your father. But, in my opinion, she did more than shield you from the truth. She shielded you from the world."

"She shielded me from nothing!"

"That was because you chose to run away. Of your own free will, you went to live with Willie. How long did it take to have your eyes opened?" he asked.

Calla glanced toward the ceiling, but didn't answer.

"My guess is you got the message the first week you were with him. You ran away from him, too, remember? Still, it took you a total of six months to own up to the truth, to swallow your pride and move back to Buffalo Valley."

Her shoulders rose and fell with a deep sigh. "Is there a point to this conversation?" she asked.

"Oh, yes, there's a very big point."

"Good, because it's exceedingly boring."

Joshua pretended he hadn't heard that. "From what I understand, you and Dennis recently had an argument."

"He's got a big mouth."

"Dennis Urlacher?" Her comment was enough to make Joshua choke back a laugh. "I've never heard that description of Dennis before."

"Whatever."

"Whatever?" he repeated. It was a word that seemed to punctuate his granddaughter's conversation. An all-purpose response.

When she didn't speak again, he said, "I heard that Dennis stood up to you and demanded to be treated with respect."

"He's a jerk."

"The hell he is," Joshua said, unwilling to mince

words. "You're the one who's been unreasonable. At every opportunity, you've mocked and ridiculed your mother."

"It's what she deserves after—"

"Your mother *deserves* your respect," he shouted. He could tell by the way she went wide-eyed that his booming voice had shocked her. Good, the girl needed a shock.

"Your mother has done nothing but love you. She's loved you so much she's overprotected you," he continued. "When I heard about your little fight with Dennis, I wanted to stand up and applaud him for having the courage to challenge your rude behavior."

Calla's lips were tightly pinched, but she said nothing.

"Good for Dennis," he said again. "Hell, I wish I'd had the courage to do it myself. You needed to be brought down a couple of pegs. It was time. Furthermore, I sincerely hope you listened."

"Grandpa, I know you mean well, but—"

"No, you don't," he muttered. "You think I don't know how anxious you are to get out of here. I expect when I'm finished, you'll leap out of that chair like a prize-winning bullfrog and make a dash for the door."

Calla merely shook back her hair, then examined her nails, painted a sparkling silver.

"I don't care if you do make a fast escape, that's up to you, but young lady, I advise you to hear me out."

Glancing at her watch, she asked. "Is this going to take much longer?"

"It'll take as long as it takes."

She sighed and fell back against the sofa cushion.

"When was the last time you saw your mother?" he asked.

"A couple of weeks ago. I see her a lot," she added defiantly.

"Visit with her, do you?"

"I have. It isn't like I ignore her."

Joshua knew Calla had sometimes visited her mother after school, but that'd happened mostly when Sarah was bedridden.

"You owe your mother respect—and you owe her more than that. You think she did you so wrong, but have you ever stopped to consider all the sacrifices she made for you? I doubt it. Did you ever once stop to consider how much she loves you and how hard she's worked to make you happy, often at the price of her own happiness?"

The bored, martyred look was back.

Joshua gripped both sides of his chair and then slowly leaned forward. "Calla Stern, listen to me. *Grow up.*" The last two words were nearly shouted. "You're seventeen, and it's well past time you appreciated your family."

She blinked, looking stunned.

"If you want to inflict your moodiness on your mother, then my advice is to stay away."

"Fine. No problem."

"If you can't treat Dennis and your mother with respect, then you and I need to have a serious discussion."

"About what?"

"Your living arrangements here," he said. "Either I see a dramatic change in your behavior or I'm going to have to ask you to pack up and leave my home."

Calla didn't say anything for several moments. "Are you telling me you want me to move out? I—I won't graduate from high school until next month."

"I didn't say you were being forced to move," he

clarified. "What I said was that if you continue to behave like an unreasonable and immature brat, perhaps you should look elsewhere for housing."

Calla stared at him as though she had trouble taking in the words. "You don't mean that."

"Trust me, Calla, I do. Shape up or ship out."

Sixteen

It'd been a week since Bob and Merrily had heard from the attorney. Every morning, Bob expected to find an empty space next to him in bed. Most days he woke before the clock radio went off. His first thought was of Merrily, wondering if she'd slipped away as she had so many times in the past.

The alarm sounded, and although he knew his wife was already awake, he gently patted her backside, and got out of bed. Some mornings it was all he could do not to ask if she intended to leave. Knowing was better than this damnable waiting. Somehow he couldn't do it, though.

They barely spoke these days. Bob buried his grief in work—cooking, cleaning, tending bar, remodeling and repairs. Only on rare occasions did he rent the hotel rooms, but with the approach of summer, this seemed a good time to spruce them up. He was repainting the rooms that needed it and freshening those that didn't.

Merrily, on the other hand, sank deeper and deeper into a pit of despair. Most every day now, she sat in front of the television, numbing her mind with soap operas and game shows. At night, she went into Axel's old room and sat on his bed, weeping silently. Bob tried to help her, but nothing he said seemed to penetrate the wall of pain.

Wednesday afternoon, Pastor Dawson stopped by. It wasn't his first visit since they'd received the news from California, but it was the first time Merrily had been downstairs.

"I thought I'd come over to—"

He'd barely started to speak when Merrily flew across the room with more energy than Bob had seen from her in days. "Get out!" she roared.

The minister stared, apparently too stunned to react.

"Merrily!" Bob had never seen her behave like this.

"It's all your fault! We'd have Axel now if it wasn't for you."

If Bob was shocked by this unexpected show of life, it didn't compare to his horror when she raised her fists and actually attacked the minister, pounding his chest as hard as she could. Acting quickly, Bob wrapped his arms around her waist and pulled her away. She started to sob then, a heart-wrenching wail that came from deep inside her. The kind of sobs that relate an unspeakable agony. Bob turned her in his arms and held her, his own throat growing thick. Closing his eyes, he battled down his pain and dismay as he attempted to comfort his wife.

Merrily clung to him, hiding her face in his shoulder.

Pastor Dawson stood close by, his eyes filled with pity and understanding. "Is there anything I can do?" he asked.

Bob shook his head sadly. There was nothing anyone could do. Merrily's outburst had come suddenly and without provocation. Bob didn't know what to think. They'd both been dealing with their disappointment in different ways; his method was to immerse himself in work, hers to drown in lethargy and tears. He would never have anticipated this type of reaction from her. It left him completely baffled.

He led Merrily to their bedroom and was grateful to find the minister waiting when he returned downstairs.

"Obviously Merrily blames me for what happened."

Bob shifted uncomfortably. "She assumes you threatened to turn us in to the authorities. I let her think that because I knew she'd never agree to contact them voluntarily."

Larry Dawson reached out and gripped Bob's forearm. "We talked about that earlier. It's not a problem. You did what you had to." He paused. "You had a difficult choice to make and I believe you did the right thing."

"*Would* you have turned us in?" Bob demanded.

"Thankfully, I didn't have to make that decision." His gaze held Bob's. "In truth, I can't tell you what I would've done. I was deeply relieved when you suggested talking to that attorney Maddy recommended."

"At the time, I thought we did the right thing, too," Bob added with bitter insight. But he'd been wrong, and he'd suffer from that mistake for the rest of his life.

"You and Merrily aren't talking much?"

Bob shook his head. "It's too painful... I don't have anything left inside to give her."

The minister followed Bob into his private office and sat across from him. "You need each other now more than ever. Merrily needs you more than you realize and—"

"Yes, I know, but—"

"And you need her," Pastor Dawson finished. "You said you don't have anything to give her. I understand your feelings, but Bob, it's together that you'll get through these next few weeks. One day at a time. Sometimes one hour or even one minute at a time. You've got to help one another and look to God for the strength to carry on. Take all the love you have for Axel and give it to your wife."

A lump filled Bob's throat, the same one that had appeared at inopportune moments all week. "Merrily didn't mean to do what she did," he said hoarsely, feeling the necessity to apologize. "Her anger is really with me."

"I know. It's forgotten, so don't worry about it."

They spoke a few minutes longer. "I'll think about what you said," Bob promised as he walked the minister to the door.

They shook hands and once again Bob was grateful for the good friends he'd made in Buffalo Valley. The pastor wasn't the only one who'd shown him love and understanding. Hassie came by nearly every day, often with the flimsiest of excuses. Bob welcomed her company and her wisdom. She'd lived through a similar ordeal and spoke to his heart in ways that others couldn't.

After the minister left, Bob waited a few minutes, then headed upstairs. He found Merrily sitting in front of the television, staring sightlessly at the screen. Taking the remote control from her limp grasp, he muted the sound. She barely noticed.

"I'm…sorry," she whispered.

"I know." Bob knelt in front of her and took both her hands in his. "We need to talk about Axel."

Immediately fresh tears threatened to spill down her pale cheeks. "No… I can't… Oh, Bob, I don't know what I'll do without my boy."

"We're going to get through this, sweetheart. It'll always hurt, but you and I are going to deal with this."

Her smile was weak but present, and his heart filled with love for his wife. "Now, about Pastor Dawson."

She glanced away, embarrassed.

"The judge's decision had nothing to do with the minister. If you want to lay the blame at anyone's feet, you don't need to go any farther than this room."

"What do you mean?"

"Sweetheart," he said, leaning forward to gently brush the hair from her cheek. "We were the ones who screwed up our lives. Just try to put yourself in that judge's shoes. He had two couples—maybe more—to choose from. All of us good people, each couple wanting Axel. He didn't have anything to look at but the facts, written in black and white on a sheet of paper. Nothing that would prove to him how much we loved Axel. Nothing that would discount our mistakes. Before we got married, you told me there were things you'd done…"

Merrily squeezed her eyes shut and shook her head.

"I have my own list of sins, and it isn't any shorter than yours. We both made errors over the years. The judge couldn't ignore that."

Merrily looked down and her hair fell forward. "I know, but no one will love Axel more than us."

"No one," Bob agreed.

"It seems so unfair when we've both worked so hard to be better people and…and we are, but—"

"We *are* better," Bob said. "We've both grown, and part of that process is learning to accept responsibility for the past. The angry drifter who got arrested for possession of a controlled substance several years ago isn't me. Not anymore. I'm a husband and a business owner, a member of the town council and the school board. But, unfortunately, I do have a past, and I have to accept the consequences of the life I once lived."

Merrily studied him for a long moment, then nodded. "I do, too." Sliding forward, she wrapped her arms around his neck and hugged him. It was the most physical contact they'd had since Doug's phone call.

"I've needed you," Merrily told him, her voice trembling. "I've felt so alone."

"I've needed you, too."

"Then why did you stay away? Why didn't you hold me when I wanted you so much?"

Bob buried his face in the curve of her neck. "I was afraid." He could tell by the way her body tensed that she didn't understand. "Afraid you'd vanish. Afraid I'd wake up and find you'd left me again. I was protecting myself."

"But, Bob—"

"Every time you walk away, something dies inside of me," he said, as he gently wiped the tears from her cheeks.

Merrily caught his hand and brought his fingers to her lips. "You're right, you know, about accepting responsibility for my past. I played a role in the judge's decision, too. You never said, but the caseworker learned about my little habit of running away, didn't she? It couldn't have looked good as a qualification for being Axel's mother."

"I don't think they knew," he lied, wanting to spare her.

"Hogwash," she said, shaking her head. "The judge had to know. You say we have to take responsibility for ourselves. I'm doing that, so don't try to make excuses for me. I did run away, but it won't happen again."

"You're sure?" Bob hated how uncertain he sounded, but he needed her reassurance.

Merrily smiled and briefly kissed him. "Very sure. I learned my lesson the last time."

She'd never spoken of where she'd gone or how she'd lived while they were apart. Not knowing had plagued Bob, filled him with doubts and gnawing questions, but he'd never press her for details. "Did someone hurt you?" he demanded, anger tightening his chest.

"No." She was quick to correct him. "I realized I couldn't leave you or Buffalo Valley. My heart is here. You're my home, this town and these people are a part of me. We *will* get through this. It won't be easy, but together we'll survive."

May 30th

Dear Kevin,

Your letter arrived today and I'm thrilled you've got some great ideas for the war memorial. I think it's way cool that the town council contacted you about the project.

So you've got a summer job, working at the Art Institute of Chicago. I have to admit I'm a bit disappointed you won't be coming home. We've been writing a couple of months now, and it'd be nice if we could sit down and talk face-to-face. Funny, when we were in school together, we didn't say more than a few words to each other. Now all I think about is seeing you and talking to you in person. I know you'll be home for the Fourth of July weekend, but that seems so far away. Actually, I was thinking about checking out Chicago— more on that later.

Believe it or not, I've got my choice of jobs. I'm working part-time at Joanie's video store, after school and on Saturday nights, but Rachel approached me about working full-time at a new day-care center after graduation. She offered to pay for the college courses I'd need in early childhood development. I'm thinking about it. Buffalo Bob's going to hire three people for the summer, and my mother's quilting business has grown to fifteen employees. When you're home, you'll be amazed by the changes here. More and more people are moving to Buffalo Valley. One of the nurses from the new medical clinic moved into town last week. There's only a couple of vacant houses now.

I recently had a bit of a run-in with my grandfather. As soon as I graduate, I'm moving out. You've got a wonderful family and I think it's great how all of you get along, but that's not the case with me. My mother's remarried and isn't interested in having me around and frankly, I wouldn't live with her and Dennis, anyway. Gramps has developed an attitude, so it doesn't look like I'll be living there much longer. I was thinking about asking my uncle Jeb about moving in with him and Maddy, but they live so far out of town. I wouldn't like being an hour away from my friends. Anyway, I've come up with an alternative idea. Hassie Knight. I've always liked Hassie. Everyone loves Hassie. She's been around forever and she knows everyone and…well, you understand. I thought she might like the company. What do you think of my idea? Not that I intend to live with her long. Only until I've got enough money to check out Chicago. Maybe I could go to school there—do Early Childhood or whatever. Plus, I'd be able to see you!

I wonder if you know how grateful I am that we're friends. It's incredible to me that someone from Buffalo Valley actually escaped. I know, I know, you talk about moving back one day and maybe you will, but for right now you're living in one of the most exciting cities in the world, experiencing things the rest of us only dream about. Minneapolis didn't work out, but I wish I could leave Buffalo Valley. I don't feel really connected with anyone here anymore. Jessica's started dating Joe, and I feel like all my friends are pairing up.

I'd better go, I'm at work just now. It's time to close down and count out the till. I'm so glad you answered my letter right away.

Write again soon. Okay?
Love,
Calla

Calla mailed the letter on her way home from school Friday afternoon. As she stepped out of the post office, she saw Hassie Knight entering the pharmacy. Not hesitating, she headed across the street. No time like the present to approach Hassie with her idea.

Not wanting to be obvious, Calla strolled into the pharmacy and slid onto a stool at the fountain.

Hassie wore a big smile as she made her way behind the counter. "Come for one of my sodas, have you?"

"I sure have," Calla said, propping her chin on her hands. "I thought about these sodas more than once when I was living in Minneapolis."

"I'll bet one of my sodas wasn't the *only* thing you were thinking about while you were away."

Calla didn't answer; no need to let Hassie know that she'd probably be leaving town as soon as she was financially able. The older woman was such a staunch defender of the community, she wouldn't understand Calla's eagerness to leave. "Actually I came for more than a soda," she said.

Hassie handed her the soda, then walked around the counter and pulled up a stool. "What's on your mind?"

Calla figured it'd help to have some kind of subtle lead-in to the question she wanted to ask, but she couldn't come up with one. Might as well wade right in. "I guess you know I've been having trouble with my mother."

"I did hear something along those lines," Hassie admitted.

Calla took a sip of her soda and smiled, letting the older woman know how much she enjoyed it. A little flattery was never a bad idea, and besides, Hassie really did make fabulous sodas.

"I don't blame my mother," Calla added, wanting to sound adult and mature. "In some families, parents and children just don't see eye to eye."

"Is that true of you and your mother?"

"It seems to be." Calla released a small sigh, as though she considered this entire situation unfortunate and one she deeply regretted.

"It's never too late, you know."

This wasn't the path Calla wanted the conversation to take. "My mother has a new life now. She's got her business and her marriage. She's happy with Dennis and they're starting a family. I don't fit into that picture, if you catch my drift."

Hassie shook her head, her expression impatient. "Fiddlesticks."

"It's true, Hassie. I love my mother, but I can't live with her."

"I imagine you're grateful for your grandfather, then." Hassie raised her eyebrows expectantly.

"Oh, yes. Gramps has been wonderful. I don't know where I'd be if it wasn't for him—but lately we seem to be having a bit of a problem, too."

"You're not getting along with your grandfather?" Hassie asked loudly. "Is that what you're saying?"

Calla forced herself to look sad and woebegone. Lowering her eyes, she whispered, "We recently had a bit of a falling out."

"You and Joshua?" Hassie made it sound like that wasn't possible. "I've known your grandfather a lot of years, and he's an absolute marvel at avoiding conflict. Hates it. In fact, he'll do just about anything to get out of it."

"He didn't have any trouble speaking his mind with me," Calla informed her, remembering all too well the bluntness of his words. She inhaled a deep breath. "Seeing that I don't get along with him or my mother," she said quickly, "I was giving serious thought to..." She hesitated, wondering if her announcement would sound too melodramatic.

"Serious thought to *what*?" Hassie asked.

Her chin came up. "Disowning my family." That idea had felt very satisfying when she'd first thought of it.

Hassie's eyes narrowed to thin slits. "You mean before they disown you?"

Calla felt that barb and would have returned an even sharper one of her own if she wasn't looking to Hassie for help. All right, in all likelihood she *wouldn't* disown her entire family. She'd probably stay in contact with Jeb and Maddy, not as relatives but as friends. Jeb was all right as uncles went and Maddy was terrific. Besides, Julianne was the only cousin she had and the sweetest baby ever.

"You don't think I should disown my family?" she asked.

"Hardly. As far as I can see, they've done nothing to deserve it."

Apparently Hassie wasn't privy to the things her mother had done, but Calla preferred to avoid discussing the sordid details of Sarah's affair with Dennis Urlacher. Nor did she wish to talk about her father's pathetic life. Both her parents disgusted her.

She reached for her soda and took a deep swallow. This conversation was more difficult than she'd bargained for. Clearly, she needed to approach it from a different angle. "Have you noticed how many people are moving into Buffalo Valley?" she asked in a determinedly casual tone.

Hassie's eyes brightened. "The way this town's coming back to life is a sight to behold, isn't it?"

"It's really cool."

Hassie laughed, and patted Calla's hand.

"You seem to be doing good business lately." She nodded at the cash, where Leta was ringing up purchase after purchase.

"Very good," Hassie agreed.

"I don't suppose you could use any extra help?" She made the question sound timid, as though she was afraid to ask.

"I thought you were working at the Wyatts' video store."

"Oh, I am, but... I was looking for more hours. Whatever you could give me." The job inquiry was meant to lead into the subject of living with Hassie.

Just until she finished school and had enough money to move away.

She'd always heard that honesty was the best policy, and seeing what a mess she'd made of this, Calla decided the direct approach would probably work better. "Actually," she said, staring down at her soda, "I was thinking I could move in with you."

"You want to live with me?" Hassie sounded kind of skeptical.

"Not for long," she promised quickly. "Just until graduation. Perhaps a while longer... I wouldn't be a bother, really I wouldn't. We could help each other. I'd do the housework and the cooking, work in the store, and you'd be helping me out."

Her suggestion was followed by a lengthy silence.

"You don't think it's a good idea?" Calla asked, chancing a look in the older woman's direction.

"No. In fact, I think this is the worst idea I've heard in twenty years."

"Oh." Calla's voice fell. A simple *no* would do, she thought resentfully. "Why?"

"First of all, you've already got more places to live than four teenagers combined. I know for a fact that your mother would love to have you with her—"

"No way!" As if Calla would deign to live in the same house as Dennis Urlacher! Not in this lifetime.

"So I understand, which is a pity. Your mother and Dennis deserve better treatment than you're giving them. So does Joshua. I don't know what happened between you two, but if he confronted you, then my guess is you damn well needed it. I can't imagine anyone with less reason to disown her family! One day you'll look back and realize how foolish you've been. For your sake, I hope it's soon."

Calla felt the heat of indignation fill her face.

"My advice, and you did ask for it, is to step back a moment, think about what you have and thank God every day of your life that there are people who love you and care about you."

Calla blinked back the hurt. She'd expected Hassie to be an ally. Obviously she'd been wrong. Slapping some money on the counter, she turned and with an indignant tilt to her head, walked out of the pharmacy.

Margaret drew in a deep, calming breath and spoke gently to the laboring heifer who was about to deliver her calf. This was her first birth and the poor thing struggled with each contraction.

"It's all right, girl," Margaret said softly. "You're doing just fine. Soon you'll have a beautiful new baby."

Margaret worried about the heifer. The birth was taking longer than expected and the animal was weakening. Rolling up her sleeves, she slipped on the long plastic glove and inserted her arm into the birth canal to feel for the hooves. They were there, thankfully. At least the calf wasn't breech. She removed her arm, slipped off the glove and patted the heifer, crooning encouragement.

"Can I help?"

At the sound of Matt's voice, she swung her head around. He stood no more than five feet away. She stared, hardly able to believe that her imagination hadn't conjured him up. She hadn't seen him in over a week.

"Say something," he said next. He seemed to need some sign of the kind of reception she was willing to accord him.

The cow bawled with pain and Margaret glanced back at her. "Yeah—I could use some help," she said.

"You've got it." A moment later, he was on his knees at her side.

"We're going to need a rope," Margaret told him.

"You sure she's ready?"

"Check for yourself."

Matt quickly washed his hands, then rolled up his sleeve. Soon his arm was sheathed in the blue glove and he was elbow-deep inside the cow. She didn't take kindly to the intrusion and protested loudly, thrashing her legs until Matt withdrew his arm.

"Apparently I'm not as gentle as you," he muttered.

Margaret let the comment slide. She wasn't there to discuss who possessed the better technique. She wanted to know his thoughts on how the birth was progressing. "Well?" she demanded.

"I agree with you. She's ready. I feel the hooves and the nose. As soon as they show, we'll put the rope to use."

The birth proved to be even more difficult than Margaret had anticipated. Soon after the calf's hooves emerged, they looped the rope around the front legs. Down on her knees with Matt, Margaret tugged and pulled, employing every ounce of strength she had. By the time the calf slid free of his mother, Margaret's arms ached and her face burned with exertion.

She had just started to rise when the first cramp hit her. An involuntary yelp escaped and she doubled over, cradling her stomach.

"Margaret!" Right away Matt was there.

"I'm fine, I'm fine." She slumped onto a bale of hay until she could assess what was happening. It didn't take long to realize she'd strained a muscle.

"Is it the baby?"

"No," she said through gritted teeth. "I'm fine. Leave me alone."

"There's something wrong. You're pale as a ghost," Matt argued.

"I said I was fine," she fired back.

"You're in pain."

Now that was a laugh. The man who'd broken her heart was concerned because she had a stomach cramp.

"Dammit, Margaret, you can't be doing this kind of physical labor. Not when you're pregnant."

The man had his nerve. "I'll do whatever I damn well please!"

"You can be angry with me if you want, but I can't allow you to do anything that'll hurt our baby."

"Like I'd intentionally do such a thing." Did he think she was an idiot?

"You're too damn stubborn for your own good."

Margaret opened her mouth to argue, then stopped. It wasn't outrage she saw in Matt's eyes, but love and concern. He'd been gone a week, seven days in which she'd had time to consider her options. Time to decide what was important. Time to consider her future and that of her child.

"Be angry if you want," he said again, "but you can't do everything by yourself. You need me."

"The hell I do!" Her response was automatic, her voice sharp.

"Okay, you don't need me," he countered just as sharply. "I'm the one who needs you. Hear me out and if you want me to leave afterward, I will."

"All right."

He sat on a bale across from her. "I've been with quite a few women over the years. I'm not proud of this, and I don't think it comes as any surprise."

She'd known the kind of man he was when she married him, but she hadn't understood exactly what that meant. She hadn't realized that he couldn't completely escape his history—as Sheryl had proven.

"You married me because I had something to offer that those other women didn't—my land and the cattle," she threw out angrily. "And because I believed in you, or so you've said."

"Yes," he said, equally angry. "But dammit, Margaret, there's more. You got to me. You're the finest cattlewoman I know. The finest rancher, period. No one's better at managing a herd than you, and I respect that. You're attractive and you're smart and you have character. Okay, so you're no beauty queen. I'm not interested in pretty, shallow girls—they're a dime a dozen. But there's only one you."

The intensity of his words, his eyes, told her he spoke with sincerity.

"There's something else you should know. Every other woman I've ever loved, I've loved from below the waist, if you know what I mean. But I love *you* with every part of me—my heart, my mind, my body."

"Oh, Matt," she whispered and slid off the bale of hay onto her knees. He knelt, too, facing her.

He reached for her and she all but fell into his arms. His mouth sought hers and they kissed with the desperation of two people who'd experienced despair... and renewal.

Their kisses were deep and long. The new calf mewled softly and his mother nuzzled her offspring while Margaret clung to her husband. When they broke apart, there were tears on her cheeks. Matt kissed them away, his tenderness profound. He'd said exactly what she'd been longing to hear.

"I wasn't sure you'd be back," she whispered brokenly.

"I wasn't, either, but I couldn't give up on us. I thought, I hoped, that if I went away for a few days, it'd give us both time to think."

"I did think," Margaret told him. "In fact, that's all I've been doing. Now it's time we talked."

They checked on the cow and her calf, then washed up in the barn and headed toward the house.

Sadie met them at the back entrance, holding open the screen door. "I've got iced tea and chocolate chip cookies waiting for you on the front porch."

The thoughtful gesture pleased Margaret. "I don't know what you did to win her over, but Sadie's certainly in your camp."

"You honestly don't?" He grinned. "All I ever did to win Sadie was show her how much I love you."

With their arms around each other, they walked through the house and to the front porch, settling in the two wicker chairs that rested there. Her father often used to sit in this very spot and Margaret liked to think he was with them now.

"I do love you," Matt told her again, "and our baby."

"I know," she said simply.

"If we reconcile, I feel I should warn you that it isn't going to be easy with Sheryl." He gave her a pained look. "My lawyer and I tried to talk sense into her, but it did no good."

"She wants to raise your daughter herself?"

He nodded. "I suggested adoption, but she made it very clear that she intends to eke every penny out of me that she possibly can. The child is a means of holding on to me—and punishing me. For leaving her, and I think, for loving you." Matt reached for her hand, entwining their fingers. "She assumed I'd divorce you and marry her. She figured the pregnancy would be the incentive—and she figured you for a source of cash." He threw back his head, eyes closed. "Not once did I even consider such a plan. I swear it."

She pressed her hand to his jaw. "I believe you."

He opened his eyes, looked her full in the face. "I don't know if it's possible, but some day I'll make all of this up to you. Maybe I can't but I intend to try. God knows I don't deserve a second chance, but I'm asking for one, anyway."

They were in each other's arms again. Margaret found it almost impossible to keep her hands off him. They hadn't slept together in months, not since she'd learned of Sheryl's pregnancy. He'd been the one to initiate her into the physical aspect of love, and in the process had created a need in her that only he could fill.

"We have a lot to overcome, but I love you, Matt. As long as you're one hundred percent committed to me and our marriage, we have a chance."

"One hundred percent."

They kissed until Margaret heard Sadie clearing her throat behind them.

"Yes, Sadie?" she asked, her voice a mere rasp.

Matt continued to kiss the side of her neck, his hands on her shoulders, his lips moist and eager.

"Mr. Eilers has a phone call."

"Mr. Eilers?" Matt repeated, sounding amused that Sadie would be so formal.

"Gage Sinclair has a question for you."

"I'll be right back," Matt told his wife.

He left and Sadie folded her arms. "Well? Are you two back together?"

Margaret nodded.

"Good." Her smile was brief but undeniably genuine. "This time don't be so quick to give up."

Margaret laughed. "I won't."

Seventeen

"Bob, what's taking you so long?" Merrily called out from the back storeroom. Her husband had worked frantically doing spring cleaning and repairs. Merrily had joined him, working equally long hours.

"Coming," he shouted brusquely from somewhere in the kitchen.

She sighed, waiting impatiently for him to move the fifty-pound flour sack so she could continue cleaning the shelves. The more involved she became in this physical labor, the better she understood why Bob had worked himself to a frazzle those first few weeks after receiving word about Axel. It did help; it distracted her and left her tired enough to sleep. And she found the resulting cleanliness and order deeply gratifying.

Now, a month since the judge's decision, Merrily was feeling a kind of contentment. The tears didn't come as readily or as often. Instead of focusing on her loss, which seemed overwhelming, she took an inventory of her blessings. At the top of her list was Robert Carr, her husband. He wasn't the best-looking man she'd ever seen—in fact, it would be a stretch to call him handsome—but he was everything she wanted in a husband. No one had ever loved her the way he did.

"All right, all right," he muttered, walking into the storeroom, a little breathless. "What do you want?"

"Hey, don't snap at me, Buffalo Man."

"I didn't snap. I happen to be busy."

"And I'm not?" She rolled her eyes. "Do you want me to move that flour myself?"

"Don't be ridiculous."

"That's what I thought."

Bob lifted the sack as though it weighed no more than a shoe box and plopped it down where she wanted. Merrily thanked him with a kiss on the cheek, then reached inside the soapy bucket for her cleaning rag.

"I've been thinking," she began as he picked up a second bag, this time of sugar.

"About what?" he grunted.

"Us," she said calmly. She waited until she had his full attention, then drew herself up straight and looked him in the eye. "Tell me, is there any reason we couldn't have a baby of our own?"

The fifty-pound bag of sugar dropped to the floor with a solid thump. It was a wonder the sack didn't burst wide open.

"What did you just say?" Bob asked.

Merrily frowned. "You heard me! I asked your opinion on us having a baby."

Bob stared at her, mouth gaping slightly.

"Is the idea that wild?" She wasn't accustomed to seeing her husband speechless.

Bob sank onto the sugar sack, shaking his head as though completely overwhelmed. He glanced up at her. "I…I suppose we could try."

Merrily wasn't pleased with his response. She'd assumed he'd welcome the suggestion. Be excited. Eager. Happy. But he was none of that. Whirling around, she resumed her task, attempting to hide her disappointment.

"What's wrong?"

Snorting softly, she ran the wet rag along the empty shelf. "You might have shown a *little* enthusiasm."

Once more he seemed at a loss. He shrugged his shoulders.

"I thought...you'd like the idea," she muttered, uncertain of her own feelings now. Bob had taken the news about Axel as hard as she had, perhaps harder. While the child was with them, Bob had loved and cared for him, had considered him their son. He seemed such a natural father, she'd expected him to jump instantly at the possibility of having a baby.

"I do like the idea," Bob insisted.

"Well, I sure couldn't tell."

He continued to stare at her. "It just takes some getting used to, is all."

She didn't reply. What was there to say?

"You honestly want a baby?" he asked.

"Would I have suggested it if I didn't?"

"I...guess it wouldn't hurt."

Merrily forced herself to look past her disappointment at his lukewarm response. Clearly she'd taken her husband by surprise, but she sensed that something else was troubling him.

"You'd better tell me what's wrong," she said.

"Nothing," he said quickly, far too quickly. "If you're finished with me here, I've got my own work to do."

"Fine, be that way." It was hard not to let her hurt feelings show, but she managed by turning her back to him and scrubbed the shelf with enough vigor to remove half the paint.

"Dammit, Merrily, if you want a baby, then we'll have a baby."

"I want *you* to want a baby, too," she snapped back.

"I do!" he bellowed.

"Everything you've said and done tells me otherwise."

He started pacing, his movements brisk and erratic. "I'm afraid."

His words stunned her, and she turned to face him. "You're afraid? Of what?"

Bob was sitting now, and he gestured weakly as he spoke. "What if something happened? You could miscarry. There's a risk with any pregnancy... And babies are so vulnerable. What about illness? Or accidents? We lost Axel and dammit, Merrily, I don't know if I could bear to lose another child. I can't deal with that kind of pain again."

"I couldn't bear it, either," she agreed, reaching for his hands and clasping them between her own. "No one will take our baby away from us. We were good parents to Axel—no one faulted us there. We'll be good parents to our own child, too." Her voice tearful, she whispered, "The risk is just part of life. You have to take all the precautions you can, and then...then you have to trust."

"You know what I think?" Bob asked. He stood up and wrapped his arms around her waist, pulling her against him. "I think you're the bravest woman I know. If you're willing to do this, then, what the hell, so am I."

"I'm throwing out my birth control pills today." She smiled widely, the tears gone.

Holding her close, Bob threw back his head and

laughed. "You do that, sweetheart, and leave the rest to me."

Despite his bravado, Merrily knew that Bob still felt some uncertainty about committing himself to this project. If you could call a baby a "project." So for the rest of the day, she formed a plan of action to lure her husband into bed. By the time she was finished with him, any lingering fears would be gone.

That night, after a lengthy shower, Bob walked into their bedroom, wrapped in his thick robe. He took one look at her and came to an abrupt standstill.

Merrily stood posed beside the bed, smiling saucily. Crooking one finger, she urged him toward her.

"What have you got on under that?" he asked, his voice husky.

"That's for you to find out."

"Merrily, I had a long, hard day. I'm tired…"

"I promise to make the night a whole lot more pleasant." Untying the sash, she let the short silk robe fall open to expose her breasts and smooth, flat abdomen.

"Ah…"

"You still too tired, Buffalo Man?" she asked softly.

"I think I've just found a new surge of energy."

Merrily beamed him an enticing smile and held out her hand, but he still hesitated. "Hey, Buffalo Man." She pouted prettily. "How much of an invitation do you need, anyway?"

He chuckled as he swung her into his arms and carried her to their bed. With a gentleness that always amazed her in a man of his size, he placed her on top of the covers. "So, you want a baby, do you?" he whispered, smiling down at her.

She nodded.

"Tonight seems the perfect time to try."

"That's what I thought, too."

"And if it doesn't work tonight, we'll just have to continue doing this until we succeed."

"Oh, I agree with that." She slid her arms around his neck.

"I hope I don't disappoint you…"

"Not a chance."

"And I hope that getting you pregnant doesn't turn out to be as easy as you think it'll be."

She giggled again and kissed his jaw. He captured her lips with his own and they were soon so caught up in their lovemaking that the only sounds they made were soft panting sighs.

Matt loved his wife. He'd come to recognize it in the first months of their marriage, but the intensity of his love had deepened after their reconciliation. His admiration for Margaret's hard work and leadership grew. But just as much as he admired her ability to manage a ranch, he loved her compassion and her capacity for forgiveness.

"Did anyone ever tell you how good you look on a horse?" he called out as they rode toward the ranch after a long day moving the herd to its summer pasture. The size of the herd was more than they could handle alone and there were several ranch hands working with them for the season.

"If you're trying to tell me I'm beautiful, just say so," she called back.

"You're beautiful," he shouted. "You're a fine rider, Margaret Eilers. You ride like you're part of the horse."

"Yeah, but which part?"

Matt threw back his head and roared with laughter. This was what he enjoyed most about their marriage, this banter and easy camaraderie. Margaret was more than his wife; she was his friend. The best friend he'd ever had. He'd never felt lonely until he'd nearly lost her. Never understood what brought a man home to a woman every night. Not just sex or domestic comfort. It was *this*—companionship. Understanding. A shared life. He couldn't imagine living without her now. Pastor Dawson was right; he had to fight to save his marriage.

Dinner was waiting for them when they arrived at the house. Soon afterward Sadie left for the day, but not before she caught Matt's eye and winked. It was the housekeeper's way of letting him know she was pleased that the situation had been resolved.

Only, everything *wasn't* resolved, and wouldn't be until after Sheryl's daughter—his daughter—was born. Matt and Margaret didn't talk about Sheryl or her baby, but they hadn't forgotten the other woman, either. Her time was drawing close and Matt expected to hear from her any day. In recent weeks, his only contact with his former lover had been through her attorney.

"Did you read that article I gave you about the new worming medication?" Margaret asked as they sat down at the table.

Matt nodded, helping himself to chicken casserole and green beans. "I did and I think it might be a good idea to give it a try." He'd run the numbers and saw a substantial savings for them if the medication did all it claimed. He described his conclusions and Margaret listened intently. The conversation then drifted to one of the newly hired ranch hands. Margaret wasn't pleased with his performance and said as much. Matt agreed with her complaints.

"If he can't get more accomplished in a day, then

he's pushing his luck with me," Margaret told him as she reached for a dinner roll.

Matt smiled. "They don't call you a tough broad for nothing."

Margaret slathered butter on the homemade roll. "You trying to get on my good side?"

"Aren't I already?"

She attempted to keep back a smile and failed.

Then the phone rang, and Margaret glanced at Matt. "You want to get it?"

What she was really asking, he realized, was whether he thought it might be Sheryl. He shrugged and reluctantly started to get up.

"No, wait," she said, stopping him. "Let the machine take it."

He sat down again, and they both strained to hear the voice at the other end of the line.

Sure enough, it was Sheryl.

Matt's appetite instantly vanished and his stomach cramped. His eyes met Margaret's and he saw that she was just as tense.

"You'd better pick up, don't you think?" she asked.

He shook his head. "I'll phone her back later."

Margaret nodded, but the mood of the evening changed. They hardly touched what remained of their dinner. Matt carried his plate to the kitchen, scraping his leftovers into the garbage, then set it in the sink. Margaret followed him and he poured them each a cup of coffee.

"Are you going to call her back?" Margaret pressed.

Matt sighed, knowing it would do no good to delay the inevitable. "I'd better, otherwise she'll phone again." One thing about Sheryl, she was tenacious.

Flustered, Margaret hurriedly rinsed the dishes and

loaded them into the dishwasher with jerky movements. "Do you want me to leave?"

"No." Already his stomach felt as if he'd swallowed hot coals. Walking over to the phone, he punched out her number, then braced his back against the wall. Margaret stood across from him, by the sink, staring at the floor.

Sheryl answered on the second ring.

"You asked me to call," Matt said, wanting to sound civil but not over-friendly.

"I had the baby."

"Did you name her?"

"Hailey Faith."

The pain in his stomach intensified with the unfamiliar and unwelcome mixture of emotions. He had a daughter, and while a part of him experienced joy and pride, another part felt fear and anger. "That's a fine name," he said after an uncomfortable moment.

"I thought so, otherwise I wouldn't have named her that."

"Was anyone with you?"

"Lee Ann came to the hospital. I wanted to phone you, but she wouldn't let me. Probably a good thing, because you wouldn't have liked the things I said about you when the labor pains got bad."

Matt couldn't keep from smiling at that. "I don't doubt it."

"Are you going to come see your daughter?" Sheryl lowered her voice, her tone confidential.

"I'm sure I will."

"When?"

Matt's gaze flickered toward Margaret. "I'll get back to you."

"Ah," Sheryl said, "the little woman's listening in, is she?"

"It's not like that."

Sheryl sighed expressively. "I'd argue if I thought it would do any good."

"As I said, I'll get back to you about when you can expect us."

"Margaret's coming with you?" Sheryl's voice rose with indignation.

"That decision belongs to my wife," Matt insisted.

"If she comes, she's an even bigger fool than I thought."

He ignored her remark. "I'll be in touch with you later."

Like everything else, Sheryl accepted this information with ill grace. "Don't you want to know about Hailey? One would think a child's father might ask when she was born and how much she weighed."

"Of course I want to know." Hearing the news of her birth had been jolt enough, although he thought he was prepared. "Tell me the rest."

"She was born two days ago. She's a little thing, only five pounds, six ounces. The doctor said if I'd quit smoking, she might have been bigger."

Matt tensed, suppressing the anger he felt at her selfishness. "Did you have a hard time?" he asked instead.

"You think giving birth is easy, you should try it. It's like shoving a watermelon through a doughnut hole."

Matt didn't know what to say.

"I have to tell you, though," Sheryl continued, her harsh voice softening, "she's beautiful."

"I'm sure she is."

"Is that a backhand way of telling me I'm beautiful?" Sheryl coaxed.

The question pulled Matt up short. "What do you mean?"

"You just said Hailey must be beautiful, and I asked if you were telling me I'm beautiful, too. I *am* her mother, you know."

"I…didn't mean anything."

Sheryl blew out an exaggerated sigh. "I don't know why you have to be so damned difficult. Nothing has to change with us—it never did. You're the one who decided to stay with Miss Moneybags, but I can forgive and forget. We had a good thing going. If you're interested in continuing our arrangement—the way it was before—I'd be willing to consider it. You can have me *and* go home to your wife."

"No, Sheryl, I'm not interested." He made sure his response was curt enough to get his message across.

"We'll see," Sheryl said after a short pause. "You come visit your daughter, and in the meantime I'll put on my thinking cap."

"What?"

She laughed softly. "I'm going to look for some inventive ways to detain you." She groaned at the ensuing silence. "Bring your wife if you wish, but it won't matter. I'm not making any secret of it, Matt, I want you back in my bed. You belong with me—and with your baby. Little Hailey needs her daddy," she whispered, and then before he could respond, she hung up.

"Well?" Margaret asked when he replaced the receiver.

"Hailey Faith—that's what she named her." Shaken by the encounter, Matt gathered Margaret in his arms. Sheryl had just demonstrated what he knew to be true:

she was determined to do everything in her power to either have him or destroy him.

"What is it?" Margaret asked, tilting her head back to meet his gaze.

He didn't answer, not knowing how to explain his own heart. Hailey Faith was his daughter, and he didn't know how to reconcile his feelings for this newborn baby. How could he love his child and at the same time detest her mother?

"Matt." Margaret held his face between her hands.

He weighed the pros and cons of letting Margaret know about their conversation and decided to tell her. "Sheryl wants to continue our arrangement," he confessed, deciding it was better to clear the air than hide anything from his wife again.

"Is that what you want?"

Her question shocked him. "Not on your life!"

"Actually it'd be *your* life. If you'd answered yes, I swear you'd be unable to walk upright without terrible pain for months."

He laughed; Margaret's sense of humor was exactly what he needed just then. But only later did he fully appreciate her wisdom and her insight into what the future held for them and Hailey.

"I have a daughter."

"No," she corrected him gently, holding his gaze. "*We* have a daughter. Hailey Faith is part of my life, too. I'm going to love her, welcome her into our home, nurture her and make her part of our family."

Matt stared at the incredible woman he'd married and couldn't find the words to thank her. They'd lodged themselves deep in his throat.

"We have a daughter," she repeated.

"We," Matt agreed, and held his wife close.

* * *

The pains started early Thursday afternoon in the last week of June. At first Sarah didn't recognize what they were. She was seven and a half months along, just getting to the uncomfortable, awkward stage of pregnancy. The baby moved often, stretching and kicking. The ache low in her back was simply muscle pain, she decided. Dennis was continually after her about doing too much. She didn't agree, but to be on the safe side, she left work and immediately went home and fell asleep.

The pains woke her an hour later. Now there was no disguising it: she was in labor. The low back pain worked its way around her abdomen with growing intensity. Checking her watch, she realized the contractions were coming regular as clockwork, every five minutes.

Not wanting to alarm her husband, the first person she phoned was Dr. Leggatt. Unfortunately he was out of the office, but she was able to talk to his nurse, Mrs. Berghoff.

"I'm in labor," Sarah cried, doing her best to control the blinding sense of panic. "It's too soon... I'm afraid I'm going to lose my baby."

"Relax," the woman told her calmly. "I'm sure everything's going to be all right."

"You don't know that," Sarah cried, clinging to the telephone receiver until her fingers went numb.

"You're right, I don't, but I do know that panicking isn't good for you or for the baby. Is anyone with you?"

"No—my husband's gone for the day." Leave it to this baby to choose a day Dennis was delivering fuel.

"Is there anyone who can drive you to the hospital?"

"Yes...of course."

"Good, then leave your husband a message and get started."

"Without Dennis? But… I want him with me."

"Mrs. Urlacher, for your sake and the sake of your child, don't delay any longer. I'll alert the hospital and they'll be waiting for you. This hasn't been an easy pregnancy. Let's not do anything to jeopardize it now."

"All right, all right," Sarah agreed, fighting back the fear and hysteria. "I'll come right away."

Dennis was out of reach, but she did take time to contact two families along his route, asking them to let him know she'd left for the hospital. With her husband unavailable, the first people Sarah thought to contact were her brother and Maddy, but they were an hour from town. She couldn't wait. Her second choice was her father. Her hand shook as she punched out the phone number.

Only it wasn't her father who answered, but Calla.

"Where's Dad?" she demanded.

"Hello to you, too, Mother," Calla said, her voice dripping with sarcasm.

"I need your grandfather," Sarah cried, unwilling to engage in pettiness. There'd been too much of that between her and Calla in the past few weeks.

Something in Sarah's tone must have alerted her daughter. "What's wrong?"

"I'm in labor. I need your grandfather to drive me to the hospital in Grand Forks." Sarah's voice trembled with urgency. A labor pain came over her, worse than the others, and she moaned softly.

"All right, all right, don't panic," Calla cried, sounding close to it herself. "I'll get Gramps and send him right over."

"Calla, please…"

"Mom, don't worry, I've got everything under control."

Sarah desperately wanted to believe that, but her fears had intensified, as well as her pains.

Within minutes, the old battered pickup that belonged to her father pulled up in front of the house. Reaching for her overnight bag, Sarah started out the door, but it wasn't her father who rushed to meet her. Instead of Joshua McKenna, there stood Calla.

"Where's my dad?" Sarah asked.

"Playing poker in Devils Lake. You ready, or are we going to stand here and argue all afternoon?"

Sarah hesitated, then nodded. Calla had a driver's license, had been driving for years. Despite their differences, she knew her daughter would get her where she needed to go.

Taking Sarah's elbow, Calla carefully helped her inside the truck, then raced around the front and climbed into the driver's seat. "Hold on," she instructed as she revved the engine and shifted into gear.

Sarah clicked the seat belt into place and closed her eyes as another labor pain seized her. An involuntary moan slipped through her lips.

"You're in pain?"

Sarah nodded. "It's too soon—oh, Calla, it isn't good for the baby to come this early."

"You're not going to lose my sister," her daughter muttered. "Not if I have anything to say about it." Then, apparently realizing what she'd said, she added, "A brother would be all right, too, but I'd prefer a little sister."

Sarah didn't have time to comment. Her full concentration went into breathing. As much as possible, she tried to give her body over to the contraction. Despite her efforts, all she could think about was her husband's inevitable panic when he got word of what was happening.

"Relax, Mom," Calla urged, gripping her hand. She squeezed Sarah's fingers.

"When did you get to be such an expert on labor and birth?" Sarah snapped.

"I'm not," Calla returned, ignoring her sarcasm. "That's just common sense."

The drive took forever. Twice Calla pulled over to the side of the road when Sarah cried out with the intensity of the contractions. They were coming hard and fast now, and it was all she could do to endure them.

"What can I do to help you?" Calla cried frantically.

Doubled over in agony, Sarah shook her head. "Nothing…nothing."

"Mom, let me do something!"

"Just drive," Sarah wailed, convinced that if it took much longer, the baby would be born in the front seat of the old truck. "Get me to the hospital."

Calla tore back onto the highway for the second time, spitting dirt and gravel as she did.

Sarah noticed that Calla's knuckles were as white and tense as her own.

By the time they arrived in Grand Forks, Sarah was weeping softly. She pressed her hands over her abdomen, afraid that with all the complications she'd already suffered, plus a premature birth, her baby didn't have a chance.

Tires squealing, Calla pulled the truck into a spot normally reserved for emergency vehicles. Slamming her hand on the horn to attract attention, she cut the engine, then leaped out of the truck and raced through the doors into the hospital emergency room.

Almost immediately an orderly hurried outside with Calla, wheeling a chair. He opened the door and helped Sarah down.

"Be careful!" her daughter yelled.

"I'm fine, I'm fine," Sarah insisted, but she wasn't.

"Did Dr. Leggatt's office phone?" Calla demanded as the orderly rolled Sarah into the hospital.

"I wouldn't know," the man responded.

"Well, find out!"

"Please," Sarah sobbed, and gripped the orderly's sleeve. "Please…"

Calla reached for her hand. "Mom, it's going to be all right."

"Why does everyone keep telling me that?" Sarah shouted. "My baby's six weeks early—"

"Mom… Mom." Calla knelt at her side by the admissions desk. The attendant was studying her computer and assembling pieces of papers, giving Sarah and Calla a few precious moments together. "Listen to me—"

"No, no. You don't know—"

"I know you love your baby and that the baby can feel your love."

"It didn't work with you, did it?" Sarah hated being so caustic, but she couldn't help herself.

To Sarah's shock, Calla's eyes filled with tears. "Actually it did." Her daughter's fingers tightened around her hand. "Despite everything I did—running away, being a real jerk—I always knew you loved me. I always knew I could turn to you for help. I've been acting like a spoiled brat for so long, I didn't know how to tell you I regret everything I've done."

Sarah stared at her daughter, certain her state of mind had conjured up those words.

"I love you, Mom," Calla whispered. "I love my little half brother or half sister, too."

"How…what happened?"

Calla brushed the back of her hand along the arch of her cheek, wiping away tears. "Does it matter?"

"No."

They hugged and Calla buried her face in her mother's shoulder. "Gramps and I had an argument about…things."

"You and my dad?" Joshua hadn't said a word. How typical of him.

"I was thinking of moving out."

"Where?"

Calla's laugh was ironic. "I thought Hassie would take me in, especially if I came to work for her."

"She wasn't keen on the idea, I assume?"

"That's putting it mildly," Calla said. "She didn't laugh in my face, but she might as well have."

The orderly waved a paper. "I have to take your mother now."

Calla nodded and stood. "I'll walk you to the elevator." Holding her mother's hand, Calla escorted her as far as the elevator.

"Say a prayer for me," Sarah cried when the big steel doors slid open.

The attendant pushed her inside and then reversed her position so that she faced Calla.

"Mom… Mom…"

Another contraction struck and Sarah was left gasping by the force of the pain. They were worse now, worse than anything she remembered. She was hardly aware of the short journey to the labor room.

"Mrs. Urlacher," Dr. Leggatt greeted her as soon as she was settled. "This is a surprise."

"I don't want to lose my baby," she sobbed.

"Good," the physician said. "I have no intention of losing either one of you."

"My husband…"

"Phoned the hospital," Dr. Leggatt told her. "Don't worry. He's on his way."

Eighteen

Matt took Margaret's suggestion that he visit Sheryl and the baby by himself as a sign of her love and trust.

"Are you sure?" he asked before he left the ranch. His arms were burdened with gifts, ones they'd purchased together for Hailey.

"Yes. For the first visit, at any rate."

Still he hesitated.

"Matt," she said, and laughed, easing him toward the door. "Hailey's your daughter. I want you to have some time with her on your own."

He understood and appreciated her reasons, but he wasn't entirely sure he wanted to do it this way. Today's visit was going to be difficult enough. If Margaret accompanied him, they'd present a united front, proving to Sheryl once and for all that there was no chance of a continuing relationship. Instead, Margaret ushered him out the door to make his own peace with his former lover.

The drive into Devils Lake seemed to require double the amount of time it normally did. His hands tightened around the steering wheel, and Matt acknowledged how nervous he was. Not about any confrontation with

Sheryl; she didn't tempt him in the least. He wasn't even worrying about her lawsuit; somehow or other, that would all be settled. In analyzing his feelings he realized his uneasiness had to do with his newborn daughter. This child was the result of his own carelessness—and Sheryl's greed. Yet Hailey was blameless. During the pregnancy Matt had avoided thinking about the baby, avoided forming an emotional attachment. Deep down, all he'd wanted was the whole thing to go away. Not exactly a mature or realistic outlook.

From the day he'd heard about Hailey's birth, he could no longer block her from his life. He was about to meet the daughter he'd fathered, the daughter he was prepared to love—already loved. The realization terrified him.

He parked outside Sheryl's rental house and saw the drapes part as she peeked out the window. The front door was open long before he reached the porch steps.

"You're right on time," she said, holding the screen door for him.

Matt had to admit she looked good, despite having given birth only a week earlier. She'd evidently gone to a great deal of trouble with her appearance. Her hair and makeup were done to perfection. She wore tight slacks and a revealing halter top, her breasts almost spilling out.

She must have caught him looking, because she instantly commented. "Nothing fits right anymore." Cupping the underside of the bra top, she shrugged her shoulders, then jiggled her breasts so they threatened to spill out entirely.

Embarrassed, Matt glanced away and set down the packages. "I brought Hailey a few gifts."

"How sweet." She leaned forward and kissed his cheek.

Matt reacted as though she'd burned him.

Sheryl giggled. "No need to be afraid. I promise not to hurt you."

An immediate argument came to him, but he squelched it. From the moment Sheryl realized he wasn't going to divorce Margaret and marry her, she'd done everything she could to hurt him. She'd tried to destroy his marriage and his life. If she couldn't get him back, she was going to make him pay.

"Where's Hailey?" he asked.

"Asleep."

"I'd like to see her."

"Don't worry, you will," Sheryl said. She motioned for him to sit. "Make yourself comfortable and I'll get you a drink."

"I'm here to see my daughter," he insisted, refusing to take a seat.

"Oh, Matt," she said with an exaggerated sigh. "Am I such a threat? I promise if you sit down I'm not going to pounce on you, although I have to admit the thought is tempting." She walked over to the liquor cabinet and brought out a bottle of Irish whiskey.

"I said I don't want a drink."

She frowned at him over her shoulder. "You might not, but I do. Frankly, I need something to help me relax. I was up half the night with the baby. She's already showing signs of a temper. Can you imagine? You should see her lower lip quiver when she doesn't get what she wants."

Sheryl poured herself a drink, then went into the bedroom.

Matt sank down on the edge of the sofa, but immediately stood as she returned with the baby. His heart pounded so loud, it echoed in his ears. Automatically he held out his arms for his child; Sheryl placed Hailey there, then stepped back as he took his first look at his daughter.

She was a tiny thing, he noted, just like Sheryl had said—so small she almost fit in the palms of his two hands. Her hair was dark and there was a lot of it. She didn't look like him, but she didn't resemble Sheryl, either.

"Don't worry, she isn't going to break."

Matt sat down and carefully folded open the blanket, then bent to kiss her forehead.

"You wake her and you get to put her back to sleep," Sheryl told him, taking a large gulp of her drink.

"I'll do my best," he whispered, awed by the strength of his emotions. He'd dreaded this for months and knew now that he had nothing to be afraid of. His daughter was incredible, beautiful, perfect.

"Pretty, isn't she?" Sheryl asked proudly.

"Beautiful," Matt whispered, using his index finger to brush a soft wisp of hair from her small face. This was the child who'd caused him such grief, yet all he could feel in that moment was love.

"People say she looks a lot like me."

He grinned, unwilling to fall into that trap again. "Time will tell."

Sheryl moved close and perched on the edge of the coffee table across from him. She leaned forward, pretending to study Hailey. Matt knew what she was really doing, and that was offering him a look at her generous breasts. He centered his concentration on his daughter, counting her fingers and toes.

"You want me to open the gifts?" Sheryl asked, gesturing at the bags.

Matt had purposely left them unwrapped. They weren't gifts for Sheryl. Everything he'd purchased was for Hailey. "Margaret and I picked up a few things we thought you'd need."

"How nice," she responded, but sounded more perturbed than grateful.

Enthralled as he was with Hailey, Matt didn't watch as Sheryl inspected the baby outfits and supplies he'd brought.

"So cute," Sheryl said.

"She really is, isn't she?"

"I was talking about this dress," Sheryl told him.

Matt looked away from the baby. "Margaret picked it out."

"Margaret, Margaret, Margaret! Is she all you can talk about?"

At Sheryl's shrill voice, Hailey woke and started to fuss. Matt didn't know much about babies, but he gently bounced her in his arms. That didn't seem to help, so he placed her ever so carefully on his shoulder and patted her back.

"Answer me, dammit," Sheryl demanded.

With Hailey wailing in his ear and Sheryl haranguing him, it took Matt a minute to compose himself. "Margaret's my wife."

"You'd never have married her if it wasn't for me," Sheryl said furiously. "You weren't supposed to fall in love with her, you idiot. Why am I surprised? Why?" She stood and slapped her sides. "That woman's no woman. I can't *believe* you actually fell for her."

Again Matt resisted correcting her. Insisting that Margaret was more woman than Sheryl could ever be wouldn't improve the situation. As much as possible, he wanted to keep his relationship with Sheryl neutral, for Hailey's sake.

"You were supposed to marry *me*," Sheryl shouted. "How could you do this?"

The baby wailed louder still, and nothing Matt did seemed to comfort her.

"I'm sorry," he said in an effort to appease Sheryl.

"Not sorry enough. What's going to happen to us?" She glared at him, her eyes spitting anger.

"I'll make regular child support payments and—"

"Not me and the baby," she interrupted. "You and me! Us."

"Sheryl," he said as gently as he could. "There *is* no us. I'm married to Margaret. All you and I share is Hailey. I was hoping we could both remain adult about this… I realize the situation's difficult, but—"

"You're damn straight it is."

"If you want to blame me, then go ahead. I accept full responsibility…"

"Of course I blame you," she yelled. "You're an idiot. Don't you get it, you could have had me *and* Margaret's money? We were good together."

Matt's heart sank. Sheryl simply didn't understand. More than that, she refused to understand. He loved his wife. Marrying Margaret was the smartest thing he'd ever done, and to his dying day, he'd be grateful that she chose to love him.

Sheryl started to sob and covered her face with both hands. "Now look what you've done."

"I'm sorry," he said again.

"Don't apologize. You're worthless, you know. Worthless."

He stood, still patting the baby's back. It was time

he left. Sheryl was in danger of exploding and his own patience was limited. Visiting his daughter shouldn't include having insults hurtled at him, and he wondered if this would be the norm. He supposed he should get in touch with his attorney, see what they could figure out. What kind of agreement or—

"Make her stop crying!" Sheryl shouted.

Matt wrapped his arm protectively around the newborn and rocked her from side to side, hoping that would work.

"Shut up!" Sheryl screamed at the baby and placed her hands over her ears. Whirling around, she glared at Matt. "This is all your fault."

"Fine, it's my fault, but screaming at a baby isn't going to help."

"Get out of here," she said, pointing at the door. "I want you out of my home."

He hesitated. Clearly, Sheryl was distraught, but there was little he could do. He carried the baby to the bedroom and lovingly settled her inside the crib. It was hard to turn his back on his daughter, especially when she was crying like this, but he had no choice.

"Get out of my home." Sheryl had apparently regained some of her composure. Tears glittered in her eyes, and he could recognize another emotion there, one that sent chills racing down his backbone. Hate.

"Sheryl," he said, determined to try one last time. "I told you before—and I meant it—if you want to blame me, do. But if the day ever comes when you feel you can't deal with the stress of the baby, call me. Margaret and I will raise Hailey."

"Now you want my daughter, too?"

"Only if she becomes too much for you."

Sheryl crossed her arms and stared at him with hatred gleaming from her eyes. "I'll rot in hell before I give you my child. Go home to your precious Margaret and may you both get what you so richly deserve."

Calla paced the waiting area outside the emergency room. She hadn't seen her mother in over an hour and each attempt to glean information had met with failure. She tried to sit and calm herself, but that didn't work for more than a few minutes. When she couldn't stand it any longer she bolted to her feet again and continued to wear a path in the floor.

Worries crowded her mind. With those worries came regrets. The last thing Calla saw before the elevator doors slid shut was the look of pain on her mother's face, mingled with a terrible fear. Although Calla knew little about pregnancy and birth, she understood that seven and a half months was too early. A premature birth would probably cause complications, especially since the pregnancy had already been difficult.

Before they'd taken her mother away, Calla had spilled out her heart. She hadn't intended to feel a thing for this baby. Dennis's baby. But she did. During the time her mother had undergone bed rest, Calla had spent a number of afternoons with her. Sarah had let Calla touch her stomach to feel the baby's movements. At first she hadn't been able to detect anything. But later, when she had, she'd felt a sense of genuine excitement.

Just then the hospital door burst open and Dennis rushed inside. He looked like a man possessed as he raced to the admissions desk. "My wife's here. Her name is Sarah... Sarah Urlacher. She's having our baby."

"Just a minute, Mr. Urlacher."

The receptionist sounded so calm. She turned to her

keyboard and typed in the name. "Your wife has been admitted."

"Can I see her?"

"It says here she's on the third floor but doesn't give a room number."

"I'll find her."

Calla didn't doubt that he would. Unwilling to be left behind, she followed him. Distraught as he was, Dennis didn't notice her until after he'd hit the elevator button for the second time.

He stared at her, and Calla shifted uncomfortably under his scrutiny. "I drove Mom here."

He nodded, but said nothing.

When the elevator arrived, they both stepped inside. It rose slowly to the third floor, and when the doors opened, Dennis virtually leaped out and ran to the nurses' station.

"I'm here to find out about my wife."

Hospital staff might not give Calla information, but they wouldn't ignore Dennis.

After asking Dennis a few pertinent questions, the woman glanced at Calla.

"I'm her daughter," Calla said.

"Mr. Urlacher, your wife's in surgery."

"Surgery?" The word exploded from Dennis.

"Dr. Leggatt will explain everything as soon as he's finished. We have a small waiting area here." She nodded toward a few chairs grouped around a low table. "It shouldn't be much longer now."

Looking defeated and broken, Dennis slumped into a chair and leaned forward, his arms braced against his knees, hands dangling.

Calla found a chair as far away from him as possible. It would have helped had there been other people in the waiting area. There weren't. Every minute claimed more of Calla's composure. The longer they were required to wait, the more certain she was that something had gone wrong. She could see Dennis had reached the same conclusion. His face was tortured with the pain of not knowing.

"Can you tell me what happened?" he finally asked, hurling the words as if he couldn't keep from asking.

"I... Mom phoned, telling me she needed a ride into Grand Forks."

"She didn't fall or anything?"

Calla shook her head. "I don't think so."

"She didn't mention what brought on labor?"

"No, only that she was afraid of losing the baby."

At this, Dennis ran his fingers through his hair and exhaled harshly. "Did they tell you why the surgery's necessary?"

"No."

He was silent again for several minutes, then started to pace, his movemnnts full of frantic compulsion. Past the table, around the chairs, back to the table, again and again. He didn't look at Calla and she didn't look at him. At least she tried not to, but soon found it impossible. Dennis loved her mother, loved his unborn child, too.

"She wanted to wait for you, but the nurse told her to get to the hospital right away," Calla told him.

Dennis stopped abruptly and glanced at Calla, as though surprised she'd spoken. He swallowed visibly, then said, "I'm thankful you were there."

Calla nodded, no less thankful.

"I realize there's no love lost between us," she said, and heaved in a deep breath, "but I can tell that you care about my mother."

"She's the only woman I've ever loved." He sank back into the chair.

"I don't hate you, you know."

He raised his head. From the expression on his face, she guessed he was sorely tempted to call her a liar.

"I don't hate you anymore," she amended.

Dennis waited for her to continue.

"I've been a…a jerk the last couple of years and, well, I guess I wanted my mother to love me more than she did you. What I did was create a tug of war between the two of us."

"Your mother loves you, Calla."

"I know, but that wasn't enough for me. I didn't want her to love anyone else. I understand now that I was asking the impossible." She squared her shoulders, and figured this was as good a time as any to make the necessary amends. "I've said and done things that I'm not proud of, and I was thinking…hoping…you might be willing to forgive me."

He studied her as though to gauge her sincerity.

"I wouldn't blame you if you decided not to, but I'm hoping that's not the case." She should've known Dennis wouldn't make this easy, but then why should he? She'd gone out of her way to make his life miserable for a very long time.

"You don't have to like me," she whispered.

"Why the change of heart?" he demanded.

"Why?" Calla wasn't entirely sure when it had come about. Sometime after she'd argued with Dennis. She'd been furious, looking for people to take her side against him. Since then, she'd had long talks with people she respected. Maddy and Jeb were two of the first. Although her aunt and uncle weren't overtly critical of her, Calla could see they felt she was in the wrong.

Her grandfather and Hassie were more inclined to state their unvarnished opinions, and neither felt any compunction about bruising her ego. Still, Calla had been able to shake off their warnings and admonitions. But Kevin's letter had reached her in a way no one else could. Although it hadn't seemed like that at first read, and although he hadn't said it in so many words, he'd told her to grow up. It was time she made peace with Dennis, his letter said, and the sooner she acknowledged her own contribution to the problems, the sooner she'd have her family back. Despite everything she claimed, Calla had missed her mother. She'd found their estrangement increasingly difficult.

"Why the change of heart?" Dennis repeated.

Calla told him, and when she finished she held out her hand for him to shake. Dennis looked at her and then slowly, cautiously, a smile appeared.

"Just get one thing straight," Calla said, feeling close to tears. "I'm not calling you dad."

"You don't have to," he assured her.

They both stopped talking when Dr. Leggatt approached, his face solemn. Calla and Dennis met him halfway. Calla's heart thudded hard against her ribs.

"Congratulations, you have a son."

"A son," Dennis repeated, his voice barely audible. "What about Sarah? Is she all right? What about the baby? How is he?"

"Unfortunately by the time your wife got here, the baby was in distress and so was she. We did what we could to stop the labor, but couldn't. In the end we were forced to perform an emergency caesarean. No fear, your wife did beautifully."

"And the baby?" Dennis asked nervously.

"Small. Three pounds, ten ounces. Our main concern isn't so much his size as his lung development. We have him in the neonatal intensive care unit now. You'll be able to see him soon, but I don't want you to be alarmed by the tubes and needles."

"He'll be all right?"

"Every indication at this point says so."

Dennis grinned at Calla, who battled back tears, then watched as her stepfather hugged the physician.

"A son!" he cried. "I have a son."

"I wanted a sister," Calla muttered, trying to lighten the atmosphere.

"Your wife is anxious to see you both," Dr. Leggatt said, then led them to her room.

Sarah looked shockingly pale against the sheets. When she saw Dennis, she stretched out a hand, and her husband moved toward her. At another time, an earlier time, Calla might have resented seeing the love between them. Although she'd made her peace with Dennis, it still hurt to know there was someone else her mother loved, but Calla recognized that what Kevin had said was true. One day she'd marry, and leave her mother for her own life. She was wrong to begrudge Sarah happiness.

Her mother *was* happy, she realized. She stood in the background and waited.

"Calla," Sarah whispered, reaching toward her now.

"I'm here, Mom," she said. She stepped close to the bed.

"Thank you…" Sarah whispered.

"Hey, I got a brother out of the deal. That's not so bad."

"Not bad at all," Dennis said, placing a hand on Calla's shoulder.

Her mother noticed the change between Dennis and

her right away. "You don't need to worry, Mom, Dennis and I are square now."

"Square?"

"Yeah, everything's going to be all right."

Tears sprang to Sarah's eyes. Dennis took her hand and pressed his lips to her palm. "We've reached an understanding," he said. "We both love you and little Josh. Who knows, before long we might even like each other."

Calla had the feeling it wouldn't take long at all.

Buffalo Bob walked over to Lily Quantrill Park and inspected the newly planted grass. The park remained roped off to prevent anyone from walking on the fresh green shoots, but that hadn't stopped folks from stopping and taking a gander. Bob was pleased.

Right now, the park revealed little of what the town council had planned for the future. By next summer, there'd be play equipment for the kids, including swings and a slide. The Boy Scout troop that met at the church on Tuesday nights was building a huge sandbox, and there was talk of installing a wading pool in a year or two. Lily Quantrill would be proud of what they'd accomplished in such a short time. A park would draw the community together, and Bob suspected that was what she'd intended all along.

Feeling good about life in general, he wandered over to the post office to pick up the mail. Merrily was busy with her friends, who were holding a baby shower for Sarah Urlacher at the restaurant. Bob used the shower as an excuse to leave. He'd prefer not to get involved in a women's gathering, with gossip and giggling and lots of talk about diapers and such.

He was greeted by a few friends as he headed into the post office, where he collected a handful of envelopes. Included was a statement from the attorney, and a few flyers. He'd open the bill later. He shot the breeze with Joshua McKenna and talked motorcycles for the better part of an hour.

By the time he returned to 3 OF A KIND, the baby shower had ended and the last of Merrily's friends was leaving.

"Is it safe?" he teased. He liked claiming that these women's get-togethers were really "weanie roasts" where no man was safe.

"Anything in the mail?"

"A bill from the California law firm."

Merrily frowned. "I thought we paid them off last month?"

Come to think of it, she was right. Merrily disappeared into his office with the mail, and Bob went into the kitchen where the prep cook was getting ready for the dinner crowd. Within a few hours, Buffalo Bob's would be bustling.

"Bob."

Merrily's voice shook, and it frightened Bob. Not understanding, he found her still in his office, her face streaked with tears. Instead of explaining, she handed him a handwritten letter.

"The attorney forwarded this to us," she whispered.

Puzzled, Bob reached for it.

July 5th

Dear Friends,

Forgive me for not using your names, but I don't know them. However, I felt compelled to write to you. Our attorney has spoken with the lawyers who represented you, and he didn't think it'd be inappropriate for me to write this letter. I beg your forgiveness if it brings you any sadness, because that isn't my intention.

After that rather lengthy prelude, I'd like to introduce myself. My name is Jenny and my husband, Michael, and I are the couple who adopted Axel. We understand there were rather unusual circumstances that led to his adoption and were given only a brief history of his life when we applied with the state adoption agency. Axel's personal history left a great deal unexplained.

When we asked to speak to his foster mother, we learned that he'd only been with the family a few weeks. For several months before that, we were later told, Axel lived with you. The caseworker informed us you'd saved Axel's life. It's hard to imagine parents who would abuse their own child and actually be willing to sell him. The purpose of my letter is to thank you from the bottom of our hearts for saving Axel from what would certainly have been a horrible fate. I can't bear to think what might have happened to him if not for you.

Our son is the joy of our lives. We waited five years for him, and had almost lost hope of ever receiving a child. You cannot imagine our delight when we learned we'd been chosen to raise Axel. He's a bright, cheerful boy, full of love and happiness. Every day is an adventure for him.

One day, when he's better able to understand, my husband and I will tell him about the brave couple who risked so much to save him. We want him to know the story of how you nurtured and loved him when he needed it most. My husband

and I will forever be grateful to you both. We wanted you to know we appreciate the loving care you gave our son.

He's adjusting well and thriving. Enclosed is a recent photo so you can see for yourselves how well he's doing.

Again we can't thank you enough.
Sincerely,
Jenny and Michael
Axel's family

Bob read the letter a second time and his throat clogged with emotion. "Look," Merrily whispered, and handed him a picture.

Bob examined the snapshot. At first all he felt was his own sense of loss. Anger filled his chest. How dared these people rip open a wound that had only half healed? How dared they invade his life, even with the best of intentions?

That feeling didn't last, however, and was quickly replaced by a stronger one. Gratitude. Two strangers had reached across the miles to offer him and Merrily a feeling of closure to a difficult time in their lives.

"He…he's grown so much," Merrily said.

Not trusting his voice, Bob nodded.

"The letter was very generous. An act of kindness."

"Yes," he agreed.

"I wonder if Axel…" She stopped midsentence and when he glanced over, expecting her to complete her thought, Merrily shook her head. "It doesn't matter anymore. He's happy… I can see it in his eyes. It isn't important if he remembers us. Not anymore."

Later that night, after the restaurant had closed, Bob read the letter yet again. The snapshot was missing, and he suspected Merrily had taken it. Axel had adjusted; the photo told him as much. The boy had a good, loving home with these people—Jenny and Michael—and was obviously doing well.

"Bob," his wife called from upstairs.

"I'll be right there," he called back. He refolded the letter and tucked it away. Despite everything, his heart was heavy as he climbed the stairs.

"Are you coming to bed soon?" Merrily asked, meeting him at the top.

"As soon as I shower."

"There's a surprise for you in the bathroom."

"A surprise?" In his present frame of mind, Bob wasn't especially interested in surprises.

"Don't you want to know what it is?" Merrily asked as she wrapped her arm around his waist.

"Then it wouldn't be a surprise, would it?"

"No. I guess you'd better look and then if you want, I'll explain."

Deciding to humor his wife, he entered the small bathroom and saw nothing out of the ordinary. "What?" he asked, wondering if this was her clever way of telling him about a blocked drain. Frankly, he could live without a plumbing problem right now. Come morning, he'd deal with it.

"See that stick?" Merrily asked, her eyes twinkling.

"What stick?" he asked, glancing about the room.

"The one on the counter."

Sure enough, there was a plastic stick on a bed of tissue. "What about it?"

"It's blue."

"And what does that mean?"

"That, my darling Buffalo Man, means we're pregnant." Her smile was filled with such joy it took Bob's breath away.

"Pregnant. But—" It was too much. Stunned and delighted by turns, he collapsed on the edge of the bathtub. "You're sure?"

"Positive, if that test can be trusted. Oh, Bob, Bob, we're going to have a baby!"

Bob closed his eyes and threw his arms around his wife. The pain they'd suffered over the loss of Axel had been replaced with the joyful promise of a child of their own.

This ebb and flow of life. Grief mingled with pain. The happy with the sad. Lost and then found. Five years earlier, he'd rolled into Buffalo Valley, never suspecting this dead-end town would end up being home. Yet here he was, a business leader, a husband and soon to be a father. Life didn't get much better than this.

Epilogue

Six months later

"Mom!" Calla burst through the door of Buffalo Valley Quilts, clutching a letter in her gloved hand. Beneath her thick coat and hat, all that was visible were her eyes, nose and mouth.

Sarah looked up from her designing board and was struck by the sheer joy she saw in her daughter. The sullen teenager who'd become a fixture over the past few years was gone, replaced by the daughter she'd desperately missed. Since Josh's birth six months earlier, a great deal had changed in Sarah's life. Her son thrived and was growing, making up for lost time. After nearly a month in the hospital, Josh had been released, and they were able to bring him home to a doting older sister and a father intent on spoiling him. Not to mention an adoring grandfather—his namesake—and an uncle, aunt and cousin. Soon afterward Calla graduated from high school and as a surprise Kevin Betts had arrived for the ceremony.

Kevin had become something of a celebrity in town. An inspiration to other young people. He was about to enter his third year of art school and had proved to all of them that it was possible to achieve one's dreams.

"What are you so excited about?" Sarah asked. Calla was home for the Christmas holidays. After delaying a decision about continuing her education, she'd applied at the last minute to the community college in Grand Forks, with plans to transfer to the University of North Dakota in her Junior year.

"I got a letter from Kevin," Calla explained.

"You get letters from Kevin all the time." Sarah was pleased with the budding relationship between her daughter and Leta Betts's son. He was a positive influence on Calla, and they seemed to understand and appreciate each other.

"First off," Calla said, sounding breathless, "he sold another sculpture and he's really excited."

"Wonderful."

"You know what else he said?"

Sarah could only imagine.

"He suggested I might apply for law school after graduation."

Her daughter an attorney. "Well," Sarah murmured as she mulled over the idea, "you certainly have a gift for arguing any side of an issue."

"That's what Kevin said, too. I've never thought about being an attorney, but I bet it'd be really interesting work. I'm going to think about it."

"Good. Buffalo Valley could use a capable attorney."

"Mother, honestly," Calla said with a groan, "what makes you think I'd want to practice *here*? The whole world's just waiting to be explored. If I do take up law, it'll be a long time before I set up an office in *this* town."

"You have years before you need to make that decision," Sarah told her.

"I'm heading back to school now, so I just came to say goodbye."

Although Calla was often home on weekends, Sarah always hated it when she had to leave. She stood and hugged her daughter, savoring the renewed closeness they shared. Their relationship wasn't perfect, and there were still times when Calla tried her patience, but it was infinitely better than it had been.

"I'll phone next week," she promised.

"Good." Sarah enjoyed their long telephone conversations immensely.

"Kiss Josh goodbye for me."

"I will," Sarah said, walking her to the front door. The wind roared and the chill factor was well below zero—a typical North Dakota winter.

Calla paused as she rewrapped the muffler. "Love you, Mom."

"Love you, too."

Still her daughter hesitated. "I'm really proud of what you've done with your quilting business. One day, your quilts will be known all over the world."

Her daughter's faith in her did Sarah's heart good. "Thank you, sweetheart. I hope you're right."

"I am, Mom, just wait and see."

"How'd the knitting lesson go?" Buffalo Bob asked his wife when he returned from the town council meeting.

Merrily, six months pregnant, sat in the rocking chair in their small living room with a pair of knitting needles and a pattern. "This isn't as easy as it looks, you know."

Bob had to grin. Once again, Leta Betts had stepped forward and volunteered to give free knitting lessons. Joanie Wyatt had sold Merrily the yarn and other necessary supplies, and before he knew it his wife was busily working on a blanket for the baby. But Merrily wasn't the only one preparing for the birth of their child.

Bob had completely refurbished the spare bedroom, converting it into a nursery. The ceiling had been re-painted, the walls papered, the floor recarpeted. His kid had yet to be born and already he or she was being showered with love. Not a bad start.

Working on the nursery, he'd found it hard to sup-press memories of Axel. Merrily's suggestion about having their own baby had been a good one, although at the time it'd shaken him. His wife's wisdom was an unexpected blessing, just like her love. These days, thoughts of Axel weren't as painful as they'd once been. The boy was happy with parents who loved him. He had a new life. Axel was a precious gift he'd been able to have for only a short time and Bob could more easily accept losing him now.

"How'd the council meeting go?" Merrily asked, her feet propped on the ottoman. The knitting needles were close to her face and the tip of her tongue appeared as she slipped a stitch from one needle to the other.

"Long," Bob said as he took the chair across from her. "There's a lot going on. It looks like Heath's going to move the corporate headquarters out of Grand Forks sooner than expected."

Merrily glanced up from her knitting. "Really?"

"The plan's in the works."

"I figured as much when he and Rachel announced they were going to build a home here in town."

The Quantrills' two-story brick house was big news. It was the first brand-new home built in Buffalo Valley in nearly thirty years. The first of many to come. It was inevitable with all the growth.

"We talked about the Summer Fest and a parade next July."

"A parade," Merrily repeated, sounding delighted. "What a great idea! Whose—no, don't tell me, let me guess. Hassie's idea, right?"

"Right. We've already chosen a grand marshal for the parade. Want to guess who?"

Merrily stopped knitting and her brow furrowed. "There are several ways that could go. Sarah's business is thriving, and with all the people she employs now, it would be a small way for the town to thank her."

"And there's always Heath, president of the bank and all," Bob pointed out.

Merrily shook her head. "Nah, Rachel wouldn't want her husband to get conceited, and as council president she might think that was a conflict of interest. It isn't, but I think Rachel would rather be on the safe side."

His wife was right again. Heath's name had come up and Rachel had mentioned that very thing.

"All right, tell me," Merrily said.

"Actually, we chose Lindsay Sinclair."

"The high-school teacher?"

Bob nodded. "You might not remember, but she was the one who started it all. She saved the town when she agreed to step in and take over classes after Eloise Patten died. The entire course of this community changed after her arrival. It seemed only fitting to thank her."

"Hassie's idea again?"

"Yeah," he said with a grin. "But we have a big surprise for Hassie, too. This summer we're dedicating the park. Kevin's doing the sculpture, of course—it's a bronze of rifles stacked against each other, to represent the fallen soldiers. There's going to be a plaque in memory of all the men from Buffalo Valley who died in the different wars. Hassie's son is listed there. She doesn't need to worry about people forgetting him or any of the other men."

"Does she know?" Merrily asked.

"She doesn't have a clue that Kevin's practically finished the sculpture. But there's going to be more than that. It's still a secret, though."

"Tell me, Bob. I promise I won't breathe a word."

He could trust his wife; Merrily was nothing if not discreet. "There'll be a flower garden in the park dedicated to Hassie. Not once did she lose faith in Buffalo Valley. She's been a source of inspiration to us all and we love her." Himself included. Hassie had been both friend and mentor.

"She'll be so pleased."

Bob leaned forward and kissed his wife's cheek. "I'd better get back to work."

"Yes, dear," Merrily murmured, and reached for her knitting.

Three-month-old David Bernard Eilers woke with a loud, lusty cry. Margaret automatically moved into the boy's bedroom and cradled him against her. "I'll bet you're hungry, aren't you?" she cooed softly. Small but strong, David kicked and thrashed about as she quickly changed his diaper. Margaret then sat in the rocking chair and freed her breast to nurse her son.

It wasn't long before Matt came. He paused when he saw her and his face softened with love.

Margaret smiled up at her husband and marveled at the changes a year had brought into her life. She'd set her sights on Matt Eilers, chosen him as her husband, convinced him to marry her. It wasn't a perfect marriage, but after a less-than-ideal beginning, she could guarantee it was a strong one. It had to be.

Now Margaret was not only a wife, but a mother twice over. Little Hailey often spent weekends with them. Their contact with Sheryl Decker was limited, which was best all the way around. The waitress was bitter and difficult, despite a determined effort from both Matt and Margaret to make the situation as tolerable as they could.

Matt claimed the chair across from Margaret. She could tell that something was troubling him.

"Problems?" No doubt they involved Sheryl.

"I got a call from her attorney this morning."

"Again?"

Matt nodded, frowning. "Only this time it isn't money Sheryl wants." Margaret knew he worried about his daughter. Margaret did, too, but they were helpless to do anything but love and support little Hailey.

"Sheryl wants to give us custody of Hailey. Apparently, someone called Child Protective Services on her. A neighbor, as far as I know."

Margaret's first reaction was to feel elated. Then her practical nature asserted itself. "She doesn't suspect *us*, does she?"

"Oh, no," he murmured. "Sheryl says she isn't cut out for this motherhood business."

What she really meant, Margaret thought, was that using Hailey as a means of controlling Matt hadn't worked. All her frustration and bitterness had been directed at the baby. While Margaret had never seen evidence of physical abuse, she feared Sheryl had often left her unattended. That was probably what had motivated her neighbor to call the authorities.

"She says she's willing to sign over all rights to us," Matt said.

This was what Matt and Margaret had wanted, what they'd prayed for almost from the first. "Matt, that's wonderful news!"

"I thought so, too, but I had to be sure two babies wasn't going to be too much for you."

"Matthew Eilers, have you ever known me to walk away from a challenge?"

"No," he admitted.

"I can do this and will do it, with a grateful heart. A year ago, I was alone. Now I'm blessed with a husband and two beautiful children."

"They're a handful. It's like having twins. I'll help in any way I can, but—"

"I love Hailey," Margaret insisted, and she did. In the beginning, she'd wondered how she'd feel about Sheryl's daughter, but soon realized that Hailey was her husband's daughter, too, and Margaret deeply loved Matt. Besides that, Hailey was simply Hailey. She was a person in her own right, an innocent child not to be held accountable for her parents' sins.

"Have I mentioned lately how much I love you?"

Margaret had to smile. Not a day passed that Matt didn't show his love for her in one way or another. A year earlier she'd vowed to love him, faults and all; she'd discovered that the alchemy of marriage had changed both of them, for the better.

Raising two children, less than three months apart in age, wasn't the way she'd expected to be introduced to motherhood, but she welcomed Hailey into her home and her heart.

"We can do this," Margaret assured him once more.

"I doubt there's anything we can't do," Matt said with a deep sigh.

"Together," Margaret added. She reached out her hand to Matt, who took it in his own, linking them.

Hand to hand.

Heart to heart.

Child to child.

* * * * *

BUFFALO VALLEY

To my mom and dad,
Ted and Connie Adler.
Boy, did I get lucky to have you for my parents!
I love you both.

One

So this was North Dakota. Gazing steadily ahead, Vaughn Kyle barreled down the freeway just outside Grand Forks. Within a few miles, the four lanes had narrowed to two. Dreary, dirt-smudged snow lay piled up along both sides of the highway. Fresh snow had begun to fall, pristine and bright, glinting in the late-afternoon sun.

His parents had retired earlier in the year, leaving Denver, where Vaughn had been born and raised, and returning to the state they'd left long ago. They'd moved north, away from the majestic peaks of the Rocky Mountains to the endlessly boring landscape of the Dakotas. *This* was supposed to be beautiful? Maybe in summer, he mused, when the fields of grain rippled with the wind, acre after acre. Now, though, in December, in the dead of winter, the beauty of this place escaped him. All that was visible was a winding stretch of black asphalt cutting through flat, monotonous terrain that stretched for miles in every direction.

After seven years as an Airborne Ranger in the U.S. Army's Second Battalion based in Fort Lewis, Washington, Vaughn was poised to begin the second stage of his working life. He had his discharge papers and he'd recently been hired by Value-X, a mega-retailer with headquarters in Seattle. Value-X was one of America's most notable success stories. New stores were opening every day all across the United States and Canada.

His course was set for the future, thanks largely to Natalie Nichols. They'd met two years earlier through mutual friends. Natalie was smart, savvy and ambitious; Value-X had recognized her skills and she'd advanced quickly, being promoted to a vice presidency before the age of thirty.

Vaughn had been attracted by her dedication and purpose, and he'd admired her ambition. His own work ethic was strong; as he'd come to realize, that was increasingly rare in this age of quick fixes and no-fault living. Natalie was the one who'd convinced him to leave the army. He was ready. When he'd enlisted after finishing college, he'd done so intending to make the military his career. In the seven years since, he'd learned the advantages and drawbacks of soldiering.

He didn't mind the regimented life, but the career possibilities weren't all he'd hoped they would be. What he lacked, as Natalie had pointed out, was opportunity. He was limited in how far he could rise through the ranks or how quickly, while the private sector was wide-open and looking for promising employees like him. He'd been interviewed by three headhunters who recruited candidates for a variety of corporations and in just a few weeks had six job offers.

At first he'd felt there might be a conflict of interest, taking a position with the same company as Natalie. However, she didn't view it that way; they would be a team, she'd told Vaughn, and with that remarkable persuasive skill of hers had convinced him to come on board. He wouldn't officially start until after the first of the year, but he was already on assignment.

Value-X was buying property in Buffalo Valley, North Dakota. Since Vaughn was going to be in the vicinity, visiting his parents in nearby Grand Forks, Natalie had asked him to pay the town a visit. It wasn't uncommon for a community to put up token resistance to the company's arrival. In most cases, any negative publicity was successfully handled, using a proven strategy that included barraging the local media with stories showing the company's "human face." After a recent public-relations disaster in Montana, Natalie was eager to avoid a repeat. She'd asked Vaughn to do a "climate check" in Buffalo Valley, but it was important, she insisted, that he not let anyone know he was now a Value-X employee, not even his parents. Vaughn had reluctantly agreed.

He'd done this because he trusted Natalie's judgment. And because he was in love with her. They'd talked about marriage, although she seemed hesitant. Her reasons for postponing it were logical, presented in her usual no-nonsense manner. She refused to be "subservient to emotion," as she called it, and Vaughn was impressed by her clear-cut vision of what she wanted and how to achieve it. They'd get married when the time was right for both of them.

He was eager to have her meet his family. Natalie would be joining him on December twenty-seventh, but he wished she could've rearranged her schedule to travel with him.

On this cold Friday afternoon two weeks before Christmas, Vaughn had decided to drive into Buffalo Valley. Because of Hassie Knight, he didn't need to invent an excuse for his parents. Hassie was the mother of his namesake. She'd lost her only son—his parents' closest friend—in Vietnam three years before Vaughn was born. Every birthday, until he'd reached the age of twenty-one, Hassie had mailed him a letter with a twenty-five-dollar U.S. Savings Bond.

In all that time, he'd never met her. From first grade on, he'd dutifully sent her a thank-you note for every gift. That was the extent of their contact, but he still felt a genuine fondness for her—and gratitude. Hassie had been the one to start him on a savings program. As a young adult Vaughn had cashed in those savings bonds and begun acquiring a portfolio of stocks that over the years had become a hefty nest egg.

An hour after he left Grand Forks, Vaughn slowed his speed, certain that if he blinked he might miss Buffalo Valley entirely. Value-X could put this place on the map. That was one benefit the company offered small towns. He wasn't sure what kind of business community existed in Buffalo Valley. He knew about Knight's Pharmacy of course, because Hassie owned that. Apparently the town was large enough to have its own cemetery, too; Hassie had mailed him a picture of her son's grave site years earlier.

Buffalo Valley was directly off the road. You didn't take an exit the way you would in most places. You just drove off the highway. He slowed, made a right turn where the road sign indicated. The car pitched as it left the pavement and hit ruts in the frozen dirt road. He'd gone at least a hundred feet before the paved road resumed.

He passed a few scattered houses, and as he turned the corner, he discovered, somewhat to his surprise, a main street with businesses lining both sides. There was even a hotel of sorts, called Buffalo Bob's 3 OF A

KIND. The bank building, a sprawling brick structure, seemed new and quite extensive. This was amazing. He wasn't sure what he'd expected, but nothing like this. Buffalo Valley was a real town, not a cluster of run-down houses and boarded-up stores, like some of the prairie towns his parents had told him about.

Hassie's store caught his attention next. It was a quaint, old-fashioned pharmacy, with big picture windows and large white lettering. Christmas lights framed the window, flashing alternately red and green. In smaller letters below KNIGHT'S PHARMACY, a soda fountain was advertised. Vaughn hadn't tasted a real soda made with hand-scooped ice cream and fla-vored syrup since his childhood.

He parked, climbed out of his rental car and stood on the sidewalk, glancing around. This was a decent-size town, decorated for the holidays with festive dis-plays in nearly every window. A city park could be seen in the distance, and Buffalo Valley Quilts appeared to take up a large portion of the block across the street. He remembered an article about it in the file Natalie had given him.

The cold stung his face and snow swirled around him. Rather than stand there risking frostbite, Vaughn walked into the pharmacy. The bell above the door jin-gled and he was instantly greeted by a blast of heat that chased the chill from his bones.

"Can I help you?" He couldn't see who spoke, but the voice sounded young, so he assumed it wasn't Hassie. The woman or girl, whoever she was, stood behind the raised counter at the back of the store.

"I'm looking for Hassie Knight," Vaughn called, edg-ing his way down the narrow aisle. This pharmacy ap-parently carried everything: cosmetics, greeting cards, over-the-counter medicine, gourmet chocolate, tooth-paste and tissues—just about anything you might require.

"I'm sorry, Hassie's out for the day. Can I be of help?"

He supposed he didn't need to see Hassie, although it would have been nice.

"I'm Carrie Hendrickson." A petite blonde in a white jacket materialized before him, hand extended. "I'm an intern working with Hassie."

"Vaughn Kyle," he said, stretching out his own hand. He liked the way her eyes squarely met his. Her expression held a hint of suspicion, but Vaughn was prepared for that. Natalie had mentioned the North Dakota attitude toward strangers—a wariness that ranged from mild doubt to outright hostility. It was one reason she worried about this proposed building site.

"Hassie and I have never officially met, but she does know me," he added reassuringly. "I was named after her son."

"You're *the* Vaughn Kyle?" she asked, her voice revealing excitement now. "Did Hassie know you were coming and completely forget? I can't imagine her doing that."

"No, no, it was nothing like that. I just happened to be in the area and thought I'd stop by and introduce myself."

Her suspicion evaporated and was replaced with a wide, welcoming smile. "I'm so pleased to meet you. Hassie will be thrilled." She gestured to the counter. "Can I get you anything? Coffee? A soft drink?"

"Actually, I wouldn't mind an old-fashioned soda."

"They're Hassie's specialty, but I'll do my best."

"Don't worry about it." On second thought, he decided something warm might be preferable. "I'll have a coffee."

She led him to the soda fountain and Vaughn sat on a padded stool while Carrie ducked beneath the counter and reappeared on the other side.

"Do you know when Hassie's due back?" he asked.

"Around six," Carrie told him, lifting the glass pot and filling his cup. "You need space for cream?" she asked.

He answered with a quick shake of his head. She didn't cut off the steady stream of weak coffee until it'd reached the very brim of his cup.

The door opened, bells jingling, and a woman dressed in a black leather jacket walked into the store. She had three scarves wrapped around her neck, nearly obscuring her face.

"Hi, Merrily," Carrie called, then scrambled under the fountain barrier. "I'll have Bobby's prescription ready in just a moment." She hurried to the back of the store. "While you're waiting, introduce yourself to Vaughn Kyle."

Merrily glanced toward the counter and waved, and Vaughn raised his mug to her.

"That's *Hassie's* Vaughn Kyle," Carrie said emphatically. "Vaughn was named after her son," she added.

"Well, why didn't you say so?" Merrily walked over to shake his hand. "What are you doing here?" she asked, unwinding the woolen scarves.

Now, that was an interesting question, Vaughn thought. He certainly hadn't anticipated anyone knowing about him.

"He came to meet Hassie," Carrie said as she returned with the prescription. She handed Merrily a small white sack. "How's Bobby feeling?"

"Better, I think. Poor little guy seems prone to ear infections." She turned to Vaughn with a smile. "Nice meeting you," she said. She wrapped the mufflers around her face again before she headed out the door.

"You, too," Vaughn murmered.

Carrie reached across the counter and grabbed a second mug for herself. "Hassie told you about the War Memorial, didn't she? We're all proud of that." Not waiting for a response, she continued, "The town built the Memorial three years ago, and it honors everyone from Buffalo Valley who died in war. The only one most of us actually remember is Hassie's son. But there were others. We lost Harvey Schmidt in the Korean War and five men in World War II, but none of their families live in the area anymore."

"You knew Vaughn Knight?" The blonde seemed far too young to have known Hassie's son.

"Not personally. But from the time I was small, Hassie told my brothers and me about Vaughn. It's been her mission to make sure he isn't forgotten."

Vaughn had heard about Vaughn Knight from his own parents of course, since they'd both been close to Hassie's son.

Carrie sipped her coffee. "Hassie told me it was one of the greatest honors of her life that your parents chose to remember her son through you."

Vaughn nodded, disappointed that he'd missed meeting the older woman. "What time did you say Hassie would be back?"

"Around six, I guess."

Vaughn checked his watch. He didn't intend to make an entire day of this.

"If Hassie had known you were coming, I don't think *anything* could've kept her away."

"I should have phoned beforehand," he muttered. "But…"

"I hope you'll wait."

Vaughn glanced at his watch again. Three hours was far longer than he wanted to stick around. "Tell her I'll come by some other time."

"*Please* stay. Hassie would feel terrible if she learned you'd left without meeting her." She hesitated, obviously thinking. "Listen," she said, "I'll phone Leta Betts and ask if she can fill in for me for a couple of hours."

Vaughn reconsidered. He might get all the information he needed from Carrie; then he could meet Hassie on strictly social terms. He'd been vaguely uncomfortable about questioning Hassie, anyway.

"Please," she said, "it would mean the world to Hassie, and I'd be delighted to give you a tour of town."

Perfect. He'd learn everything Natalie wanted to know and more. "That's a generous offer. Are you sure you don't mind?"

"I'd consider it a pleasure," she said, and smiled.

With her looking up at him that way, smiling and appreciative, Vaughn couldn't help noticing that Carrie Hendrickson was a very attractive woman. Not that Natalie had anything to worry about, he told himself staunchly.

Working closely with Hassie as an intern pharmacist, Carrie Hendrickson was keenly aware of how eager the older woman was to meet her son's namesake. A few months ago, Hassie had heard that the Kyles had retired in Grand Forks and she'd mailed off a note, inviting them to visit Buffalo Valley. Apparently they planned to do that sometime in the new year. Hassie would be ecstatic about finally meeting their son.

Carrie loved Hassie Knight, who was her mentor and her friend. Following Carrie's divorce, Hassie had given her sympathy—and good, brisk, commonsense advice.

She'd guided her through the fog of her pain and encouraged her to look toward the future. Many an afternoon they'd spent talking, reminiscing, sitting quietly together. Hassie had shared the grief of her own losses and helped Carrie deal with Alec's betrayal in ways her own mother never could. Hassie was the person who'd suggested she return to college. Carrie had taken her advice; nearly six years ago she'd enrolled at the University of North Dakota in Grand Forks. Now she was about to finish her internship with Knight's Pharmacy and achieve her Pharm.D and become a Doctor of Pharmacy. The last few years had been bleak financially, but the reward would be worth all the sacrifices.

After her divorce, she'd moved back in with her parents. She felt deeply grateful for their generosity but she *was* twenty-seven years old and longed for more independence and a home of her own. Well, it would happen eventually; she'd just have to wait.

Meanwhile, working side by side with Hassie, Carrie had learned a great deal. When it came time for the older woman to retire, Carrie would be willing and able to assume her role in the pharmacy and in the town. People knew and trusted her. Already they approached her with their troubles and concerns as naturally as they did Hassie. Alec's infidelity had reinforced the importance of trust and honor for Carrie. Those were precepts she lived by. The people of Buffalo Valley knew she would keep their problems to herself.

The town was a success story in an area where there'd been few. The Hendrickson farm, like many others, had fallen victim to low crop prices. Unable to make a living farming the land that had supported them for three generations, her father had leased the acreage to his older sons and moved into town. Together with Carrie's two younger brothers, he'd opened a hardware store.

For as long as she could remember, Knight's Pharmacy had been the very heart of this town. Hassie was getting on in years and probably should've retired long ago. She wouldn't, though, not while the community still needed her, not only to dispense prescriptions and basic medical advice but also to be their counselor and confidante.

Carrie knew she could never replace Hassie, because that would be impossible. But she'd always been good at chemistry and math, and had done well at her pharmaceutical studies. She also cared about the town and had an intense interest in people. Hassie had often told her she was naturally intuitive and sensitive toward others; Carrie was pleased by that, although her intuition had been notably absent during her ex-husband's affair. Hassie said she was exactly the pharmacist Buffalo Valley needed and had given her the faith in herself to believe she could complete the six years of schooling required to obtain her license.

"I'll get my coat and hat and be right back," she told Vaughn after calling Leta. Hassie's friend worked at the pharmacy part-time and was as eager as Carrie to make sure that Hassie met Vaughn.

"You're certain this isn't an imposition?"

"Absolutely certain," she told him.

Leta arrived promptly and after making swift introductions, Carrie removed the white pharmacist's jacket and put on her long wool coat.

"What would you like to see first?" she asked when she rejoined him.

"Whatever you'd like to show me."

"Then let's go to the City Park." Although there were

a number of places she wanted to take him, the park seemed the best place to start. As they left the pharmacy, Carrie noticed it had stopped snowing, but she suspected the temperature had dropped several degrees. She led him across the street and then down a block, past the quilt store and several others.

"I know Hassie would want you to see the War Memorial," she said, glancing up at Vaughn. Now that she stood beside him, she was surprised to see how tall he was—possibly six-two. All four of her brothers were six feet, but Carrie took after her mother's side of the family and was small-boned and petite. His dark good looks didn't escape her notice, either.

"First came the park," she explained, walking briskly to ward off the cold. Carrie loved the City Park and everything it said about their community. The people of Buffalo Valley had worked together to make this barren plot of land a place of which to be proud. "The land itself was a gift from Lily Quantrill," she said. "Heath Quantrill, her grandson, is the president of Buffalo Valley Bank." She pointed toward the brick structure at the far end of Main Street.

"Isn't there a branch in Grand Forks?"

"There are branches all across the state," Carrie told him.

"The headquarters is here?"

She nodded. "Heath moved everything to Buffalo Valley two years ago. I know it was a hard decision, but this is his home now, and he was tired of commuting to Grand Forks three days a week."

"It's an impressive building."

"Heath's an impressive bank president. I hope you get the chance to meet him and his wife, Rachel."

"I do, too," Vaughn said.

"Heath donated the lumber for the children's play equipment," she said as they entered the park and strolled past the jungle gym, slides and swings. "But Brandon Wyatt, along with Jeb McKenna and Gage Sinclair, actually built all these things." She realized the names didn't mean anything to Vaughn, but she wanted him to get a sense of what the park stood for in this community. Each family had contributed something, from planting the grass to laying the concrete walkway.

"It looks well used."

An outsider like Vaughn couldn't possibly understand how much the children of Buffalo Valley cherished the park. "My family owns the hardware," she continued, pointing to the opposite side of the park toward the store. "We donated the wood for the picnic tables."

"I notice they aren't secured with chains," Vaughn said.

"We don't have much crime in Buffalo Valley." It distressed her to visit public areas where everything, including picnic tables and garbage cans, was tied down by chains to prevent theft. But no one had ever stolen from the park or any other public place in Buffalo Valley. There'd never been any real vandalism, either.

"No crime?" He sounded as though he didn't believe her.

"Well, some, but it's mostly petty stuff. A few windows soaped at Halloween, that kind of thing. The occasional fight or display of drunkenness. We did have a murder once, about eighty years ago. According to the stories, it was a crime of passion." Quickly changing the subject, she said, "The War Memorial was designed by Kevin Betts. I don't know if you've heard of him, but he was born and raised right here."

"Sorry, I haven't," Vaughn said with a shrug.

"He's Leta's son, and he's an artist who's making a name for himself." Everyone in town was proud of Kevin. "This sculpture—" she gestured as they neared it "—was one of his very first." She watched Vaughn's expression when he saw it and was stirred by the immediate appreciation that showed in his eyes.

Kevin was a gifted artist, not only because he was technically skilled but because his work evoked emotion in people. The bronze sculpture was simple and yet profound. Half-a-dozen rifles were stacked together, upright and leaning against one another, with a helmet balanced on top. Beside the guns a young soldier knelt, his shoulders bowed in grief. No one seeing the piece could fail to be moved, to respond with sorrow and a bittersweet pain.

Vaughn stood before the memorial and didn't say anything right away. Then he squatted down and ran his finger over the name of Vaughn Knight. "My parents still talk about him. He was the one who brought them together," Vaughn said, and slowly straightened. "I'm glad he won't be forgotten."

"He won't be," Carrie assured him. "With this memorial, his name will always be here to remind everyone."

Vaughn thrust his gloved hands into his coat pockets.

"Cold?" Carrie asked.

He shook his head. "I know about the pharmacy and you've mentioned the hardware store. Tell me about the other businesses in town."

They walked toward Main Street and Carrie told him about each one in turn, starting with Joanie Wyatt's video-rental and craft store and ending with her parents' place.

"It was a leap of faith for you to move into town, wasn't it?" Vaughn said.

Carrie nodded pensively. "Yeah, but it's paid off. My two oldest brothers are still farming and the two younger ones work exclusively with Mom and Dad. It's a good arrangement all around."

"Are you hungry?" Vaughn asked unexpectedly.

She laughed. "You offering to feed me?" It was a bit early, but dinner would pass the time until Hassie returned.

"Unless there's a reason for you to hurry home."

"No reason. I'm divorced." Even now, six years later, the words left a bitter taste on her tongue. She focused her gaze directly in front of her.

"I'm sorry," he said.

"I am, too." She forced a cheerful note into her voice, as if to say she was over it.

"I thought I'd suggest Buffalo Bob's 3 OF A KIND. I was intrigued by what you told me about him."

"He's certainly a character," she agreed. "But before we go there, I'd like to show you Maddy's Grocery." Carrie loved the wonderful and witty Christmas display Maddy put up every year. Eight reindeer were suspended from the ceiling, with the front half of Santa's sleigh coming out of the wall.

Vaughn laughed when he saw it. His reaction was one of genuine enjoyment and not the short derisive laugh of someone mocking Maddy's efforts. On their way to 3 OF A KIND, they strolled past Buffalo Valley Quilts.

"This is the success story of the decade," Carrie boasted as she motioned to the holiday quilt displayed in the first set of windows. "Sarah Urlacher started the business in her father's house, dyeing the muslin herself from all-natural products. The designs are her own, too."

Vaughn stopped to look at the quilt in the window.

"It all began when Lindsay Sinclair introduced Sarah's quilts to her uncle. He owns an upscale furniture store in Atlanta, and before she knew it, Sarah had trouble keeping up with the demand. Now people all over the country buy her quilts."

"That's great."

"Sarah's business has boosted the economy of Buffalo Valley to the point that we can now afford things that are commonplace in other towns."

"Such as?"

"The sidewalks got refurbished last summer, and the town could never have paid for that without the tax revenue Sarah's business brings in." Carrie didn't mention the new community well and several other improvements that had taken place over the past few years.

"I'll let Leta know where we are so she can tell Hassie," Carrie said, and made a quick stop at the pharmacy. She was back within moments. Vaughn waited for her outside.

There was no one at the restaurant or in the bar when they arrived. Studying Buffalo Bob with fresh eyes, Carrie could only guess what Vaughn must think. The ex-biker was a burly man. He was an oddity here in a town where most men came off the farm. With his thinning hair drawn back into a ponytail and his muscular arms covered in tattoos, he looked as though he'd be more comfortable with a biker gang than waiting tables.

"How ya doin', Carrie?" he greeted her when she took a seat across the table from Vaughn.

"Good, Bob. Come meet Vaughn Kyle."

"Welcome to Buffalo Valley," Bob said, extending his hand for a hearty shake. "Merrily told me you'd dropped by." Bob gave them each a menu. "Take a look, but the special tonight is Salisbury steak. I don't mind telling you it's excellent." He grinned. "And who would know better than me?"

"I'm convinced," Vaughn told him with an answering smile. "I'll have the special."

"Me, too," Carrie said, returning the menu.

Bob left them, and Carrie tried to relax but found it difficult. She hadn't been alone with a man, other than her brothers, in a very long time. Following her divorce, she'd only dated twice, and both occasions had been awkward. Her schooling, plus her internship, didn't leave much room for a social life, anyway.

Vaughn sat back in his chair. "Tell me about Hassie," he suggested easily.

Carrie felt the tightness leave her shoulders. On the subject of Hassie, she could talk his ear off. "What would you like to know first?"

"Whatever you feel is important."

"She's been my hero for as long as I can remember. I don't know what would've happened to this town without her." Carrie wanted him to realize how deeply Hassie was loved by everyone in Buffalo Valley. "She's older now, and she's slowing down some." Carrie had seen the evidence of that in the months since she'd come to work as an intern. She almost suspected that Hassie had been holding on until she got there.

Vaughn glanced at Buffalo Bob as he brought their salads and nodded his thanks. "Every year, along with my birthday card and a U.S. Savings Bond, she wrote me a short message." His mouth lifted in a half smile. "She called it *words to live by.*"

"Give me an example," Carrie said, curious.

"I don't remember them all, but…okay, she told me about the importance of being on time. Only, she did it by making up this little poem..." He hesitated and a slow grin crossed his face. "She once wrote that if at first I don't succeed, it just means I'm normal."

"That sounds like Hassie."

"She has a wonderful way of putting things." He paused, a reflective look on his face. "When I was sixteen, she told me the grass isn't greener on the other side of the fence, it's greener where it's watered."

"I think it's wonderful that you remembered them."

"How could I not, when she made them so much fun? She was like an extra grandmother."

Hearing that warmed Carrie's heart, because she knew Hassie felt toward him the way she would a grandson.

They were silent as they ate their salads. Buffalo Bob had made even a plain lettuce, cucumber and tomato salad taste delicious with the addition of a tart-sweet cranberry dressing. They were just finishing when Bob reappeared, carrying two plates heaped with food. He placed them in front of Vaughn and Carrie, then stepped back, and said, "Enjoy."

Vaughn stared after him as he returned to the kitchen. "He's not the typical sort of person you find in a place like this, is he?"

"Bob's a sweetheart," she said defensively. "He's hardworking and well-liked and a wonderful father and—"

"Tell me how he happened to land in Buffalo Valley," Vaughn broke in. He reached for his fork, tasting the fluffy mashed potatoes and tender gravy-covered steak.

"He came here when the town was at its lowest point. My uncle Earl owned this hotel and he'd been trying to sell it for years. Seeing that there weren't any buyers and he was losing money every month, my uncle devised an unusual poker game. It cost a thousand dollars to play, but the winner walked away with the hotel, restaurant and bar. Lock, stock and barrel."

Vaughn's brows arched. "And Bob won it with three of a kind."

"Exactly."

Vaughn shook his head. "More power to him."

"A lot has changed since then, all of it for the better. Bob married Merrily, and two and a half years ago, they had little Bobby."

"The one who's prone to ear infections?"

She nodded. "You've never seen better parents. Those two dote on that little boy something fierce. In fact, Bob and Merrily are terrific with all the kids in town." Carrie paused long enough to sample her dinner. "Hey, this is terrific."

Vaughn agreed with her. "In addition to his other talents, Buffalo Bob's a good cook. He wasn't kidding about that."

"I don't know what his life was like before he came to Buffalo Valley, but he's one of us now."

Vaughn was about to ask a question when the door opened and Hassie hurried inside.

Carrie was instantly on her feet. One look told her Hassie was exhausted. Her shoulders were slumped and she seemed close to collapse.

"Hassie," Carrie said, wrapping her arm protectively around the older woman's waist. "This is Vaughn Kyle."

It was almost as if Hassie didn't hear her at first. "Vaughn," she repeated, and then her face brightened visibly. "My goodness, did you let me know you were coming and it slipped my mind?"

Vaughn pulled out a chair for her to sit down. "No, I very rudely showed up without an invitation."

"I wish I'd known."

"It's no problem. Carrie was kind enough to spend the afternoon with me."

"Let me take a good look at you," Hassie said. She cupped his face with both hands and a smile emerged. "You're so handsome," she whispered. "You have such kind eyes."

If her praise embarrassed or flustered him, Vaughn didn't reveal it.

"How long can you stay?" she asked.

"Actually, I should probably think about heading back to Grand Forks soon."

"No," Hassie protested. "That's hardly enough time for me to show you everything."

"Carrie already gave me a tour of town."

"That's good, but I have a number of things I've saved that I'd like you to have—things that were my son's."

Her disappointment was unmistakeable, and Carrie glanced at Vaughn, trying to signal him, hoping he'd change his mind.

"I want to see them."

Carrie could have hugged him right then and there.

"But," he added, "you've had a long, tiring day. Perhaps it would be better if I came back later."

Hassie didn't bother to deny what was obvious. "Would it be too much to ask you to come here on Sunday?" Both her hands gripped his, as if she was afraid to let him go.

Carrie found herself just as eager to hear his response.

"I'll meet you at the store shortly after noon," he said. "I'll look forward to seeing you then."

Carrie felt a surge of relief—and anticipation. She couldn't help smiling, first at Hassie, then at Vaughn.

Happiness shimmered in the old woman's eyes as

she placed one hand on Carrie's shoulder and leaned heavily against her.

"That would be perfect," she said quietly. "Thank you, Vaughn."

Two

Hassie felt old and weary, especially after a day like this. But God had rewarded her patience by sending Vaughn Kyle to Buffalo Valley. Seeing him, however briefly, had lifted her spirits. Best of all was his promise to return on Sunday afternoon.

Tired though she was, Hassie brewed herself a cup of tea and sat at her kitchen table, mulling over the events of the day. Ambrose Kohn had been a thorn in her side for many years. His family had lived and worked in town for generations, but with impeccable timing, the Kohns had moved to Devils Lake just before the economy in Buffalo Valley collapsed.

Ambrose owned several pieces of property here and a building or two. The theater belonged to him, and he'd been quick enough to close it down, despite the town council's efforts to convince him otherwise. The old building still had plenty of life in it, but it'd sat abandoned and neglected until the first year Lindsay Snyder came to Buffalo Valley as the high-school teacher. She'd wanted to use it for a Christmas play. If Hassie remembered correctly, Ambrose had demanded she go out with him first before he gave permission. That annoyed Hassie even now, several years later.

Lindsay had attended some social function with Ambrose, and it had nearly ruined her relationship with Gage Sinclair. But she and Gage had resolved their differences.They'd been married for more than five years now and were parents of two beautiful daughters.

Ambrose, despite his underhanded methods, had walked away a winner, as well. After the community had cleaned up that old theater and put on the high-school Christmas program, he'd reopened the movie house and it'd been in operation ever since.

Unfortunately Ambrose hadn't learned anything from that experience. He hadn't learned that people in Buffalo Valley loved their town and that they supported one another. He hadn't figured out that for them, Buffalo Valley was *home*, not just a place to live. Now the middle-aged bachelor held the fate of the community in his hands. Value-X, a huge retailer, wanted to move into town and they wanted to set up shop on land owned by Ambrose. The company had a reputation for sweeping into small towns and then systematically destroying independent and family-owned businesses. Six months earlier, Hassie had watched a television report on the effect the mega-retailer had on communities. At the time she'd never dreamed Buffalo Valley might be targeted. Naturally the company insisted this was progress and a boon to the town's economy. There were already articles in some of the regional papers, touting the company's supposedly civic-minded attitudes. Profit-minded was more like it.

No one needed to tell Hassie what would happen to Buffalo Valley if Value-X decided to follow through with its plans. All the small businesses that had recently started would die a fast and painful death. Her own pharmacy wouldn't be immune.

Ambrose owned twenty acres just outside of town; this was the property Value-X was interested in acquiring, and he wasn't opposed to selling it—no matter how badly it damaged the community.

Nothing Hassie said had the least bit of impact on him. Buffalo Bob, as president of the town council, had tried to reason with him, too, again without success. Heath Quantrill had thrown up his hands in frustration at the man's stubborn refusal to listen.

While Ambrose didn't live in Buffalo Valley, he did have a powerful influence on its future. For that reason alone, he should think carefully about his decision to sell that parcel of land. Progress or not, it wasn't the kind of future she or anyone here saw for Buffalo Valley. Jerry, her husband, might have been able to talk sense into Ambrose, but Jerry had died the year after Vaughn. She'd lost them both so close together.

The TV report on Value-X had made a strong impression on Hassie. What had stayed in her mind most clearly were the interviews with business owners, some with three-and four-generation histories. They'd been forced to close down, unable to compete. Local traditions had been lost, pride broken. Men and women wept openly, in despair and hopelessness. Downtown areas died out.

Hassie couldn't bear to think what would happen to Buffalo Valley if Ambrose sold that land to those outsiders. Why, it would undo all the work the town council had done over the past six years. The outcome was too dismal to consider.

Joanie Wyatt's video-rental and craft store would probably be one of the first to fold. And the Hendricksons—

they'd sunk everything they had in this world and more into AceMan Hardware. Value-X would undercut the lowest prices they could charge and ring the store's death knell for sure.

Dennis Urlacher supplied car parts to the community at his filling station. Although that was only a small portion of his business, Dennis had once mentioned that his largest profit margin came from the auto parts and not the fuel. It wouldn't be long before his business was affected, too. Even Rachel Quantrill's new hamburger stand would lose customers. Maddy's Grocery would suffer, too; how long she'd be able to hold on depended on Value-X's plans. It was said that many of the newer stores included groceries.

None of that concerned Ambrose. All he knew was that he'd been offered a fair price for a piece of land that had sat vacant for years. He'd let it be known that he fully intended to sell those acres. If anyone else was interested, he'd entertain other offers. Ambrose had made one thing perfectly clear: the offer had to be substantially higher than the deal Value-X had proposed. No one in town, not even Heath Quantrill, had a thick-enough bankroll to get into a bidding war with the huge retailer.

Hassie sipped her tea and purposely turned her thoughts in a more pleasant direction. What a fine-looking young man Vaughn Kyle was. After all these years, she was grateful to finally meet him. His letters had meant so much to her, and she'd saved each thank-you note from the time he was six years old.

For a short while after her son was buried, Hassie and Barbara, the boy's mother, had been close. They'd stayed in touch, but then a year later the wedding announcement arrived. Barbara, the beautiful young woman her son had loved, was marrying Rick Kyle, who'd been one of Vaughn's best friends.

Hassie didn't begrudge the couple happiness, but she hadn't attended the wedding. Their marriage was a painful reminder that life continues. If circumstances had been different, this might have been her own son's wedding.

Two years later, Rick and Barbara had mailed her the birth announcement. They'd named their first child after Hassie's son. Two years later came another birth announcement, this time for a girl they named Gloria. Sight unseen, Hassie had loved that boy and thought of him as the grandson Vaughn could never give her. Her own daughter, Valerie, had two girls and Hassie adored them, but since Val and her family lived in Hawaii, there was little opportunity to see them. Vaughn Kyle had assumed a special significance for her. Neither his parents nor anyone else knew how deep her feelings ran. With a determined effort, she'd remained on the sidelines of his life, writing occasional letters and sending gifts at the appropriate times.

Now she would have the opportunity to give Vaughn the things she'd set aside for him so many years ago. It'd been her prayer that they meet before she died.

She had to stop herself from being greedy. She would gladly accept whatever time Vaughn Kyle was willing to grant her.

Carrie found herself smiling as she walked into the family home shortly after six. She paused in the entryway to remove the handknit scarf from around her neck and shrug out of her coat. Softly humming a Christmas tune, she savored the warm feelings left by her visit with Vaughn. She'd enjoyed getting to know him. Even though it'd been years since she'd spent this much time in a man's company, the initial awkwardness between them had dissipated quickly.

Vaughn seemed genuinely interested in learning what he could about Hassie and Buffalo Valley. What she appreciated most was that he hadn't asked any prying questions about her divorce. A lot of people assumed she wanted to tell her side of it, but Carrie found no joy in reliving the most painful, humiliating experience of her life.

Their dinner conversation had flowed smoothly. He was easy to talk to, and Carrie loved telling him about Buffalo Valley. She was proud to recount its history, especially the developments of the past five years. The improvements could be attributed to several factors, but almost all of them went right back to Hassie Knight and her determination and optimism. Hassie refused to let the town fade into nothingness, refused to let it die like countless other communities throughout the Dakotas.

When Carrie walked into the living room, her mother glanced up from her needlework and her two younger brothers hurried in from the kitchen. All three fixed their eyes on her. Everyone seemed to be waiting for her to speak.

"What?" Carrie demanded.

"We're curious about your dinner date," her mother said mildly.

Carrie should've realized her family would hear she'd gone out with Vaughn. *How* they knew she could only speculate, but in a small town word traveled even faster than it did on the Internet.

"How'd it go?" Ken asked, looking as though he'd welcome the opportunity to defend her honor should the occasion arise.

Part of the pain of her divorce came from knowing that she was the first in their family's history to whom it had happened. Long-standing marriages were a tradition she would gladly have continued. But she couldn't stay married to a man who didn't honor his vows, a man whose unfaithfulness undermined her self-respect, as well as their marriage. Her four brothers had hinted that things with Alec would have worked out differently if they'd been around to see to it. Needless to say, the last thing she wanted was her brothers, much as she loved them, playing the role of enforcers.

"He's very nice," she said, carefully weighing her words. She didn't want to give the impression that there was more to their meeting than a simple, friendly dinner.

"He didn't try anything, did he?" Chuck asked.

Carrie nearly laughed out loud. "Of course he didn't. Where's Dad?" she asked, wondering why her father hadn't leaped into the conversation.

Before anyone could respond, her father shuffled into the room, wearing his old slippers, a newspaper tucked under his arm and his reading glasses perched on the end of his nose. He stopped abruptly when he saw her.

"So how was your hot date?" he asked. He stood in front of his easy chair and waited for her to answer.

"It was just dinner," she protested. "The only reason he asked me out was to kill time while he waited for Hassie." It was unlikely they'd be doing this again, which she supposed was just as well. She had to admit she *wanted* to, but from what he'd said, he was only in the area for the Christmas holidays and then he was going home to Seattle. There was no point in starting something you couldn't finish, she thought. Not that she knew if he was even interested in her...or available.

"Will you be seeing him again?" her mother asked, but Carrie wasn't fooled by her nonchalant tone.

"He's coming back Sunday afternoon to—"

"That's great." Her mother smiled, clearly pleased.

"He isn't returning to see *me*." It was important her family understand that she had nothing to do with his decision. The sole reason for his visit was to spend time with Hassie.

"That's a shame." Her father claimed his chair, turning automatically to the sports page.

"Did you invite him to the tree-lighting ceremony?" Ken asked.

Her father lowered the newspaper and her mother paused in the middle of a stitch to await her response.

"No," Carrie admitted reluctantly. She'd thought of mentioning it, but couldn't see the purpose. She glanced around the room, looking at each hopeful face.

What she didn't say was that she would've welcomed the opportunity to know Vaughn Kyle better. The few hours she'd spent with him had helped her realize that her heart was still capable of response, that it hadn't shriveled up inside her like an orange left too long in the fruit bowl.

For that she was grateful.

As Vaughn pulled the rental car into the long driveway that led to his parents' home, he saw that his mother had turned on the back porch light. It wasn't really necessary, since the outside of the entire house was decorated with Christmas lights.

He knew his mother had made tentative plans for a dinner with friends on Sunday afternoon and might not be pleased by his absence. However, Vaughn didn't mind returning to Buffalo Valley. He'd enjoyed meeting Carrie and learning some of the town's recent history. He'd report this information to Natalie; she might find it useful. Carrie Hendrickson was an interesting contrast to the women he'd met and dated in Seattle during the past few years—including Natalie, his sort-of fiancée. Carrie had shied away from talking about herself, which was a refreshing change from what he'd grown accustomed to hearing. A recent dinner date with Natalie had been spent discussing every aspect of her career and the Value-X corporation—as if their work was all they had to talk about. He'd come away with a letdown feeling, feeling, somehow, that he'd missed out on something important…only he didn't know quite what. After all, he *admired* Natalie's drive and ambition and her unemotional approach to life.

His mother was finishing the dinner dishes when he entered the kitchen. "How was your visit?" she asked, rinsing a pan before setting it on the drainboard.

"Wonderful."

"How's Hassie?" she asked, looking expectantly at him as she reached for the towel to dry her hands. "You did give her my love, didn't you?"

"She was exhausted." He explained that the pharmacist had been at a meeting when he arrived and that her assistant had convinced him to wait until she got back. Neither she nor Carrie had mentioned the reason for the meeting, but whatever it was had drained her, emotionally and physically.

His mother's brow furrowed with concern. "She's not ill, is she?"

"I don't think so, but I didn't want to tire her out any more than she already was, so I told her I'd be back on Sunday."

His mother's face clouded and he knew what was

coming. The subject of Vaughn Knight always distressed her. Every time his name was brought up, she grew quiet. He suspected she'd postponed a promised visit to Hassie because, for whatever reason, she found it hard to talk about Vaughn. More than once he'd seen tears fill her eyes. His mother wasn't the only one; his father also tended to avoid conversations about Hassie's son. All Vaughn knew was that both his parents thought a great deal of the friend who'd lost his life in a rice paddy thirty-three years earlier. So much that it still caused them pain.

"I'm glad you're doing this," she said. "Over the years I've wanted to talk about Vaughn, but I get choked up whenever time I try."

She grabbed a bottle of hand lotion and occupied herself with that for a few moments, but Vaughn wasn't fooled. She didn't want him to see that her eyes were brimming with tears.

"Hassie will do a far better job of telling you about Vaughn than your father or I could."

Impulsively Vaughn hugged his mother, then joined his father, who was watching television in the living room.

On Sunday the drive into Buffalo Valley seemed to go faster than it had on Friday. He knew exactly where he needed to go, and the very landscape he'd found monotonous two days earlier now seemed familiar, even welcoming.

When he pulled into town, Buffalo Bob was spreading salt on the sidewalk in front of his own place and the businesses on either side. He waved, and Vaughn returned the gesture, then eased into a parking spot near the pharmacy. Once again he was struck by what an appealing town Buffalo Valley was. It felt as though he'd stepped back in time, to an era when family and a sense of community were priorities, when neighbor helped neighbor and people felt responsible for one another.

A sign on the door stated that the drugstore was open from noon until five on Sundays during December. When he walked inside, Vaughn found Hassie behind the counter. He automatically looked for Carrie and wasn't disappointed when he saw her over by the cash register, checking receipts. She paused in her task as soon as she saw him.

To his surprise, his mind had drifted toward her a number of times since Friday. He was attracted by her charm, which was real and uncontrived. She was genuine and warm, and he liked the pride in her eyes when she talked about her town.

She froze, as if she, too, had been thinking of him. That was a pleasant thought and one that sent a shiver of guilt through him. He was as good as engaged to Natalie, and the last thing he should be doing was flirting with another woman.

"Right on time," Hassie said, sounding much livelier this afternoon than she had two days earlier.

"I'm rarely tardy when I have a date with a beautiful woman," he teased, and watched both Hassie and Carrie smile. He generally didn't have much use for flattery, but occasionally it served a purpose. In this case, his rather silly statement had given everyone, including him, a moment of pleasure.

"You going to be all right here by yourself?" She turned to Carrie.

"Of course. You two go and visit, and don't you worry about a thing."

"I'll just get my coat," Hassie said, and disappeared

to retrieve it. While she was gone, he had a few minutes with Carrie.

"I'm glad you're doing this for Hassie," she said. "It means so much to her to be sharing her son's life with you."

"I'm not doing it out of any sense of charity." Vaughn was truly interested in learning what he could about his namesake.

Hassie returned, wearing a long, dark coat, and they walked over to her house, which was one street off Main. Vaughn slowed his gait to match hers, tucking her arm in the crook of his elbow. Together they strolled leisurely down the newly shoveled sidewalk.

The house resembled something out of a 1950s movie. The furniture was large and bulky, covered in thick navy-blue fabric. Doilies decorated the back of the chair, and three were strategically placed across the back of the matching sofa. Even the television set was an old-fashioned floor model.

"It'll only take me a minute to make tea," Hassie announced heading toward the kitchen. He was given instructions to sit down and to look through the photo albums she'd already laid out.

Vaughn opened the biggest album. The first photograph he saw was a black-and-white version of a much younger Hassie standing with a baby cradled in her arms. A tall, handsome man stood awkwardly beside her, grinning self-consciously. His hand was on the shoulder of a little girl about four or five who stood in front of them, her dark brown hair in long braids.

Thereafter, photograph after photograph documented the life of Vaughn Knight. He was in Boy Scouts and active in his church. His school pictures showed increasing growth and maturity. When he reached high school, Vaughn had grown tall and athletic; a series of newspaper articles detailed his success on the basketball court and the football field. The year he was a senior, Buffalo Valley High School won the state football championship, with Vaughn Knight as the star quarterback. Another article named him Most Valuable Player.

His high-school graduation picture revealed the face of a young man eager to explore the world.

Hassie rejoined him, carrying a tray with a ceramic pot and two matching cups, as well as a plate of small cookies.

Vaughn stood and took the tray from her, placing it on the coffee table, and waited while she poured. He noticed that her hands were unsteady, but he didn't interrupt or try to assist her.

When she'd finished, she picked up a round, plain hatbox and removed the lid. "The top letter is the first one that mentions your mother."

Vaughn reached for the envelope.

September 30, 1966

Dear Mom and Dad,
I'm in love. Don't laugh when you read this. Rick and I went to a hootenanny last night and there was this terrific girl there. Her name's Barbara Lowell, and guess what? She's from Grand Forks. She's got long blond hair and the most incredible smile you've ever seen. After the hootenanny we drank coffee and talked for hours. I've never felt like this about any other girl. She's smart and funny and so beautiful I had a hard time not staring at her. Even after I left her, I was so wrapped up in meeting her I couldn't sleep. First thing this

morning, I called her and we talked for two hours. Rick is thoroughly disgusted with me and I don't blame him, but I've never been in love before.

As soon as I can, I want to bring her home for you to meet. You'll understand why I feel the way I do once you see her for yourselves.
Love,
Vaughn

"The Rick he's writing about is my dad?" Vaughn asked.

Hassie nodded. "Here's another one you might find interesting." She lifted a batch of letters from the box. It was apparent from the way she sorted through the dates that she'd reread each letter countless times.

July 16, 1967

Dear Mom and Dad,
I've made my decision, but I have to tell you it was probably the most difficult I've ever had to make. I love Barb, and both of us want to get married right away. If I were thinking just of me, that's exactly what we'd do before I ship out. But I'm following your example, Dad. You and Mom waited until after the war to marry, and you came back safe and whole. I will, too.

Barb cried when I told her I felt it was best to delay the wedding until after my tour. Although you never advised me one way or the other, I had the feeling you thought it was better this way.

Vaughn stopped reading. "Did you want him to wait before marrying my mother?"

Hassie closed her eyes. "His father and I thought they were both too young. In the years that followed, I lived to regret that. Perhaps if Vaughn had married your mother, there might have been a grandchild. I realize that's terribly selfish, and I hope you'll forgive me."

"There's nothing to forgive."

"I always wondered if Jerry would've lived longer if we'd had grandchildren. Valerie was still in college at the time and wasn't married yet. A few years after that, she moved to Hawaii to take a job and met her husband there, but by then it was too late for Jerry."

"So your husband took the news of Vaughn's death very hard?"

"Once we received word about Vaughn, my husband was never the same. He was close to both children, but the shock of Vaughn's death somehow made him lose his emotional balance. Much as he loved Valerie and me, he couldn't get over the loss of his son. He went into a deep depression and started having heart problems. A year later, he died, too."

"Heart attack?"

"Technically, yes, but Vaughn's death is what really killed him, despite what that death certificate said. He simply gave up caring about anything. I wish…" Her voice trailed off.

"I'm sorry," Vaughn said, and meant it.

"Don't be." She patted his hand. "God knew better. Had your mother and my son married, you would never have been born."

It must have hit her hard that her son's fiancée and closest friend married each other within a year of his death. "Were you upset when my parents got married?" he asked.

"A little in the beginning, but then I realized that

was exactly what Vaughn would have wanted. He did love her, and I know in my heart of hearts that she loved him, too."

"She did." Vaughn could say that without hesitation.

Hassie plucked a tissue from the nearby box and dabbed at her eyes. "I'd like you to have this." She reached for a second box and withdrew a heavy felt crest displaying the letters BVHS. It took Vaughn a moment to recognize that it was from a letterman's jacket.

"Vaughn was very proud of this. He earned it in wrestling. He was a natural at most sports. Basketball and football were barely a challenge, but that wasn't the case with wrestling. Many an afternoon he'd walk into the pharmacy and announce to his father and me that he was quitting. By dinnertime he'd change his mind and then he'd go back the next day." She paused, dabbing at her eyes again. "Our children were the very best of Jerry and me. Vaughn was a good son, and losing him changed all of us forever."

"I'd be honored to have this letter," Vaughn said.

"Thank you," Hassie whispered. She smiled faintly through her tears. "You must think me an old fool."

"No," he was quick to tell her. "I'm very glad you showed me all this." For the first time Vaughn Knight was more than a name, someone remembered who'd been lost in a war fought half a world away. He was alive in the words of his letters, in the photographs and in the heart of his mother.

"His letters from Vietnam are in this box," Hassie said. "They'll give you a feel for what it was like. If you're interested…"

Having served in the military, Vaughn was, of course, interested. He sat back and read the first letter.

When he'd finally finished them all, it'd grown dark and Hassie was busy in the kitchen.

"What time is it?" he asked.

"It's after six."

"No." He found that hard to believe. "I had no idea I'd kept you this long. I apologize, Hassie. You should have stopped me."

She shook her head. "I couldn't. Your interest was a pleasure to me. Everything was fine with the store— Carrie's fully capable of handling anything that might come up. Besides, we're closed now."

"He could've been a writer, your son," Vaughn said, setting aside the last letter. For a few hours he'd been completely drawn into Vaughn Knight's descriptions of people and landscapes and events. Although the details were lightly sketched, a vivid picture of the young soldier's life had revealed itself through his words.

"I often thought that myself," Hassie agreed. After a brief silence she said, "I didn't want to interrupt you to ask about dinner. I hope it wasn't overly presumptuous to assume you'd join me."

"I'd like that very much."

Hassie nodded once, slowly, as if she considered his company of great worth.

While she put the finishing touches on the meal, Vaughn phoned his parents to tell them he'd be later than anticipated. "Be sure and give Hassie my love," his mother instructed. "Tell her your father and I plan to visit her soon."

"I will," he promised.

When he ended the phone conversation, he found Hassie setting the table. He insisted on taking over, eager to contribute something to their dinner. His admiration and love for the older woman had grown this afternoon in ways he hadn't thought possible on such short acquaintance. She'd opened his eyes to a couple of important things. First and foremost, he'd learned about the man he'd been named after and discovered he had quite a lot to live up to. Second, he'd come to see his parents in a new light. He understood how their fallen friend had shaped their lives and their marriage. It was no wonder they didn't often speak of Vaughn Knight. The years might have dulled the pain, but the sense of loss was as strong in them as it was in Hassie.

They chatted over dinner, and his mood lightened. Hassie was wise and considerate; she seemed to understand how serious his thoughts had become.

"The community is lighting the Christmas tree this evening," she said casually as Vaughn carried their dishes to the sink.

"Are you going?" he asked.

"I wouldn't miss it for the world," Hassie informed him. "The Christmas tree is set up beside the War Memorial. Nearly everyone in town will be there—" she paused and looked at him "—including Carrie."

"Are you playing matchmaker with me, Hassie Knight?" he asked. He had a feeling she didn't miss much—and that she'd seen the way his gaze had been drawn to Carrie when he'd entered the pharmacy.

Hassie chuckled. "She's smitten, you know."

Smitten. What a wonderful old-fashioned word, Vaughn mused. It would take a better man than him not to feel flattered.

"You could do worse."

"And how do you know I don't already have a girlfriend waiting for me in Seattle?" he asked, and wondered what Hassie would think of Natalie. For some reason he had the impression she wouldn't think much of her sharp-edged sophistication. It'd taken him a while to see past Natalie's polished exterior; once he had, he'd realized she was just like everyone else, trying to be noticed and to make a name for herself.

"You don't," Hassie returned confidently.

He was about to tell her about Natalie, when Hassie said, "Come with me. Come and watch the community tree being lit. There's no better way to learn about Buffalo Valley."

Vaughn's purpose, other than meeting Hassie, was to do exactly that. Still, seeing Carrie again appealed to him, too—more than it should.

"That's just what I need to put me in the Christmas spirit," Vaughn said. "I'd consider it an honor to accompany you."

"Wonderful." Hassie clasped her hands together as though to keep herself from clapping with delight. "I can't tell you how happy this makes me."

He helped her on with her coat, then grabbed his own. Taking her arm again, Vaughn guided her out the door and down the front steps. By the time they rounded the corner to Main Street and the City Park, the town was coming to life. There were groups of people converging on the park and cars stopping here and there. The air was filled with festivity—carols played over a loudspeaker, kids shrieking excitedly, shouts of welcome…and laughter everywhere. Vaughn could practically *feel* the happiness all around him.

"This is about as close as it gets to a traffic jam in Buffalo Valley," Hassie told him.

As soon as they appeared, it seemed everyone in town called a greeting to Hassie. Vaughn had never seen anything to compare with the reverence and love people obviously felt for her.

"You've been holding out on me, Hassie Knight," an older man teased as he approached. "I didn't realize I had competition."

"Cut it out, Joshua McKenna." Hassie grinned. "Meet Vaughn Kyle."

"Mighty pleased to meet you." The man thrust out his hand for Vaughn to shake.

"Nearly everyone in a fifty-mile radius is coming," Joshua said, glancing around him. More and more cars arrived, and the park was actually getting crowded.

"I don't see Calla. She's not going to make it home this year?"

"And miss spoiling her baby brother?" Joshua returned. "You're joking, right?"

Hassie laughed delightedly. "I should have known better."

"Jeb, Maddy and the kids are already here."

The names flew over Vaughn's head, but it was apparent that Hassie loved each family.

"Maddy owns the grocery," Joshua explained as they strolled across the street and entered the park. "She's married to my son. Best thing that ever happened to him."

"Oh, yes—I saw the grocery," Vaughn said. "Maddy. I remember. The fantastic reindeer."

Joshua grinned widely. "Yup, that's our Maddy. Loves any excuse to decorate—and does a great job."

"They have two of the most precious children you'll ever want to see," Hassie added, "with another on the way."

"The first pregnancy and this latest one were real surprises."

"I'll bet Jeb's developed a liking for blizzards," Hassie murmured, and the two older folks burst into laughter.

"You'd have to know the history of that family to understand what's so amusing," Carrie said, joining them.

"Hello again," Vaughn murmured.

"Hi."

Vaughn had trouble looking away.

"How about you and Carrie getting me some hot chocolate?" the older woman asked.

"Bring some for me, too, while you're at it," Joshua said.

"I think we just got our marching orders," Carrie told him, her eyes smiling. "Is that okay?"

"I don't mind if you don't," Vaughn replied.

The cold had brought color to her cheeks, and her long blond hair straggled out from under her wool hat. "It's fine with me. Buffalo Bob and Merrily are serving cocoa and cookies over there," she said a little breathlessly.

"I'll be right back," Vaughn said over his shoulder as he followed Carrie.

"Don't rush," Hassie called after him…and then he thought he saw her wink at him.

Three

The Christmas lights strung around the outside of the old house welcomed Vaughn back to his parents' home. His mother had been born and raised in Grand Forks, but his grandparents had moved to Arizona when he was six. Vaughn had no recollection of visiting the Dakotas, although he was certain they had. His memories centered on the Denver area and his father's family. Not until Rick was accepted for early retirement did they decide to return to the home that had been in the Lowell family for more than a hundred years.

The television blared from the living room as Vaughn let himself into the house, entering through the door off the kitchen after stomping the snow from his shoes on the back porch. He unzipped his jacket and hung it on a peg, along with his muffler.

"Is that you, Vaughn?" his mother called.

"No, it's Santa," he joked.

He watched as his mother, still holding her needlepoint, hurried into the kitchen. "You're not hungry, are you?"

"I filled up on cookies and hot chocolate."

His mother studied him as if to gauge how the meeting with Hassie had gone—the *real* question she wanted to ask, he suspected. "Did you have a...good visit?"

"Yes." He nodded reassuringly. "We talked before dinner, but afterward there was a tree-lighting ceremony in the park."

"You attended that?" His mother sounded pleased.

"Sure, why not?" His response was flippant, as though this was the very thing he'd normally do. In truth, though, Vaughn couldn't recall attending anything like it since he was in grade school. The evening had been quite an experience. The whole town had come alive with music and laughter and people enjoying one another's company. Christmas had never been a big deal to Vaughn—but he'd never seen an entire community join together like this, either. He knew it had made a lasting impression on him, that it left him longing for the same kind of warmth. For a true spirit of celebration, far removed from sophisticated parties and decorator-trimmed trees.

"How is Hassie?" his mother asked.

Vaughn wasn't sure what to say. Hassie was without a doubt one of the most dynamic women he'd ever met. She possessed character and depth and a heart that poured out love for her family and her community. He'd immediately seen how deeply she was loved and respected. After these hours in her company, Vaughn had understood why. "She's an extraordinary woman."

"I know." His mother's voice was soft, a little tentative. Before Vaughn could say more, she'd retreated into the living room.

Vaughn followed and his father muted the television, obviously waiting for him to enlighten them about his visit.

"Hassie let me read the letters her son wrote from Vietnam."

His mother resumed her needlepoint and lowered her head, as though the stitches demanded her full attention.

"They were riveting. I learned about the war itself, things I could never have learned from a book, and about the man who wrote them." At the time, Hassie's son had been younger than Vaughn was now. In his letters, Vaughn had recognized the other man's sense of humanity, his hatred of war and his desire to make a difference, to share in a struggle for freedom.

"We met at the University of Michigan during our freshman year of college," his father said, and his eyes went blank. He seemed to be back in a different place, a different time. Vaughn knew he hadn't been accepted into the service himself because of poor eyesight. "He was my roommate. Both of us were away from home for the first time and in an environment completely foreign and unfamiliar. I suppose it's only natural that we became close."

His mother added in a low voice, "He was the most generous person I've ever known."

"He got a part-time job tutoring a youngster who had leukemia," his father continued, his gaze focused on the television screen. "He was hired for three hours a week, but Vaughn spent much more time with him than that. He played games with Joey, talked to him, cheered him up, and when Joey died at thirteen, the boy's mother said Vaughn had been his best friend."

"That's the kind of person he was," his mother said.

"Hassie gave me the school letter he earned in wrestling. And then, after I walked her back home, she said there was something else she wanted me to have." His parents looked up when he paused. Even now, Vaughn could hardly believe Hassie would give him such a gift.

"What, son?"

"Her husband's gold pocket watch. It would've been Vaughn's had he lived." Hassie had placed it in his hands with tears filming her eyes, then closed his fingers around it.

"Treasure it, Vaughn," his mother whispered.

"I do." Vaughn's first reaction had been to refuse something that was clearly a valuable family heirloom, something that meant a great deal to the old woman. He'd felt the significance of her gift and was moved by the solemnity of her words and gestures when she'd presented it to him.

He would always keep it safe. And he would pass it down to his oldest son or daughter.

"What else did Hassie tell you?" his father asked.

"She…said how much Vaughn had loved Mom."

"He did."

Vaughn studied his father, looking for any sign of jealousy. If he'd been in his father's shoes—well, he wasn't entirely sure *how* he'd feel.

"We planned to marry," his mother said, "but Hassie probably told you that."

He nodded. "She showed me the letter in which Vaughn explains why it would be best to wait until he returned from Vietnam."

"Only, he didn't return. And everything worked out in a completely different way." His mother took his father's hand and held it and they gazed at each other for a moment. "But a good way," she said quietly.

"I often wondered what Hassie really thought about the two of us getting married," his father said. He stared at Vaughn as if, after meeting Hassie, he could supply the answer.

Indeed, Vaughn had seen the look that came over her face when she mentioned his parents' marriage. "At first I think she took it hard." This didn't appear to surprise either of his parents.

"Our marriage was a reminder that Vaughn was never coming home," his mother said, "and that no matter how much pain the world brings us, life continues."

"She said as much herself."

"I think…she was disappointed in us both."

"Perhaps in the beginning," Vaughn agreed, "but she changed her mind later. She told me she felt that her son approved."

"I'm sure he did," his mother whispered.

His father reached abruptly for the remote, indicating that the conversation was over. Sound flared back, and Vaughn got up and went to the kitchen to pour himself a cup of coffee before rejoining his parents.

"Oh, dear, I almost forgot to tell you," his mother said. "Natalie phoned."

Vaughn's first reaction was that he didn't want to talk to her. Not tonight. Not after such an emotionally overwhelming day. Knowing Natalie, she'd want to discuss business, and that was the last thing on his mind. He needed to think before he returned the call, needed to absorb what he'd learned first—about the town, about Hassie…about himself.

"It isn't too late to call her back," his mother said. "With the time difference, it's barely eight on the West Coast."

"I know," he said absently, his thoughts now on Carrie Hendrickson. Much of the evening had been spent with her. After they'd brought hot chocolate to Hassie and Joshua McKenna, she'd introduced him to her family.

Vaughn had seen the wary look in her brothers' eyes and realized how protective they were of her. He wished he'd had more of a chance to talk to Carrie, but they were constantly interrupted. She was a favorite with her nieces and nephews, who were forever running up to her, involving her in their games and their squabbles. She was a natural peacemaker, he observed, one of those people whose very presence brought out the best impulses in others. Like Hassie. And the people in town valued Carrie in much the same way; that was easy to tell. They came to her for advice and comfort. They were drawn to her just as he was.

"Your father and I are looking forward to meeting Natalie," his mother said, breaking into his musings.

Vaughn started guiltily. He was as good as engaged— although, he supposed, all they'd really done was discuss the possibility of marriage. He hadn't divulged his plans to either of his parents. At Natalie's request, he hadn't even told them about his job. "She's anxious to meet you, too," he said, but without a lot of enthusiasm. The contrast between Natalie and Carrie flashed like a neon sign in his brain. One was warm and personable and focused on the needs of her community, the other sharp, savvy and ambitious. When he'd arrived in North Dakota, he thought he knew what he wanted; all at once, he wasn't sure.

"You've been seeing her for two years now," his mother went on, watching him.

"Barbara, the boy doesn't need you to tell him that."

Vaughn sipped his coffee. This was one conversation he had no wish to continue. "Carrie and I are going Christmas shopping tomorrow," he said, instead.

His mother lowered the needlepoint to her lap and stared at him. "Carrie? Who's Carrie?"

Vaughn didn't realize his mistake until it was too late. "A friend."

His mother raised her eyebrows as if his answer didn't please her. "When did you have time to make friends?"

"She works with Hassie at the pharmacy."

"I see." It appeared his mother did see, because she said nothing more.

Vaughn wished he understood his own feelings. A week ago he would have rushed to return Natalie's call. He wasn't avoiding *her*, he decided, but the subject of Value-X and Buffalo Valley. In a matter of days— one day, really—he'd become oddly protective of the town…and its people. Hassie, of course, but Carrie, too. Natalie was bound to ask him questions he no longer wanted to answer.

One thing was clear; he needed to think the situation through very carefully.

Craving solitude, Vaughn swallowed the last of his coffee, then announced he was heading for bed.

His mother glanced up at the wall clock. "Aren't you calling Natalie?"

He frowned. "Later. Don't worry about it, Mom."

"Vaughn has to rest up for shopping," his father teased.

"Ah, yes, the great shopping expedition. Where will it be, by the way?"

"The mall here in town."

"You're actually going to a mall at this time of year?" His father looked at him as though he'd lost his sanity.

Vaughn gave a nonchalant shrug. He didn't know what had possessed him to suggest he and Carrie meet at Columbia Mall. His excuse had been that Carrie was a wonderful source of information about the town. He'd never had the opportunity to bring up the subject of Value-X, and wanted to get her reactions to it. Or so he told himself.

The truth was, he wanted to know her better.

Hassie sat up in bed, her eyes on the photograph of her son on the bedroom wall. She looked at Jerry's picture next and Valerie's, then turned back to Vaughn's. It was only natural that she'd be thinking about her son tonight.

Time passed with such inexorable swiftness, she reflected. She had startlingly clear memories of Vaughn as a toddler, stumbling toward her, arms outstretched. If she closed her eyes, she could almost hear his laughter. She'd loved to scoop him into her arms and hug him close until he squirmed, wanting to run and play with his older sister. As they grew older, Valerie had listened to his confidences and offered a big sister's sage advice.

How carefree life had been for her and Jerry in the early 1950s. Simple pleasures had meant a great deal back then. She could think of no greater comfort than sitting with her husband after a day at the pharmacy, a day they'd spent working together. Jerry would slip his arm around her shoulder and she'd press her head against his. He'd loved to whisper the sweetest words in her ear, and oh, she'd enjoyed being in his arms. In those days, it seemed the sun would never stop shining and the world would always be filled with happiness.

Turning out the light, Hassie nestled under the covers and let her memories take her back. Valerie and Vaughn used to come to the pharmacy every afternoon after school. To this day she could still picture the two of them sitting at the soda fountain, waiting to be served an after-school snack. They were a normal sister and brother, constantly bickering. Valerie always teased Vaughn, and when she did, he'd tug her pigtails hard enough to bring tears to her eyes. Then it would be up to Hassie to chastise them both. Softhearted Jerry had left the discipline to her. Hassie hated it, but knew her children needed to understand that their actions had consequences.

The years flew by so fast! Looking back, Hassie wished she'd appreciated each day a little more, treasured each moment with her children while they were young. Before she could account for all the years that had passed, it was 1960, and Vaughn was in high school.

Jerry was especially proud of Vaughn's athletic talent. He, too, had been a sports star in his youth. Vaughn had played team sports throughout his four years in high school, and they'd never missed a game. One or the other, and often both of them, were at his games, even if it meant closing the pharmacy, although they didn't do that often. They always sat in the same section of the stands so Vaughn would know where to find them. When his team came onto the field, it wasn't unusual for him to turn toward the bleachers and survey the crowd until he located his parents. Then he'd smile and briefly raise one hand.

Without even trying, Hassie could hear the crowds and recall the cheerleaders' triumphant leaps, while the school band played in the background.

Watching Vaughn play ball had been hard on Hassie's nerves. Twice that she could remember, her son had been injured. Both times Jerry had to stop her from running onto the field. She stood with the other concerned parents, her hands over her mouth, as the coaches assessed his injuries. On both occasions Vaughn had walked off the playing field unaided, but it'd been pride that had carried him. The first time his arm had been broken, and the second, his nose.

His high-school years had been wonderful. The girls always had eyes for Vaughn. Not only was he a star athlete and academically accomplished, he was tall and good-looking. The phone nearly rang off the hook during his junior and senior years. There'd never been anyone special, though, until he met Barbara Lowell in college. She'd been his first love and his last.

Hassie recalled how handsome he'd looked in his brand-new suit for the junior-senior prom, although he'd been uncomfortable in the starched white dress shirt. The photo from the dance revealed how ill at ease he'd been. His expression, Jerry had said, was that of someone who expected to be hit by a water balloon.

Hassie had suggested he ask Theresa Burkhart to the biggest dance of the year. He'd done so, but he'd never asked her out for a second date. When Hassie asked him why, Vaughn shrugged and had nothing more to say. Every afternoon for a week after the prom, Theresa had stopped at the soda fountain, obviuosly hoping to run into Vaughn. Each afternoon she left, looking disappointed.

Packing Vaughn's suitcase the day before he went off to the University of Michigan was another fond memory. She'd lovingly placed his new clothes in the suitcase that would accompany him on this first trip away from home. Although saddened by his departure, she took comfort in knowing he'd only be gone for a few years. This wasn't a new experience, since Valerie had left four years earlier and was attending Oregon State. She was working part-time and seemed in no particular hurry to finish her education. Jerry and Hassie had been reassured by Vaughn's promise to return as a pharmacist himself. He shared their commitment to community and their belief in tradition.

Soon the kitchen table was littered with his letters home. The letter in which he first mentioned meeting Barbara had brought back memories of Hassie's own—like meeting Jerry at college just before the war. The day that letter arrived, she'd sat at the kitchen table with her husband and they'd held hands and reminisced about the early days of their own romance.

Then the unthinkable happened. News of a war in a country she'd barely heard of escalated daily. The papers, television and radio were filled with reports, despite President Johnson's promises to limit the United States' involvement. Then the day came when Vaughn phoned home and announced, like so many young men his age, that he'd been drafted. A numbness had spread from Hassie's hand and traveled up her arm. It didn't stop until it had reached her heart. Vaughn was going to war. Like his father before him, he would carry a rifle and see death.

This wasn't supposed to happen. For a while, men in college were exempt, but with the war's escalation, they were now included. Vaughn took the news well, but not Hassie. He had to do his part, he told her. It was too easy to pass the burden onto someone else. Citizenship came with a price tag.

Suddenly bombs were exploding all around her. Terrified, Hassie hid her head in her hands, certain she was about to die. Bullets whizzed past her and she gasped, her heart cramping with a terrible fear. All at once she was cold, colder than she could ever remember being, and then she was flat on her back with the sure knowledge that she'd been hit. The sky was an intense shade of blue, and she was simultaneously lying there and hovering far above. But when she looked down, it wasn't her face she saw. It was the face of her dying son. His blood drained out of him with unstoppable speed as the frantic medic worked over him.

Her son, the child of her heart, was dying. He saw her and tried to smile, to tell her it was all right, but his eyes closed and he was gone. Her baby was forever gone.

A crushing load of grief weighed on Hassie's heart. She cried out and, groaning, sat upright.

It was then she realized she'd fallen asleep. This had all been a dream. Awash with memories, she'd drifted into a dream so real she could hear the fading echoes of exploding ammunition as she dragged herself out of a past world and back to reality.

As her eyes adjusted to the dark, her gaze darted from one familiar object to another. From the bedroom door where her housecoat hung on a hook to the dresser top with the silver mirror and brush set Jerry had given her on their tenth anniversary.

"Vaughn." His name was a broken whisper, and she realized that she couldn't remember what he looked like. His face, so well loved, refused to come. Strain as she might, she couldn't see him. Panic descended, and she tossed aside the blankets and slid out of bed. It wasn't her son's image that filled her mind, but the face of another young man. Another Vaughn.

Vaughn Kyle.

"Of course," she whispered, clutching the bedpost. Leaning against it, she heaved a deep, quivering sigh and climbed back into bed.

Wrapping the quilt around her, she tucked her arm beneath her pillow and closed her eyes. Yes, it made sense that she'd dream of Vaughn that night. Her

Vaughn. It also made sense that it was Vaughn Kyle's face she now saw. After all, she'd spent much of the day with him.

Barbara and Rick had done a good job raising him. Vaughn was a fine man, honest and genuine, sensitive yet forthright. She was grateful she'd had the opportunity to meet him before she died.

Giving him the gold watch had been a spur-of-the-moment decision. It was the one possession of Jerry's she'd held back from Valerie and her two granddaughters. Valerie lived in Hawaii and although they were close, they rarely visited each other. Hassie had flown to the island once, but all those tourists and hordes of people had made her nervous. Not only that, she wasn't comfortable in planes, and the long flight made her nervous. A few years back, after a scare with Hassie's heart, Valerie had flown out to spend time with her, but had soon grown bored and restless.

Hassie didn't think Val's daughters, Alison and Charlotte, would have much interest in their grandfather's watch. But it was precious to her, so she'd kept it.

She knew when she pressed the watch into Vaughn's palm that this was the right thing to do. He looked as if he was about to argue with her, but he didn't and she was glad. Still, his hesitation told her more clearly than any words that he understood the significance of her gift.

Warm once more, Hassie stretched out her legs, enjoying the feel of the sheets against her bare skin. She smiled, remembering the exchange she'd witnessed between Carrie and Vaughn Kyle last night. She hoped something came of it. After her divorce Carrie was understandably wary about relationships, but Hassie felt confident that Vaughn would never intentionally do anything to hurt her.

* * *

"Can't something be done?" Carrie asked, pacing in front of Heath Quantrill's polished wood desk. As the president of Buffalo Valley Bank, he just might know of some way to stop Value-X from moving into town. In the past day or so, news of the retailer's plans had spread through town faster than an August brushfire. Carrie had first heard of it that morning. She suspected Hassie knew and had been protecting her; she also suspected there'd been rumors last night, but she'd been too involved with Vaughn to notice.

Heath's frown darkened. It went without saying that he wasn't any happier about this than she was. "I'm sorry, Carrie, but Ambrose Kohn is a difficult man to deal with. The town council has spoken to him several times. Hassie tried and I did, too, but he isn't willing to listen."

"You knew before this morning?" she fired back. "Hassie, too?" That was what she thought—and it explained a great deal. Hassie just hadn't been herself lately, but every inquiry was met with denial.

Heath nodded.

"Doesn't Mr. Kohn realize what he's doing?" Carrie found it hard to believe he could be so callous toward the town.

"He knows all too well."

"People have a right to know that the entire future of our town is at risk." She could only imagine what would happen to her father's store if Value-X set up shop.

Heath obviously agreed with her. "Hassie suggested we keep this under wraps until after Christmas, and the rest of the council decided to go along with her. I don't know how the news leaked." He scowled and rolled his gold pen between flat palms.

Delaying the bad news changed nothing. This morning at breakfast her father had announced what he'd learned. He was already alternating between depression and panic. He'd heard it from Joanie Wyatt at the tree-lighting ceremony. The Wyatts had sent away for stock information, and Joanie had read over a prospectus; she'd seen that Buffalo Valley was listed as a possible expansion site. She'd immediately phoned Buffalo Bob, who'd reluctantly confirmed it.

"Nothing's been signed yet," Heath said, as though that should make her feel better. It didn't.

She glanced at her watch, wishing she had more time to get all this straight in her mind. Although she was eager to meet Vaughn at the Columbia Mall as promised, she wasn't in the mood for Christmas activities. Not with this Value-X problem hanging over all their heads.

"Have you talked to anyone at the corporate office?" she asked.

Heath nodded.

"They weren't interested in listening, were they?" Heath's disheartened look was answer enough. "It's *progress*, right?"

"Right," Heath muttered. "Listen, I've got a meeting in ten minutes. I'm sorry, Carrie. I know what this will mean for your father's business and Knight's Pharmacy, too. I'm doing the best I can."

"Can't you buy the property yourself?"

"I approached Kohn about that, but…"

"He won't sell it to you?" Carrie asked in an outraged voice.

"Let's say he'd love a bidding war—one I'd be sure to lose." Heath stood and retrieved his overcoat from a closet.

Her gaze pleaded with his. "You've *got* to find a way
to keep Value-X out of Buffalo Valley."

"Kohn hasn't heard the last of this," Heath promised
as he escorted her out of the bank.

Carrie accompanied him to his four-wheel-drive vehicle.

"Is there anything *I* can do?" she asked, feeling the
need to act.

Heath shook his head as he opened his car door. "Don't
worry, Carrie, this isn't over yet. Not by a long shot."

All Carrie could do was trust that, somehow or other,
he'd convince Ambrose Kohn to be reasonable.

The drive into Grand Forks passed in a fog. Burdened by the news, Carrie was surprised when the two
lanes widened to four as she reached the outskirts of
the big city.

Vaughn was waiting for her inside the mall at a coffee shop they'd designated as their meeting place. He
stood as she approached. She was struck again by what
an attractive man he was. Her ex-husband had been attractive, too, but Alec's good looks had belied his selfish, arrogant nature. She'd learned, the hard way, that a
handsome face proved nothing about the inner man. No,
handsome is as handsome does, her grandma always
said. Which made Vaughn Kyle very handsome, indeed.

He'd been so gentle and caring with Hassie. He'd
spent time with her, listened to her talk about her son.
Carrie marveled at his patience and his good humor
and the respect he seemed to genuinely feel for Hassie and for the town. When he'd asked her to meet him
in Grand Forks to help him finish his shopping, she'd
agreed. It'd been a long, long time since a man had impressed her as much as Vaughn Kyle.

"Thanks for coming," he said now.

Although it was relatively early, the mall was already frantic. With exactly a week left before Christmas, the entire population of Grand Forks had apparently decided to cram itself inside.

"The only person I still need to buy for is my mother," he told her, looking around as though he already regretted this.

"What about perfume?" Carrie wasn't feeling too inspired, either.

"She's allergic to a lot of those scents."

"Okay, how about…" Carrie proceeded to rattle off several other suggestions, all of which he categorically dismissed for one reason or another.

"Do you have any more ideas?" he asked, looking desperate.

"Not yet, but we might stumble across something while we're here."

Vaughn sighed. "That doesn't sound promising." He glanced around. "How about if we find a quiet restaurant and discuss it over lunch?"

He didn't need to ask twice. She was as anxious to get away from the crowds as he was. They found an Italian place Joanie and Brandon Wyatt had once recommended and were seated almost immediately. Sitting at their table with its red-and-white-checkered tablecloth, Carrie could see why her friends liked it here. The casual atmosphere was perfect. If the food was half as good as the smells wafting from the kitchen, she was in for a treat.

Carrie quickly made her decision and closed the menu. Lowering her gaze, she pushed thoughts of Value-X from her mind for the umpteenth time. Her worries kept intruding on the pleasant day she was hoping to have.

"You'd better tell me," Vaughn said. His hand reached for hers and he gently squeezed it. "Something's wrong."

Apparently she hadn't done a very good job of hiding her concerns. Rather than blurt everything out, she stared down at the tablecloth for a long moment.

"We learned this morning that Value-X is considering Buffalo Valley as a possible site," she finally said. "Apparently they've already negotiated for a piece of land. I don't need to tell you what that'll do to our community."

"It might be a good thing," he said slowly. "Try to think positive."

"If this is progress, we don't want anything to do with it," she muttered. Vaughn couldn't *possibly* understand. She was sorry she'd brought up the subject. "We happen to like our town just the way it is."

"It isn't that—"

"We're going to fight it," she said confidently.

"How?" Vaughn asked. "Isn't that a little like David fighting Goliath?"

"Perhaps, but like David, you can bet we aren't going to idly sit by and do nothing." Already plans had started to form in her mind. "Other communities have succeeded. We can, too."

"You're serious about this?"

"Damn straight I am."

"Don't you think you're overlooking the positive aspects of a company like Value-X opening a store in Buffalo Valley? They have a lot to offer."

Carrie glared at him. "You don't get it, do you?"

"I guess not. Help me understand." Vaughn leaned back in his chair, his expression serious.

"Value-X will ruin *everything*. We don't want it, we don't need it." Carrie struggled to keep her voice even.

Vaughn studied her. "I imagine you're a formidable opponent when you put your mind to something."

"It isn't only me," she told him. "The entire town is up in arms. We haven't come this far to let some heartless enterprise wipe out all our efforts."

Vaughn frowned. "Value-X will mean the end of Knight's Pharmacy, won't it?"

That was only the beginning as far as Carrie could tell. "And AceMan Hardware." She ran one finger across the tines of the fork. "The only business I can't see it affecting is Buffalo Valley Quilts." Carrie shot him a look and wondered why she hadn't thought of this earlier. "That's it!"

"What is?"

"A quilt. It's the perfect Christmas gift for your mother."

Vaughn didn't appear convinced. "A quilt?"

"They're special. Hand-sewn, and you could go traditional or innovative."

"How much are they?"

"I don't know the full range of prices," she said, "but if the quilt is more than you want to spend, there're table runners and place mats and lap robes."

"Hmm." The idea seemed to take hold. "That does sound like a gift she'd enjoy."

"I'm sure she would," Carrie said. "I can't believe I didn't think of it earlier."

"So how do I go about this?"

"If you don't want to drive back to Buffalo Valley so soon, I could choose one for you," she offered.

"Perhaps Mom should pick it out herself."

"Great idea—and I know Hassie would love to see her."

"I think it would do my mother a world of good to renew her friendship with Hassie."

The waitress arrived and took their orders. Seafood linguine for her, lasagna for him. And a glass of red wine for each. "Hey, it's Christmas," Vaughn said with a grin.

He took his cell phone from his jacket and flipped it open. Within seconds, he had his mother on the line.

"What about tomorrow?" he asked, looking at Carrie.

"I'm sure that'll be fine."

"Hassie will be there, won't she?"

Carrie nodded. "She's scheduled to work in the morning, but she has the afternoon free. I'll cover for her, if need be."

He relayed the information to his mother, then ended the conversation and slid the phone back inside his jacket. Smiling at her, he said, "Thanks, Carrie."

A warm feeling came over her, and once again she lowered her gaze. Vaughn Kyle—kind to old women and a thoughtful son. He was exciting and he was interesting and he made her heart beat furiously. She could only regret that he was heading back to Seattle so soon after Christmas.

Four

"I suppose you heard," Hassie said when Leta Betts came bustling into the pharmacy late in the afternoon. The word about Value-X had filtered through Buffalo Valley, and the town was rife with speculation. Nearly everyone she knew had stopped by to talk it over with her, as though she had a solution to this perplexing problem.

"I don't like it," Leta muttered, walking behind the counter of the soda fountain and pulling out a well-used teapot. "Want me to make you a cup?"

"Please." Hassie had filled prescriptions all afternoon, between interruptions, and she was ready for a break. She'd known that Leta would come by at some point; fortunately, there was a lull just now, which made it a good time to talk to her dearest friend.

"Where's Carrie?" Leta found two mugs and set them on the counter.

"It's her day off."

"I heard she went to see Heath."

Hassie had heard about that, as well. Carrie had a good heart and cared about this community with the same intensity as Hassie did. Once Carrie received her

Pharm.D., Hassie had planned to turn the business over to her. That was before the threat of Value-X, however. If that threat became a reality, Hassie couldn't sell the pharmacy, not in good conscience. In all likelihood the place would be out of business within a year after the big retailer moved in.

"It's a shame, you know," Leta murmured. She dragged a chair closer to the counter and perched on the seat. Leaning forward, she braced her elbows on the edge, sighing deeply. "Who'd have thought something like this would ever happen?"

Hassie shook her head helplessly. She'd worked so hard to save this town. And now, even if oblivion wasn't to be its fate, a corporation like Value-X could make Buffalo Valley unrecognizable, could turn it into something that bore no resemblance to the place it had been. The place it *should* be.

"What are we going to do?" Leta asked.

Hassie sat next to her and assumed the same slouched pose. Leta was her friend and employee, and there wasn't anything Hassie couldn't tell her. But this situation with the conglomerate had her poleaxed. She was at her wit's end. "I don't know," she admitted.

"We'll think of something," Leta insisted, and poured tea into the mugs. She set one in front of Hassie and then added a teaspoon of sugar to her own.

"Not this time," Hassie said as she reached for the mug, letting it warm her hands. She was too old and too tired. A few years back she'd fought for her town with determination and ingenuity, but this new war would have to be waged by someone else. She'd done her part.

"This was how we both felt when we learned Lindsay had decided to return to Atlanta, remember?" Leta prodded.

As though Hassie would ever forget. At the last minute Leta's son, Gage, had realized he'd be making the worst mistake of his life if he let Lindsay leave without telling her how much he loved her. As a result, Lindsay had not only stayed on as a high-school teacher, she'd married Gage. Leta was a grandmother twice over, thanks to the young couple.

"Value-X is too powerful for me." A bit of research had revealed that the retailer was accustomed to exactly this kind of local resistance. They had their battle plans worked out to the smallest detail. Hassie remembered from the television exposé that the company had a legal team, as well as public-relations people, all of them experts at squelching opposition. Hassie knew the town council couldn't afford any high-priced attorneys to plead their case. Even if they banded together, they were no match for the company's corporate attorneys. They were cutthroat, they'd seen it all, done it all. According to the documentary, they'd won in the majority of their cases. Like it or not, Value-X simply overran a community.

"We can't give up," Leta insisted. She glared at Hassie, as though waiting for some of the old fight to surface.

It wouldn't, though. Not anymore. Slowly Hassie lowered her gaze, refusing to meet her friend's eyes. "It's a lost cause," she murmured.

"This doesn't sound like you, Hassie."

"No," she agreed, glancing at her tired reflection in the mirror above the soda fountain, "but it won't matter that much if I lose the pharmacy."

Leta's jaw sagged open. "Wh-what—"

"I should've retired years ago. The only reason I

held on as long as I did is the community needs a pharmacy and—"

"What about Carrie?"

Hassie had been so pleased and grateful when Carrie had come to work as an intern. This was what she'd always wanted for the pharmacy. Years ago she'd expected her son to take over, but Vietnam had robbed her of that dream. The hopelessness of the situation settled squarely over her heart.

"I'm sure Value-X will require a pharmacist. Carrie can apply there."

Silent, Leta stared into the distance.

"I'm tired," Hassie said. "Valerie's been after me to retire, move to Hawaii… Maybe I should."

"You in Hawaii? Never!" Leta shook her head fiercely. "I've always followed your lead—we all have. I don't know what would've become of us if not for you."

"Fiddlesticks." Hassie forced a laugh. "Value-X is coming to town, and that's all there is to it. We might as well accept the inevitable. Not long from now, both of us will be shopping there and wondering how we ever lived without such a store in town."

"You're probably right," Leta returned, but her words rang false.

"Let's just enjoy Christmas," Hassie suggested, gesturing at the garlands strung from the old-fashioned ceiling lights. "What are your plans?"

"Kevin won't be home, but he'll call from Paris on Christmas Eve. Gage and Lindsay invited me to spend Christmas Day with them." Hassie knew that Leta would take delight in spoiling four-year-old Joy and two-year-old Madeline.

"Bob and Merrily invited me over in the morning to open gifts with them and Bobby," Hassie told her friend. They thought of her as Bobby's unofficial grand-mother. Early in their marriage, Bob and Merrily had lost a son—although not to death. They'd fostered a child from an abusive environment and had wanted to adopt him, but in the end, the California authorities had seen fit to place the boy with another family. It'd been a difficult time for the couple. Having lost a son her-self, Hassie had understood their grief as only some-one who'd walked that path could understand it. She'd tried to bring them comfort and the example of her en-durance. Bob and Merrily never forgot her kindness, little as it was. Over the past few years, they'd become as close to her as family.

"You finally met Vaughn Kyle," Leta said. "That's definitely a highlight of this Christmas season."

"Yes," Hassie agreed, somewhat cheered. It'd been an unanticipated pleasure, one she'd always remember. In the hours they'd spent with each other, she'd forged a bond with the young man. Meeting Vaughn had left Hassie feeling closer to her own son, although he'd been dead for thirty-three years. Hard to believe so much time had passed since his death…

"That was him with Carrie at the tree-lighting cer-emony, wasn't it?"

Hassie felt a small, sudden joy, sending a ray of light into the gloom she'd experienced earlier. "She's spend-ing the afternoon with him in Grand Forks."

"It's time she put the divorce behind her."

Hassie felt the same way but didn't comment.

"Do you think something might come of it?" Leta asked, her voice slightly raised.

Hassie couldn't answer. Her hours with Vaughn had been taken up with the past, and she hadn't discov-ered much at all about his future plans. She knew he'd been honorably discharged from the military and had accepted a position with a Seattle-based company, although he'd never said which one. Probably a big software firm, she decided. From what she understood, he'd be starting work after the first of the year. She felt it was a good sign that he'd come to spend two weeks with his parents.

"He's been to town twice already," Leta offered. "That's encouraging, don't you think?"

"I suppose."

A small smile quivered at the edges of Leta's mouth. "I remember when Gage first got interested in Lindsay. That boy drummed up a hundred excuses to drive into town."

"Remember Jeb and Maddy?" Hassie murmured, her eyes flashing with the memory. These were the thoughts she preferred to cling to. Stories with happy resolutions. Good things happening to good people.

Leta's responding grin brightened her face. "I'm not likely to forget. We hadn't seen hide nor hair of him in months."

"Years," Hassie corrected. Following the farming accident that cost Jeb McKenna his leg, the farmer-turned-buffalo-rancher became a recluse. Hassie recalled the days Joshua had to practically drag his son into town for Christmas dinner. Then Maddy Washburn bought the grocery and started her delivery service. After those two were trapped together in a blizzard, why, there was no counting the number of times Jeb showed up in Buffalo Valley.

"Do you remember the day Margaret Eilers stormed into town and yanked Matt out of Buffalo Bob's?" Leta asked, laughing outright.

"Sure do. She nearly beat him to a pulp." Tears of

laughter filled Hassie's eyes. "Can't say I blame her. Those two certainly had their troubles."

Margaret had set her sights on Matt Eilers and wanted him in the worst way, faults and all. That was what she got, too. Not three months after they were married, Margaret found out that Matt had gotten a cocktail waitress pregnant. Granted, it had happened *before* the marriage, but Margaret had still felt angry and betrayed.

"Look at them now," Leta said, sobering. "I don't know any couple more in love." She drank a sip of her tea. "If Margaret and Matt can overcome their problems, why can't Buffalo Valley sort out this thing with Value-X?"

For the first time all week, Hassie felt hopeful. "Maybe you're right, Leta. Maybe you're right."

Carrie sat down at the kitchen table and reached for the cream, adding it to her coffee. Even though she was twenty-seven years old, she found it comforting to watch her mother stir up a batch of gingerbread cookies. The house was redolent with the scent of cinnamon and other spices.

Her morning had been busy. After a lengthy conversation with Lindsay Sinclair, who'd been in contact with the Value-X corporate offices, Carrie had spent an hour on the Internet learning what she could about the big retailer.

"Did you have a good time yesterday afternoon?" Diane Hendrickson asked. She set the mixing bowl in the refrigerator, then joined Carrie at the table.

"I had a *wonderful* time." She was surprised to realize how much she meant that. Lowering her eyes momentarily, she looked back up. "I told Vaughn about Alec."

Her mother held her gaze. Carrie didn't often speak

of her failed marriage, especially not to new acquaintances.

"It came up naturally, and for the first time I didn't feel that terrible sense of…of defeat. I don't think I'll ever be the same person again, but after talking to Vaughn, I knew I don't want to be."

Her mother smiled softly. "There was nothing wrong with you, Carrie."

"That's true, Mom, but I was at fault, too. I suspected Alec was involved with someone else. I simply preferred not to *face* it. The evidence was right in front of my eyes months before he told me. I don't ever again want to be the kind of woman who ignores the truth."

"You've never—"

"Oh, Mom," she said, loving her mother all the more for her unwavering loyalty. "It's time to move forward."

"With Vaughn Kyle?"

Carrie had thought of little else in the past three days. "Too soon to tell."

"But you like him?" her mother pressed.

She nodded. "I do." It felt good to admit it. Good to think that her life wouldn't be forever weighed down by a mistake she'd made when she was too young to understand that her marriage was doomed. Her husband's betrayal had blindsided her. Outwardly she'd picked up the pieces of her shattered pride and continued her life, but in her heart, Carrie had never completely recovered. Alec had shattered her self-esteem. Somehow she'd convinced herself that there must've been something lacking in *her*; it'd taken her a long time to realize the lack had been his.

Carrie drank the rest of her coffee and placed the cup in the sink. "We spoke about Value-X, too, Vaughn and I. At first he didn't seem to see how a company like that would hurt Buffalo Valley. In fact, he felt it might even have a positive effect. If so, I don't see one. But he let me vent my frustrations and helped me clarify my thinking."

"Will you be seeing him again?" her mother asked innocently enough.

"Most likely. He's bringing his mother into town this morning. He's buying her one of Sarah's quilts for Christmas and thought she'd like to choose it herself."

"What a thoughtful gift."

Carrie didn't mention that she'd been the one to suggest it. "They're meeting Hassie later." They hadn't made any definite plans, but Carrie hoped to meet Vaughn's mother. She was almost sure he'd stop by, either here or at the store; in fact, she was counting on it.

The doorbell chimed right then, and fingers crossed, Carrie decided it had to be Vaughn. Her mother went to answer the door.

"Carrie," she called from the living room, "you have a visitor."

"I hope you don't mind me dropping by unexpectedly," he was saying to her mother when Carrie walked in. Vaughn stood awkwardly near the door. He removed his gloves and stuffed them in his pockets.

"Hello, Vaughn." Carrie didn't bother to disguise her pleasure at seeing him again.

"Hi." He looked directly into her eyes. "Would you be free to meet my mother? I left her a few moments ago, drooling over Sarah's quilts."

"I'd like that." Carrie reached into the hall closet for her coat and scarf. "What did you think of the quilts?" she asked, buttoning her coat. She wanted him to appreciate Sarah's talent.

"They're incredible. You're right, it's the perfect gift for Mom."

Carrie supposed she had no business feeling proud; the quilt shop wasn't hers and she had nothing to do with it. But everyone in Buffalo Valley took pride in Sarah's accomplishments. It was more than the fact that Sarah had started the company in her father's living room. People viewed her success as a reflection of what had happened to the town itself—the gradual change from obscurity and scant survival to prosperity and acclaim. Her struggles were their own, and by the same token, her successes were a reason to celebrate.

"I wanted you to know how much I enjoyed our time together yesterday," Vaughn said, matching his steps to hers as they took a shortcut through the park. "I appreciate the suggestion about the quilt. And I learned a lot about you—and Buffalo Valley. You helped me see the town in an entirely different way."

"I was grateful you let me talk out my feelings about Value-X…and everything else."

Vaughn's arm came around her and he briefly squeezed her shoulder. There was no need to refer to the divorce. He understood what she meant.

"I talked to Lindsay Sinclair earlier," Carrie said, changing the subject. "She phoned the corporate office and asked if the rumors are true."

"I thought you said they were negotiating for property."

"That's what I told Lindsay, but she doesn't trust Ambrose Kohn. She said she wouldn't put it past him to let people *think* Value-X was interested in the property so Heath or someone else would leap forward and offer to buy it. He's not exactly the kind of person to generate a lot of trust."

"What did your friend find out when she talked to the corporate people?"

"First they said they didn't want to comment on their plans, but when Lindsay pressed the spokeswoman, she admitted that Buffalo Valley's definitely under consideration." Carrie's shoulders tensed. "Lindsay took the opportunity to let her know they aren't welcome in Buffalo Valley." When she'd heard about that part of the conversation, Carrie had cheered.

"What did the company spokeswoman say then?"

Carrie laughed. "Apparently Value-X's official response is that according to their studies, a growing community such as Buffalo Valley doesn't have enough retail choices."

Vaughn snorted.

"That's what I thought. They're sending a representative after Christmas. This person is supposed to win us over and show us everything Value-X can do for Buffalo Valley." She couldn't keep the sarcasm out of her voice.

"It wouldn't hurt to listen," he said mildly.

Carrie whirled on him. "We'll listen, but having a huge chain store in town is *not* what we want. Joanie Wyatt's already started a petition, so when the company representative arrives, he or she will be met with the signature of every single person in town."

Vaughn said nothing.

"What Value-X doesn't understand is that Buffalo Valley is a small town with small-town values and that's exactly the way we want to keep it. If they move in, they'll ruin everything that makes us who we are."

Vaughn stopped in front of a picnic bench, cleared away the snow with his arm and sat down. "What about jobs? Value-X will offer a lot of opportunity to young people. I've heard repeatedly that farming communities are seeing their young adults move away because of the lack of financial security."

"That's not necessarily true, the part about Value-X bringing jobs. After I talked to Lindsay, I got on the Internet and did some research myself. I learned that most of the positions Value-X brings into a town are part-time and low-paying. They offer few benefits to their employees. The worst aspect is that they destroy more jobs than they create."

Vaughn's frown deepened.

"I apologize," she said. "I didn't mean to get carried away about our problems with Value-X."

Standing, Vaughn still seemed deep in thought. "No, I want to hear this. It bothers me that the company isn't listening to your concerns."

"They don't *want* to listen."

"But you said they're sending a representative."

"Right," she said with a snicker. "To talk to us, not to listen. They're under the mistaken impression that we'll be swayed by a few promises and slick words. They've decided we need to think bigger and bolder and stop acting like a small town."

"But Buffalo Valley *is* a small town."

Carrie gave a sharp nod. "Exactly."

As they approached Buffalo Valley Quilts, Carrie noticed the middle-aged woman standing inside by the window, looking out into the street. When Vaughn and Carrie appeared, she smiled and waved, then pointed to the quilt on display.

Carrie waved back, silently applauding his mother's choice.

Mrs. Kyle smiled. Her eyes moved to her son and then to Carrie; her expression grew quizzical. Carrie didn't have time to guess what that meant before Mrs. Kyle opened the glass door, stepped out and introduced herself.

* * *

Barbara Kyle knew that when she agreed to accompany Vaughn into Buffalo Valley, she'd be seeing Hassie Knight. A meeting was inevitable. They hadn't been together since the day they'd stood in the pouring rain as a military casket was lowered into the ground.

Following the funeral, she'd kept in touch with Vaughn's mother. They'd called each other frequently. But despite the war, despite her grief, Barbara's college courses had continued, and she'd had to immerse herself in a very different kind of reality.

Rick had lost his best friend, and they began to seek solace from each other. Falling in love with him was a surprise. Barbara hadn't expected that, hadn't thought it was possible to love again after losing Vaughn. Rick wasn't a replacement. No one could ever replace the man she'd loved. He understood, because in his own way he'd loved Vaughn, too.

When they announced their engagement, Hassie had pulled away from Barbara. Neither spoke of it, but they both knew that their relationship had fundamentally changed and that their former closeness could no longer exist. Vaughn's parents didn't attend the wedding, although they'd mailed a card and sent a generous check.

Barbara thought now that naming their son after Vaughn Knight had as much to do with Hassie as it did with their feelings for Vaughn. Perhaps she'd hoped to bridge the distance between them...

Until he was twenty-one, Hassie had remembered Vaughn Kyle every year on his birthday, but that was the only time Barbara and Rick heard from her. When Rick accepted early retirement and they'd decided to move back to North Dakota, Barbara recognized that, sooner or later, she'd see Hassie again. A month or so after they'd moved, Hassie had welcomed them with a brief note. It seemed fitting that Barbara's son had been the one to arrange this meeting, to bring them together again.

"Hassie wanted me to bring you to the house, instead of the pharmacy," Vaughn said as they left the quilting store.

"You're coming with us, aren't you?" Barbara asked Carrie. She'd quickly grasped that Vaughn was attracted to this woman, and she could understand why. However, she didn't pretend to know what was happening. Natalie had phoned several times, wanting to speak to Vaughn; she wasn't amused that he'd apparently turned off his cell phone. Barbara didn't feel it was her place to inform the other woman that Vaughn was out with someone else. The situation concerned her, but she couldn't interfere and had to trust that he was treating both women with honesty and fairness.

"I'd love to come to Hassie's with you," Carrie told them, "but I said I'd fill in at the store for her. You two go and have a good visit, and I'll see you later."

As they crossed the street, Carrie headed toward the pharmacy, and Barbara and Vaughn went in the opposite direction.

"Does the pharmacy still have the soda fountain?" Barbara asked her son.

"Sure does. In fact, I thought I'd leave you and Hassie to visit, and I'd steal away to Knight's to let Carrie fix me a soda."

"You're spending a lot of time with her, aren't you?" Barbara couldn't resist asking.

"Am I?"

Barbara didn't answer him. There was probably some

perfect maternal response, but darned if she knew what it was.

Hassie's house came into view, and Barbara automatically slowed her pace. It'd been thirty-three years since she'd walked up these steps. Thirty-three years since she'd attended the wake, sat in a corner of the living room with Vaughn's older sister and wept bitter tears. At the end of a day that had been too long for all of them, Vaughn's mother had hugged her close and then instructed a family friend to make sure Barbara got safely home to Grand Forks.

"Mom?" Vaughn studied her and seemed to sense that something was wrong.

"It's all right," she said. Funny how quickly those old emotions resurfaced. Her stomach churned as if it'd been only a few months since she'd last walked this path. But thirty-three years, a lifetime, had passed.

Hassie opened the door before Barbara could ring the bell. They stood there for a moment, gazing into each other's eyes.

Hassie smiled then, a welcoming smile that seemed to reach deep inside her with its warmth and generosity. "Barbara," the older woman said, flinging open the screen door.

When she'd entered the house, Hassie hugged her for long minutes, and Barbara felt the tears gather in her eyes.

"I'm so glad you came." Hassie finally released her and embraced Vaughn, who stood quietly behind his mother. "I assume Vaughn told you about our visit?"

"Yes, he did. I can't tell you how honored we all are that you'd give him Mr. Knight's gold watch."

"It seemed right that he have it." She took Barbara's coat and hung it in the hall closet. "I won't take yours," she said to Vaughn, her back to them both. "You're probably planning to sneak over to the shop for a soda."

"How'd you guess?"

"I was young once myself," Hassie said, and shooed him out the door.

"Carrie's a wonderful young woman," Hassie told her as soon as Vaughn had left.

"They certainly seem to have taken a liking to one another," Barbara said noncommittally. She liked what she'd seen of Carrie—but what about Natalie? Well, that was Vaughn's business, she reminded herself again.

Hassie led her into the living room. "I hope you don't mind, but I've already poured the tea."

"Not at all."

The silver service was set up on the coffee table and two delicate china cups were neatly positioned, steam rising from the recently poured tea. A plate of cookies had been placed nearby.

"I don't often get an excuse to use my good tea service and china these days," Hassie murmured.

The two women sat side by side on the dark-blue sofa and sipped their tea. Neither really knew where to start, Barbara reflected. She took a deep breath.

"I've thought of you often," she said. "Especially since you were so generous with our son."

"He must have thought me a silly old woman, writing him little tidbits of advice."

"Hassie," Barbara said, and touched Hassie's forearm. "*No one* could think that." She shook her head. "He saved every birthday card you ever sent him. And he remembered what you wrote. He grew up honorable and generous, and I can't help thinking you played a part in that."

Hassie smiled her appreciation. "Nonsense, but it's very kind of you to say so."

Barbara glanced around the room. "Being here brings back so many memories," she said. The house, this room, was exactly as she remembered. She suspected that even after all these years, Vaughn's bedroom was virtually untouched. She remembered the high-school banner he had pinned to the wall and the bedroom set, old-fashioned even then. Valerie's old room was probably the same as it had been, as well, just like the rest of this house.

Hassie didn't comment, and Barbara sensed that the older woman had hung on to the past as much as she could and found comfort in what was familiar. Hassie's strength was considerable, but her loss had been too great. *Losses*, Barbara recalled. Jerry had died not long afterward, and Valerie had moved to Hawaii.

"Do you like living in Grand Forks?" Hassie asked, turning away from reminders of grief.

"Very much. My parents leased out the house when they moved to Arizona. Rick and I always intended to move here one day, and I'm really happy we did. This will be our first Christmas in North Dakota since Vaughn was five or six."

"With family again."

"Actually, there'll only be Rick, Vaughn and me. All my family has moved away, and Gloria, our daughter, lives in Dallas."

"Have Christmas here with me," Hassie urged, and then as if she regretted the impulse, she shook her head. "No, please forget I asked. I'm sorry to impose. It's just the rambling of an old woman."

"Hassie, if you're serious, we'd love nothing better than to spend the day with you."

Hassie's eyes shone. "You mean you'd actually consider coming?"

"We'd be honored. I know Rick would love to see you again. He wanted to join me today, but he was already committed to something else—some volunteer work he's doing."

"You're sure about Christmas?"

"Very sure," Barbara insisted. "But I can't allow you to do all the cooking."

"Oh," Hassie said, "it's no problem. I'd enjoy preparing my favorite recipes."

"We'll share the meal preparation, then," Barbara compromised, and Hassie agreed.

"We'll be having Christmas dinner," Barbara murmured, "with a dear, dear friend."

"I can't think of anything I'd enjoy more."

Barbara couldn't, either.

Five

Carrie found Leta tending Knight's Pharmacy when she arrived after saying goodbye to Vaughn and his mother.

"Thanks for filling in for me," she said, hurrying to the back of the store. She stored her coat and purse and pulled on her white jacket.

"I don't mind staying," Leta told her. "In fact, Hassie asked me if I would. She thought you and Vaughn might like a few hours together." Leta wiped down the counter, and Carrie noticed how the other woman's eyes managed to evade hers.

"Aren't you two being just a little obvious?" she teased.

"Perhaps," Leta said, "but we both think it's high time you got into circulation again."

"Like a library book?" Carrie said with a grin. "I've been on the shelf too long?"

"Laugh if you want, but it's true. You've been avoiding a social life. That's not good for a woman of your age."

Carrie was about to explain that, while she appreciated their efforts, she'd already spent time with Vaughn. Before she could, though, the bell above the door chimed, and Lindsay Sinclair and her two daughters stepped into the warmth of the pharmacy.

"Grandma." Four-year-old Joy ran toward Leta, who scooped the girl up in her arms for an enthusiastic hug.

"I've had the most incredible morning," Lindsay announced.

"Value-X?" Carrie asked.

Lindsay nodded. "The spokeswoman actually phoned me back."

"She called you?" Leta asked, voice incredulous, as she set Joy back on the floor.

"Yes, and for some reason, she seemed to view me as a contact who represented the community. That's fine, since everyone in town shares my opinion." Lindsay removed her hat and shook out her hair. "She wanted me to understand that Value-X intends to be a good neighbor, quote, unquote."

"Yeah, right!" Carrie muttered sarcastically.

"I'll just bet," Leta added. "They assume we're nothing but a bunch of dumb hicks."

"To be fair," Lindsay said, glancing between the other two women, "we don't know *what* they think of us—not that we have any interest in their opinion. But we are fully capable of mounting a campaign to keep them out."

"I was thinking the same thing," Carrie said.

"Organization is the key," Leta put in.

"You'll be at the Cookie Exchange tonight, won't you?" Lindsay asked Carrie. "I know Leta will." She smiled at her mother-in-law. "I thought that would be the best time to get all the women together. We can talk then."

"Good idea. Mom and I will be there for sure." The women's group at the church held the Cookie Exchange every Christmas. Joyce Dawson, the pastor's wife, had been instrumental in organizing the event, and every woman in town and the surrounding community could be counted on to attend.

"Value-X won't know what hit them," Leta said happily.

The bell chimed a second time, and Vaughn entered the store. For a moment, he seemed startled to see the three women, but then his gaze sought out Carrie's. "Should I come back later?"

"Not at all," Leta said. "There's no need for Carrie to work today. I've got everything covered."

Carrie was grateful for what her friends were trying to do, but she did have responsibilities. Leta seemed to read her thoughts. "If any prescriptions get phoned in, I'll find you," she promised. "I'll leave a message with your mom."

"Ever hear the expression about not looking a gift horse in the mouth?" Lindsay whispered.

"Well, it appears I'm not wanted or needed around here," Carrie said before Leta and Hassie's intentions became any plainer than they already were. She walked past Lindsay, who winked at her. After collecting her coat and purse, Carrie left with Vaughn.

"Where would you like to go?" he asked as soon as they were outside.

She hadn't had lunch yet and suspected Vaughn hadn't, either. "I know we had Italian yesterday, but I love pizza."

"Me, too."

"Buffalo Valley has some of the best homemade pizza you'll ever eat."

He lifted his eyebrows. "Sounds good to me."

They started down the street, their pace relaxed.

Snow had just begun to fall, drifting earthward in large, soft flakes. Christmas-card snow, Carrie thought. As they walked, she told him the story about Rachel's pizza, and how it had led to her restaurant and subsequent success.

"You mean she makes the sauce herself?"

Carrie nodded. "I worked for Rachel one summer and I watched her make a batch. She starts with fresh tomatoes straight from her garden. It's amazingly good. I think she could sell her recipe, but of course, she doesn't want to."

A pickup approached and slowed as it came alongside Vaughn and Carrie. Glancing over her shoulder, Carrie saw her two older brothers, Tom and Pete. She tried to ignore them, but that was impossible.

"Hey, Carrie," Tom called, leaning his elbow out the open passenger window.

She acknowledged his greeting with a short wave, hoping he'd simply move on. Not that this was likely. Apparently Chuck and Ken had mentioned Vaughn, and now they, too, were looking for an introduction.

"Don't you want us to meet your friend?"

"Not right now," she called back, and sent Vaughn an apologetic glance. Because she was the only girl, all four of her brothers were protective of her, even more so after her divorce.

"You ashamed of your family?" This came from Pete, who was driving.

Carrie sighed, praying that her brothers wouldn't say or do anything to further embarrass her. Pete parked the truck and both men climbed out, slamming their doors extra hard. Both wore thick winter coats and wool caps with the earflaps dangling. They were large men and did their best to appear intimidating.

She made the introductions, gesturing weakly toward her brothers. Vaughn stepped forward and shook hands with both of them.

"Nice to finally meet you," Tom said, resting his foot on the truck's bumper. "Now I'd like to know what your intentions are toward my sister."

"Tom!" Furious, Carrie clenched her fists. "This is *none* of your business."

"The day you stop being my sister is the day I stop caring who you date."

"Well..." Vaughn clearly had no idea what to say.

Her brothers putting him on the spot like this was outrageous. Picking up a handful of snow, Carrie immediately formed a ball and threw it at her oldest brother, hitting him square in the chest. Not waiting for his reaction, Carrie grabbed Vaughn's arm and shouted, "Run!"

"You asked for this, Carrie Ann," Tom shouted as Carrie and Vaughn raced across the street. They had just entered the park when Carrie felt her backside pelted by two snowballs.

"This is war," Vaughn yelled when he saw that she'd been hit. He leaned down and packed his own snow, then hurled two balls in quick succession, hitting both Pete and Tom. Her brothers reacted with stunned surprise.

Laughing and dodging around the play equipment with her brothers in hot pursuit, Carrie had trouble keeping pace with Vaughn. He yelled instructions and pointed toward the back of Hamburger Heaven. The stand was closed for the winter and offered ample protection, but a few moments later, her brothers found them and began to bombard them with a flurry of snowballs. Although most of them hit the side of the building, it was obvious that Vaughn and Carrie couldn't stay there long.

"You ready to surrender yet?" Pete demanded.

"Never," Vaughn answered for them.

"This way," Carrie told him. With the community Christmas tree blocking their movements, she led him across the street. Hidden by a loaded hay truck that passed behind them, Carrie steered him toward her parents' store.

"This is what I'd consider enemy territory," Vaughn whispered as they slipped behind the building and out of view.

"But it's the last place they'll look," she assured him.

"Smart thinking." Vaughn beamed her a delighted smile.

She smiled back—and realized she hadn't felt this kind of pure, uninhibited pleasure in…years. Since childhood, probably. When she didn't break eye contact and started to laugh, he said, "What?"

She shook her head, not wanting to put into words the joy she felt.

A sound startled them both, and they froze. Carrie was certain her brothers had found them again, but if it *was* Pete and Tom, they left without searching farther.

Relieved, Carrie sighed and slumped against the wall. "I believe we're safe for the moment. Are you still interested in that pizza?"

Vaughn nodded, but she saw a strange expression in his eyes as he continued to gaze down at her. Carrie tried to look away and couldn't. She knew he intended to kiss her, and she shut her eyes as he moved closer. She'd been waiting for this moment, anticipating it. Wrapping her arms around his neck, she leaned into him. He drew off his gloves and then her wool hat and dropped them. Weaving his hands into her hair, he kissed her...and deepened the kiss until they were both breathless. Carrie trembled and buried her face in his shoulder. Neither spoke. As he held her tight, it seemed for those few moments that their hearts beat in unison.

He kissed her again, his mouth both firm and soft. When he eased away, Carried noticed that his brow had furrowed, and she thought she read doubt in his eyes. Uncertainty. She touched his face, wondering at the confusion she saw in him. "Is anything wrong?" she asked.

He answered with a quick shake of his head. "Everything is right."

And yet he sounded reluctant. She wanted to ask him more, but he moved away from her and peeked around the back wall. "Do you think it's safe now?" he asked.

"It should be. Pete and Tom were just having fun with us."

"Protective older brothers."

"Exactly."

"I watched over Gloria, too," he said. "She's two years younger than me."

"Just imagine that four times over."

"I don't need to," Vaughn said, ostentatiously brushing evidence of the snow battle from his sleeves.

They didn't see Pete or Tom on their way over, so Carrie assumed they'd gone about their business. As she'd told Vaughn, it'd been all in fun and at least her brothers knew when to admit defeat.

Predictably enough, Vaughn raved about the pizza. In fact, he bought a second one to take home and reheat. When they'd eaten, they returned to Hassie's, where his mother had just finished her visit. All four of them walked to where Vaughn had parked the car outside

Sarah's quilt store. When they reached it, Hassie and Barbara Kyle hugged for a long moment.

"Thank you for coming," Hassie said, dabbing at her eyes.

Carrie knew it had been an emotional visit for both women.

"No—thank *you* for…for being Hassie," Barbara said, and they hugged again. "I'll be in touch about Christmas."

Vaughn opened the car door for his mother and helped her inside, an old-fashioned courtesy that reminded Carrie of her father and uncles.

Carrie stood on the sidewalk next to Hassie as Vaughn placed his pizza carefully on the back seat.

"They're coming to spend Christmas with me," Hassie said. "I haven't looked forward to anything so much in years. It'll be like when the children were still home."

Carrie knew Hassie intended to spend Christmas morning with Bob and Merrily and little Bobby, but she'd turned down invitations from almost everyone in town for dinner. Carrie was relieved that Hassie wouldn't spend the afternoon alone—and she envied her Vaughn's company.

He climbed into the car beside his mother and started the engine. Before he backed out of the parking space, his eyes met Carrie's. She raised her hand and he returned the gesture. She felt as if her heart was reaching out to him…and his to her.

Six

Hassie had been looking forward to this night. The Dawsons had moved to Buffalo Valley four years earlier; at that time the only church in town had been Catholic and was closed after Father McGrath's retirement. Then Reverend John Dawson and his wife had arrived.

What a blessing the couple had turned out to be! Joyce knew instinctively what to say to make people feel welcome. John's sermons were inspiring, and his advice was both sensitive and practical.

Her first Christmas in Buffalo Valley, Joyce had organized the Cookie Exchange, which had become a yearly event.

Hassie had baked oatmeal-cranberry cookies early that morning and set out a plate for her visit with Barbara. Both had gotten so involved in their conversation that they hadn't tasted a single one. Hassie shook her head, smiling. It was as though all those years of not seeing each other had simply vanished after their initial awkwardness had passed. The visit had gone by far too quickly; Barbara had to leave long before Hassie was ready. What amazed Hassie was that she'd found herself saying things she hadn't even realized she felt.

Her daughter's decision to live in Hawaii was one example. She'd never understood what had prompted Valerie's choice. Yes, there'd been a job offer, but Valerie had *pursued* that job. The fact was, she'd wanted to get as far away from North Dakota as she possibly could. Hassie understood this for the very first time.

When Barbara had inquired about Valerie, Hassie explained that her daughter had chosen to remove herself from the pain of losing her only brother and then her father. Never before had Hassie consciously acknowledged that. Yet the moment she said the words, she knew they were true.

Later that evening when Hassie got to the church for the Cookie Exchange, the place was blazing with light. Although she was twenty minutes early, the parking lot was already half-full. The first person she saw once she'd set her platter of cookies on the table was Calla Stern. Sarah's once-rebellious daughter had become a lovely young woman. She was in her junior year of college now, if Hassie recalled correctly, and there was talk of her applying for admission to law school. She attended the University of Chicago and shared an apartment nearby, but at heart Calla remained a small-town girl.

As soon as Calla saw Hassie, she broke off her conversation and hurried across the room, arms outstretched.

"When did you get home?" Hassie asked, hugging her close.

"This afternoon. Oh, Hassie, I just heard about Value-X. What are we going to do?"

"I don't know, Calla, and this might shock you all, but I've decided I'm too old to fight them."

Calla frowned.

"That's what Leta told us."

"We can't stand in the way of progress." *If progress it is.* Change, anyway. Perhaps if Hassie repeated that often enough, she might come to accept it. This wasn't what she wanted, but as she'd learned long ago, the world didn't revolve around what she assumed was best.

"Let's enjoy this evening," Hassie urged, "and put these worries behind us until the new year."

"I'll try," the girl promised.

"Good." Hassie slid her arm through Calla's. "Now tell me, are you still seeing Kevin?" Calla had been dating Leta's boy off and on since her last year of high school.

"Occasionally. He's so busy, and I'm in school most of the time. Anyway, with him in Paris for six months..."

"Calla would make a wonderful daughter-in-law," Leta said, joining them.

"Oh, you!" Calla hugged her tightly, laughing as Hassie seconded Leta's remark.

"Stop it, you two," the girl chided. "I'm dating someone else at the moment and so is Kevin. We're good friends, but that's all. For now, anyway."

"Damn," Leta muttered.

"Give them time," Hassie told her.

"Exactly," Calla said with a soft smile, and after kissing them both, added, "Now excuse me while I go mingle."

Hassie watched her leave. She thought Calla and Kevin would eventually get married, but probably not for some years. Not until educations were completed and careers launched. Still, they understood each other and shared the experience of having grown up in Buffalo Valley.

No sooner had Calla wandered off than Maddy appeared with four-year-old Julianne. She was heavily pregnant with her third child, but she'd lost none of her composure or contentment.

"Maddy," Hassie said, pleased to see her. "Here, let me help you with all that." Maddy was juggling her coat and purse, plus a huge box of homemade cookies.

"Mommy, can I play with Joy?" Julianne asked, tugging at Maddy's sleeve.

"Yes, sweetheart, and tell Lindsay I'll be right there."

"Where's little Caleb?" Hassie asked.

"With his daddy. After all, this is a *girls'* night out," Maddy said. Hassie knew this third pregnancy was as unexpected as their first. With three babies in five years, Jeb and Maddy were sure to have their hands full for quite a while.

Jeb's mother must be looking down from heaven, mighty pleased with her son, Hassie mused. Thanks to Maddy, he'd gone from curmudgeonly recluse to good husband and proud father.

Hassie and Leta busied themselves arranging platters of cookies on the long tables. Joyce made several trips to the business office to run recipes off on the copier so they'd be available for whoever wanted them.

Margaret Eilers and her daughter, Hailey, were among the last to arrive. Hailey, at three, bore a strong resemblance to her father and to her brother, David. Looking at Margaret and the child, no one would guess she wasn't the girl's birth mother. Hassie had nothing but praise for the way Matt and Margaret had worked out the awkward situation involving their children.

In the beginning Hassie hadn't been keen on Matt Eilers. No one in town held a high opinion of the rancher. But Margaret had fallen hard for Matt; she wanted to marry him and nothing would change her mind. After Bernard died and left her the ranch, Matt started seeing more and more of her. A few months later, there was a wedding. Then, lo and behold, Margaret turned up pregnant—at the same time as that woman in Devils Lake.

The babies were born within a few weeks of each other, Hailey first and then little David. Hailey had been living with the couple for most of her three years. She was a darling little girl, which Hassie attributed primarily to the love and attention Margaret lavished on her.

The room rang with laughter and cheer, and Hassie basked in the sounds that ebbed and flowed around her. Her day had started early and been an emotional one. When she noticed chairs arranged along the wall, she slipped quietly off and sat down. A few minutes later Leta came to sit beside her.

"Just listen," Hassie said, closing her eyes.

"What am I supposed to be listening to?" Leta asked.

"The joy," Hassie told her. "The friendship. These women are the very breath of this community." Hassie was grateful she'd lived long enough to witness the town's reversal of fortunes. It was because of women like Lindsay and Rachel and Maddy and Sarah and Joanie Wyatt... And maybe she herself had played a small part.

"What I can't get over is all the babies," Leta said. "Future generations for Buffalo Valley."

"Rachel Quantrill is pregnant again," Hassie said, nodding at the young woman on the other side of the room talking with Sarah. Hassie was particularly fond of Rachel. She'd watched the young widow struggle to get by after the death of her first husband. She'd driven a school bus and worked as a part-time bookkeeper for Hassie. Later she'd opened the pizza-delivery service. That was how she'd met Heath. New to the banking business, Heath had rejected her loan application. His grandmother, who'd started the bank, had been furious with him, Hassie recalled. But things had a way of working out for the best. Lily Quantrill had lived to see her grandson and Rachel marry. Rachel had brought a son into the marriage, and later she and Heath had a daughter they'd named after Lily. A third child was expected in early summer.

"I'll have to remember that," Hassie murmured absently.

Leta gave her a puzzled look. "What?"

Hassie wasn't aware she'd spoken aloud. "About things working out for the best." Despite her efforts, her thoughts had returned to Value-X and the potential for disaster. All her hopes for this town and the people she loved so dearly were at stake.

"You feeling all right?" Leta asked in a concerned tone.

"I'm fine," Hassie assured her. "Just tired. It's been a busy day."

Joyce Dawson sat down at the piano, and soon the room was filled with sweetly raised voices. The women and children gathered around, breaking naturally into two-part harmony. To Hassie it sounded as though the very angels from heaven were singing.

"Hassie—" Carrie Hendrickson crouched by her chair "—are you ill?"

Leta answered for her. "She's just tired."

"No wonder," Carrie murmured. "She was up before dawn baking cookies and then there was the visit from Barbara Kyle, plus a big order came in for the pharmacy."

Hassie grinned, amused that they spoke as if she wasn't even there.

"Let me walk you home," Carrie suggested, taking her hand.

"Fiddlesticks. I'm perfectly capable of walking back on my own. No need for you to leave the party."

"I insist," Carrie said. "It'll only take a few minutes and no one will miss me."

Hassie was weary, wearier than she cared to admit, so she agreed. Carrie retrieved their coats and led the way outside, sliding her arm through Hassie's to lend her support. They walked slowly, in companionable silence. The night sky was bright and clear, the stars scattered against it like diamonds. Most of the snow had been swept aside and the sidewalks salted.

As they crossed the street, a truck pulled up to the curb and rolled down the window. "You two need a ride?" Chuck Hendrickson asked.

"We're fine, thanks, anyway," Carrie told her brother.

"Say, that fellow you had dinner with phoned a few minutes ago."

"Must be Vaughn," Hassie said. It did seem that Carrie and Vaughn were seeing a lot of each other, and that pleased her. From now on, Hassie resolved to look only at the positive side of things. She refused to let herself fret over situations she couldn't control.

"I'll call him back once I'm finished over at the church," Carrie told her brother, who drove off.

"You could do worse, Carrie," Hassie said. "He's a fine man."

"I think so, too."

"Not every man is another Alec."

"I know," she said.

Hassie patted Carrie's hand. She would go home and think good thoughts for the young woman and for Buffalo Valley. Happy, positive thoughts.

* * *

"It's about time you called," Natalie snapped. There'd been no word of greeting.

Vaughn sat on the bed in his parents' guest room and pressed his cell phone to his ear. He felt guilty about not returning Natalie's repeated calls. He'd delayed it, needing to put his thoughts in order first. He felt guilty about other things, too, but he didn't want to think about Carrie, not when he had to deal with Natalie.

No one in Buffalo Valley knew he'd taken a job with Value-X. Not his parents. Not Hassie. And certainly not Carrie. His visit to North Dakota at a time when the company was considering an outlet in this area had seemed a fortuitous coincidence. Now it felt like the very opposite. He'd agreed to check out the town, but that had been a mistake he regretted heartily. And Natalie was hounding him for information.

"You're right, I should've phoned sooner," he admitted.

"Yes, you should have." Her voice softened. "I've missed hearing from you."

He didn't have an excuse to offer her, and the truth was…well, difficult to explain. Not only did he have serious doubts about working for this company, he'd met Carrie, and the attraction between them was undeniable.

Just a few days ago his future had seemed assured, but now, after meeting Hassie and Carrie, his entire sense of what was right had been challenged. And his assumptions about love and marriage, about Natalie—they'd changed, too.

Natalie's voice was hard when she spoke again. "I was beginning to wonder if I made a mistake recommending you for this position. I put my reputation on the line."

"I assumed I'd been hired on my own merits."

"You were but..." She sighed heavily. "Let's forget all that, shall we? I didn't know what to think when you didn't phone." She gave a stilted laugh. "I realize you're not officially on the payroll until January, but it's so advantageous for you to be near this little town."

"The town has a name."

"I know that," she said, and some of the stiffness returned to her voice. "I'm sorry, Vaughn, but I've had a trying day. Apparently Buffalo Valley is mounting opposition against Value-X."

"I know."

"You do?" She slowly released her breath. "You can't imagine how hectic everything is here, with the holidays and everything else. Now *this*. I spoke with a woman in town. I can't remember her name exactly. Lesley, Lindy..."

"Lindsay Sinclair."

"You know her?"

"I've met her."

"She made the town's position very clear," Natalie continued. "It seems we've got some public-relations work ahead of us. Okay, we can deal with that—we've done it before. We know how to present our case in a positive light. It won't take much to change their attitude, and really, at this point, they really don't have much choice."

Vaughn was sorry to hear that. So it was too late; Value-X had obviously succeeded in buying the property. This was what he'd feared. "Lindsay told me Value-X is sending someone out after Christmas."

"I volunteered for the job myself," she said, excited now. "It was providential, don't you think? I can meet your parents and settle this unfortunate matter with

Buffalo Valley at the same time. Combine business with pleasure, in other words." She sounded pleased with herself for having so neatly arranged this trip. "I've got everything in motion for a Value-X campaign."

"I hope you'll be willing to listen to the town's concerns."

"Well, yes, of course I'll listen, but I'm hoping to present our case, too. In fact, I've already authorized a letter to be delivered to every family in Buffalo Valley. It's scheduled to arrive just after the first of the year."

"A letter?"

"Everyone thinks it's a great idea." Her satisfaction was unmistakable. "I wrote it myself for a personal touch. I want the town to understand that they've unfairly prejudged Value-X. I told them not to look at any negatives they might've heard about the company, but at the positives—everything we can do for their community. We plan to be a good neighbor."

Vaughn knew that Natalie's letter would most likely anger the people of Buffalo Valley, not reassure them. "I didn't realize you'd signed the deal on the land," he muttered. Without being completely aware of it, Vaughn had held out hope that the controversy would die a natural death if the land deal fell through. His heart sank. It looked as if he'd have no choice but to get involved. The question was: on which side would he stand? If he followed his heart, he'd join Hassie and Carrie in their fight, but if he did that, he'd compromise his future with Value-X and Natalie...

Natalie hesitated before she answered. "There've been a few snags with the property deal. Mr. Kohn isn't an easy man to work with."

Vaughn's relief was swift. So there *was* hope. "That's what I hear about Ambrose Kohn."

"Have you met him?"

"No, he lives in Devils Lake. Listen, Natalie, I have to tell you I'm not convinced Buffalo Valley is a good site."

She laughed, but he could tell she wasn't amused. "You haven't even started work yet and you're already telling me my job?"

"*You* chose Buffalo Valley as a development site?"

"I sure did," she said smugly. "We did a study on small towns that have shown substantial growth over the last five years. Buffalo Valley is a perfect target area for retail expansion."

Vaughn's hand tightened around the telephone receiver. "They don't have enough retail choices," he muttered.

"Exactly." Apparently she hadn't noticed the sarcasm in his voice.

Vaughn felt tension creeping across his shoulders. He probably couldn't influence her to change her letter or withdraw it; he was in no position to tell Natalie news she didn't want to hear.

She returned to the subject of Ambrose Kohn. "I'm interested in what you know about him," she said.

"I don't know him, but I have heard about him." Vaughn didn't feel comfortable saying anything more than he already had. As it was, he felt traitor enough.

"He *will* sign, and soon." Natalie's confidence sounded unshakable. "The transaction is as good as done."

Vaughn rotated his neck in order to ease the tension.

"I know what's happened," she said, catching him by surprise. "You've seen this little town and now you have doubts that Value-X is doing the right thing."

It was as though she'd read his mind. He found himself nodding.

"You're confused," Natalie continued. "It happens

to a lot of us when we first hire on with the company. Don't worry, it's something we all work through. Trust me, Vaughn, Value-X knows what it's doing."

"Buffalo Valley is afraid of losing its character."

"Every town is in the beginning. They get over it. Sooner or later, each town comes to realize that we know what's best for them. Buffalo Valley will, too."

This was worse than he'd thought. Vaughn rubbed his hand down his face. Still sitting on the edge of his bed, he tilted his head back to stare up at the ceiling. This was *really* bad.

Value-X had no intention of listening to the concerns of Buffalo Valley's citizens. In its arrogance, the retailer had decided on a course of action, one that reflected solely its own interests.

"I'm looking forward to seeing you," Natalie told him, lowering her voice seductively.

It was almost more than Vaughn could do to echo the sentiment.

When he finished the conversation, he returned to the kitchen to find his mother dishing up ice cream.

"You interested?" she asked, holding up the scoop.

"Sure, why not?" he muttered. He took a third bowl from the cupboard and handed it to his mother, who pried open the carton lid.

"Tell me more about Natalie," she said.

Vaughn didn't know what to say. "You'll meet her soon enough."

"She's joining us after Christmas, right?" She studied him hard, and Vaughn knew what she was thinking. He'd spent almost every day of the past week with Carrie. He was with one woman and had another waiting in the wings—that was how it looked. His mother's eyes filled with questions.

"Natalie is coming, then?" she repeated when he didn't answer.

"So it seems." He sighed. She'd show up even if he asked her to stay home. Value-X was paying for the trip.

"You don't sound too happy about it," his mother murmured, her eyes narrowed. "What about Carrie?"

"Mom…"

"I know, I know, but I can't help wondering if you're really sure of what you want. I saw the look Carrie gave you as we left Buffalo Valley earlier today."

Vaughn frowned.

"She deserves your honesty."

He was in full agreement; he owed Carrie the truth, and not only about his relationship with Natalie. He had to tell her about Value-X.

As soon as his mother left the kitchen, Vaughn reached for the phone. Unfortunately Carrie wasn't home. He recalled now that she'd mentioned something about meeting with the church women's group, but that'd slipped his mind. He left a message with one of her brothers.

After that, he joined his parents in the living room. He settled on the sofa next to his mother and focused his attention on a television show about Christmas traditions around the world.

An hour later the phone pealed and his mother automatically rose to answer it. She returned almost immediately. "It's Carrie for you."

Vaughn went into the kitchen.

"Hi," she said excitedly when he picked up the receiver. "I just got back from the Cookie Exchange and got your message."

"How was it?"

"Great, as usual. There was a lot of talk about this

Value-X problem. We're going to take active measures to keep the company out of town."

She'd given him the perfect lead. This was his chance to explain the whole confused mess. But Vaughn didn't. He couldn't, not over the phone. It was something that needed to be said face-to-face, he decided. Okay, so he was a coward.

Carrie seemed to be waiting for a response, so to keep the conversation going, he asked, "What can be done?"

"According to Hassie, nothing. She's afraid we can't win, especially after everything she's heard and read. According to all the news stories, the company practically always comes out on top. Still, there are a few towns that didn't give in, including one in Montana, I think." She paused. "Hassie's real problem is that she's just tired out. But I'm not, and neither are the rest of us."

Vaughn could hear the fighting spirit in her voice.

"I suggest you start with Ambrose Kohn." That was probably more than he should've said, but the words escaped before he could judge their wisdom.

"We're having an organizational meeting as soon as it can be arranged, and I'll recommend that."

"Great," he mumbled, wishing he could tell her he didn't want to hear any of this. It put him in a terrible position. He'd be a traitor to Value-X and Natalie if he withheld these facts, and a traitor to Carrie if he relayed them.

"...tomorrow night."

"I'm sorry," Vaughn said, trapped in his own dilemma. "What did you say?"

"Can you come? It's the high-school play. I know it doesn't sound like much, but we're all proud of it. The play's about the history of Buffalo Valley and the families that settled here. It'll give you a feel for the town."

Vaughn's own great-grandparents on his mother's side had settled in the Dakotas in the late 1800s. He pondered Carrie's words. Knowing more about the town's past might help him decide what to do about his relationship with Value-X—and Natalie. It was a faint hope—and maybe just another delaying tactic—but he had nothing else to cling to.

"Will you come as my guest?" she asked.

"I'll look forward to it."

She gave him the details and Vaughn hung up the phone feeling as vulnerable and unsure as ever.

"How'd it go?" his mother asked when he returned to the living room.

"Fine," he muttered. "Just fine."

Seven

The theater was filled to capacity. People crowded the aisle, chatting and visiting with one another. Carrie had been fortunate to get good seats for herself and Vaughn, thanks to Lindsay Sinclair.

"I didn't know there were this many people in Buffalo Valley," Vaughn said, twisting around to glance over his shoulder.

"There aren't. Folks come from all over. The Cowans drove down from Canada. Her great-grandmother is one of the main characters in the play."

Vaughn looked at his program. "So, Lindsay Sinclair is the producer and director of Dakota Christmas."

Carrie nodded. "Lindsay's the person responsible for all this," she said, gesturing toward her friend. "None of it would've happened without her."

Carrie went on to explain how the play had been created and described everything Lindsay had done to make sure it got performed. At the end of the story she told him that the theater belonged to Ambrose Kohn.

"*The* Ambrose Kohn?" Vaughn's brows arched.

"When Lindsay first arrived, the theater was nothing but cobwebs and dirt. She was a first-year teacher and one of the stipulations when she accepted the job was that the community would pitch in and help."

"In what way?"

"In whatever way she required. She asked the town's older people to talk to the kids. It started with Joshua McKenna. At the time he was president of the town council, plus he knows quite a bit of local history. After that, Lindsay lined up community representatives to come to the school on Friday afternoons. Joshua was the one who gave her the idea of having the kids write the play."

"The high-schoolers wrote the play?"

"The original script was created by the kids Lindsay taught six years ago. Each new group of students refines it a little bit."

"This is the sixth year?" He glanced around with what appeared to be renewed appreciation. "Pretty impressive audience."

"It's a fabulous play. Why else would so many people return year after year?"

"What's your favorite part?"

"I love all of it. There's a scene early on when a tornado hits the town and everything's destroyed. The people lose heart. Entire crops are wiped out and families are left homeless. You can just *feel* their agony." She didn't mean to get carried away, but no matter how often she'd seen it, the scene brought tears to Carrie's eyes.

"What happens then?" Vaughn asked.

"Everyone pulls together. The people whose fields were spared share their crops with the ones who lost everything. With everyone working together, they rebuild the farms destroyed in the tornado and save the town."

Vaughn nodded slowly. "Teamwork," he murmured.

"That was a message that really hit home for all of

us. So many of the farmers continue to struggle financially. The play helped remind us that we need to work together. Then and now."

"Are you talking about Value-X?"

Carrie shook her head. "Not only Value-X. We have more problems than just that. As you probably know, farm prices are low and have been for years. Most folks around here feel that no one appreciates the contribution of the small farmer anymore. A lot of people were demoralized by what was happening."

"Is it better now?"

"Yes, but only because farmers in the area have banded together. They still aren't getting decent prices for their crops, but they've found ways around that."

Carrie looked away; she had to swallow the lump in her throat. Her own family had been forced off the farm. The land had produced record yields, and it still wasn't enough to make ends meet. After several years of dismal wheat prices, the family had realized the farm could no longer support them all. That was when her parents and younger brothers had moved into town.

This had happened shortly after she'd filed for divorce. At first it had seemed inevitable that they'd have to sell the land, but then her two older brothers had decided to lease it. Pete and Tom were married by this time, and along with their wives, they'd made the decision to stay.

Buffalo Valley had started to show signs of new life—with the reopening of the hotel and bar, as well as Rachel's pizza restaurant. And Lindsay, of course, had brought fresh hope to the community in so many ways...

Carrie's mother had come into a small inheritance, and her parents chose to invest it in a business. Buffalo

Valley was badly in need of an all-purpose hardware store. Carrie's father felt confident that if people could shop locally, they would, so the family had risked everything with this venture. To date, it had been a wise choice, but now with the mega-chain threatening to swallow up smaller businesses, the Hendricksons were in grave danger of losing it all.

"The American farmer refuses to be discounted," Carrie said, clearing her throat. "When was the last time you purchased pasta?"

"Pasta? As in noodles?" Vaughn asked in a puzzled voice. "Not recently. What makes you ask?"

"Ever hear of Velma brand?"

"Can't say I have."

Carrie tucked her arm through his. "It's made with wheat grown right here in Buffalo Valley. Brandon Wyatt and Gage Sinclair are part of the program. A year ago they joined several other local farmers, including my brothers, and some not so local, and cut out the middleman."

"You mean a group of farmers decided to start their own pasta company?"

"That's exactly what I mean."

"Ingenious," Vaughn said. "Incredible. So that's what you were talking about when you said they'd found ways around the poor prices."

"Yeah. There's often a solution—but sometimes you have to find it yourself."

"Carrie."

Carrie looked up to see Lindsay and Gage Sinclair standing in the aisle near them.

Carrie started to make the introductions, then remembered that Vaughn had met Lindsay in the pharmacy two days before.

"Vaughn, this is my husband, Gage," Lindsay said.

Vaughn stood and held out his hand to Gage. He and Carrie made their way into the aisle.

"I understand you're an Airborne Ranger," Gage said.

"Was," Vaughn corrected.

The two men began a conversation about military life, and Lindsay stepped closer to Carrie.

"Thanks for getting us such great seats," Carrie said. Lindsay was a substitute teacher now but still worked on the play every year.

"No problem." Lindsay glanced pointedly at Vaughn. "How's it going?"

Carrie didn't know how to answer. Her divorce had devastated her, and since then she'd thrown herself into her studies, forging ahead, insulating her heart. She'd been protecting herself from any risk of pain, but at the same time she'd eliminated any hope of finding love. Then Vaughn entered her life. His patience with Hassie had touched her. His willingness to hear her concerns about the changes that seemed to be coming to Buffalo Valley inspired her to fight for what she knew was right.

Carrie looked at Vaughn and sighed. "He gives me hope," she whispered.

"I remember the first time I saw Gage," Lindsay whispered back. "He looked at me and... I know it's a cliché, but it was as if someone had zapped me with an electrical jolt. I didn't even know this man's name and it was as though I'd *connected* with him."

The music started and Gage reached for Lindsay's hand. "We'd better find our seats."

Gage and Lindsay left, and Carrie and Vaughn returned to their own seats. No sooner had they settled in than the curtain went up.

Several times during the evening, Carrie caught

Vaughn studying her. She felt his eyes on her, and when she turned to meet his gaze, he took her hand and entwined his fingers with hers. Carrie had the sensation that something was troubling him, but now wasn't the time to ask.

"Kids in high school actually wrote the play themselves?" Vaughn asked Carrie for the second time. He found it difficult to believe that a group of teenagers could have created and put on such a high-quality production. The acting was a bit amateurish, true, but the emotion and heart that went into each scene stirred him more than he would've thought possible.

After seeing the play, Vaughn realized he could no longer evade a decision regarding Value-X. Not after these vivid depictions of the struggles Buffalo Valley had faced. Through the years, bad weather and bouts of pestilence had plagued the land. The tales of the "dust bowl" years had given him a small taste of the hopelessness the farmers endured. The play ended with a farm family standing in the middle of a wheat field, their heads held high, their arms linked. Just thinking about that scene raised goose bumps onhis arms.

"High-school kids," he repeated before Carrie could respond.

"It was as good as I said it was, don't you agree?"

Words fell short of describing the powerful sensation he'd experienced throughout the play.

"Would you like to come over to Buffalo Bob's for hot cider? A lot of folks do," Carrie said. "But I should warn you, Pete and Tom will be there."

Vaughn would enjoy going another round with Carrie's brothers, but unfortunately he had a long drive back to Grand Forks. "Another time," he told her. He wasn't in the mood to socialize.

As they stepped from the warmth of the theater into the cold night air, his breath became visible in foggy wisps. The cold seemed to press against him with an intensity he hadn't expected.

"Let me get you home," Vaughn said, placing his arm around her. He wasn't accustomed to cold so severe it made his lungs ache just to draw a breath.

Carrie wrapped her scarf more securely about her neck and pulled on her wool hat. Normally they would have walked the short distance, but not when the cold was so bitter, the wind so vicious.

Vaughn helped her into his rental car, then hurried around the front and climbed into the driver's seat.

Neither spoke as he drove the few short blocks to her family's home. Vaughn wondered if Carrie had realized no one would be there. The house was dark. Had he asked, she would've invited him inside, but he preferred talking to her there, in the dark.

"Carrie, listen, there's something I have to tell you." He stared straight ahead, unable to look at her.

"I know what you're going to say."

He jerked his gaze to hers. Her blue eyes were barely visible in the moonlight, but he saw enough to be aware that she only *thought* she knew.

"We've known each other a very short time," she said. "You'll be leaving soon."

"It doesn't have anything to do with you and me."

"Oh." He could hear her surprise and embarrassment. "I'm sorry. I didn't mean to speak out of turn."

"At the same time, it has *everything* to do with us," he said, and slid his arm around her neck and drew her to him. He breathed in her scent—clean and light and floral; he felt her body against him, softly yielding. After a moment of debating the wisdom of what he was about to do, he exhaled harshly.

"Vaughn, what is it?"

He didn't know where he'd find the courage to tell her. She raised her head to look at him, her eyes full of warmth and concern. Kissing her was wrong; he knew it even as he lowered his mouth to hers. He didn't care, he *had* to kiss her one last time before he was forced to watch the transformation that would come over her when she learned the truth. In a few seconds he was going to hurt and disillusion her.

His mouth was on hers with excitement, with need. The kiss was intense. Real. It seemed to him that the woman in his arms had flung open her life for him, and that thought left his senses reeling.

The guilt he felt was nearly overwhelming.

Her hat had fallen off, and Vaughn slipped his fingers into her hair. He held her close, refusing to release her. From the way she clung to him, she didn't want him to let her go.

"Tell me?" she pleaded.

"Carrie..." He shut his eyes and held his breath for a moment. "I came to Buffalo Valley for more reasons than you know."

"Hassie?"

"For Hassie, yes, but... I'd also been asked to check on something for a friend."

"Check on what?"

"The only way to say this is straight out. I work for Value-X."

Carrie froze. *"What?"* she asked, her voice confused. Uncomprehending.

"Value-X's corporate headquarters are in Seattle."

"I thought you were just discharged from the army."

"I was."

She pulled away from him and scraped the hair back from her face as though to see him more clearly. "I don't understand."

"I don't expect you to. I took a job with Value-X after my discharge."

"They sent you here?" Her back was stiff now, and she leaned away from him. A moment earlier she couldn't get close enough, and now she was as far from him as the confines of the vehicle would allow. "Are your parents involved in this?"

"No! They don't even know."

She shook her head over and over, raising both hands to her face. "I need to think," she said.

"I don't officially start with the company until January."

"You're a *spy*?"

"No. The vice president of new development asked me to check out the town. I was going to be in the area, anyway. It made perfect sense, and..."

"And so you did."

He couldn't very well deny it. "You have every right to be furious."

"You're damn straight I do," she said, grabbing the door handle.

Vaughn stopped her by reaching for her hand. "I can't do it."

She glared at him. "Can't do what?"

"Work for Value-X. I'm faxing in my resignation first thing tomorrow morning." No one would be in the office to read it until after Christmas, but that couldn't be helped.

Carrie still appeared stunned. "I don't know what to say," she muttered. "I need time to think."

"All right. I know this is a shock. I won't blame you if you decide you want nothing more to do with me. That decision is yours." He sincerely hoped his honesty would prove his sincerity.

She climbed out of the car and without another word, ran toward the house. Vaughn waited at the curb until she was safely inside and then, with a heavy heart, he drove back to Grand Forks.

His parents were still up, playing a game of Scrabble at the kitchen table, when he walked in.

His mother looked up and smiled. "How was the play?"

"Excellent," he answered.

His father picked up four new alphabet squares. "I heard it was put on by a bunch of kids."

"That's true, but they did an incredible job." Vaughn turned a chair around and straddled it.

"How's Carrie?" his mother asked innocently enough.

Vaughn's response was so long in coming that Barbara frowned. She seemed about to repeat her question when he spoke, intending to forestall her.

"If no one minds," he said quickly, "I think I'll go to bed."

"Sure," his father said, concentrating on the game.

"You don't want a cup of tea first?" his mother asked, still frowning.

"I'm sure," he said.

Inside the guest room, Vaughn threw himself on the bed. The guilt and remorse that had haunted him on the sixty-minute drive from Buffalo Valley hadn't dissipated.

He folded his hands beneath his head and gazed up

at the ceiling, his thoughts twisting and turning as he attempted to reason everything out. Now that Carrie knew the truth, he should feel better, but he didn't.

Resigning from Value-X was only a small part of what he had to do. He wouldn't be this attracted to Carrie if he truly loved Natalie. He closed his eyes and could only imagine what Natalie would say once she discovered what he'd done. Avoiding a confrontation with her would be impossible. She was coming to Buffalo Valley, and what was that old adage? *Hell hath no fury like a woman scorned.* He could feel the flames licking at his feet even now. Oh, yes, this was only the beginning.

He trusted that Carrie would eventually forgive him for his deception concerning Value-X and his role with the company. He'd been as candid with her as he could.

Unfortunately Value-X wasn't the only issue. He didn't have the courage to tell Carrie about Natalie. Not yet. He didn't want to force her to accept more than one disappointment at a time. Once she'd dealt with the fact that he was connected with Value-X, he'd explain his relationship to Natalie. By then, that relationship would be over.

Sitting up, Vaughn swung his legs over the side of the bed and sat there for several minutes. His mind wasn't going to let him sleep, so it was a waste of time to even try.

The kitchen light was off when he stepped into the hallway. He assumed his parents had finished their game and retired for the night. Perhaps if he had something to eat, it might help him relax. To his surprise, he found his father sitting in the darkened living room, watching the late-night news. The Christmas tree in the corner twinkled with festive lights that illuminated the gifts piled beneath.

"I thought you'd gone to bed," his father said.

"I thought I had, too," Vaughn answered, joining him. They both stared at the screen, although there was nothing on except a too-familiar commercial. Yet anyone might have thought they were viewing it for the first time.

His father suddenly roused himself and turned off the TV. "Something on your mind?" he asked after an uncomfortable moment of silence.

Vaughn hesitated, wondering if he should share his burden.

His father yawned loudly. "You'd better start talking soon if you're inclined to do so, because I'm about to hit the sack."

Vaughn laughed despite himself. "Go to bed. This is something I've got to settle myself."

"All right," Rick Kyle told him. "If you're sure..."

"'Night, Dad," Vaughn said, grateful for having been raised by two loving parents.

"You coming to bed or not?" Gage Sinclair called to his wife. Lindsay had been fussing ever since they'd driven back to the farm. After they'd put the girls down for the night, she'd decided to sort laundry. Then it was something in the kitchen. He had no idea what she was up to now.

"Lindsay," he shouted a second time, already in bed himself.

"I'll be there in a minute." Her voice came from the living room.

"That's what you said fifteen minutes ago."

Tossing aside the comforter, he got out of bed and

reached for his robe before walking into the other room. Sure enough, he found her sitting on the sofa, knitting. This particular project looked like it was going to be a sweater for Joy. "Tell me what's bothering you," he said, sinking down in his recliner.

"Things," she returned a moment later.

"You're not upset with me, are you?"

She lowered her knitting and stared at him. "Has there *ever* been a time I was afraid to tell you exactly what I thought, Gage Sinclair?"

Gage didn't have to consider that for very long. "No," he said decisively.

"Exactly."

"Then what is it?" he pressed. All at once he knew. The answer should have been obvious. "Value-X?"

His wife nodded. "My mind's been buzzing ever since I talked to the company. That woman was so arrogant. I don't doubt for a moment that Value-X will be as ruthless as they need to be."

"Sweetheart, there isn't anything we can do about it now."

"I know, but I can't stop thinking. We've got to get organized."

"I agree."

"It's just that with Christmas only a few days away, everyone's so busy we can't find even a couple of hours."

"That's what happens this time of year."

"But the future of the entire *town* is at risk."

"Don't you think other towns have tried to keep them out?" He didn't mean to be a pessimist, but truth was truth. No matter what kind of slant they put on it, nothing was going to change.

"What worries me most is Hassie's attitude," Lindsay admitted. "I've never known her to give up without one hell of a fight."

"Sweetheart, she's single-handedly slayed dragons for this town. It's someone else's turn."

"I know." This was said with a sadness that tugged at his heart. Gage knew his wife had a special relationship with Hassie. He also knew that without Hassie Knight, he might never have married Lindsay. Now it was impossible to imagine his life without her and their daughters. It wasn't anything he even wanted to contemplate.

"I saw you talking to Maddy," Gage said. The two women had been friends nearly all their lives, and they still relied on each other when either had a problem. This problem, though, was shared by the whole town. Predictably, Lindsay had taken on Buffalo Valley's latest dilemma—taken on Hassie's role, too, he thought.

That was what he loved about her, and at the same time dreaded. His wife didn't know the meaning of the word *no*. She simply refused to give up. When she'd first moved to Buffalo Valley, they'd been constantly at odds; he was crazy about her, yet couldn't say a word to her without an argument erupting.

They'd met one hot summer afternoon at Hassie's. Lindsay had left town but she'd stayed in his mind. For weeks afterward she filled his thoughts, and if that wasn't bad enough, she invaded his dreams. When he learned she'd accepted the teaching position at the high school, he managed to convince himself that this Southern belle wouldn't last longer than the first snowflake. His behavior toward her had been scornful, even combative—an attempt to keep from making a fool of himself. It hadn't worked, since he'd done a mighty fine job of looking like a dolt.

Then there was the matter of finding their aunt, the

illegitimate child of her grandmother and his grandfather. Gage had wanted no part of that. He'd violently disagreed with her decision to intrude on this unknown woman's life.

He'd been wrong about that, and during the past few years, Angela Kirkpatrick had become an important figure in their lives.

It didn't stop there. Lindsay had known what was best for Kevin, too. His much younger brother was never meant to be a farmer. Kevin hated what Gage loved most. But Kevin's talent meant that he would one day be named among the country's major artists. Lindsay had recognized his brother's gift when Gage had turned a blind eye to it.

Having seen the error of his ways—repeatedly— Gage had come to trust his wife's judgment and intuition. "What do you suggest we do?" he asked, getting up and sitting next to her on the sofa.

"I just don't know, and neither does Maddy," Lindsay told him, shrugging helplessly. She put aside her knitting, muttering that she couldn't concentrate anymore. Not *his* fault, she assured him. It was just this Value-X thing.

He clasped her hand and she gripped his hard. She scrambled into his lap, pressing her head against his shoulder. Gathering her close, Gage savored the feel of his wife in his arms.

"I tried to talk to Hassie about it, but she said I should turn my thinking around and try to look at the positive side of the situation."

"Have you?" Gage asked, dropping a kiss on her forehead.

"No. I can't get past what'll happen to Buffalo Valley once Value-X arrives."

The prospects for the future weren't bright in view of what had become of other communities the retailer had entered.

Neither spoke for several moments, then Gage changed the subject. "I enjoyed meeting Vaughn Kyle."

"You two certainly seemed to hit it off."

"We got to talking about army life."

"Wouldn't it be wonderful if he moved to Buffalo Valley and he and Carrie got married?" his wife said. Sometimes he forgot what a romantic she could be. And yet...time and again, her instincts about people proved to be correct. She was the one who'd claimed Maddy and Jeb were falling in love, although Gage would've sworn on a stack of Bibles that it wasn't happening.

"Carrie and Vaughn?" he repeated.

"Mark my words, Gage."

Lindsay wasn't going to get an argument out of him. "You ready for bed now?"

"Ready," she told him, kissing his jaw and sending shivers down his back.

"Me, too," he whispered.

Eight

"I've got a meeting in town this morning," Margaret Eilers announced at the breakfast table Saturday morning, three days before Christmas.

This came as news to Matt. His wife hadn't mentioned anything about going into Buffalo Valley. Something was in the air, though. The phone had been ringing off the hook for the better part of a week. He knew the women around here were up in arms about the Value-X problem, although Matt didn't see what could be done. Neither did any of the other men in town.

"Can you watch the kids for me, Sadie?" His wife smiled at the housekeeper, who'd been with the family since Margaret's childhood.

Sadie brought a stack of pancakes to the table and wiped her hands on her apron. "Not this morning," she said in that brusque way of hers.

Anyone who didn't know Sadie might assume she was put out by the request. She wasn't. This was simply her manner, and they were all used to it. Matt had learned more than one lesson from the highly capable housekeeper. She'd become an ally and friend shortly after he married Margaret, and he was forever grateful for all she'd done to see him through his troubles.

"I'm leaving at noon, remember?" Sadie reminded them.

"That's right," Margaret muttered, glancing at Matt.

"What's going on in town?" he asked. Margaret wasn't one to make unnecessary trips, nor was she the type of woman to find an excuse to shop.

"I'm meeting with the other women. We're going to discuss ideas on how to deal with the threat from Value-X," she told him.

"Sweetheart, that's already been discussed to death. The town council has tried, Hassie's—"

"Everyone's been talking to Ambrose Kohn individually. We've got to mount a defense as a community."

"And do what? Sign petitions?" He didn't mean to sound negative, but he sincerely doubted that Value-X cared what the community thought. They'd already set the wheels in motion. Matt suspected many a town such as theirs had tried to mount a defense, but it had been hopeless from the start. Value-X knew how to win.

"We can't sit by and do nothing," Margaret insisted.

"But it's almost Christmas."

"Exactly, and Value-X is counting on the community to delay a response until after the holidays. By then it could be too late. That's what the meeting's about. I'm willing to fight now, and so are the other women in town."

"What about the men?"

"You're welcome to join us, but..."

"But the women are spearheading this."

"That's because none of you men believe it can be done." Her smile belied the sharpness of her words. "You can still come if you want."

"No, thanks," Matt said, waving a hand in dismissal. "I've got the kids to look after."

Margaret smiled and reached over to spear a hot-cake with her fork. They'd been married three years, and Matt fell more in love with her every day. Times had been hard in the beginning, but it seemed that once they'd survived that rough period, they'd grown closer than ever. Of one thing Matt was certain—his wife brought out the very best in him. He loved her with an intensity that gave him strength.

"So I can leave Hailey and David with you?"

"I did have plans this morning, but they can wait." He'd hoped to finish the gift he was working on for Margaret. The antique rocker had belonged to her father. Matt had stumbled upon it in the loft up in the barn, and Sadie had told him its history. Joshua McKenna had repaired it earlier, and Matt had sanded and varnished the wood. Sadie had sewed new cushions for the seat and back. Matt had hoped to add a final coat of varnish that morning so it would be ready for Margaret on Christmas morning. Well…he'd have to find time tonight.

"I don't know what you women think you're going to accomplish," he said, "but if you sincerely believe it'll make a difference, then I'll do my part—and I'll wish you well."

Margaret thanked him with a brilliant smile, rose from the table and kissed him. The kiss was deep and full of promise. She was letting him know he'd be rewarded a hundred times over at a more appropriate hour.

Soon afterward Margaret headed into town. Once the kids were up, dressed and fed, Matt decided he wanted to know exactly what the women intended. Reaching for the phone, he called Jeb McKenna, his closest neighbor.

"Is Maddy gone, too?" he asked. Matt heard children crying in the background.

"I've got my hands full."

"Me, too," Matt confessed.

"Do you know what they're planning?" Jeb asked.

"I don't have a clue, but I'm sorry now that I didn't go with her. They have great intentions, but what can they do that hasn't already been tried?"

"You signed the petition?"

"Along with everyone else in town," Matt told him.

"Buffalo Bob contacted the governor and asked for help."

"Did he hear back?" Now, that was promising.

"Not yet."

Matt sighed impatiently. "I feel like we should be there."

"I do, too."

"Daddy." Hailey tugged at his jeans. "Can we go to town and have a soda?"

Matt grinned at his daughter. "Just a minute, honey." What an inspiration. "I'll meet you at the soda fountain," Matt suggested. "That way we can keep the kids occupied and we can talk ourselves."

"Good idea," Jeb said.

Matt pushed a tape into the truck's console and sang Christmas songs with his children as he drove into town. When he parked outside Hassie's, he noticed several other vehicles there, too. The two youngsters followed him excitedly into the drugstore.

The soda fountain appeared to be the most popular place in town; Gage Sinclair was there with his two daughters, and Jeb McKenna had arrived ahead of him. So had Brandon Wyatt and six-year-old Jason. Every stool at the fountain was occupied.

Matt acknowledged his friends with a quick nod.

"Hey, Matt," Jeb said in a jocular tone, "seeing that you called us together, I'm hoping you've come up with a few ideas to share."

"Me?" Matt glanced at Jeb, who shifted his weight. "I called a couple of the other guys, too. I think we made a mistake by taking such a negative attitude. Now the women are stuck trying to cope with the problem all by themselves."

The door opened and Dennis Urlacher walked in with his three-year-old son. Little Josh might be named after Sarah's father, but he was the spitting image of his own.

"I'm not late, am I?" Dennis asked, taken aback by the sight of all the children.

Leta was doing her best to keep up with orders, but she was obviously overwhelmed. As soon as she delivered one soda, she got an order for two more. Apparently Hassie was at the meeting over at Sarah's shop, as well. The men stood in a small circle while the children sat at the counter. Their joyous laughter made all the fathers smile, none more than Matt.

"So, does anyone have any ideas?" Dennis asked.

"Did you get anywhere with the governor's office?" Jeb asked Bob.

Bob shook his head. "I got the runaround. Reading between the lines, I could tell the politicians don't want to get involved in this fight. Buffalo Valley is on its own."

"Okay," Matt said, "maybe the politicians don't want to take sides in this issue, but there are plenty of other influential people who aren't afraid of challenging Value-X."

"Who?"

A flurry of names followed—writers and filmmakers and media personalities—along with a volunteer to contact each one immediately after the holidays. This was exactly the kind of pressure necessary to get the company's attention.

Soon the men were talking excitedly, their voices blending with those of their children. Various ideas were considered, discarded, put aside for research or further thought. The women were right—they had to become a united front.

"Do you seriously believe anyone at the corporate level will listen?" Gage asked. "They've dealt with organized opposition before."

Matt shrugged, although he suspected that if Margaret was the one doing the talking, those muck-a-mucks would soon learn she refused to be ignored. A smile formed on his face as he imagined Margaret standing before the conglomerate's board of directors. They'd listen, all right.

"What's so funny?" Brandon Wyatt asked.

"Nothing." Matt shook his head, dispelling the image. "Joanie's been real upset about all this."

"Maddy, too," Jeb said. "I don't think the grocery will be too badly affected, but that's not the point. She's worried about how everyone else will fare."

"Value-X would ruin Joanie's and my business," Brandon said. "But I don't think a bunch of suits in some fancy office in Seattle really care what'll happen to a small video store in Buffalo Valley."

The other men agreed.

"We could hold a rally," Gage suggested.

"The women have already thought of that," Leta inserted, speaking from behind the counter. "They figured it wouldn't have enough impact unless we got major media coverage."

Several of the men nodded; others seemed prepared to argue.

"Hassie's probably got a few ideas," Gage said next. "When she comes back from the meeting, we'll—"

Leta broke in. "Hassie's not with the others," she informed them as she set a chocolate soda on the polished mahogany counter.

"She's not?" The question came from two or three men simultaneously, including Matt.

"Nope. She's at home this morning."

This was news to them all.

"Hassie's not with the other women?" Dennis repeated, frowning. "But…"

"How many of them are over at Sarah's, anyway?" Matt wanted to know.

"They're not at Sarah's," Dennis told them.

"Then where are they?" Matt had assumed that was where the women had met. Sarah had the most space for such a gathering.

"I think they're over at the church with Joyce Dawson," Brandon Wyatt said. "I'm not sure, but something Joanie said…"

Matt figured it wasn't all that important where the women had congregated. The community was coming together, bringing forth ideas. Value-X might be a powerful corporation, but the men and women of Buffalo Valley weren't going to submit humbly to this invasion.

Sleep had eluded Vaughn Kyle all night. The message of the Christmas play had stayed with him. A community standing together, enduring through hard times, its unique character created by that history of struggle and victory. Not *a* community, *this* community. Buffalo Valley.

His confession to Carrie after the performance had played no small part in his inability to sleep. Unfortunately Carrie wasn't the only woman he needed to talk to, and the conversation with Natalie would probably be even harder.

He waited until eight, Seattle time, before calling her. His decision to resign and the reasons for it would infuriate her. And his plan to end their relationship— he didn't even want to think about her reaction to that. He wasn't convinced that she truly loved him, but the humiliation of being rejected would be difficult for her to accept. He sighed; he'd betrayed Carrie twice over and now he was doing the same to Natalie.

The house was still quiet when Vaughn brought the portable phone into his room. Sitting on the bed, he dialed Natalie's home number and waited four long rings before she picked up.

"Hello." Her voice was groggy with sleep. Normally she'd be awake by now. He'd already started off on the wrong foot, and he had yet to say a word.

"I got you up, didn't I," he said.

"Vaughn," she said sleepily, then yawned. "Hello, darling."

Vaughn tried to ignore the guilt that rushed forward. Mere hours ago, he'd been holding and kissing Carrie.

"This is a surprise," Natalie cooed. "You must really be missing me."

"I need to talk to you about Value-X," Vaughn said, getting directly to the point. There was no easy way to do this.

"Now?" she protested. "You're always telling me all I think about is work. I didn't get home until after eleven last night, and work is the last thing I want to think about now. You know we're under a lot of pressure just before the holidays. There's so much I have to get done, especially since I'll be leaving on this trip."

"I do know, and I apologize." He honestly felt bad about this. "I'll be sending in a fax this morning."

She sighed as if to say she was already bored. "Why?"

He hesitated, bracing himself for her angry outburst. "I've resigned."

"What?" Her shriek was loud enough to actually startle him. "If this is a joke, Vaughn, I am *not* amused."

In some ways he wished it was. He doubted this was one of those situations he'd look back on years from now and find amusing. "You asked me to check out Buffalo Valley."

"So?" she asked. "You mentioned an aunt or someone you knew who lived there. What's the big deal?"

"The big deal is that the town isn't interested in Value-X setting up shop."

Natalie didn't so much as pause. "Honey, listen, we've already been through this. Few communities fully appreciate everything we can do for them. Invariably there's a handful of discontented, ill-informed people who take it upon themselves to make a fuss. For the most part it's a token protest. Rarely is it ever a threat."

"If that's the case, why did you ask me to report back to you on Buffalo Valley?" She'd been worried, Vaughn knew; otherwise she'd never have suggested he check the place out.

"After the bad publicity in that Montana town, I overreacted. That was a mistake," she said quickly. "I see that now. A big mistake! I can't allow you to throw away the opportunity of a lifetime because I sent you into battle unprepared."

"Battle?"

"You know what I mean," she said irritably. "I wasn't thinking clearly. You were going to be in the area and it seemed like such a little thing. I should've known…"

"I'm grateful you asked me to do this," Vaughn countered. "I've learned a whole lot."

"No! No…this is all wrong." Natalie sounded desperate now.

"Buffalo Valley is a nice town. The people here are worried about what'll happen if Value-X moves in."

"But they don't understand that we—"

"They want someone to listen, and it's clear the company isn't going to do that." The purpose of Natalie's visit was to convince the people of Buffalo Valley that they needed Value-X.

"Of course the town wants us to listen, they all do, but what would happen to our jobs if we actually did?"

Natalie made her point without contradiction by Vaughn, although he doubted she recognized the real import of her words.

"Don't do anything stupid," Natalie pleaded. "At least wait until I get there and we can talk this out."

Her arrival was an entirely separate issue. "That brings up another…problem."

"Now what?" she snapped. "I suppose you're going to tell me you've met someone else and you want to dump me."

Vaughn rubbed his hand along his thigh and said nothing.

"This has *got* to be a joke." She gave a short, humorless laugh. "Talk about the Grinch stealing Christmas!"

"I realize my timing is bad—"

"Bad! You don't know the half of it."

"Natalie, listen, I'm genuinely sorry."

"You asked me to be your wife."

Technically, that wasn't true. They'd talked about marriage, but Natalie had shown no great enthusiasm. Now, however, didn't seem to be the time to argue the point. "If you'll recall, you were pretty lukewarm about the idea. That has to tell you something about your feelings for me."

"I was playing it cool," she insisted, sounding close to tears.

Vaughn had never known Natalie to cry, and he experienced deep pangs of regret. "I didn't mean to hurt you, but I had to say something before you showed up here." He hoped she'd cancel the trip, although he figured that was unlikely.

"I wanted you to be thrilled when I finally agreed to marry you. Now you're saying you don't love me."

"Not exactly…" He did hold tender feelings for her, but he knew with certainty that they were never meant to be together.

"You love me—but you love someone else more?"

Vaughn wasn't sure how to respond. He hadn't declared his feelings for Carrie, but the promise he felt with her outweighed his feelings for Natalie.

"I suppose she's one of the crusaders against Value-X. That would make sense, now that I think about it."

Vaughn didn't answer.

"I'm not giving up on us," Natalie insisted, "not until we've had a chance to speak face-to-face."

He'd already guessed she wouldn't make this easy. "I'd rather you just accepted my decision."

A painful pause followed. "Just what do you plan to do with your life if you resign from Value-X?" she demanded.

"I don't know." His future was as much a mystery

to him as it was to her. All Vaughn could say was that he had no intention of remaining with the company.

"You're not thinking clearly," Natalie said.

"Actually, I'm thinking about settling here." He wasn't sure where the words had come from, but until he said them aloud the possibility hadn't even occurred to him.

"In North Dakota," she blurted out, as though he was suffering from temporary insanity. "Now I *know* this is all a bad joke. Who in their right mind would live there? You know the demographics as well as I do. *No one* lives in a place like that on purpose."

"I would."

"This is ridiculous! I wouldn't believe it if I wasn't hearing it with my own ears. You can't be serious."

Although he knew it was probably a waste of breath, Vaughn felt obliged to tell her about Buffalo Valley. He wanted her to know the people he'd met. She couldn't begin to grasp what he felt unless she understood who and what they were.

"This farming community is small-town America at its best," he said, and wondered if she was even listening. "They have a history of banding together in hard times—and there've been plenty of hard times." He wanted to make her understand the depth of his respect for them, so he relayed to her the plot of the Christmas play.

"That's all very interesting," Natalie told him, her tone bored, "but that was then and this is now. Value-X will come into Buffalo Valley with or without you. With or without me. It doesn't matter how many times you sit and watch a group of teenagers act out the town's history, nothing is going to change."

"It will," Vaughn said.

"I'm not letting you quit. One day you'll thank me."

"Natalie, what are you doing?"

"First I'm going into corporate headquarters to make sure no one reads your resignation letter. Then I'm flying out on the twenty-seventh, just the way I planned, so we can talk this out."

"I wish you wouldn't. Let it go, Natalie."

Her returning laugh sounded like a threat. "I don't think so. You didn't really believe I'd allow you to cut me loose with a simple phone call, did you?"

He didn't bother to respond. What was the point?

"You see yourself as this hero, this knight in shining armor, and while that's fine and good, it isn't going to work."

Vaughn could see the storm clouds gathering on the horizon.

Sunday morning while his parents attended church, Vaughn drove into Buffalo Valley. He'd made the trek so often in the past week that it seemed almost second nature to head in that direction.

Everything about the town appealed to him. It'd started when he'd first met Hassie and accepted the gold watch that had belonged to her husband. With the watch came an implied trust. He refused to be part of anything that would betray their relationship.

He hadn't heard from Carrie, but he would once she was ready. He didn't think it would take her long to come to terms with his confession. Because of her ex-husband's betrayal, it was vital that he be as open and honest with her as possible. However…he still hadn't explained Natalie's role in his life. Poor Carrie was about to be hit with a second shock, but there wasn't a damn thing he could do to prevent it.

He parked just outside town, at the twenty-acre site for the proposed Value-X. With the wind howling, he climbed out of the car and walked onto the property. Either he was becoming accustomed to the bone-chilling weather or it'd warmed up in the past twenty-four hours. He discovered he could breathe now without feeling as though he was inhaling ice particles.

He'd been there for several minutes when he saw a truck pull up and park next to his vehicle. Two men climbed out and started toward him. He instantly recognized them as Carrie's younger brothers.

"Chuck and Ken, right?" he said as they approached.

Chuck, the older of the two, touched his hat. "Vaughn Kyle?"

Vaughn nodded.

"Did you have a falling-out with Carrie after the play?" Chuck asked. The man was nothing if not direct. His brow had furrowed and the teasing friendliness was gone. "You hurt her and you have me to answer to."

"I have no intention of hurting her."

"Good." He nodded once as if to suggest the subject was closed.

"What are you doing out here?" Ken muttered.

Vaughn wasn't sure what to tell him. He hadn't asked Carrie to keep the fact that he was employed by Value-X a secret, but it was apparent that she had. If either Chuck or Ken knew the truth, they'd have him tarred and feathered and run out of town.

"Just looking," Vaughn told him.

"Looking at what? Empty land?"

"If you had this twenty acres or any portion of it, how would you develop it?" Vaughn asked the pair.

"That's easy," Ken said. "This town needs a feed

store—been needing one for years. Most everyone has to drive to Devils Lake for their feed."

A feed store. Now that was interesting. "Why don't you do it?" he suggested.

"No time. The hardware store keeps us busy. Dad needs us there, but if someone were to come along with enough investment capital and a head for business, they'd be guaranteed success."

"Dad carries some of the more common feed, but he doesn't have room for much."

"We got to talking about a feed store just the other day," Ken said, glancing at his brother. "Wondering who might be able to open one."

This morning, Vaughn had casually told Natalie that he might settle in Buffalo Valley. A few days earlier his future was set, and now all at once he was cast adrift. His carefully ordered life was in shambles, and Vaughn didn't like the uncomfortable feeling that gave him.

"It'd take someone with ready cash," Ken told him, his expression pensive, "and that's in short supply around here." He kicked at the snow with the toe of his boot. "People in these parts invest everything in their land."

"You interested?" Chuck asked him bluntly.

Vaughn looked in the direction of town, suddenly aware that this venture piqued his interest. He wanted to be part of Buffalo Valley, part of its future. It'd be a risk, but he'd never backed down from a challenge before and he wasn't planning to start now.

"I don't know a damn thing about running a feed store," he said, meeting the other men's eyes.

Chuck and Ken studied him for a long moment.

"You serious about this?" Chuck finally asked.

Vaughn nodded.

"Between Dad, me and my brothers, we could show you everything you need to know."

"You'd do that?" Vaughn found it hard to believe that these men, who were little more than strangers, would willingly offer him their expertise.

"I saw a light in my sister's eyes that hasn't been there since her divorce," Ken told him. "That made me decide you might be worth taking a chance on." He stared down at the ground, then raised his head. "Now, I realize you moving into town and opening a feed store might have absolutely nothing to do with Carrie. Personally, I hope it does, but I want you to know that whatever happens between you and my sister is your business."

"That's the way it would have to be."

Her two brothers shared a glance and seemed to reach the same conclusion. "You're right about that." Chuck spoke for the pair. "This has nothing to do with Carrie."

"There are a lot of *if*s in all this," Vaughn reminded them. He could see that they were getting excited, but then so was he. Naturally, all of this depended on a dozen different factors. Right now it was little more than the glimmer of an idea. Little more than a possibility. But it gave him a glimpse of what he might do...

"At the moment the future doesn't look all that promising for Buffalo Valley," Ken said, surveying the bare land around them. It went without saying that if Value-X came to town, that would be the end of any talk about a feed store.

On the verge of leaving, Vaughn returned to the subject of their sister. "Have either of you seen Carrie?"

"She's gone for the day," Ken told him.

"All day?"

Chuck shrugged. "She's over with our brother Tom and his family. Did you two have plans?"

"No." How could he expect her to be at his beck and call? "I'll talk to her later," he said with reluctance. Their conversation had to take place soon. He'd rather this business with Natalie was over, but it now seemed that would require a protracted...discussion, for lack of a better word.

"She was upset when you dropped her off at the house after the play." Ken frowned at him in an accusatory way, suggesting Vaughn had some explaining to do. "What happened? What did you do?"

"That's Carrie's and my business. Remember?"

Chuck agreed. "She'd have our heads if she knew we were talking to you about her. We'll stay out of it, but like I said, you hurt her and you'll have me to answer to."

Vaughn nodded and resisted the urge to laugh. Melodramatic though they sounded, her brothers were serious.

"I heard you and your parents are spending Christmas Day with Hassie," Ken said.

News sure traveled fast in a small town. "We're coming for dinner."

"Then I think we might be able to arrange something." The two brothers exchanged another look.

"Arrange what?" Vaughn asked.

"Nothing much, just an opportunity for you to have some time alone with our sister." Chuck and Ken left then, both of them grinning broadly.

Nine

Hassie spent Christmas morning with Buffalo Bob, Merrily and little Bobby, upstairs at the 3 OF A KIND. Sitting around the Christmas tree with the family reminded her of what it'd been like years ago, when Valerie and Vaughn were young. The good feelings started right then, and she suspected this would be her best Christmas in a very long while.

Bobby's eyes got round as quarters when his father rolled out a shiny new miniature bicycle with training wheels. It amazed her that a three-year-old could actually ride a bicycle. In another three or four months, the park would be crowded with kids on bikes, enjoying the Dakota sunshine. When Hassie closed her eyes, she could almost hear the sound of their laughter. That would happen, she comforted herself, with or without Value-X.

She exchanged gifts with the family—magazine subscriptions for Bob and Merrily, a book of nursery rhymes for Bobby. Their gift to her was a new pair of lined leather gloves. After coffee and croissants—and hugs and kisses—she left.

Home again, Hassie set the dining-room table with

her finest china. Not much reason to use it these days. Yet twice this week she'd had cause to bring it out of the old mahogany cabinet. The first time was her visit with Barbara and now Christmas dinner.

Already the kitchen counter was crowded with a variety of food. Carrie and her mother had thoughtfully dropped off a platter of decorated sugar cookies. Those cookies, plus the ones she'd collected the night of the exchange, added up to enough for the entire town.

Sarah Urlacher and Calla had given her a plate of homemade fudge. Maddy, Lindsay and several of the other women had stopped by with offerings, too—preserves and homemade bread and mincemeat tarts. It was far more than Hassie could eat in two or three Christmases.

Then word had leaked out about Vaughn Kyle and his parents coming for dinner. Before Hassie could stop them, her friends and neighbors had dropped off a plethora of side dishes. Joanie Wyatt sent over baked yams. Rachel Quantrill delivered a green-bean-and-cauliflower casserole. Soon all that was required of Hassie was the bird and dressing. The tantalizing aroma of baking turkey, sage and onions drifted through the house.

Living alone, Hassie didn't bother much with meals. At night, after she closed the pharmacy, her dinner consisted of whatever was quick and easy. When Jerry had been alive and the children still lived at home, she'd been an accomplished cook. Now she considered cooking for one a nuisance. Many a night she dined on soup or a microwave entrée.

The doorbell chimed at exactly one o'clock, and Hassie, who'd been occupying herself with last-minute touches, was ready to receive her company.

"Merry Christmas," Barbara Kyle sang out, hugging Hassie as soon as she opened the front door.

"Merry Christmas. Merry Christmas." Hassie hugged them all.

For the next few minutes the men made trips back and forth between the car and the house. They hauled in festively wrapped presents, plus various contributions to the meal, including three beautiful pies.

"How in heaven's name are the four of us going to eat all these pies?" Hassie asked, giggling like a schoolgirl over such an embarrassment of riches. Pies, cookies, candies. Oh, my, she'd be on a diet till next June if she tasted everything in her kitchen.

"Pecan pie is Rick's favorite," Barbara explained.

"Pumpkin is mine," Vaughn said.

"And fresh apple mixed with cranberry is mine," Barbara said, setting down the third pie. She had to rearrange other dishes on the crowded counter to find room for it.

"Apple mixed with cranberry," Hassie mused aloud. "That sounds delicious."

"I'm willing to share," Barbara said with a laugh.

The meal was even better than Hassie had dared hope. The turkey was moist and succulent, and the sage dressing was her finest ever, if she did say so herself. The four of them sat around the table and passed the serving dishes to one another. They talked and laughed as if each was part of Hassie's family. Anyone seeing them would never have guessed there'd been a thirty-three-year lapse in their relationship.

This was the way Christmas was meant to be, Hassie thought, immersing herself in the good feelings. Barbara had always been a talker, and she effortlessly kept the conversation going. The years had changed

Rick Kyle considerably, Hassie noted, smiling over at him. She doubted she would've recognized him now.

The last time Hassie had seen Rick, he'd had shoulder-length brown hair, a bushy mustache and narrow-rimmed glasses. A wooden peace sign had dangled from his neck. As she recalled, he'd worn the craziest color combinations with tie-dyed bell-bottom jeans and sandals.

His hair was mostly gone now, but Barbara claimed bald men could be exceedingly sexy. Hassie wouldn't know about that, but it did her good to see that they were happy and obviously still in love.

Perhaps it was selfish of her, but she liked to believe that if her son had lived, Vaughn would've found the same happiness with Barbara.

"If I eat another bite, I swear someone might mistake me for a stuffed sausage," Barbara declared, pushing back her chair.

"Me, too." Rick wrapped his arms around his belly and groaned.

Hassie looked at Vaughn, who winked and said, "Could someone pass me the mashed potatoes and gravy?"

Laughing, Barbara hurled a roll at him from across the table. Vaughn deftly caught it. "Hey, I'm a growing boy."

When they'd finished, the men cleared off the table and Hassie brewed a pot of coffee. They gathered in the living room around the small Christmas tree, where Hassie had tucked three small gifts, one for each of her guests. Shopping in Buffalo Valley was limited and there hadn't been much time, so Hassie had found items with special meaning to share with her friends. Three little gifts she knew each would treasure.

For Barbara, it was a pearl pin Jerry had given her

after Vaughn's birth. For Rick it was a fountain pen— an antique. Choosing a gift for Vaughn had been difficult. In the end she'd parted with one of the medals the army had awarded her son for bravery. Since Vaughn had recently been in the military himself, she felt he'd appreciate what this medal represented.

They seemed truly touched by her gifts. Barbara's eyes brimmed with tears and she pinned the pearl to her silk blouse. Rick, who didn't appear to be the demonstrative sort, hugged her. And Vaughn seemed at a loss for words.

"I have something to tell you," Vaughn said after several minutes of silence.

"This sounds serious." Hassie saw the look Barbara and Rick exchanged and wondered at its meaning.

Vaughn leaned forward and took Hassie's hands in both his own. "I told Mom and Dad earlier, and they urged me to be honest with you, as well. First, I want you to know I'd never deliberately do anything to hurt you."

"I know that. Honest about what?"

"Value-X. When I left Seattle, I'd accepted a job with them."

Hassie gasped, and her hand flew to her mouth. This was almost more than she could take in. Vaughn an employee of Value-X?

"I knew the company was planning to expand into Buffalo Valley, but I didn't understand the threat they represented to the community."

"He isn't working for them any longer," Barbara quickly inserted.

"Since I wasn't going to be officially an employee until after the first of the year, one of the vice presidents suggested I not mention my association with the company," Vaughn explained. "It was never my intention to deceive you or anyone in Buffalo Valley." He took a deep breath. "I faxed in my resignation and made it effective immediately."

Hassie felt a little dizzy. It was hard enough to grasp what he was saying, and she could only imagine what Carrie must think, so she asked, "Does Carrie know?"

Vaughn nodded. "I told her the night of the play. I didn't want to wait until after the holidays."

"What did she say?" Hassie asked. She feared that the news might mean the end for this budding relationship, which would be a dreadful shame.

"I haven't had a chance to speak to her since."

Barbara moved forward to the edge of the sofa. "There's more."

Vaughn cast his mother a look that suggested he'd rather she hadn't said anything.

"Tell me." As far as Hassie was concerned, it was too late for secrets now.

Vaughn glanced at his mother again. "I don't want to get anyone's hopes up, because it's much too soon."

"Yes, yes, we know that," Barbara interjected, then waited for him to continue.

Vaughn's reluctance was evident. At last he said, "I'm investigating the possibility of opening a feed store here in town."

For the second time in as many moments, Hassie gasped. Only this time, the shock was one of excitement and pleasure. "Oh, Vaughn, that's an excellent idea. The town could use a feed store."

Rick wrapped his arm around his wife's shoulders, and both of them smiled broadly.

"Vaughn spoke with two of the Hendrickson brothers about it yesterday morning," Barbara said. "They actually suggested it."

Hassie's heart surged with hope. Vaughn was right of course; there was no reason to get carried away. But she couldn't help it. The thought of having Vaughn right here in Buffalo Valley—she was almost afraid to believe it could happen.

"I've got an appointment with Heath Quantrill first thing Wednesday morning," Vaughn explained. "I'll need to put together a business plan and look into financing. The Hendricksons recommended I start there."

"Yes—Heath will give you good advice." Some of the excitement left her as reality came rushing back. "Everything hinges on what happens with Value-X, doesn't it?"

"True." Vaughn gave her a lopsided smile. "But I have a good feeling about this." As Hassie fought the emotion that threatened to overwhelm her, he added, "I want to invest in Buffalo Valley."

Keeping the tears at bay was impossible now. "Why would you do such a thing?" she asked between sniffles. Reaching into her pocket, she withdrew a linen handkerchief and blew her nose. She must be getting old, because normally she wasn't a woman prone to tears.

"I arrived in North Dakota thinking I knew exactly what I wanted and where I was headed," Vaughn said, "but everything changed. I probably shouldn't have said anything about my idea." He frowned at his mother. "But now that it's out, I'm glad you know."

"God bless you," Hassie whispered, stretching her arms toward Vaughn for a hug. Their embrace was warm. "If God had seen fit to give me a grandson, I would have wanted him to be just like you."

"That's a high compliment," Vaughn said, sitting down again.

"I meant it to be," Hassie told him. She rubbed her

wet cheek with the back of her hand. "Look what you did," she said. "It isn't just anyone who can make this old lady weep."

"Shame on you, son," Rick teased, and they all smiled.

It took Hassie a few moments to compose herself.

"Look," Barbara said, pointing outside, "it's snowing."

Sure enough, the flakes were falling thick and soft, creating a perfect Christmas scene. "This is the way I always dreamed Christmas would be," Hassie whispered. "Surrounded by family—" she used the word purposely "—on a beautiful winter day."

This was the best Christmas she'd had in many years, and all because of the Kyles—people who'd been brought into Hassie's life by her son. Somehow she could picture Vaughn smiling down, wishing them a Merry Christmas.

Hassie had invited Carrie to join Vaughn and his parents for dessert on Christmas Day, and Carrie had yet to decide if she'd go. Vaughn's confession about working for Value-X had shocked her. The fact that he'd come into town, gained her confidence and that of everyone else—so he could collect information for the company—had been a betrayal of trust and goodwill. He'd withheld the truth from her and she should be outraged. She *was* outraged.

All week Vaughn had listened to everyone's objections to Value-X and said nothing. As she thought back on their numerous conversations, she realized how often he'd defended the company. At the time she'd assumed he was playing devil's advocate. Now she knew otherwise. Carrie wasn't sure what had happened to make him resign. Whatever it was, she was grateful. Still…

Trust was a basic issue with Carrie. Vaughn had betrayed her, Hassie and the entire town, and she couldn't conveniently look the other way. *Forgive and forget* might work for others, but not for her.

She didn't think Vaughn had told anyone else. Carrie hadn't determined whether that was a good thing or not. She did know she had to hide this from Hassie, who would be heartbroken if she found out. If she didn't show up at Hassie's and then claimed she'd forgotten, Hassie would immediately conclude that something was wrong. Then she'd start asking questions. Questions Carrie didn't want to answer. She could invent plausible excuses, but the problem was that Carrie *did* want to see Vaughn again, despite what he'd told her.

She needed to talk to him, needed to vent her feelings. The shock of his confession had robbed her of that chance. But finding a private time to speak with him today might prove difficult, if not impossible. In any event, she hadn't given verbal shape to her emotions yet. Talking to him should probably wait, she rationalized.

"Where you going?" Ken asked, following her into the hallway as she gathered her coat, gloves and scarf.

"I bet she's going off to see that new friend of hers," Chuck teased.

"I'm going over to Hassie's," she informed her two younger brothers smugly.

"I suppose *he's* there."

How Pete knew that, Carrie could only guess. She shoved her arms into the silk-lined sleeves of her coat.

"He's there, all right," Tom said, leaning against the door jamb. "His car's parked outside Hassie's."

Carrie ignored him and went to get her purse. She and Hassie had exchanged their gifts on Christmas Eve, but Carrie had borrowed a book on traditional remedies that she needed to return. She retrieved it from the bookcase.

"Will you guys leave me alone?" she cried. All four of her brothers were trailing her from room to room. "Don't you have anything better to do?"

Her brothers glanced at each other and shrugged, then Pete announced, "Not really."

"Do you want to hear what we think of your new boyfriend?" Ken asked.

If they could be this obstinate, so could she. "No."

Carrie headed for the front door. If her four guardian angels wanted to follow her into the cold and snow, that was their choice.

"I like him, Carrie," Ken called after her.

"Me, too." Tom crowded beside him in the doorway.

"He's all right," Pete concurred.

Chuck simply winked and gave her a thumbs-up. This had to be a record. Never before had she dated a man all four of her brothers approved of. Little did they know. She wondered what they'd say if they knew that, until recently, he'd been a Value-X employee. The answer didn't bear considering. She couldn't disillusion them any more than she could Hassie. Against her will, she'd been pulled into his subterfuge, and she hated it.

The snow was falling hard by the time Carrie reached Hassie's house; she barely noticed.

Vaughn answered the door and surprised her by closing it after him as he stepped onto the porch. "Merry Christmas," he said, his eyes never leaving hers.

As much as possible, she avoided looking at him.

"We need to talk, Carrie."

"Here? Now?" She faked a short laugh. "I don't think so, Vaughn."

"Later, then?"

She nodded.

He sighed with unmistakable relief. "Thank you."

She didn't *want* to feel anything. She longed to ignore him, make a token visit and then be on her way. But it was too late for that. Her emotions were painfully confused; she wanted to kiss him and at the same time, she wanted to scream and rage and throw his betrayal in his face.

He pressed his hand to her cheek. "I'm glad you're here."

She'd intended to slap his hand away, but instead, her fingers curled around his, and she closed her eyes and leaned toward him. Then she was angry with herself for being weak and jerked back.

"Come in out of the cold," Hassie called just as Vaughn opened the door and Carrie stepped inside. She took off her coat and tossed it onto the stair railing.

"Have you met my dad?" Vaughn asked, taking Carrie by the elbow and escorting her into the living room. He made the introductions.

"Pleased to meet you," she said, hoping none of the stiffness she felt came through in her voice.

Hassie was on her way to the kitchen. "You're just in time for pie."

"I'll help dish up," Barbara said, following Hassie.

"Me, too," Carrie offered, eager to escape Vaughn.

Barbara Kyle shook her head. "Well take care of it."

The two older women disappeared, which meant that Carrie was left alone with Vaughn and his father. She would've preferred the women's company and felt awkward alone with the two men. Vaughn was obviously eager to talk to her, and she was just as eager to avoid any conversation with him. Yes, there were things she needed to say; she wasn't ready, though—not nearly ready. She glanced in his direction and he mouthed something, but she looked away.

"Hassie and Barb are trying to keep you and Vaughn together," Rick confided to her frankly. Vaughn scowled fiercely. "So you may as well play along," he advised. "Here, sit down, Carrie, and make yourself comfortable."

She sat on the sofa and Vaughn joined her, sitting so close that their thighs brushed. In an effort to ignore him, she stared out the picture window.

"Isn't it a lovely day?" she asked, making conversation with his father. "The snow—" A flash of color outside caught her attention. It was her younger brothers. Gasping, she leaped to her feet.

"What?" Vaughn asked, getting up, too.

"It's Chuck and Ken," she said, and pointed at the window. Sure enough, they were outside—in an old-fashioned sleigh pulled by two draft horses.

"That's my great-great-grandfather's sleigh," Carrie explained. "He used it to deliver the mail. Dad and Mr. McKenna have been fixing it up. It's been in the barn for the last hundred years."

"That sleigh looks like something straight out of a Christmas movie," Vaughn's father remarked, standing by the window. "Whose horses are they?"

"I think they belong to a friend of Pete's," Carrie said.

Despite her mood, she giggled. Her brothers must have planned this all along. How they'd managed to keep it a secret she could only guess.

The doorbell chimed, and when Hassie answered it, she found Chuck grinning down at her.

"Anyone here interested in a sleigh ride?" he asked, looking around Hassie to where Carrie and Vaughn stood. "There's room for five."

"I'm game," Rick said. "Come on, Barb."

"Hassie?" Vaughn turned to their hostess.

She seemed about to refuse, then smiled broadly and said, "Don't mind if I do."

Vaughn helped Hassie on with her coat and made sure her boots were tightly laced before they ventured outside. Carrie tried not to be affected by the tenderness he displayed toward Hassie, especially when he bent down on one knee to lace her boots. There was nothing condescending in his action, only affection and concern. Meanwhile, Rick held Carrie's coat for her and then Barbara's. By the time they left the house, the old sleigh, pulled by twin chestnut geldings, had attracted quite a bit of attention from the neighborhood. The horses were festively decked out in harnesses decorated with jangling bells.

Barbara, Rick and Hassie sat in the back seat, which fortunately was nicely padded. Once they were settled, Ken handed them a blanket to place over their laps. Carrie and Vaughn took the front seat, which was narrower and made of wood, forcing them close together.

Chuck and Ken walked in front of the horses, leading them down the unfamiliar street.

"Where are you taking us?" Carrie shouted as her brothers climbed onto the sleigh.

"The park," Ken called back.

"Shouldn't we be singing Christmas songs?" Barbara asked.

"Go right ahead," Rick answered, and taking him at his word, Vaughn's mother started with "Jingle Bells." What could be more fitting? Even if it was a "two-horse open sleigh."

Moments later Hassie's rough voice joined Barbara's soft soprano.

Carrie began to sing, too, and soon Vaughn's rich

baritone blended with the women's voices. He and Carrie looked at each other. Perhaps it was the magic of the season or the fact that they were in a sleigh singing while they dashed through the snow, their song accompanied by the muffled clopping of hooves and the jingling of harness bells. Whatever the reason, Carrie realized her anger had completely dissipated. Vaughn seemed to genuinely regret what he'd done. He wasn't involved in a plot to destroy Buffalo Valley. To his credit, as soon as he'd recognized the threat Value-X represented to the town, he'd resigned from the company. It couldn't have been easy to walk away from a high-paying job like that.

Vaughn noticed the transformation in her immediately. He stopped singing and leaned close enough to ask, "Am I forgiven?"

Carrie nodded.

His eyes brightened and he slid an arm around her shoulders. Carrie was convinced that if their circumstances had been different, he would've kissed her.

When they reached the middle of the park, they found Carrie's entire family waiting there, applauding their arrival.

Effortlessly they segued from one Christmas carol to another. Everyone seemed to have a favorite. Amid the singing and the laughter, Carrie's mother served hot chocolate from large thermoses.

Vaughn and Carrie left their places in order to give others an opportunity to try out the sleigh. After several trips around the park, Chuck and Ken drove Hassie and Vaughn's parents back to Hassie's. Carrie and Vaughn remained with her family.

With pride, Carrie took Vaughn around and introduced him to everyone he had yet to meet.

"What were Chuck and Ken talking about earlier?" Tom asked, standing next to his wife, Becky.

Vaughn glanced at Carrie. "We discussed a few ideas, nothing more."

"That's not what I understood," Tom said. "Chuck said you'd made an appointment to talk to Heath Quantrill."

"You've got an appointment to see Heath?" Carrie asked. "About what?" She'd suspected earlier that something was up involving her two younger brothers. Sunday night they'd sat with their father at the kitchen table, talking excitedly in low voices. Carrie couldn't figure out what they were doing, and when she asked, their replies had been vague.

Rather than answer her directly, Vaughn looked away.

"More secrets?" she asked him under her breath.

"Vaughn's thinking about opening up a feed store in town," Tom supplied.

"Is this true?" she asked. If so, it was the best kind of secret.

"Nothing's certain yet," he told her, and she could see that he wasn't pleased with her older brother for sharing the news. "Everything's just in the planning stages. The *early* planning stages."

"You'd actually consider moving to Buffalo Valley?"

Vaughn nodded and smiled down on her, but then his gaze clouded. "I still need to talk to you."

"Of course."

"Privately," he insisted.

The park was crowded with her family. Carrie knew that the instant they broke away, one of her brothers or nieces and nephews would seek her out. "We can try," she promised.

"It's important."

Her heart was in her eyes, but Carrie didn't care if he saw that or not. "I'm so excited you might move here."

"I'm excited, too."

He didn't sound it. If anything, he seemed anxious. "What is it?" she asked. She wanted to hear what he needed to say, and she wanted to hear it *now*, even if they couldn't escape her family.

"Someone from Value-X is coming to Buffalo Valley," he murmured.

"You mean the representative Lindsay mentioned?" Carrie was well aware that the company intended to wage a public-relations campaign to win over the community; that was part of their strategy. She suspected the corporate heads at Value-X had only the slightest idea how unwelcome the retailer was in Buffalo Valley. Whatever they were planning simply wouldn't work.

"Yes. Her name's Natalie Nichols and—"

"It doesn't matter," she told him.

"Yes, it does," he countered.

Carrie lowered her voice, wanting him to know he could trust her. "I didn't tell anyone—no one knows."

"Hassie does. I told her myself."

She didn't understand what had prompted that confession, but wasn't sure it had been the wisest thing.

"She deserves honesty, the same way you do." Vaughn's brow creased with concern. "I would've come to meet her, with or without Value-X."

"I know."

"It isn't going to be pretty, Carrie, when Natalie Nichols arrives. Value-X has proved that it's capable of bulldozing its way into a town. They've done it before."

"Not here, not in Buffalo Valley. We won't let it happen." When he shook his head, she whispered, "It's going to be all right, Vaughn." Because her fears about him had been laid to rest, she leaned forward and kissed him.

Vaughn wrapped his arms around her and held her close.

"Hey, what's this?" Pete shouted.

Carrie laughed. "Leave us be," she replied. "Go on! Shoo!" She wasn't about to let her brothers ruin the most romantic moment of her life.

"Never," Tom hollered.

"There's something else," Vaughn said, ignoring her brothers.

"I have a feeling it's going to have to wait," she said, and ducked just in time to miss a flying snowball. Vaughn, however, wasn't quick enough. Snow exploded across his shoulder and he whirled around to face four large Hendrickson males.

"You shouldn't have done that," he said mildly.

"You gonna make me sorry?"

"Oh, yeah." Vaughn's chuckle was full of threat. "Prepare to die, Hendrickson."

Three hours later a cold and exhausted Vaughn made his way back to Hassie's. The snowball fight had eventually involved everyone in Carrie's large family, from two-year-old Eli to his grandfather. They'd stopped only long enough to build snow forts before the battle had resumed with peals of laughter and more hilarity than Vaughn could remember in years.

He'd sincerely meant to tell Carrie about his relationship with Natalie, but the opportunity never arose again. It became easy to let it ride once they were caught up in the family fun. Come morning, he was driving back to town to meet with Heath; he'd stop by the pharmacy and tell her then.

It was dark when he returned to Hassie's, and his parents were ready to head home to Grand Forks. When they got there, he discovered that Natalie had left five messages on his parents' machine. He was stunned to learn that she'd already arived in North Dakota.

The first message, from the Seattle airport, had been soft and coaxing, claiming she needed to speak to him at his earliest convenience. By the final one, her tone had become hard and demanding. The last part of the message, telling him she'd call early the next morning, had sounded more than a little annoyed.

"Trouble?" his father asked, standing next to the phone as the message finished playing.

Vaughn shook his head. "Nothing I can't handle."

"Good."

"This has been the most wonderful Christmas," his mother said as she turned off the lights. They all went to bed, wishing each other good-night and a final Merry Christmas.

The following morning Vaughn woke early. He showered, shaved and dressed for his meeting with Heath. Sooner or later, he'd have to talk to Natalie, but he wanted as much information as he could gather before the inevitable confrontation. He gulped down a cup of coffee, eager to be on his way, to begin this new phase of his life. His mother hugged him before he left. "What do you want me to say if Natalie shows up?"

"No need to tell her anything," he advised. He'd deal with her when he had to, but not before. The letter she'd mentioned would be in the community post office soon and with that, the campaign would officially start. Vaughn was prepared to do whatever was necessary to keep the retailer out of Buffalo Valley. He had a stake in the town's future now.

He parked near the bank, then hurried inside; to his surprise, Heath's glass-enclosed office looked empty.

"I have an appointment with Mr. Quantrill," Vaughn told the receptionist.

"You're Mr. Kyle?"

Vaughn nodded.

"Mr. Quantrill left a message. He had some last-minute business to attend to and said I should reschedule the appointment. He sent his apologies and asked me to tell you that the Kohn property has sold."

It wasn't until he was standing outside that Vaughn understood the significance of the message. The Kohn property was the land Value-X wanted. So the battle lines had been drawn. No wonder Quantrill was out of the office. There was no longer any reason for Vaughn to meet with him; Quantrill and the community had far more important issues to worry about.

Vaughn walked over to the pharmacy, his steps slow. No doubt Hassie and everyone else in town had heard the news. He knew how discouraged they'd be.

When he entered the pharmacy, Carrie was behind the prescription counter. As the bells over the door cheerfully announced his arrival, she glanced up, and from her disheartened expression, it was clear she'd heard. Her eyes seemed dull and lifeless. For a long moment she stared at him, almost as though he was a stranger.

"I guess you know?" he asked, stepping toward her.

"Oh, yes," she said with such sadness it nearly broke his heart.

"I'll help, Carrie," he told her. "We can beat Value-X if we stand together." He tried to sound positive, but truth was, he didn't know if they could.

"That's not the news I'm talking about," she said,

moving out from behind the counter. "I wonder if you've ever heard the old saying, *Fool me once, shame on you, fool me twice, shame on me.*"

Vaughn frowned, not understanding. "What are you talking about?"

"You mentioned the name Natalie Nichols yesterday."

"Yes, she works for Value-X. She—"

"I met her this morning."

"Natalie's here?" Foolishly he'd assumed she'd spent the night in Grand Forks.

"She stayed at the 3 OF A KIND last night. She's been trying to reach you—and here you are, right under her nose."

"I don't know what she told you, but—"

"She told me she was your fiancée."

It was all starting to make sense to Vaughn, a sick kind of sense. Natalie's declaration certainly explained that "shame me twice" stuff. "She spoke to your mother this morning," Carrie went on. "Your mother said if you weren't over at the bank to check here with Hassie. Only it was me she found."

"I can explain," he began.

"I'm sure you can, but frankly I'm not interested in listening." With that, she returned to the pharmaceutical counter and resumed her work as if he was no longer there.

Vaughn waited uncertainly for a moment, but she didn't look anywhere except at her task, at the pills she was counting out.

It was too late for explanations. Too late to regain her trust. Too late for him.

Ten

Vaughn didn't think anything could happen to make this day any worse, but he was wrong.

As soon as he pulled into the driveway at his parents' home, he saw the unfamiliar car. Even before he'd climbed out of his own vehicle, he knew who'd come to visit.

Natalie.

Sure enough, the instant he walked into the house, his father cast him a sympathetic glance.

"You're back," his mother said, her voice strained and unnaturally high.

"Hello, Vaughn," Natalie said from the living room. She held a cup of coffee balanced on her knee. She looked out of place—and decidedly irritated.

He nodded in her direction.

"I think we'll leave the two of you to talk," his mother announced, and exited the room with the speed of someone who's relieved to escape. His father was directly behind her.

With a silent groan, Vaughn turned toward Natalie.

"You didn't answer my phone messages." She set aside her coffee, glaring at him. "When I couldn't find you, I drove straight to Buffalo Valley, where I spent the night at some hole-in-the-wall. Merry Christmas, Natalie," she said bitterly.

She didn't appear to expect a comment, so he sat down across from her and waited. When she didn't immediately continue, he figured he'd better take his stand.

"I'm finished with Value-X." Nothing she could say or offer him would influence his decision. "You aren't going to change my mind."

"I'll say you're finished. I'll be fortunate to have a job myself after this."

Vaughn doubted that. Natalie was the type who'd always land on her feet. Yes, she'd recommended Vaughn to the company, but they couldn't hold that against her.

"You intend to go through with this…this craziness, don't you?"

No use hedging. "Yes, I do. I've resigned, and since I hadn't officially started work yet, I didn't bother to give any notice."

She sighed and stared down at her coffee. "I wonder if I ever knew you."

Vaughn said nothing. He'd let her say what she wanted, denounce him, threaten him, whatever. She had cause; he wasn't exactly blameless in all this.

"You think I don't know what this is about?" she challenged. She stood, crossing her arms. "It all has to do with you and me."

Vaughn didn't know a kind way to tell her there *wasn't* any "you and me." There'd probably never been a "you and me." Not with Natalie. Looking at her, Vaughn wondered how he could ever have believed he was in love with her. The very traits that had once attracted him now repulsed him. Her ambition blinded her to everything that was unique and special about Buffalo Valley.

"Say something!" she shrilled.

"I'm sorry."

"That's a good start." Her stance relaxed somewhat.

"It doesn't change anything, though." He wasn't being purposely cruel, only frank. "I'm going to do everything I can to keep Value-X out of Buffalo Valley."

"You're mad at me," she insisted. "All this craziness about moving to some backwoods town is a form of punishment. You're trying to make me regret what I said. Vaughn, you simply don't understand how important Value-X is to me and to our future."

"Natalie—"

She ignored him and started pacing. "We've always been good together, Vaughn, you know that."

"Have we, Natalie?" he asked, hoping she was capable of admitting the truth.

"I can't let you do this," she said, clenching her fists.

He shook his head. "It's done."

"But you're destroying your career!"

"I don't want to work for a company like Value-X. Not now and not in the future."

"What are you going to do, then?"

"I don't know," he told her, and it was true. He'd fight the big retailer for as long as his money held out, but after that…he didn't have any answers.

"I can help you," she said. "You're this rough-and-ready Airborne Ranger, trying to be a hero. But you've got to face reality. No one goes against Value-X and walks away a winner. This will cost you more than you can afford to lose."

He ignored her threat. "Thanks but no thanks," he muttered.

She looked crestfallen.

Vaughn had a few questions of his own. "Why did you tell Carrie we're engaged?"

"Because we are!" she cried. "Did we or did we not discuss marriage?"

He didn't respond. She already had her answer.

"Oh, I get it," Natalie raged, her eyes spitting fire. "You found yourself a little side dish while you were away visiting Mom and Dad. You forgot all about me. Is *that* it?"

"We aren't engaged and we aren't getting married." She couldn't seriously believe he intended to continue this relationship when it was obviously a dead end for both of them.

"But we *did* discuss marriage on more than one occasion, and I never said I *wouldn't* marry you. We both understood we'd get married someday."

"I didn't see it that way. Yes, we talked about marriage, but there was no commitment—and very little interest on your part."

"Now you're lying, too."

He bristled, but bit his tongue before he said something he'd regret.

"Well…it's sort of a lie." Natalie lowered her head. "I made a mistake, but not once did I say anything about breaking off our relationship."

"It's over." He didn't know how much plainer he could be.

"I know." She sighed. "Well, if you insist on this lunacy, you're on your own."

He nodded.

"We could've been very good together," she whispered.

"I'm sorry."

"I know, and you'll be a whole lot sorrier once Value-X is through with this town." She rallied then, jerking her head up, chin tilted. "If you want to freeze your butt off in this horrible place, then go right ahead." She reached for her coat and yanked it toward her.

The sound of several car doors closing distracted Vaughn. He glanced out the window to see all four of Carrie's brothers standing in the driveway. He could only surmise that they'd come en masse to finish him off.

"Who's here?" Natalie asked.

"The firing squad," Vaughn answered.

"Terrific. Can I fire the first shot?"

Vaughn didn't respond to her sarcasm. He headed toward the front door, opening it for the four men who marched, single file, into the house. Soon Carrie's brothers stood in the middle of the room, looking from Vaughn to Natalie and then back.

"What happened?" Chuck demanded. "You left town without saying a word."

"I didn't meet with Heath," Vaughn started to explain, but wasn't given the opportunity before another question was hurled at him.

"Aren't you going to introduce us to your sister?"

"I'm Natalie Nichols." She introduced herself, stepping forward and offering each of the Hendrickson brothers her hand. "And I'm not Vaughn's sister."

"Then who are you?" Ken asked, frowning.

"His fiancée. Or I was," she said, "until recently, but now Vaughn's met someone else. He just told me that he no longer wishes to marry me." She appeared to be making a brave effort to hold her chin high and keep her lower lip from trembling. He'd never realized what a good actress Natalie was.

Vaughn resisted rolling his eyes. He remained silent, preferring not to get drawn into a theatrical scene in which *he* was identified as the villain.

"Someone will need to give me directions back to my hotel." She pulled a tissue from her pocket and dabbed at her eyes, being careful not to smear her mascara.

"I can get you there." Ken stepped forward. "I'll be happy to help."

Tom's gaze narrowed on Vaughn. "Did she have something to do with the fact that you didn't see Heath?"

Vaughn shook his head, surprised the Hendrickson brothers hadn't already heard. "The land sold."

"What the hell?"

All four brothers started speaking at once. As luck would have it, Vaughn's parents chose that precise moment to reappear.

"I thought I heard voices," his mother said as she came into the living room.

Tom motioned with his head toward Natalie. "You'd better have a good explanation," he muttered. "You'd better not be engaged to her and seeing Carrie."

"Yeah," Pete agreed. "This is all some kind of misunderstanding, isn't it? Didn't I tell you I'd make you pay if you hurt my sister?"

"He was never actually engaged," his mother said, hurrying to defend Vaughn. "What he told us is—"

That was when his father stepped into the fray. "Barbara, let Vaughn answer for himself, would you?"

This was impossible. Everyone talked at once. Part of the conversation had to do with the land; everyone was clearly upset about that. Then Pete and his mother got involved in a debate about whether Vaughn should be dating Carrie. In the meantime, Ken and Natalie had apparently struck up a friendly conversation. They sat next to each other on the sofa, so close that their knees touched. Vaughn could only guess what she was saying, but frankly, he couldn't care less.

Before everything blew up in his face, Vaughn walked through the kitchen, grabbed his coat and stepped out the back door. He got into his car, which fortunately hadn't been blocked by the other vehicles. Glancing toward the house, he saw everyone gathered in front of the big window in the living room, staring at him. They must have been dumbfounded, because no one seemed to be speaking.

When he reached the end of the long driveway, Vaughn had to make a decision. He could go searching for solitude, a quiet place to recover his dignity. Or he could drive back to Buffalo Valley.

He chose Buffalo Valley. When he'd finished breaking Hassie's heart, he'd do what he could to mend Carrie's.

He'd never meant to hurt Carrie, but that didn't discount the fact that he'd misled her. This wasn't exactly his finest hour.

When they'd first met, he'd found her charming. Later, when he got to know her, he'd been enchanted by her warmth, delighted by her love of family and home. Those were qualities that had come to mean a great deal to him. Carrie was *genuine*, and she was authentic in her relationships. Unlike him...

Vaughn wanted to kick himself for not being honest with her from the start. He didn't have a single excuse. All he could do now was pray that she'd be willing to accept him—and that she'd give him an opportunity to prove himself.

The hour's drive into town passed in a blur, and practically before he knew it he'd pulled off the highway and turned onto what were now familiar roads. Buffalo Valley stretched before him, but he viewed it with new eyes. He recalled his first visit, recalled how stark and bare the town had seemed, almost as if it were devoid of personality. He'd soon recognized how wrong he was.

While the buildings might be outdated and the lampposts antiques, the town itself represented the very heart of the country. The heart of America's heartland. It was where he wanted to be, how he wanted to live.

His mind was clear now. Easing the car into a parking space on Main Street, Vaughn forced himself to consider what he'd say to Hassie. It wasn't a task he relished.

All his talk of opening a feed store had done nothing but build up her hopes. Now he was about to disillusion an old woman who'd invested her whole life in a town that couldn't be saved. Whatever happened, though, he was staying in Buffalo Valley; he'd be part of its struggle and part of its future.

He dared not put this off any longer, and drawing a deep breath, he walked into the pharmacy.

The instant she saw him, Hassie cried out his name. "Vaughn, oh, Vaughn." Tears streaked her weathered cheeks as she hurried across the store, her arms stretched out toward him.

Apparently someone had already brought her the news. Holding open his own arms as she came to him, he hugged her, the sound of her sobs echoing in his ears.

"I'm so sorry," Vaughn whispered, wondering what he could say that would comfort her.

"Sorry?" Hassie eased back, gazing at him through watery eyes. "In the name of heaven, why would you be *sorry*? This is what we've hoped for all along."

Vaughn stared at her, not knowing what to think. "The land sold, Hassie."

"Yes, I know." She clapped her hands, eyes sparkling with delight. "This is better than anything I could've imagined."

"I'm...confused."

"I know." She patted his back and led him to the soda fountain. "Sit down," she ordered. "If there was ever a time for one of my chocolate sodas, this is it."

"What about Value-X?"

"They lost the land. The women of Buffalo Valley got to Ambrose before he signed the deal with Value-X and they bought it out from under the company. The ladies convinced Ambrose he'd be making a mistake."

Vaughn knew that several of the women in town owned businesses; he knew they had a big stake in the community. It floored him that they'd managed to do what no one else had deemed possible.

"But how...when?"

"Do you recall when the women got together?" Hassie asked, leaning over the refrigeration unit, scooping up the ice cream.

"I remember a Cookie Exchange." Carrie had mentioned something along those lines earlier in the week.

"The meeting took place after that," Hassie said. "Then a committee of six paid Ambrose a visit. I don't know everything they said, but apparently they convinced him to sell *them* those twenty acres. I hear they twisted his arm by appealing to his vanity—promising to name the school after him. He liked that. He also liked the fact that he could sell his land at the same price Value-X offered."

"Is Value-X seeking out any other property?"

Hassie grinned. "They can try, but there isn't a single person in this area who'd sell to them—not at any price."

Vaughn nodded, still feeling a little numb. "What do the women intend to do with the property?" he asked.

Hassie's grin widened. "You mean you don't know?"

He didn't. Since they were all capable, business-minded individuals, Vaughn suspected they already had plans.

Hassie chuckled softly. "You'll have to ask them, but my guess is they'd be willing to sell you a portion of it— that is, if you're still inclined to settle in Buffalo Valley."

Vaughn could barely take it in. "You mean that?"

"Talk to Sarah Urlacher and she'll give you all the details."

"I need to see Carrie first."

Hassie set the glass on the counter. "Ah, yes, Carrie." She made a tsking sound and plunked a paper straw into the thick chocolate soda. "You've got your work cut out there."

Vaughn wrapped his hand around the glass, feeling the cold against his palm. "I assume she's upset."

"That's one way of putting it."

Vaughn slid off the stool. He didn't want to offend Hassie by not drinking the soda, but he'd feel worlds better once he resolved the situation with Carrie. "She at home?"

"Doubt it." Hassie reached for the soda herself and took a long sip before she continued. "My guess is she's sitting on the swings over in the park. I found she likes to go there when something's troubling her. Look there first and if you can't find her, then check the house."

Vaughn thanked her and left immediately. He jogged across the street to the park. The snow forts he'd helped build on Christmas Day—was that only yesterday?— were still standing, a little the worse for wear. Following the freshly shoveled walk, Vaughn made his way toward the play equipment.

Hassie had, as always, given him the right advice.

Carrie sat in the middle swing. Her face was red from the cold, and he wondered how long she'd been there.

Vaughn ached to tell her how sorry he was, but he feared that if he said or did the wrong thing now, he might lose her forever.

As he approached, Carrie glanced up, but she didn't acknowledge him. Vaughn, needing to gather his thoughts, didn't say anything, either. Instead, he settled into the swing beside her and waited for the words to come.

"I hurt you, didn't I?" he asked after an awkward moment.

"Were you engaged to her when you came to town?"

This was the difficult part. "No. No, I wasn't."

"She seemed to think so."

He gripped the chain and shifted sideways to see Carrie more clearly. "Before I left Seattle, Natalie and I talked about marriage."

The words seemed to hit her hard.

"She wasn't interested."

"Apparently she's changed her mind."

Vaughn saw that Carrie was staring straight ahead, as though mesmerized by whatever she was watching. "So have I."

Carrie turned toward him, but when their eyes met, she turned away again. "Why?"

"I met someone else."

"You must be a very fickle man, Vaughn Kyle, to ask one woman to marry you and then, while she's making up her mind, start seeing another."

"I realize how bad it sounds."

"Sounds, nothing! Underhanded and unfair is more like it."

"You're right," he said simply. "I have no excuse."

"You must've really enjoyed hearing me spill out my heart." She covered her cheeks with both hands and closed her eyes, as if remembering the things she'd said. They seemed to embarrass her now.

"Carrie, no! It wasn't like that." He thought about the afternoon she'd told him about her ex-husband. He didn't know how to put into words what her trust had done for him. How her straightforward devotion had wiped out the cynicism he'd felt after Natalie's opportunistic approach to love and marriage.

"You're certainly not the kind of man I'd want in my life."

"I need you, Carrie…"

"For what, comic relief?"

"We've only known each other a short while. Who can say where this relationship will take us? Maybe you're right. After you get to know me better, you could very well decide you don't want any more to do with me. If that's the case, I'll accept it. All I'm asking for is a chance."

"To break my heart?"

"No, to give you mine."

She didn't answer him for the longest time. Finally her mouth twisted wryly and she said, "You're afraid of what my brothers will do to you once they learn about… Natalie, aren't you?"

"No man in his right mind would voluntarily tangle with your brothers," he replied, deciding this was not the moment to tell her they'd already met the woman in question. "However, I figure I can take them on if it comes to that. What I'm telling you now has nothing to do with your brothers. It's how I feel about you."

"Don't!" she cried with such passion that Vaughn jumped. "Don't say things you don't mean."

"I am completely sincere." He slid off the swing and crouched down in front of her. He wanted her to see how vulnerable he was to her. Taking her right hand in his, he removed her glove and kissed the inside of her palm.

She pulled back her hand.

"I plan to stay in Buffalo Valley," he continued, undaunted.

Her eyes widened, but she bit her lower lip as if to suppress her reaction.

"I'm going to invest in the community, become part of it, make a contribution."

Carrie's gaze darted away and then returned. "Don't tell me things like that just because you think it's what I want to hear."

"It's true, Carrie."

She closed her eyes and lowered her chin. "I want so badly to believe you."

"Believe me," he whispered, then nuzzled her throat. He didn't kiss her, although the temptation was strong. "All I'm asking for is another chance," he said again.

"Oh, Vaughn." She pressed her hands against his shoulders—to bring him closer or push him away?

Vaughn helped make the decision for her. Crouched down as he was, his face level with her own, he leaned toward her and grazed her lips with his. Her mouth was cold, yet moist and welcoming. She moaned softly and he rubbed his warm lips over hers, seducing her into deepening the kiss.

One moment he was crouched in front of Carrie and she was leaning forward, giving herself to the kiss. The next he was losing his balance and tumbling backward.

Carrie let out a small cry of alarm as she went with him. Vaughn did what he could to protect her. He threw his arms around her waist and took the brunt of the impact as she landed on top of him in the snow.

"You've knocked me off balance from the moment we met," he said.

Carrie smiled then, for the first time since he'd joined her. "You've done the same thing to me."

"Good."

"No promises, Vaughn."

"I disagree." He brushed the hair from her face, barely aware of the snow and the cold.

She frowned. "What do you mean?"

"There's promise every time I look at you, Carrie Hendrickson. Promise each time I kiss you." Then, because he couldn't keep himself from doing so, he showed her exactly what he meant.

As soon as their lips met, Carrie whimpered and he wrapped his arms more firmly around her.

"This is only the beginning for us," he whispered.

Carrie placed her head on his shoulder and gave a shuddering sigh.

"I was never really worried about your brothers," Vaughn confessed. "*You* were always the one who terrified me." He laughed and rolled, reversing their positions in the snow. Her eyes were smiling as he gazed down on her.

"So you want to give me your heart?" she said, looking up at him. She flattened her hand against his coat.

"Don't you know?" he asked her.

"Know what?"

"You already have it." And then he went about proving it.

Mr. and Mrs. William Hendrickson

and

Mr. and Mrs. Richard Kyle

Request the honor of your presence at a reception

to celebrate

the marriage of their children

Carrie Ann Hendrickson

and

Vaughn Richard Kyle

When: December 15th

Where: Buffalo Bob's 3 OF A KIND

Main Street,

Buffalo Valley, North Dakota

RSVP

* * * * *

HARLEQUIN
PLUS

Try the best multimedia
subscription service for romance
readers like you!

Read, Watch and Play.

Experience the easiest way to get
the romance content you crave.

Start your **FREE TRIAL** at
<u>www.harlequinplus.com/freetrial</u>.